Guardians of the Sword

The Warrior's Road

All Rights ereof may not be reproduced or used in any manner whatsoever without the express permission of the author.

Copyright © Jason Pope 2013

This is a work of fiction. Although there is some historical basis for some of the events and characters herein, any resemblance to any place, event or incident or any person, living or dead, is entirely coincidental.

Popius3@gmail.com

https://twitter.com/popius3

Maps and Locations

Britannia, 5th Century AD

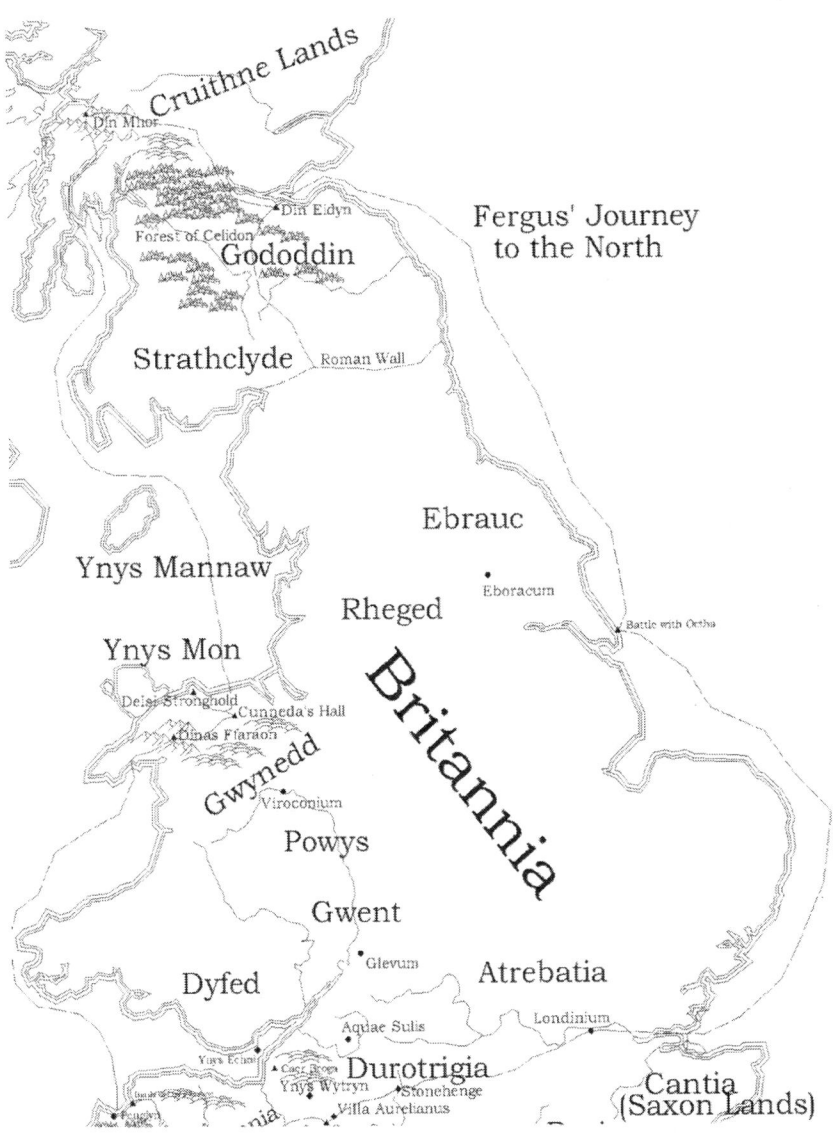

Guardians of the Sword

Book 2

The Warrior's Road

Jason Pope

Contents:

Map 1

Map 2

Prologue

Chapter 1 - Uther

Chapter 2 - The Siege

Chapter 3 - A Cry for Help

Chapter 4 - The Duke of Cerniw

Chapter 5 - Ambrosius

Chapter 6 - The Reunion

Chapter 7 - Villa Aurelianus

Chapter 8 - The Silver Mask Slips

Chapter 9 - Londinium

Chapter 10 - The Votadini

Chapter 11 - The Old North

Chapter 12 - The Forest of Celidon

Chapter 13 - In the Land of the Cruithne

Chapter 14 - The Fomoiri

Chapter 15 - The Price of the Gods

Chapter 16 - In the Hall of the Enemy

Chapter 17 - A Reluctant Freedom

Chapter 18 - Into the Night

Epilogue

Cast of Characters

Locations

Glossary of Terms

"The barbarians drive us to the sea; the sea throws us back on the barbarians: thus two modes of death await us, we are either slain or drowned".

"Groans of the Britons", sent to the Roman military leader Flavius Aetius in Gaul

BOOK TWO

The Warrior's Road

****

Prologue

The old man hunched before the fire with his gnarled hands outstretched, reaching out occasionally to turn the hazelwood spit upon which a spatchcocked hare was roasting. He looked up momentarily at the starlit sky and sighed as though reliving some distant memory, his eyes distant and unfocused.

Godric and his two thegns sat swathed in thick fur cloaks, their swords close at hand, passing around a skin of mead. He regarded the enigmatic old man with curiosity. There was something about him which he found fascinating, despite the fact that he had evidently spent most of his life fighting against Godric's people. The old man had been true to his word so far, just as Godric had supposed and although he had grown to respect him, he was not sure yet whether he could be trusted completely. They had travelled all day and were now close to the boundary of Godric's land, land that had once belonged to the Britons and the tension that he and his men felt at being in such close proximity to their mortal enemies was obvious.

"Tomorrow we will cross the River Isca, lord," the old bard said, his curious, gold flecked eyes still fixed on the distant stars. "We will then be in the territory of the Britons."

"I am well aware of that, old man," Godric replied with a note of slight irritation which he forced to cover up his nervousness. "We are putting our lives in your hands, so you had better be true to your word."

The old man fixed Godric with a curious stare. "The forest is several days travel to the north and west. I need you to fulfil your side of the bargain, so why would I wish to betray you?"

The Jutish lord stared hard at the elderly bard sat opposite him. "Why me of all people?"

The Irishman cocked his white aired head to one side. "My Lord?"

"Why choose me, an enemy of your people, to pass your tale on? Why not find a British lord instead, or one of your monks to write it down?"

The bard shrugged and thought for a while and then grinned mischievously. "It is said by many that your skill in battle is matched only by your formidable memory, my lord. It is also said that you can recite both your mother and your father's lineage all the way back to Woden and that you remember the deeds and battles of all of your ancestors, is this not true?"

Godric shrugged modestly. "Aye, that is so. But it is not unusual, many of my kinsmen can do the same."

"You do yourself a disservice lord," the old man replied. "Besides, I could not entrust a Christian monk to record my tale without bias. They wish for the Old Ways to be forgotten completely, for the Gods of old to be silenced forever, but they will not go quietly. But there is also another reason."

The Jutish lord raised his eyebrows. "And that is?"

The Irishman poked at the fire with a stick of hazel before continuing. "As Myrddin once predicted, the land will pass into the hands of your people, lord. You bring with you your own gods and your own stories and the spirits of this land, who have dwelt here since time immemorial and the people that fought for it will eventually be forgotten forever. I am the only one who remembers and once *my memories have been passed on, then my time in this world will be done."*

Godric glanced at his two men, feeling uneasy about his agreement to end the old man's life. "When you have finished your tale and the deed is done, how then will you guarantee our safe passage back through the lands of the Wealas?"

The bard smirked and tapped the side of his nose. "I will give you something that will guarantee you safe passage back my lord. Have no worries about that."

Lord Godric huffed loudly as he drew a whetstone down the blade of his sword. "I am gambling a lot on this tale of yours, old man. Forgive me if I remain unconvinced about your guarantees of our safety."

The old man shrugged and gave the roasting hare another turn on the spit and as he leaned forwards Godric noticed the sword which had been concealed beneath his long cloak, sheathed in a scabbard that bore Saxon runes.

He was about to ask him how he had acquired such a weapon when the old man spoke again.

"Do you wish for me to continue with my tale?" he asked as he rocked back onto his heels. He frowned as he tried to recall the distant events.

Godric nodded. "Please do. The last time we met, you told me about the Holy Chalice and how you had lost it."

The bard's eyes lit up suddenly, catching the orange glow of the fire as his memories returned. "Ah, yes, the Chalice. I remember now. We had sought the wisdom of Myrddin following the death of my lord, Drustan Pendragon and had persuaded him to return with us to Caer Dor, Drustan's stronghold, which lies several day's travel to the west of here," he gave a vague gesture westward with a wave of his arm. "At least it did once. Nothing remains of it now, just burned timbers and shattered rocks atop a mound of earth," he sighed deeply and stared into the flames "Such is the way of things."

"Caer Dor was destroyed?" Godric asked.

The stranger nodded wistfully. "Not just Caer Dor. Many of the places that I once knew and called home have met the same fate, but I shall come to those later. For now I shall continue my tale where I left it, at our arrival back at Caer Dor..."

Chapter 1

Uther

Several days after our arrival back at Caer Dor, all of the Pendragon clan chiefs along with their hearth troop were assembled in the Great Hall to hear Myrddin's words. The hall was hot and crowded and stank of stale ale and fetid, unwashed bodies. The druid stood at the Lord's Table, raised on its platform at the end of the large hall with Branwen sitting to one side. He wore his ceremonial dark green robe along with a simple crown of woven willow, a symbol of wisdom which he had cut and made the night before under the light of the full moon, calling upon the divine winter hag Cailleach for her insight. In his right hand he held a staff of rowan topped with holly, so that he could draw strength from the gods Dagda and Lugh.

Myrddin banged the staff three times on the floor to gain the attention of the assembled warriors.

"Noble men of the Pendragon you are gathered here to hear me speak wisdom. Drustan Pendragon has left us and is now in the Otherworld, but his legacy lives on. Last night I wandered between the worlds to seek guidance from the gods and they told me this; The Pendragon line must not be broken. The throne must pass to Branwen and in time to her only son, Uther. But they also told me that the great red dragon will fall to the white dragon and a kingdom would be lost. But the red dragon will rise again across the sea and return stronger than ever before to reclaim what it had once lost and the land shall fall under the dominion of the red dragon once and for all."

There was an expectant pause before one of the lords spoke up.

"Is this the wisdom that we have waited for?" Wynfor shouted from the crowd of warriors. "I swore fealty to Drustan Pendragon, not his daughter!"

There were several shouts of dissent before Cynyr, who was seated on Myrddin's left stood to address the crowd. "You swore that you would abide by Myrddin's decision. And his decision is made. Branwen takes the throne of the Pendragon until such times as Uther comes of age. Any man who breaks this oath shall be considered an enemy of the Pendragon."

"By whose authority do you make these claims, Cynyr?" Wynfor shouted back. "I did not hear the druid mention your name in his prophecy."

The hall erupted into shouts and insults from all sides and I looked at Brynmor who raised his eyes to the roof and shook his head. We were amongst the only armed men in the hall as we had been assigned as guards for the evening and we stood either side of the thick oak door of the hall leaning on our spears and our shields.

Branwen stood and spoke out, her voice was loud and strong and her father's fire glinted in her pale blue eyes. "Cynyr speaks on my authority. It is true that I cannot lead you into battle, but Cynyr shall be my right hand and he shall enforce my will. Remember that you are not swearing loyalty to me, but to the name of Pendragon. The decision has been made under the guidance of the Old Gods.

Those of you who feel that you cannot kneel before a woman, feel free to leave now."

The shouting subsided to a murmur as the men looked from one to another to see who would be the first to swear their loyalty to Branwen Pendragon or to leave the hall.

Wynfor laughed derisively as he looked around at his fellow warriors. "Look at you all. You call yourselves men? Ready to cringe and bow before a woman? Too afraid to stand up and speak your mind? This land will be torn apart, you mark my words."

He turned and strode out along with his hearth troop, pushing his way through the crowd. Several other chiefs followed him, but most stayed.

Branwen calmly watched them leave before speaking again. "What of the rest of you? Will you stay and swear loyalty to the name of Pendragon or will you leave?"

There was a moment's hesitation and then one of the clan chiefs, a man from the west whose lands bordered Gorlois' came forwards and knelt before Lady Branwen with his head bowed.

"I, Alwyn ap Glyn swear my undying loyalty to the Pendragon. I offer you my service and the spears of my men until the day I die. I swear this on the names of my ancestors."

Branwen walked over to the man and placed her hand gently on his shoulder.

"And in return Alwyn ap Glyn, I swear that you shall never want for food, land, shelter or riches. I shall strive to serve you as you serve me. Go now with my blessing."

One by one the other clan chiefs and their soldiers followed Alwyn ap Glyn's example until only myself and Brynmor remained. As one, we knelt before Lady Branwen and swore our loyalty to her.

Finally, Myrddin spoke. "It is done. The seeds of the future have been sewn and now I must depart for the far north. I bid you all farewell."

With that, the druid strode from the hall, his green robes flowing out behind him. I wanted to stop him, to remind him that he had promised to help me find Nivian, but as I was on guard duty, I was not permitted to speak out of turn.

I tried to catch his eye as we held the great oak doors open for him, but he did not acknowledge me. Perhaps it was his way of punishing me for allowing the Chalice to be taken.

As we closed the doors behind him I thought to myself I did not need him anyway. I was more than capable of finding Nivian and Fiachu mac Niall on my own.

My plans for finding Nivian however were to be dampened with the news that I was to become one of young Uther's protectors. I was invited to go out riding with Lady Branwen one day in early spring, along her favourite route which followed the course of a nearby river and took us through pleasant wooded glades. After the murder of her father she took no chances and surrounded herself and her son with at least a dozen armed men whenever she ventured from Caer Dor.

She rode slightly ahead of us on her white mare with Cynyr at her right side and young Uther on her left and a contingent of four hand maidens directly behind her. Uther reined his dark brown horse back until he was level with me.

"My mother wishes to speak with you," he said rather impudently, regarding me with his grandfather's steely blue eyes. He seemed to have a permanent scornful expression on his face and only ever seemed to laugh when it involved the misfortune of others. Uther was large for his age and physically very strong with a thick mat of black hair which accentuated his pale, freckled complexion. He wore a black bearskin like his grandfather's, held with an enamelled dragon brooch and a tunic of red and gold.

"Very well, master Uther," I said with a stiff nod. I spurred my horse on until I was level with Branwen. I was aware of her handmaidens behind me whispering and giggling, but I ignored them.

"Ah, Fergus. I wish to speak with you," Branwen said, her tone slightly aloof as she sniffed at the fresh but still cold spring air. The first shoots of green were beginning to force their way through the dead leaves on the forest floor and there was the definite earthy smell of new growth and life returning to the land. "Ride with me for a while," she added. Like her father, she was a formidable presence who seemed to demand respect. Her long, red braided hair was tied back and she wore her father's silver diadem on her head.

"What is it you wish to speak about my lady?" I enquired.

"You have served my family well, Fergus Halfhelm. Cynyr would never say this to your face, but he is proud of what he has made of you."

"Thank you my lady," I said a little self-consciously, glancing at Cynyr who was smirking beneath his thick moustache. We cantered through a small tributary stream that joined the river nearby in a swirling rush.

"As you know, the Pendragon have many enemies," she continued. "And I fear that those enemies may move against us very soon. I hear rumours that King

Vortigern is gathering his army and intends to march to war. Whether that is against us or someone else, I do not yet know. But Uther will need the best protection that we can provide."

I nodded in response. "Naturally, my lady."

"Therefore he will need a personal guard who will also double as a trainer and a mentor. I have chosen you for that role. You have all the virtues a Pendragon should aspire to. Bravery, intelligence, strength in battle and more importantly, compassion where necessary. I wish for you to teach these virtues to my son and to protect him with your life."

I thought about her proposal with a growing sense of dread. Teaching compassion to one such as Uther would be like trying to teach a salmon to sing.

"I don't know what to say my lady. I am truly honoured." I spoke with as much conviction as I could muster, hoping that I sounded convincing. Lady Branwen's cold demeanour melted slightly as she smiled at me and reached over to pat the back of my hand.

"I knew I could rely on you. Your three friends will also aid you in your task."

I tried to imagine Geraint's reaction when I told him that he was to be Uther's bodyguard for the rest of his life and grimaced behind the cheek plates of my helmet.

"There is one other thing," she added. "The other day we had a visit from a contingent of monks accompanied by warriors from Ynys Wytryn to formally protest about your involvement in an incident involving the Holy Chalice and the burning of their church. Cynyr insisted that we did not have the Chalice, but they demanded that you and your friends were handed over to face justice."

I swallowed nervously. "I do not have the Chalice, my lady and even if I did, I would not give it to them. It is not theirs to demand anyway as they stole it from the druids long ago. We took it as part of the bargain we had to strike to get Myrddin to come to Caer Dor. Unfortunately things did not go completely to plan and a couple of monks were killed."

Branwen's eyes widened slightly at this revelation and she pursed her lips thoughtfully.

"It seems we have made an enemy of Lord Glaesten then. He departed vowing that he would take the Chalice by force if necessary. A shame, for I have met him before and found him very amenable. Several times he fought alongside the Pendragon, but this whole turn of events worries me. If Glaesten formally complains to the High King, which I have no doubt he will do, it could give Vortigern the excuse he needs to march upon our lands. Others would flock to his banner to punish the sacrilegious heathens and assure themselves a place in heaven as well as the favour of the High King. Vortigern himself would also have much to gain through such an attack. Not only would he gain a foothold in Dumnonia, but he would also have the blessing of the Holy Church in Rome. It would help to salve the public humiliation that he endured at the hands of Bishop Germanus during his visit several years ago," Branwen leaned towards me in her saddle and spoke in hushed tones. "Did you know the Bishop accused Vortigern of lying with his own daughter?"

I shook my head. "I did not, my lady," I twisted my reins tightly in my hands, feeling guilty for having been responsible for possibly bringing war to the lands of the Pendragon. "My lady, please accept my apology for this unfortunate turn of events. If protocol demands it, I will hand myself over to Lord Glaesten to face justice, but not to Abbot Neirin."

Lady Branwen chuckled and gave me a wry grin. "Do not be foolish, young Fergus. Lord Glaesten is the Abbot's enforcer and I would not hand you over to either of them. You did what you thought you had to in my service and for that I am grateful. Myrddin should have known better than to send a warrior to do the job of a thief. Deaths will be inevitable."

"So what happened to the monks?" I asked.

"Cynyr sent them on their way after threatening to crucify them." Branwen laughed and I saw a glimmer of her father's humour in her eyes. "So what became of this Holy Chalice? Did you sell it for an evening of whoring and drinking?"

I smiled and shook my head. "No, my lady. A friend of mine, a monk of good virtue decided to take it one night whilst we were sleeping. Where he went, I do not know, but he is a good Christian and I would rather see it in his hands than in the grasp of that Abbot at Ynys Wytryn."

Branwen nodded in agreement. "I met Abbot Neirin once a few years ago in Caer Cadwy, my husband's fortress. Not a nice man. I did not like the way he looked at Uther."

"Abbot Neirin defiles that monastery with all kinds of depravities. It is supposed to be a holy place, but he has corrupted it and abused his position of power for his own twisted ends. I would never surrender myself to a man such as he."

Branwen again laid her hand on my armoured forearm. "And you will not have to, Fergus Halfhelm. Loyalty runs both ways and you have served my family well and with good grace and I would not betray you to a man such as that."

I thanked Branwen and she dismissed me with a smile and a wave of her hand and I found myself wondering how to break the news to Geraint and the others.

In the first few weeks of our new roles as personal guards we found Uther to be petulant, surly and disobedient. His personal tutor, an elderly, grey bearded sycophant by the name of Gwyllim bowed to his every whim and enforced his unruly master's will whenever possible, threatening to report our every move to Uther's mother. We knew that Lady Branwen was fiercely protective of her son, who in her eyes could do no wrong and that if we acted or spoke out of turn we would have to face her wrath. Worst of all, Uther reminded me of a younger version of Corryn and I quickly grew to dislike the child intensely. He was rude, disrespectful, spiteful and vain and quite often I shuddered to think of what sort of an adult he would become.

"If you ask me, we'd be better off if someone just slit the little bastard's throat in the night," Geraint said one evening as we sat around the fire sharing a skin of ale in our personal quarters in Caer Dor.

"If that happened, our lives wouldn't be worth living," Brynmor replied, wiping ale from his chin. "Lady Branwen worships the ground he walks on. If we failed in our duty to protect him, she'd see us hang for sure."

"Balls to that, I'd lend them the bloody rope," Geraint said with a loud belch. "At least we'd be released from his service."

"Don't talk like that," I berated Geraint. "We are sworn to protect young Uther and that is what we will do, whether we like it or not."

"The shock of a good battle may shake some sense into him when he's older."

Diarmuid added, his speech slurred from too much ale.

"Uther? I doubt it," I replied. "I think it will make him even more callous than he already is."

Geraint raised the skin of ale in a toast. "Here's to the little bastard falling off his horse and breaking his neck tomorrow."

The next day we took Uther out to indulge in his favourite pastime of hunting. We rode down to the nearby woods the next morning, the ground carpeted with purple bluebells that filled the air with a woodland fragrance. By mid-morning, Uther had managed to shoot a young fallow deer which staggered on through the woods for a while before collapsing through exhaustion and blood loss.

"Good, it still lives," Uther said triumphantly as he dismounted his horse and ran over to the struggling animal. He drew a knife from his belt and began stabbing the deer in its hindquarters, making the animal bellow piteously.

"That'll teach you for making me chase you half the morning," he said as he stabbed the animal repeatedly. He then knelt beside it and began cutting the arrow from the deer's flank while it writhed helplessly on the ground.

Furious, I strode over and pulled Uther aside by his shoulder. "At least kill the damned creature first before causing it any more suffering."

The boy glared up at me defiantly. "Why should I do that?"

I turned away from him with a look of disgust and drew my own knife, pulling the deer's head back by its antlers and drawing the blade across its throat. It thrashed for a moment before lying still. "No animal should have to suffer needlessly. It has given itself to you, it is a gift from Carnun, Lord of the Wildwoods," I said, wiping the blade on the deer's fur.

"But you've spoiled my fun," Uther protested.

"Torturing an injured animal is not fun," I yelled back at him.

Uther gave me a look of utter contempt. "And you call yourself a warrior?" he sneered.

Anger clouded my mind and without a thought I swung out, catching Uther across the face with the back of my gauntleted hand. He fell to the ground with the force of the blow and I heard

Gwyllim yell out in astonishment from somewhere behind me.

Uther looked up at me with a look of hateful disbelief, his pale blue eyes clouded with tears. He held his hand to his cheek and checked his nose for blood.

"You struck me," he muttered incredulously. "How dare you strike me?"

Gwyllim quickly ran over to the boy's aid, helping him back up. "You dare to strike the future king? You wait until his mother hears about this outrage."

I ignored him as I hefted the young deer onto my shoulder and draped it over the back of Uther's horse.

"Do you hear me?" Gwyllim shrieked. "This will not go unpunished."

"The boy had it coming," I replied as I tied the deer in place on the back of the horse. "He needs a lesson in respect and manners, something you have obviously failed to teach him."

"One day he will be a king and you will be at his mercy," the old man retorted, trembling with rage.

"One day he will thank me for keeping him on the right path." I looked at Uther but he seemed distracted by something.

"What's that noise?" He asked, his humiliation momentarily forgotten. We stopped and listened. Besides the usual hum of insects, birdsong and other woodland noises we could hear a low rumbling, like thunder rolling across the ground.

"Horses," Brynmor said. "Lots of them."

Quickly we mounted up and rode back the way we had come, climbing a high ridge that looked down through a wooded slope to the river below. It was here, following the course of the river that we saw the source of the noise. Armed men mounted on horseback, more than I had ever seen in my life were riding two abreast along the riverbank, their spears held high with the sun glinting off of their bronze helmets and their round shields bearing the emblem of a white dragon on a dark green background.

"Vortigern's army are on the move," Brynmor whispered. "And they're headed for Caer Dor."

Behind the cavalry came countless ranks of spearmen, stretching into the distance as far as I could see. In their midst, towed by oxen and rolling along ponderously on thick wheels were large wooden contraptions the likes of which I had never seen before. Some had long arms that terminated in a sling arrangement whilst others had the appearance of enormous bows turned on their sides and mounted on a sturdy wooden body. But the most fascinating to me were the huge towers that moved slowly and rocked from side to side on the uneven ground as they creaked and rumbled, towed by oxen that moved ponderously along the riverside.

"What in the name of Holy Christ is that?" Geraint whispered with awe.

"Roman war engines," Gwyllim muttered ominously. "They intend to besiege our fortress."

"We must get back to Caer Dor and raise the alarm," I said. I rode over to Uther's horse and cut loose the deer carcass, letting it slide off the horses back and drop to the ground.

"What are you doing with my kill?" he protested.

"Making sure you can ride fast," I said.

We galloped out of the forest and headed for the hills, riding as quickly as possible back to Caer Dor. It would only be a matter of hours before Vortigern's army reached the Pendragon's fortress and Lady Branwen would need as much time as possible to rally her troops.

By the time we got back, the walls were already bristling with the spears of hundreds of men. Outside of Caer Dor armed men were assembling, some on foot and some on horseback. War horns blared and drums thundered, warlords shouted orders to their men to form up into ranks with their shields overlapping. Some men sang to raise their morale while others stared silently and intently at the horizon, awaiting the inevitable approach of the enemy. It looked as though news of the approaching army had already reached Lady Branwen.

Cynyr approached us on horseback flanked by two other horsemen. His steel helmet shone brilliantly and he wore a coat of metal scales that reached down to his mid-thigh.

"I am glad to see you have returned safely," he said. "The enemy approaches from the north and the east. Scouts report Irish to the north and Saxons coming in from the east, most likely Vortigern's mercenaries."

I looked at my companions with dread. "They come from the west too. King

Vortigern's men approach with siege weapons."

Cynyr bared his teeth behind the cheek plates of his helmet and spat. "This is no opportunist raid. This is a coordinated attack. They mean to wipe us out."

"Where is Gorlois in all of this?" I asked.

In reply, Cynyr pointed out across the rolling hills to the sea beyond. There I could just make out the sails of many boats.

"I'll wager my balls that is his fleet out there, making sure they prevent us escaping by sea."

"So what do we do now?" Diarmuid asked, unable to hide the slight tremor in his voice.

Cynyr turned and looked at him. "We do what we do best. We fight. Come, Lady Branwen wishes to speak with you."

We followed Cynyr past large groups of armed men, some praying silently, some chattering nervously while sharpening the blades of their weapons with whetstones. We met Lady Branwen in the compound outside of the Great Hall surrounded by heavily armed men. Nearby came the clank of Meuric the blacksmith's hammer as last minute adjustments were made to weapons and armour. The stables were a hive of activity as stable boys prepared the horses for battle.

Lady Branwen's face seemed drawn with tension, but she visibly relaxed when she saw that her son was safe and well. "Thanks be to Dagda you still live." She came forwards and hugged her son.

"An army approaches from the west as well my lady," Cynyr announced grimly. "King Vortigern's men. With siege weapons."

Branwen looked visibly shaken and she strode back and forth as she thought. "I was right about Vortigern. He and his allies mean to destroy us," she muttered. "We must take the fight to them. Strike them hard before they have a chance to assemble. Cynyr, take as many horses as you need and strike at Vortigern's forces. Strike hard and fast, do as much damage as possible and then return here. The rest of our forces will hold their position here."

Cynyr bowed. "Yes my lady. But what of Uther? We need to get him to safety."

"Uther shall remain in Caer Dor for the time being. He will be safe here."

Cynyr looked uncertain. "But my lady, if Caer Dor falls, Uther may be captured or even killed."

Branwen regarded him with an icy stare. "Caer Dor will not fall. My decision is final."

Cynyr hesitated before finally turning to leave. He put a gauntleted hand on my shoulder as he passed. "May the Morrigan protect you," he said. The Morrigan was the Phantom Queen, the Goddess of Death and War, revered by my people when facing battle. Cynyr nodded towards the palisade where a single large raven had settled. "It looks as though she hears our prayers."

I smiled at Cynyr, the man who had forged me through sweat, blood and misery into the warrior that I now was. I remembered the time when I had hated this stern faced, no nonsense soldier who had battered us black and blue and trained us until we vomited. Now I regarded him as a friend, an older brother even. "And may Lugh's blessings shine upon you, Cynyr. Stay strong my friend."

He gave me a powerful slap on the shoulder before departing, shouting for men and horses as he went. I wished that I were going with him as there was no man, save Geraint who I would rather have at my side in battle.

"Uther is to stay with Gwyllim in my personal quarters at all times," Branwen said. "No one is to enter or leave unless myself or Cynyr commands it, understood?"

"Yes my lady," we said in unison.

"May the Morrigan be with us all. We will need all the help we can get," she added quietly. She looked at each of us in turn. "You four will protect Uther with your lives. Gwyllim, take Uther to my quarters."

The old man gave a deep bow. He shot me an accusatory look and then spoke. "My lady, I feel it is my duty to report to you an incident that took place earlier. This man took it upon himself to strike young Uther around the face over a trivial matter involving a deer."

I could not believe that the old man was bringing this up at such a time. In a couple of hours we could all be dead. "I hardly think torture is a trivial matter. Besides, is this really a good time to be discussing such things?"

"You should not have raised your hand to the young master," Gwyllim replied, his lizard like tongue darting between his lips.

"It really hurt, mother," Uther said in a wheedling tone, giving me a sidelong glance. "He made my nose bleed."

Branwen raised her hands. "We will discuss this matter later. For the moment there are more pressing things to worry about. Fergus, take your companions and ready yourself for battle."

I bowed and left Lady Branwen for the time being. We returned to our quarters to retrieve our shields and sidearms before paying a visit to Meuric the smith to put a keen edge on our swords, spearheads and seaxes, the long, single bladed knife made popular by the Saxons and carried by most warriors. By the time Meuric had finished, my sword's blade was sharp enough to draw blood at the touch of my thumb.

I was running through some basic attack and defence manoeuvres with Diarmuid, when a messenger came running through the gates.

"King Vortigern sends an envoy to speak with Lady Branwen," he shouted breathlessly.

We went into the Great Hall to inform Lady Branwen. She emerged from her personal quarters at the back of the hall with a look of concern etched on her face. She was wearing a coat of mail and had a long, slender bladed sword strapped to her waist. It was an ancient sword, the sort her ancestors would have wielded when the Romans had first arrived, iron with a curved bronze bar for a pommel.

"I shall ride out to speak with this envoy. Assemble the clan chiefs and be ready to ride with me."

Chapter 2

The Siege

Clouds were rolling in from the sea as we rode through the gates of Caer Dor to meet the High King's envoy. Apart from Diarmuid and I who were acting as Branwen's personal guard and carrying the dragon banner, we were accompanied by half a dozen clan chiefs, all clad in shining mail and war helms with great plumes of red horsehair that billowed out behind us as we rode. My breath caught momentarily in my throat as I looked out and saw an imposing sight. To the east was a great host of warriors, stretched out across the hills with their large round shields of all colours, bearing many different motifs and decorations, their ranks bristling with spears like the quills of a hedgehog. Banners and pennants beyond counting punctuated the ranks, each one proclaiming the allegiance of a warrior chief to Vortigern's cause.

"By the tits of Danu, I've never seen so many men," Diarmuid whispered fearfully. I was too stunned to answer and instead I looked northwards to where Cynyr had said the Irish were approaching. Sure enough there were more men and my heart froze as I saw amongst their ranks the crescent banner of the Masraighe.

"Fiachu is here," I uttered grimly, nodding north.

"Dagda be with us," Diarmuid said quietly.

Ahead of us were half a dozen armed and armoured men, one of whom carried

King Vortigern's banner, a white dragon on a dark green background. They waited until we stopped a dozen paces from them before one of them, a man whose face was hidden by a mail aventail that hung from his helmet trotted forwards and spoke.

"Vortimer, son of High King Vortigern wishes to address Lady Branwen Pendragon."

"Then let him come forth and speak," Branwen said firmly.

One of the men trotted forwards, flanked on either side by two formidable looking identical Saxon warriors. Behind them were another two men, one armed and clad in a coat of mail, the other frail looking and wearing only robes for protection, his head tonsured in the style of a Christian monk. I knew this man immediately and felt my blood chill when his haughty gaze fell upon me. It was Abbot Neirin and the man accompanying him carried a shield bearing the Chalice symbol of Lord Glaesten of Ynys Wytryn.

The man who had ridden forward gave a curt bow, gazing at Branwen with protuberant, reptilian eyes. He was well dressed, with a red velvet cloak that covered his long shirt of enamelled scale armour and a polished helmet encrusted with rubies with a decorated bronze crest that ran from front to back. He had a neatly trimmed brown beard and he spoke with a clipped, precise tone.

"Lady Branwen, it is a pleasure to meet you. Despite appearances, my father does not wish to destroy you. We seek only your fealty to the High King of the Britons. Bend your knee before me and you will be spared. Refuse and you will be destroyed."

Lady Branwen gave a thin smile. "I'm sorry my lord, but you seem to have confused the noble Pendragon people for that coward Gorlois, whose lands you travelled through to get here, who no doubt even now is trembling in his stronghold at Din Tagel. Maybe word of the Pendragon has not reached your lands in the north but if it had, you would have known that the Pendragon kneel before no man. Not even the Romans could defeat us."

"There is also the small matter of the Holy Chalice, my lady," Abbot Neirin said, stepping forward with a supercilious smile. "Hand over the Chalice and the ones responsible for the cold blooded murder of God's holy servants and you will save your immortal soul from the eternal torment that awaits you."

Branwen shot the Abbot a withering glance. "And what of your immortal soul, Abbot? I have heard all about the depravities that you inflict upon others within your monastery. Save yourself and look elsewhere, the Chalice is not here."

Abbot Neirin's thin face grew taut with rage but he remained silent and turned towards the Prince. "You see, your Highness. Precisely the reaction that I expected. These pagans must be wiped from the face of God's Earth."

Vortimer's mouth tightened and he sighed irritably. "Word has reached us that you are a stubborn people, but by no means stupid. If we cannot appeal to you, then maybe we can appeal to your lords and chieftains. None of you have to die this day. You will still hold the lands you once did, but instead you will swear allegiance to the High King and return that which does not belong to you."

"We do not recognise the usurper Vortigern as High King of anything," said Alwyn ap Glyn gruffly, speaking on behalf of the half dozen clan chiefs present. "Our loyalty was to Drustan Pendragon and in turn to his daughter, Lady Branwen. Do not think that because a woman has taken the throne of the Pendragon that we are any the less willing to fight. We know exactly how you and your father operate. You will usurp Lady Branwen's position, make false promises of land and riches and divide us and turn us against one another to weaken us. Then you will turn us out of our halls and take our land, just as your father has done with the lords of Cantia and Regia in the east. As for this Chalice of which you speak, none know of its whereabouts, so save yourself a lot of bloodshed and go home to your father, boy."

Vortimer looked beyond Alwyn's grizzled bulk at the fortress of Caer Dor with a self-satisfied smile on his face. He sighed and shook his head with mock regret. "Do you really think your little wooden fence will protect you? May I introduce you to Hengist and Horsa. They are Saxon chieftains and behind us is their army, paid for by my father. I have seen what these men are capable of and I implore you one final time to see sense for your own sake."

My eyes fell upon the twin Saxon warlords. They were immense men who would have dwarfed even Drustan Pendragon, clad in filthy bearskins with their straw coloured hair greased and tied back. Their thick arms were adorned with golden armbands and each wore a simple conical iron helm with a nose guard. Around the neck of one of the brothers hung a hammer pendant on a leather cord. They regarded us with a surly silence, their ice blue eyes calm and calculating in faces scarred and battered from innumerable battles. One of them fingered the blade of an immense war axe that hung from a thick belt at his waist, as if itching for it to taste our blood. The other sported a large sword strapped to his back and held the reins of his horse in two mighty red fists that looked as though they were capable of crushing a man's skull. A sneer played on his lips as he stared directly at me.

I held the Saxon's gaze unfalteringly, trying to convince myself that despite his size and formidable appearance, he was just a man and a well-placed sword thrust would kill him as easily as any other man.

"My father has gold enough to pay for many times the number of men you see here today. You cannot possibly hope to win," Vortimer continued arrogantly, brushing at the sleeve of his enamelled scale armour.

"I hope your father lives to rue the day he hired these foreign barbarians and brought them to our land," Branwen said. "They are like wild dogs. They cannot be tamed or reigned in. They know only how to kill and one day they will turn on you."

One of Vortimer's aids leaned across and whispered to one of the brothers whose pale eyes flashed murderously as Branwen's words were translated into his barbaric tongue. He replied in his harsh, guttural language, his eyes never leaving Branwen.

Vortimer gave a little depreciative laugh and translated the barbarian's words for us.

"Hengist says that after all of his men have filled you with their seed, he will hack the ribs from your back and honour you with the death of the blood eagle."

At that time I did not know what a blood eagle was. Since then, with the coming of the Saxons, I have seen it more times than I wish to remember. It was a particularly hideous way to die.

"The time for talking is obviously over," Branwen said contemptuously. "Prepare yourself for battle, Vortimer son of Vortigern."

With that she wheeled her horse around and rode back towards the high, wooden walls of Caer Dor with the rest of us bringing up the rear.

I glanced north again, to where the Masraighe army was assembled and knew that somewhere amongst that horde of warriors was Fiachu mac Niall. Dark storm clouds were gathering to the north, rolling towards the gathered armies like an omen of death and I wondered briefly whether the storm had been summoned by Fiachu's black druids.

My hand went to the triple spiral around my neck, and I offered a prayer to Danu and to Brighid.

"I wonder what Duke Gorlois, the so called protector of Western Dumnonia thinks he is getting out of all this?" Alwyn ap Glyn said, sidling his horse up to Lady Branwen.

"He will be getting exactly what he has always wanted if they succeed, which they won't," Branwen looked ahead as she spoke, her expression unreadable. "Namely complete control over Western Dumnonia and Cerniw. He has obviously struck some kind of deal with King Vortigern, allowing his armies unhindered access through his lands. But I fear his ambitions will not stop there. I'll warrant that he is after the throne of Dumnonia itself, albeit under the high kingship of Vortigern."

Alwyn frowned. "But surely Gorlois has sworn to uphold the rule of King Erbin, just as Julianus has done in the east?"

Branwen let out a humourless laugh. "Oaths of loyalty do not hold men such as Gorlois, especially oaths made to a crippled boy king. He will do exactly what he has to do to further his own ambitions. Gold and riches are all he cares about and King Vortigern has plenty of both."

"So why wait until now to attack us?" One of the other lords accompanying us asked.

"Is that not obvious, Macsen? They saw the Pendragon weakened by the death of Lord Drustan. They think that a mere woman cannot unify her warlords and are hoping that they will defect and swear fealty to King Vortigern, especially now that he has righteousness on his side. The theft of the Holy Chalice and the burning of the church at Ynys Wytryn has given him the perfect excuse to attack. He will then have a foothold in Dumnonia from which to attack Julianus in the east. Once Dumnonia has fallen, the other lands still resistant to Vortigern's rule will capitulate. Unfortunately for him, the Pendragon remain unified."

"Then someone must get word through to King Erbin, or better still, Julianus," Macsen said. "Surely he would come to our aid if we can hold out long enough."

Branwen considered this and nodded. "My ex-husband's army is second to none. Many of them are Romans who came over with him from Armorica and they fight with the discipline of the legions of old. If he thinks his son is in danger, he will come. As for King Erbin, he is just a boy who will likely never see manhood and I fear that his advisors wield the real power and I'm not sure where their loyalties lie, but I do know that he has little love for the Pendragon. The other problem is, Vortimer has us surrounded and intends to besiege us."

"I will go, my lady," I said humbly.

Branwen, Macsen and Alwyn all turned to look at me.

"I could leave under cover of darkness and get through their lines. I will go and speak to Lord Julianus personally and get him to send aid."

"And risk getting caught by those Saxon animals?" Macsen said incredulously.

"Do you know what they would do to you if they caught you, lad?"

"I am fully aware of what could happen," I replied. "But I would say we have no choice. We are outnumbered by two, maybe even three to one. If no one goes for help, then we are doomed."

"Young Fergus speaks sense," Alwyn said with a shrug. "Duke Julianus' forces could make all the difference to us."

Branwen pursed her lips thoughtfully. "If it comes to it Fergus, then I may be calling upon your services. Be ready."

I gave a dutiful nod and looked at the ranks upon ranks of spearmen assembled outside of Caer Dor as we rode up the slope towards the fortress. It was an impressive and terrifying sight to see so many warriors ready for battle, their shields forming a wall of painted limewood and I wondered briefly how our forces looked to the enemy, who were even now approaching at a steady pace from the east and the north.

From the Irish ranks to the north, I could hear the distant skirl of pipes and the thundering of war drums. From the Saxon ranks to the east came the occasional guttural, barbaric chant and the blaring of horns. My blood stirred as our own war drums began to beat in response to the enemy and our warriors began to sing one of their many battle songs, their voices lifting through the spring air and drowning out the distant foe.

Branwen drew her sword and held it aloft, riding before her assembled soldiers. Eventually an expectant silence fell as the men looked upon the daughter of Drustan Pendragon for some words of encouragement.

"Noble warriors of the Pendragon. On this day we face a foe the likes of which we have not faced since the arrival of the legions of Rome. They outnumber us and surround us, but our reputation as fierce warriors precede us. I see this not as the end, but as an opportunity. An opportunity to show our foes that they have met their match. An opportunity to send a message to the usurper Vortigern that the Pendragon will not be subjugated or beaten. That we are the descendants of a long line of proud warriors that have bled and fought for their rights to live in this land since time immemorial. Proud and noble warriors of Dumnonia, will you bleed with me now?"

A great cheer erupted from the ranks and men thrust their spears into the air and banged the shafts against the backs of their shields to create a thunderous noise that echoed through the valleys. I felt a surge of pride at being amongst such people at a time like this. The warriors of the Pendragon were feared by all and their reputation for ferocity and tenacity was well known throughout the land. The clan chiefs who had accompanied us rode off to their men, strengthened by Branwen's words.

We rode back to the gates of Caer Dor, the ranks of cheering men parting to let us through.

"I want you to stay within the palisade," Branwen said to me. "You will help to defend the walls if the enemy comes near, I hear you are a good shot with that bow of yours. If the walls are breached you are to defend Uther with your life. Understood?"

I gave a slight bow. "Yes, my lady."

"Now I must go out and lead my men to battle. May the gods be with you, Fergus Halfhelm."

"And with you, my lady."

Branwen left to ride before her men again to more uproarious cheers while I climbed one of the ladders up to the wooden walkway on the inside of the palisade so that I could get a better view of the battle. Men waited tensely with bows, spears and slings, ready for the assault that many felt was inevitable. A couple of young boys ran along distributing sheaves of arrows behind us.

From my vantage point, I could see the enemy forces clearly. I was looking east, towards the horde of Saxons and estimated their number to be six hundred at least. To the north was a confederation of Irish and Picts, numbering around four hundred, led no doubt by Fiachu mac Niall, the sound of their pipes and drums growing ever closer. But somewhere to the west was Vortigern's main force, eight hundred men with Roman siege weapons. If they were to reach Caer Dor, our defences would be smashed in a matter of hours.

Somewhere overhead came the distant rumble of thunder as the sky blackened and the temperature dropped considerably. I felt the first spattering of rain on my face and I could overhear men muttering about bad omens. I could not help thinking that they were right and bit my lip with frustration, annoyed at Branwen's stubborn decision to reject my offer to find help.

"I've never seen so many men before," Diarmuid said with a terrified awe. He was clutching his spear and I could see his hand was shaking. "Have you ever fought in a battle this size before, Fergus?"

I shook my head. Up until then, I thought that I was a seasoned warrior, but realised that all the battles that I had fought in had been mere skirmishes compared to this.

"Don't worry lads, we'll hold them."

We turned to see the portly figure of Enfys, a seasoned veteran in his forties who had been appointed captain of the defences. He carried a burning torch in one hand and had his other hand over the head of a Frankish war axe, no doubt a souvenir of some campaign years ago on the continent.

"Those Saxons are going to take some beating, mind. They have no fear of death you see. They are taught from the moment they stop sucking on their mother's tit that the most glorious thing is to die in battle. They believe that if they die well that they will spend eternity in Valhalla with their warrior god, Woden, eating, drinking, fucking and fighting forever."

"Sounds good to me," Diarmuid said with a nervous grin.

"Well let's do the bastards a favour and send them on their way. And one word of advice. Don't let them catch you alive, they are the cruellest most ruthless sons of whores I have ever known."

The Saxons were chanting and thumping their shields as they closed the distance between our army and theirs. Suddenly, two men, naked except for bear skin cloaks, broke the Saxon ranks and sprinted forwards, hurling their spears high into the air. The spears sailed clear over the heads of our men and landed harmlessly in the ground behind.

Our troops jeered derisively at the two hopelessly long spear throws and began their own chant.

Enfys shook his shaggy, grey haired head. "Fools. They think they missed. They don't realise that those two Saxons did that on purpose."

"Why did they do that?" I asked.

"They are offering our souls to Woden. It's what they do before battle."

Our men responded with a barrage of javelins, arrows and slingshots, causing the Saxons to crouch behind their large round shields as the lethal missiles pummelled into their ranks.

They responded in turn with their own barrage and I heard several cries from our men and saw some of them drop.

Filled with anger, I knocked an arrow onto the string of my short bow and fired it in a high arc that sailed over our army and landed amongst the Saxons. Before it had landed, I had fired another one and then the other men on the ramparts were following my lead, firing volley after volley into the Saxon ranks.

Suddenly a great cry went up and the Saxons surged forwards, screaming in their guttural, barbaric language. I was glad not to be in the front line of our shieldwall. The Saxons were big, averaging at least half a head taller than the Britons, fair haired and blue eyed demons filled with battle frenzy, welcoming death like an old friend, seasoned warriors who had been weaned on war and death.

As the two opposing armies clashed there was the familiar thunderous thump of shield on shield accompanied by loud grunts as the men of both sides put their weight behind their shields in an attempt to break the opposing ranks. I raised my bow again, but Enfys stilled my arm with a hand on my shoulder.

"Too risky now, lad. You could hit our own men. Quickly, to the northern ramparts, the Irish are attacking."

We made our way along the narrow walkway to the northern end of the palisade. Here our men were spread more thinly, but were still a force to be reckoned with. The Irish were still beating their drums and I could see the blue painted faces of Picts and Masraighe amongst their ranks. On their left flank, I could see the war banner of Wynfor, the chieftain who had declined to swear loyalty to Lady Branwen. He had brought around fifty men to the field and they stood with their shields touching.

"Treacherous bastards," Enfys shouted at them, but his voice was lost in the clamour of pipes and drums from the Irish.

One Irish warrior stepped forwards holding aloft a sword and an axe in defiance of his enemies to the cheers and chants of his comrades.

My blood chilled when I heard the name they were chanting. That name was Fiachu, chanted over and over again whilst banging their shields with their weapons.

I looked down upon the man who had destroyed my friends and family, who had enslaved the girl that I had loved and I watched with boiling hatred as he swaggered back and forth, shouting encouragement to his men.

I drew the string of my bow back to my ear and let the arrow fly. It was a long shot and I knew that it was more than likely wasted, but anger had overcome rationality and I wanted to do something, anything even if there was only a slim chance of killing the youngest son of King Niall. The arrow shot through the air and landed in the ground at Fiachu's feet. He reached down, pulled it from the ground and snapped it, laughing derisively before returning to his men.

Suddenly the Irish ranks parted and a group of black robed druids bearing a litter came forwards. At the head of the procession was Malbach, holding his staff before him with his one hand and yelling curses at our men. Seated on the litter was Sinusa, her thin white hair flailing in the growing wind, her skeletal white arms raised to the heavens as she called down the wrath of Crom Cruach upon us.

"What's happening to the sky?" Diarmuid said breathlessly, looking up.

My eyes were drawn upwards, away from the screeching druids to the sky above. Dark clouds were swirling and boiling, accompanied by the angry growl of thunder. A cold wind whipped around us and a flurry of hail blew into our faces.

"Men of flesh and blood I can face, but this is sorcery. This does not bode well for us," Enfys said, turning his face away from the whipping hail.

"They call upon Crom Cruach to destroy us," I shouted back over the wind.

Suddenly there was a blood chilling shriek and the Pictish and Masraighe warriors charged forwards into a shower of missiles from our ranks. I loosed off several arrows before the two armies collided down below. Some of the Picts leapt up high, placing one foot on their opponent's shield and attempted to leap over the front ranks of our men, stabbing down at their exposed backs with sword and spear. It was a tactic I had seen them use before with deadly efficiency and it was one that my own people also employed.

"What do we do now?" Diarmuid asked as we stared down at the men hacking and stabbing at one another.

"We watch and we wait," Enfys replied. "And if those bastards come anywhere near our walls, we let them have everything we've got."

The air was filled with the clash of steel on steel, the thud of sword and axe on wooden shields and the cries and shouts of men murdering one another.

I stood transfixed by the carnage below. I had never seen a battle from such a vantage point before as previously I had only ever witnessed a battle as a participant where all you see is a tangle of hacking limbs, the flash of steel blades and faces contorted with rage and pain. From where I was, I was thankful that I could not smell the smells as well; the cloying odour of spilled blood, of heaving, sweating bodies and the stench of opened bowels.

The battle raged on in the ferocious storm, hail and blood turning the ground into a quagmire of thick mud. Several times the Irish, Picts and Saxons fell back to rest and reform, unable to break our shield wall and our men jeered and cursed them, pelting them with javelins and slingstones as they fell back exhausted. Injured men were retrieved by both sides from the carpet of corpses that littered the ground and bodies were looted for jewellery and weapons by several daring individuals. During the lulls in hostilities, the moans and cries of the injured and dying rang out poignantly. Men sobbed like babies, some crying out for their mothers and wives as their lives gradually slipped away into the mud. Exhausted warriors sat on the wet ground leaning on their spears and staring into nothingness whilst women sallied forth from the fortress to tend the wounded and strengthen the troops with warm soup from a large black cauldron.

"We must break them before the main force arrives otherwise we will be in trouble," Enfys said, accepting a bowl of soup handed to him by a young boy.

The black druids were once again raining down their curses upon us and Sinusa was carried forwards again on her litter, just out of arrow shot. She had her arms raised once again and was screaming out in the Sacred Tongue to her dark god.

"I wish someone would shoot that damned witch," Enfys said, peering over the palisade.

"Believe me, I would dearly love to, but my bow string is wet and next to useless," I replied.

As we watched, the hail storm stopped and the thunder died away to a distant roar.

"By the gods will you look at that," Enfys muttered in quiet amazement.

A great ring of mist was rising up from the ground before our very eyes, its spectral tendrils enshrouding and obscuring the enemy armies until they were virtually invisible, leaving us looking out incredulously at a surrounding wall of swirling white fog.

"How do we fight an enemy we cannot see?" One of the defenders on the ramparts cried out.

The men around us began to murmur nervously about sorcery and dark magic and I knew then that Caer Dor would fall unless something drastic was done.

A loud hiss filled the air and several men yelled out as a great ball of fire descended out of the mist and landed within the enclosure with a crash, setting light to the stables. Another fell and another, smashing the timber buildings and setting them alight. These were followed by a rain of flaming ballista bolts the size of spears, thudding into the walls and ground. The people down below began to panic and scatter, some seeking shelter, others seeking a means to douse the flames.

"They're using the siege weapons!" Enfys yelled. "They used the mist to cover their advance. Now they're just going to pound us until Caer Dor is nothing but flaming timbers."

"We can't just sit here and do nothing," I said. "I must find Branwen."

I ran along the ramparts and down a wooden ladder. On the ground within the enclosure, chaos had ensued. Animals and people ran wildly in all directions. Pigs squealed and horses bucked and panicked as missile after missile rained down upon us.

I saw Brynmor approaching across the enclosure, his sword raised in salutation. suddenly, he looked up and yelled out, pushing me aside as a flaming ballista bolt missed me by a hand's breadth and struck him in the stomach, the force of the bolt knocking him backwards and impaling him against the wall of the blacksmith's workshop.

I ran towards him to try to help, but the flames from the spear sized shaft drove me back. They licked up his chest and seared his face as he let out an agonized, gasping scream. He tried to cover his face with his arms, but the flames caught quickly and he began to burn and soon he was shrieking in agony, begging for me to kill him.

I drew my sword and asking his forgiveness with tears in my eyes I plunged the blade into his chest, piercing his heart and killing him instantly. His flaming body slumped, pinned to the log wall of the blacksmith's workshop and I turned away, numbed with grief, barely aware of the shouting people and the great chunks of burning pitch soaked timber landing nearby.

After a while the rain of missiles ceased, but shortly afterwards someone up on the ramparts yelled out, snapping me out of my sorrow.

"The Saxons have breached our lines! They are attacking!"

I ran over to a nearby ladder and climbed back up onto the fighting platform, putting an arrow to the string of my bow and looking down upon the battlefield. The Saxons and the Irish had indeed taken advantage of the lull in the bombardment and using the fog as cover had managed to infiltrate our lines, surrounding our troops whilst others charged forwards with ladders ready to scale our palisade. I noticed too the Chalice banner of Lord Glaesten approaching our left flank rapidly. His mounted men, who up until now had been holding back in reserve, now came galloping out of the mist with their Chalice pennants fluttering on their lances, charging at full speed into the flanks of our army.

The shield wall was at last broken and now individuals and small groups fought isolated, chaotic battles of survival against the oncoming enemies.

Some of our men broke ranks and ran for the safety of the fortress. The gates were opened briefly to let them in, only to be closed again and barred shut with timbers as thick as a man's waist slotted into iron brackets.

I fired arrow after arrow into the horde of Saxons directly below until my fingers were raw and slick with blood from the friction of my bow string. Barrels of flaming pitch, rocks and cauldrons of boiling water were thrown down upon the besieging foe below, but still they came, breaching our defensive ditch with wooden planks and holding their shields over their heads as our missiles pounded down on them, several of our men fell screaming from the ramparts into the ditch below as the enemy fired back sporadically with arrows and sling stones.

I ran over to assist Diarmuid and another man trying to push back a ladder that had landed against our palisade, but it was too heavy to move as a number of Saxons were already climbing it with their shields held over their heads as they came.

We waited until the first man was nearly up, then Diarmuid and the other man grabbed him by his bearskin cloak and hauled him over the ramparts. I put my foot on his back to hold him down and then smashed his skull open with my sword. We hurled his limp corpse down into the enclosure below and then waited for the next man, a ferocious looking red bearded giant who leapt over the ramparts before we could grab him, swinging a great axe that splintered Diarmuid's shield, the force of the blow knocking him off of the fighting platform and sending him tumbling into the enclosure. I looked down to see that Diarmuid had landed on the corpse of the man that I had despatched and he was doubled over and clutching his sides, but I could not see any blood and assumed that the fall had merely cracked a few ribs and knocked the wind out of him.

The other man leapt onto the barbarian's back, holding a dagger, but the Saxon swung him easily over his shoulder and over the palisade into the heaving mass of warriors, who hacked his body into a bloody mess.

With a bellow of rage, the huge Saxon turned to face me and swung his heavy axe in a great circle around his head. I ducked the first swing, which sailed over my head with a rush of air, but he skilfully reversed the attack and I was forced backwards to avoid his backswing.

I waited again for the split second between his powerful attacks and then lunged forwards, punching out with the iron boss of my shield and feeling it crunch against the bones of his face. The Saxon staggered backwards, spitting out shards of teeth, his beard stained with blood from his smashed nose and mouth, giving me an opportunity to bring my blade down at an angle, burying it deep between his neck and his shoulder. The man's blue eyes glazed as he sank to his knees and I pulled the sword free with a grunt, feeling the blade squeak against bone as he toppled sideways off of the walkway. I ran back to the ladder, but more Saxons had already pulled themselves over the palisade. One of them thrust his spear at me and the tip of it snagged on my mail shirt. I felt the blade slice my flesh, but fortunately my mail had absorbed and deflected most of the blow, so that the spear head did not pierce any organs.

With a grunt of pain, I struck down with my sword, breaking the shaft of his spear in half, quickly advancing on the Saxon warrior who now only held a splintered stick as a weapon.

I swung my shield at him, knocking him sideways off of the walkway and ignoring the pain in my abdomen, advanced into the fray ahead of me.

I saw Enfys attacking from the opposite side to me and between us, we managed to clear the ramparts of the few Saxons that had scaled the palisade, pushing the ladder aside with a grunt of effort.

"You're hurt lad." Enfys said, breathing heavily after the brief but desperate fight.

I shook my head, looking down at the ragged hole in my mail and the blood leaking out of it.

"It's a flesh wound," I replied through gritted teeth. "I'll be fine."

The assault continued until the sound of war horns in the distance signalled for the enemy to fall back. We cheered as they retreated, shouting insults and pelting rocks and arrows at them as they vanished into the mist to rest and reform.

I slumped down onto the walkway next to Enfys, exhausted and bleeding. He insisted that I went down to have the wound seen to, so I eventually relented and climbed down from the ramparts into the enclosure below.

Most of the fires that had been started by the pitch soaked timber missiles from the catapults and ballistae were now out or under control, but the dead bodies of men and animals lay scattered all around. Women tended to the wounded under the shelter of an old lean to used for storing firewood. I made my way over to them, my hand clasped over the leaking wound in my side.

A small woman, elderly but not old, came over and took my arm, leading me to a bale of hay on which I sat.

"Are you hurt bad my dear?" she enquired, her voice kind and full of concern.

I looked around at the scores of wounded, moaning men. Some had lost limbs or had them smashed by falling missiles whilst others had been burnt beyond recognition, or had their insides seeping out from ragged wounds caused by axe and sword and spear. I shook my head and gave her a reassuring grin.

"Such a brave lad," she said absently as she helped undo my sword belt. "Now let's get this armour off and see what we can do."

The woman cleaned, sewed and dressed my wound while I sat and listened to the war drums and pipes outside of the palisade. A loud whoosh was followed by a destructive crash as Vortimer's men resumed their bombardment of Caer Dor. Panicked shouts went up as the missile landed harmlessly in a patch of clear ground, sending a shower of sparks in all directions. The old woman did not flinch, but carried on tending my wound.

"Where the hell have you been hiding?" Someone said, sitting on a hay bale beside me. It was Geraint, a thick, blood stained bandage tied around his head at an angle. He was chewing on a piece of salted pork with as much care as if he were attending a wedding feast...

"Manning the palisade," I replied, wincing as the woman severed the thread binding my wound with her teeth. "Brynmor's dead." I added flatly.

Geraint turned his face away, but I could still read the emotion and grief in the tension of his body and the set of his broad shoulders.

"How?" he asked.

"Ballista bolt hit him. It wasn't quick or pleasant."

Geraint shook his head and gritted his teeth in frustration. "We can't just sit here and let them pound us like this. We won't last until sunrise."

I nodded in agreement as I watched the fiery trail of another missile come smashing into the enclosure, sending men and horses scattering for cover. I heard a familiar woman's voice shouting orders and I saw Branwen striding through the enclosure, flanked by her bodyguard, her slender sword stained with blood.

I stood, thanking the old woman and made my way over to Lady Branwen. She turned towards me, her burning eyes and braided red hair making her look like a goddess of war.

I knelt before her, head lowered. "My lady, my offer still stands."

Branwen silenced her clamouring warriors with a raised hand.

"Do you think you can get through their lines without being caught?"

I looked up at the surrounding mist. "With this fog on my side, I think so."

She bit her lip as she considered my proposal. The crash of another missile and the sound of splintering wood seemed to sway her opinion.

"Very well. You must take Uther with you. Ride with all haste to Caer Cadwy and get him to his father at any cost. Where are your companions?"

"Brynmor is dead my lady and Diarmuid is incapacitated. Geraint is the only other who can make the journey with me."

"Then he must go with you too," she turned to one of her men. "Bring the swiftest horses you can find for these men and my son. Gather the others for an attack. We will create a diversion so that they can get away with Uther," she turned back to me again, pulling a gem encrusted ring from her finger and handing it to me.

"This was given to me by Julianus, when we were once lovers." Her mouth became twisted by the bitterness of distant memories and her eyes began to fill with tears. "He no longer cares for me, but he will come for the sake of his son. Hand this to him personally and he will know you speak the truth."

I took the ring and placed it in a leather pouch on my belt. "I will return with Lord Julianus," I said resolutely.

Branwen forced a smile. "Go then, Fergus Halfhelm. And may Lugh's blessing be with you."

In a short while, Alwyn ap Glyn had organised two score of armed horsemen ready to sally forth and assault the enemy.

I was given a sleek black stallion, whose owner had perished earlier in the day and Geraint had a chestnut mare with a white patch on its forehead, whilst Uther rode his dark brown palfrey. He was also wearing a coat of mail, custom made for his size and a helmet with a bronze faceplate, cast in the likeness of a Roman god, which also helped to disguise his identity.

The faceplate was raised and he looked at me with a desultory stare.

"When we get through the gates, stay close to me, Uther," I said, checking the keenness of my blade. "You must ride hard and fast. Don't hesitate and do not stop under any circumstances, understand?"

"I don't want to go to my father," Uther said petulantly. "I want to stay here and kill Saxons."

"You want to kill Saxons, boy?" Geraint interjected. "Then we'll leave you outside these walls with a sword and a shield. See how far you get."

Uther gave him a hateful glare but remained silent as Alwyn cantered over to me on his sturdy mount, his face hidden by an aventail of mail that hung from the eye protectors of his helm.

"Here's the plan my lad," he said, accepting a lance and shield from a retainer. "We ride out and smash through those Saxon scum like a hot knife through butter. Cynyr's horsemen are out there as well waiting for us. They will lead the charge and we will follow. Once through, you carry on going. Ride like your arse is on fire and don't stop until you reach Caer Cadwy. Is that clear?"

I nodded in reply, taking my place near the rear ranks of the horsemen. The order was given and several men raised the thick wooden bars and the gates were opened. Alwyn ap Glyn gave the signal and one of the horsemen sounded a war horn and with a ferocious yell, we rode forth into the mist.

Chapter 3

A Cry for Help

As Alwyn had predicted, we smashed through the unsuspecting Saxon lines with ease. They were unprepared for our counter attack and had relaxed their shield wall, and as we rode out, we saw Cynyr and his remaining horsemen waiting nearby. They had been wreaking havoc in the ranks of Vortigern's army, striking hard and fast and vanishing into the mist, rendering several of the siege engines and towers inoperable. Now they rode with us, charging the Saxon lines front on and allowing us to plough through them easily. Men fell under our onslaught like sheaves of wheat falling before a scythe, hacked down and trampled under the hooves of our steeds. As we reformed, following the charge, Cynyr sought me out. I held the broken stump of a lance in my hand, having buried the rest of it in the chest of an unfortunate Saxon.

The barbarians had reformed and strengthened their shield wall, hammering sword hilts and spear shafts against their shields and challenging us with their guttural war chant.

"You're all clear now. Ride like the wind."

Cynyr slapped my stallion's rump and I galloped off into the mist, with Uther and Geraint close behind, riding eastward. I cast one last glance over my shoulder as our horsemen rode into the Saxons again with a Pendragon war cry and kicked my heels into my horse's flanks and bent low over his neck, spurring him into a sustained gallop over the moors, splashing through streams and traversing rocky hills.

We passed several settlements on the way, abandoned and burned out by the marauding Saxon army, sometimes smelling the ominous odour of burned flesh in the acrid smoke.

By nightfall we had reached the barren, rocky eastern hills that marked the edge of Pendragon territory. A light but persistent rain fell in flurries that soaked us through and so we sheltered for a while in a cleft between two large rocks. We did not have time to light a fire, but sat with our cloaks pulled over our heads, eating dried bread and goat's cheese from our saddlebags, staring out across the bleak, dark hills while our horses rested.

"My mother told me these hills are plagued by spirits," Uther said apprehensively, his pale blue eyes wide and frightened.

There were many tales about these moors that I remembered from the hearth fires of Caer Dor. Tales of restless spirits that roamed at night, of man eating giants and a huge, grey skeletal horse that wandered the moors and portended death for any who saw it, carrying the souls of the dead on its bony back. And then there were the stories of bandits and outlaws who would cut your throat for a chunk of bread. I put these tales to the back of my mind, but I still found myself jumping at the slightest sound. Despite this, I tried to soothe the boy's fears. "Do not be afraid, Uther," I said reassuringly. "They are just stories, nothing more."

"You are afraid as well," the boy said disparagingly. "I can see it in your eyes."

I ignored the boy's acerbic comment and pulled my cloak further over my head, watching water droplets drip from the hem.

"We must be moving on soon," I muttered.

"I'm tired, I need to rest." Uther replied petulantly.

Geraint returned with two limp hares dangling from his fist.

"What are you going to do with those?" Uther asked with a sneer. "You can't cook them because we haven't even got a fire. You won't let us have a fire."

Geraint strung the two hares from his horse's saddle. "These are for Fergus and I tomorrow," he said without looking up. "Not sure what you're going to eat though."

"Don't worry. When I get to my father's fortress there will be plenty to eat for me," Uther replied. "You can keep your stinking hares."

Geraint chuckled to himself as he swung a leg over his horse's back. "We should get moving. We've already wasted too much time here."

Reluctantly we left our meagre shelter and mounted up. Uther moved lethargically, shuffling over to his mount and untying the reins from a nearby stunted tree with deliberately slow and ponderous movements, much to our annoyance.

"If you don't hurry up, I'll tie you to the back of my horse and drag you to Caer Cadwy," Geraint snarled impatiently.

The boy made a show of slowly mounting his horse whilst glaring defiantly at Geraint. "You cannot speak to me like that. My father will punish you for your insolence."

In response, Geraint smacked Uther's faceplate, slamming it shut over the boy's face and then cuffed the side of his helmet with a hefty swipe, causing Uther to nearly fall from his horse.

The boy cursed and ranted as he tried to raise the elaborate faceplate which had jammed shut and I looked at Geraint and had to stifle a snigger. Eventually, I took pity on the boy and helped to raise his faceplate. Uther's face was red with fury as he glared at Geraint who ignored him and stared indifferently over the barren, hilly landscape.

"I'll see you hang for that, cur," Uther spat viciously, but Geraint was unfazed by the boy's fury and merely chuckled, infuriating the young lord even more.

We set off again, our cloaks pulled up high against the driving squalls of rain, with Uther tagging along behind.

"How long do you think Caer Dor can hold out?" I asked Geraint when Uther was out of earshot.

"If we can convince Duke Julianus to come to our aid, it could turn the tide of the battle."

Geraint snorted. "Too little too late my friend. It will take us the best part of tomorrow to reach Caer Cadwy. It will take Julianus a further day to mobilise his forces and then three days to force march back to Caer Dor. Do you honestly think Branwen can hold out for five days against that?"

I turned in my saddle, looking at Uther behind us, tired and bedraggled and swaying with the horses movements. I remembered the words of the Saxon leader, Hengest and I hoped for the sake of Uther and his mother that Caer Dor would not fall.

We rode at a steady pace, slightly north of east by my reckoning though it was difficult to tell in the darkness, over rough, hilly terrain. Uther was silent and brooding over his humiliation and rode deliberately slowly, causing us to have to stop and wait for him to catch up. By the time the sky began to lighten in the west, we had left the high moorland and were riding through pleasant, wooded valleys and our mood improved slightly, but it was short lived when Uther's mount caught its leg in a badger set, twisting it and rendering the animal lame.

We struggled on with Uther's horse limping badly and eventually, by early morning we came to a wide, slow moving river crossing our path, flowing from north to south.

"The River Isca," Geraint said. "Marks the eastern end of Pendragon territory. Beyond that is the realm of King Erbin of Dumnonia." He pointed south. "There lies Caer Isca. King Erbin's city and the capital of Dumnonia."

I followed Geraint's pointing finger and could see in the distance to the south a vast stone wall surrounding dozens of crowded buildings. A pall of smoke hung over the city and I stared in wonder at the size of it. "Do people really live on top of each other like that? I have never before seen a city."

"They are best viewed from a distance, believe me," Geraint said. "Crowded, filthy, stinking shit holes."

"I wonder if Rome looks like that?" I said half to myself.

"Like that but an even bigger shit hole, I'd wager. I have no desire to go to either," Geraint grumbled. "Especially seeing as Drustan Pendragon killed King Erbin's father. We would hardly be made welcome. But I'm afraid my need for ale and a warm stew are greater than my fear of King Erbin."

"We're not here to drink and feast, Geraint," I replied. "We must get a fresh mount for Uther so that we can continue on to Caer Cadwy."

"Surely we can stay long enough to down a pitcher of ale before we go on our way?" Geraint replied with a grin. He turned to Uther. "And get rid of that ridiculous helmet unless you want everyone in the city to know who you are."

"Why shouldn't they know who I am?" Uther replied haughtily. "I am of the Pendragon and proud. I will not skulk around the city like a common thief."

"Did you not hear what I said earlier, boy?" Geraint said with impatience. "Your grandfather killed King Erbin's father, Custennin. If it is known that you are in his city, things could get rather uncomfortable for all of us, so lose the helmet and keep your mouth shut."

Uther sat upright in his saddle and lifted his chin defiantly. "This helmet was a gift from my grandfather, who inherited it from his father."

I could tell from Geraint's expression that he was losing patience and was on the verge of doing something foolish, so I stepped between them to diffuse the situation, eventually persuading Uther to hand his helmet over to me.

"We should be able to exchange this for a fairly good horse," I said with a wink towards Geraint.

Uther was outraged and his face was crimson with fury, but we ignored his outbursts as I placed the helmet into a sack and then into one of my saddle bags and we rode on, spurring our exhausted mounts towards a covered wooden bridge that spanned the river. We were challenged by two surly, overweight guards and we told them that we were envoys on our way to Caer Cadwy seeking refreshment and rest and a replacement horse and they reluctantly let us pass.

As we reached the great wooden gate in the western wall of Caer Isca, we were challenged again. We gave the guards the same story and they let us go, with a strict warning to stay out of trouble. The gates creaked open and we rode into the city.

It was not what I had expected. The buildings were tall, built of both wood and stone and crammed close together, with sloping roofs of red tiles, but most were derelict, with great gaping holes in the tiles and empty window and door frames. The main street down which we were riding, once cobbled evenly with stone was now uneven and potholed, strewn with waste, with weeds growing from between the cobbles and gutters overflowing with all kinds of filth.

A number of Roman statues stood on plinths either side of the street and although many were broken beyond recognition, I still marvelled at the quality of the workmanship reflected in the marble effigies. They looked like real people who had been turned to stone, caught forever in poses of oration, arms outstretched or in mid stride and for a moment I tried to imagine how this city must have once looked in its prime, when the Romans had ruled the land.

A few ragged looking people and a three legged dog watched us with lethargic interest as we passed, but they soon ignored us when they realised we posed no threat, apart from a handful of children who followed us for a short distance, laughing and shouting childish insults at us.

We rode into what must have once been the forum, but the once grand Roman buildings surrounding the open public space were now nothing but ruins, their roofs open to the sky, now homes to pigeons and stray cats and dogs with flimsy hovels leaning against their walls. We passed a small market, where people bartered and argued over vegetables and scraps of meat that smelled like they had seen better days, finally stopping at a nearby tavern, its timbers so warped that it looked as though it would collapse at any minute and the sign, now flaking with age, bore a picture of a fish leaping from a cup. We decided that this would be a good place to enquire as to where we could get a horse and so we dismounted and Geraint tossed the emaciated stable boy two small iron bars as payment for feeding and watering our horses and we entered the dimly lit, low roofed hovel. The inside stank of fish and stale beer and a number of unsavoury looking men glanced in our direction and began speaking in whispers over their mugs of ale, casting us furtive looks every now and then.

The tavern keeper, a large, portly man with a grey, drooping moustache and a stained leather apron bustled over to us and forced a smile on his ruddy face as we sat at a table in the tavern's corner.

"Good day to you, weary travellers. What can I do for you? A room maybe? A young girl for company?" He leered over at a grossly overweight girl with a bad squint on the other side of the tavern who grinned at us coquettishly and brushed back her greasy, brown hair with one hand and cupped a huge white breast in the other.

"That's my daughter there," he added proudly, running a filthy rag over our table. "She likes warriors. The more you pay, the more she'll do if you know what I mean." He finished his sentence with a wink and a salacious chuckle.

"We're not staying," Geraint said. "Just get us a jug of ale and some food and we'll be on our way."

"Also, one of our horses is lame," I added. "Could you tell us where we can get a new one?"

The man looked disappointed and a little put out that he had put on his pleasant facade for nothing.

"Well, I have a friend, Motios near the west gate," he said, rubbing a hand over his balding pate. "He has a few old nags he'd be willing to part with. I'm sure I could arrange something for you. Depends what you have to offer though."

I produced the sack containing Uther's ceremonial helmet and the innkeeper's face paled as though he half expected me to produce a bloodied head from it.

"What could he give us for this?" I asked, knowing that the helmet alone was worth all of the horses in Caer Isca. I kept the helmet half in the sack, shielding it from prying eyes.

The tavern keeper's jaw dropped open and he swallowed hard. He looked back at me with greedy, porcine eyes. "I'll see that you get the very best, sir. I'll send my boy to fetch Motios and one of his finest mounts. In the meantime I'll arrange some food and ale for you. But he will have to take the helmet with him, or else Motios may not believe him." He ran a fat tongue over cracked lips as his eyes fell once again to the sack as I carefully wrapped the helmet.

I hesitated, reluctant to hand over something so valuable to a complete stranger before hesitantly pushing the sack and its contents over the ale stained table towards the tavern keeper.

He shot out a fat, trembling hand and grabbed the sack. "Will there be anything else, gentlemen?" he enquired in hushed tones.

I reached out and grabbed his thick wrist and squeezed. My grip was like iron from my years of weapons practice and I saw the tavern keeper wince fearfully as I increased the pressure. "Just one more thing. If your son doesn't return, you die and if he returns with a worthless nag, I'll cut your hand off, understood?"

The tavern keeper nodded brusquely, his jowls shaking as he did so. "Do not worry, I am an honest man," he stammered and I released him, convinced that fear would prevent him from swindling us.

"Very well then, sirs," he winked at me, regaining his composure and rubbing his wrist. "I'll send my boy straight away. Make yourselves at home." He turned back to the ugly girl and shouted. "Gwenda, get over here. A jug of ale and some stew for the gentlemen, quick about it."

The tavern keeper went back to cleaning beakers and mugs and after a short while his daughter waddled over carrying a tray with a jug of ale, three pitchers and three clay bowls of steaming stew. She placed it on the table before us and loitered, trying to look seductive, but we ignored her and ate and drank voraciously.

"Is there anything else I can do for you handsome gentlemen?" she said, running her fingers over Geraint's broad shoulders.

"Go back to the kitchens my dear," Geraint muttered between mouthfuls of stew. "You're blocking the light, I can't see what I'm eating."

The girl muttered something under her breath and stomped off and I chuckled to myself. Geraint looked up and grinned mischievously.

"So when did Lord Drustan kill King Erbin's father?" I asked.

"About nine or ten years ago, when Erbin was still a baby. His father, King Custennin of Dumnonia wanted to bring the Pendragon under his rule. Naturally, Drustan was having none of it." Geraint spoke between mouthfuls of stew, wiping his mouth with the back of his hand.

"But now there is peace between the Pendragon and King Erbin?" I said.

Geraint shrugged and grimaced, removing a chunk of gristle from the stew and throwing it to the floor. "When they realised they could not beat the Pendragon, a peace conference was held between Drustan, King Erbin's steward and his two battle dukes, Gorlois and Julianus. An accord was reached and a great feast was held in the King's hall in this very city. That was when Julianus fell for Branwen and after a brief fling, she was with child," he nodded towards Uther who was looking around at his surroundings with a look of contempt. "Drustan was furious, and so a marriage was hastily arranged to seal the new found fragile peace."

"And the result was Uther Pendragon," I added. Uther looked up as he heard his name mentioned and Geraint nodded. "With the added convenience of the merging of two great households," he ruffled Uther's dark hair playfully but the young lord merely glared at him, still furious that we were willing to sell his precious helmet. "And Uther is now the best candidate for the throne of Dumnonia. He could unite the Dumnonii, the Cornovii and the Durotriges under one banner, which is why King Vortigern and no doubt Gorlois are keen to be rid of him before he becomes old enough to rule."

"That is why you must get me to my father," Uther stated with a self-important air.

"And King Erbin as well? Does he want rid of him?" I asked.

"More than likely, seeing as Drustan killed his father. But in the meantime, he can see the benefits of having the Pendragon on his side. But he also fears the wrath of Julianus if he were to do something rash. The Battle Duke of Durotrigia is a force to be reckoned with, believe me."

I glanced at Branwen's son who was following our conversation with a worried scowl. "But that could change if he sees that the Pendragon are weakened and beset by enemies on all sides."

Geraint nodded in agreement. "Exactly."

We hurriedly ate another bowl of stew each and shared another jug of ale whilst waiting impatiently for the tavern keeper's son to return. As we were finishing our meal, the door of the tavern opened and in walked an officious looking, thin haired man flanked by two burly warriors. He wore an expensive looking cloak of white wolf fur and around his neck was a thick gold chain and in his hands he held a familiar looking sack.

The skinny, squint eyed lad from the stables was being held by the arms by the two warriors and when he saw us he nodded towards us fearfully.

The small man turned and looked at us with a pinched, stern looking face and came striding over with his two guards who dragged the boy with them.

He stopped before us and dumped the sack on the table with a dull metallic clatter and with a flourish he removed the sack to reveal Uther's cavalry helmet, its burnished, mirror like dome reflecting the weak light of the tavern.

"You are the travellers who have come from the Pendragon lands?" He enquired brusquely.

"Who wishes to know?" Geraint asked without looking up from his stew bowl.

The man gave Geraint a distasteful look. "King Erbin wishes an audience with you. I have been sent to escort you to his palace."

"We're on urgent business. We can't go." Geraint replied bluntly.

The man's cheek twitched with irritation and his nostrils flared. He leaned forward so that his face was close to Geraint's ear. "When King Erbin requests your presence, you go immediately."

Geraint continued eating, unfazed by the man's attempt to intimidate him. "We swear loyalty to Lady Branwen Pendragon. Erbin is no king of ours."

The official's face turned bright red and I saw the two soldiers reach for their short, broad bladed swords. I quickly stood with both hands raised in a placatory gesture. "Very well, we will come. My friend is drunk, he does not mean what he says."

The official's rage quickly passed and he recomposed himself. "At least one of you has the sense he was born with. Please come with us."

We were led outside and taken across the forum, attracting the attention of the crowds of threadbare people in the market who looked on with an idle curiosity.

"We don't have time for this," Geraint complained under his breath.

I leaned over to Geraint and muttered in his ear. "Next time, keep your mouth shut and let me do the talking."

Across the other side of the forum was a large building surrounded by marble pillars which presumably once supported a roof which had now been replaced with timber and thatch. We climbed a wide set of stone steps where two armed guards stood outside of a set of ornately decorated double doors which swung open at our approach. The official went in first with Geraint, Uther and I escorted by the two guards and I stared in wonder at the inside of the vast, bright hall.

It was lit by high windows made up of squares of coloured glass that bathed the mosaic floor with green, blue and red light. It was the first time I had ever seen glass and I was amazed at the magical colours that it created. In the centre of the mosaic floor was a fire pit with long tables either side and beyond this, near the walls the hall was lined with white pillars and exquisite statues of smooth, pale marble. Guards clad in leather armour stood silently at regular intervals between the statues and pillars, their spears held straight and their large oval shields bearing the Chi-Rho initials of Christ.

At the far end of the hall stood a group of well-dressed people, clad in expensive furs and wearing brooches and bracelets of gold and silver, but my attention was drawn to the sickly, emaciated young boy sat on an ornate throne on a raised marble dais.

He was small, fair haired and frail looking, a little older than Uther but nowhere near as sturdy. His legs were as thin as twigs and hung uselessly from beneath his embroidered robe. He looked upon us with sunken hazel eyes that peered listlessly from a pale, skeletal face and despite the warmth of the hall he was wrapped in a thick fur cloak with an oversized golden crown perched on his swollen head that had been padded out with red velvet so that it would fit. He pouted petulantly and leaned over to a corpulent, unattractive woman at his side.

"Look at them mother, they're absolutely filthy," the young king wrinkled his nose in disgust. "I can smell them from here."

The fat woman at his side spoke up, her voice sibilant and high pitched. "His majesty wishes to know your business. What brings you to Caer Isca?"

I took a step forwards and knelt respectfully with my head lowered. "Forgive our appearance your majesty. But we have been in battle and have travelled from the lands of Lady Branwen Pendragon, whom we serve. We seek the aid of Duke Julianus and only stopped at your city to rest our horses and quench our thirst."

"And you did not think to seek the aid of the rightful king of this land?" The overweight woman said, casting a sidelong glance at the young monarch.

"We seek the aid of Duke Julianus only because the mother of his son is in grave danger. Caer Dor is besieged by the forces of King Vortigern, led by his son

Prince Vortimer. We would be grateful for any assistance, my lady. One of our horses is lame and we need to find another. Once we do, we will be on our way and will trouble you no more."

At the mention of Vortigern's name, the young king and his aides looked startled and began to whisper amongst themselves nervously and after a short discourse, King Erbin spoke.

"Vortigern's armies are in my lands? How can that be? Duke Gorlois' galleys protect us from any invasions by sea, surely?"

"We fear that Duke Gorlois is in league with King Vortigern, your majesty," I replied, my eyes still downcast.

"But he's my western Battle-Duke!" The king exclaimed shrilly. "He swore an oath to my father, to protect Dumnonia's western coasts and in return, my father granted him dominion over the land of the Cornovii. Gorlois is loyal, he would never betray us, would he mother?" The boy turned to his mother who sat next to him on a plain chair with her fat hands neatly folded on her lap.

"I do not think Gorlois would do that, dear," she said indulgently, giving me a look of dismissive disdain.

"We have good reason to believe that is not the case, your majesty," I said, ignoring the young king's mother. "Duke Gorlois sent assassins to kill Drustan Pendragon. These assassins were Picts who were also in the employ of King Vortigern. We believe that Gorlois let Vortigern's army land on his shores and allowed it to cross his lands unmolested so that he could attack us and gain a foothold in Dumnonia."

"These are very serious allegations you are making," an elderly priest said, who was standing on the other side of King Erbin. "What evidence do you have to back these claims?"

"Before he died, one of the assassins gave us a name," I replied. "That name was Merrion, Lord Drustan's steward. After interrogation, he revealed that he was in the pay of Gorlois of Cerniw."

The elderly priest shook his head slowly. "Interrogated you say? More than likely tortured. Anyone knows that confessions extracted under torture are unreliable. He probably told you exactly what you wanted to hear, giving your lord free reign to continue his harassment of Duke Gorlois and his lands."

"We did not torture him," Geraint spat suddenly. "Gorlois is a treacherous, conniving dog who needs to be brought to justice before the King."

The King's mother stared up at the thatched ceiling with a bored expression. "And of course, Duke Gorlois would have no reason to bring the Pendragon under control, would he? Years of raids and plundering of his lands, the rape and murder of his people. Harassment of his trade routes with the rest of Dumnonia. Need I go on?"

"The land you refer to belongs to the Pendragon people," Geraint replied, barely able to contain his anger. "It was stolen off of them and handed to Gorlois' father. We have never recognised his authority."

The woman gave a thin, supercilious smile. "No, the Pendragon have a habit of kicking against authority, don't they? That is part of the problem. Maybe the beast needs taming after all these years."

"But Gorlois has allied himself with Vortigern," I interjected. "His ships were just off the coast preventing any escape by sea whilst Vortimer attacked Caer Dor with

Irish and Saxon mercenaries. He has betrayed your son, his king and he has betrayed Dumnonia."

The woman looked thoughtful for a moment before the elderly priest spoke once again. "How do you know that Gorlois was against you? I mean, did he have warriors on the ground? Was his army directly involved in the siege?"

A cacophony of whispers and hushed voices passed through the assembly of advisors and nobles.

"Gorlois has never had the stomach to face the Pendragon directly," I said. "He was using his fleet to blockade us."

"But how can you be sure about this?" The King's mother interjected. "How do you know that he was not merely observing? Waiting for the opportune moment to strike at Vortimer's forces? I think this far more likely than your prejudicial assumptions." The woman sat back with a smirk and raised her flaccid chin in self-satisfaction.

Geraint gave a derisive snort and I too could feel my patience wearing thin. "He had plenty of opportunity to strike at Vortimer's forces if that was his intention. But instead, he sat and watched. It was a blockade, have no doubts about it, my lady."

The King's mother toyed with one of the many rings adorning her chunky fingers as she looked at Uther. "One more thing. Who is the boy who travels with you?"

Before I could answer, Uther spoke loudly and full of arrogant confidence. "I am Uther Pendragon. Heir to the lands west of the river and I must be allowed access to my father."

The woman's eyebrows rose in mild surprise and she smirked to herself. Her expression was unreadable, but I detected the hint of a sneer pass her lips. "Uther Pendragon? An honour to meet you, young lord." She bowed condescendingly, her gaze cold and unfaltering.

There was a moment of tense silence before the young king spoke in his high, reedy voice, addressing his mother. "So what do you advise that we do, Mother? I cannot pretend that I am not glad to hear that my father's murderer is dead." He turned and looked at Uther with contempt.

"Nor I, my son," the woman bit her lower lip as she pondered, a flicker of resentment crossing her face. "We will keep them here and we will send out a scouting party of our own to find out exactly what has happened. Lord Uther must remain under our protection and if what they say is true, we mobilise our armies and send them forth to face Vortimer's forces and drive them from the land. In the meantime, these gentlemen get to indulge in your Majesties hospitality until we see fit to release them." She finished her sentence with a sly, half smile that was filled with spite and gave another condescending bow.

A young girl, well dressed in the style of a Roman lady pushed her way past the assembly of nobles and stepped forward. "Mother, you cannot do this," she protested. "These men must be allowed to get to uncle Julianus. If the Pendragon fall, there will be no one to stop Vortigern sweeping into our lands and seizing the throne of Dumnonia."

The King's mother turned to face her daughter, her corpulent face growing red with indignation.

"You would do well to remember your place, Meinwen," she retorted in a measured tone. "For all we know, this could be an elaborate trap. These men will remain here until our scouts return. There will be no further discussion on the matter."

The young girl huffed in frustration, her pale cheeks growing red but she held her tongue. I caught her eye momentarily but she quickly averted her gaze.

"But we can't stay here," I protested loudly. "In a few days there will be nothing left of Caer Dor. If you wish to help, then please give us a steed and let us deliver our message to Julianus so that he can help as well. There is no time to send scouting parties back and forth, we must act now."

"The King has made his decision," the boy said suddenly in his falsetto voice. "You will remain here until we find out what is going on."

"For your own safety, of course," the King's mother added, her condescending smile returning.

Uther took a step forward and spoke again, his face red with frustration and his eyes filling with tears. "But my mother will die unless something is done now."

Geraint stood at Uther's side, his face contorted with anger, one hand on Uther's shoulder, the other closing around the hilt of his sword. "Young Uther is right. If you keep us here against our will, you will answer to the blades of the Pendragon."

Immediately the sound of swords sliding from their scabbards echoed throughout the hall as Erbin's soldiers drew their weapons and moved forwards to block Geraint. He stopped in his tracks with half a dozen steel blades pointing towards his chest.

The King's mother continued calmly, a smirk on her lips. "I would say that you have no choice but to stay here, wouldn't you? Unless of course you would like your heads to adorn the gates of the city. It is entirely up to you whether you stay in Caer Isca as guests or prisoners." She turned to a nearby servant and clicked her fingers. "Show our guests to their quarters."

****

Geraint stared gloomily out of the small window of our chamber at the pretty courtyard garden beyond. We had been escorted to our accommodation, a small but comfortable room in one of the wings of the King's palace that overlooked a spacious central courtyard. Uther had been taken to another chamber, somewhere else in the building and we both feared for his safety. Outside, slaves tended the various aromatic herbs that grew within the lush green garden that surrounded a shallow rectangular pool ringed with white marble statues of gods and emperors. It was a stark contrast to the crumbling squalor that seemed to affect the rest of the town.

"I can't believe this is happening," Geraint said again. It was about the fifth time he had said it since he had woke that morning. We had been fed well the previous evening, having been brought roast goose by the King's servants and had our every need attended to, but neither of us were under any illusions that we were being held here against our will.

"I don't care how they try to dress it up, we're prisoners here," Geraint said as he paced around the small chamber. "Why else would there be guards outside the door?"

"They want Branwen and Uther out of the way," I said as I stared out the small window. "They mean to end the Pendragon reign forever as they have been a thorn in the side of Dumnonia for too long. Uther is nothing more than a hostage now and a valuable one. As for us, who knows? They'll probably dispose of us before long as well because we know too much. We have failed, Geraint." I stood despondently and walked to the door.

"Where are you going?" Geraint asked.

"I need some air. I can't just sit here hoping that Duke Julianus arrives. If he ever arrives at all."

Two guards escorted me silently through a torch lit corridor to the courtyard and I walked out into the crisp spring air, breathing in the fragrances of the herb garden. I walked several times around the garden, pacing like a caged wolf, lost in my own thoughts as the two guards looked on in wary silence.

I felt both anger and frustration as I breathed in the cool morning air. If Caer Dor fell and Branwen were killed, once again I would be lost. Caer Dor was my home, its warriors were my brothers and they were the closest thing to family that I had. And I knew that as I strolled through King Erbin's pretty gardens, my comrades were fighting and dying against overwhelming odds. I thought of Diarmuid and Alwyn, Cynyr and Enfys and Sarn, all noble men and brave warriors who could be depended upon in the chaos of the shield wall and I wondered whether they were still alive. I felt angry for allowing myself to have walked into this bear pit and I felt impotent anger towards the young King Erbin and his mother for preventing us from completing our task.

I sat on a stone bench underneath a willow tree, picked up a handful of small white stones from the path and tossed them one at a time into the dark pool that reflected the white clouds in the sky above, watching the image become distorted by the ripples. I briefly considered whether it would be possible to break out, but there were armed guards at every corner of the enclosed courtyard. Our weapons had been taken from us and I felt naked and vulnerable without them.

I flicked several stones at a female stone effigy pouring water from an amphorae into a marble basin and jumped suddenly when I heard a female voice beside me.

"Throwing stones at Egeria won't help."

I looked up to see the young woman whom I had seen earlier in the King's hall. She was several years younger than me in a long white dress, gathered in at the waist by an embroidered girdle. She was pale skinned and thin but attractive, with wavy brown hair tied back and gathered on top of her head to reveal a long, slender neck. The jewels that she wore and the cut of her dress indicated that she was of high status.

"I'm sorry?" I muttered, taken aback by her sudden appearance.

"The statue. It is Egeria, the water nymph." She was softly spoken and she smiled slightly as she nodded towards the statue.

"Oh. Forgive me, I meant no disrespect."

"Don't worry, I won't tell anyone. What is your name, warrior?"

"Fergus. Of the Pendragon."

The girl cocked her head to one side thoughtfully. "Fergus does not sound like the name of a Briton," she said with an astute glint in her eye.

"It isn't. I originally came from Eire, the land of the Gaels. I am of the Deisi clan."

Her blue eyes widened with excitement. "A Gael? I never thought I would ever meet a Gael. But you look like a Briton."

"That's because they removed my tail when I arrived here," I said with a wry smile.

The girl laughed and the sound of her gentle, joyous laughter touched my heart and I laughed too despite my dark mood.

The girl pursed her red lips and looked me up and down with curiosity. "What brings you to this land, Gael? Why did you leave your homeland?"

I hesitated and swallowed hard at the bitter lump that had formed in my throat. "It wasn't through choice. My home was destroyed and I had to leave."

"Do you have family?" the girl asked tenderly.

I shook my head and turned away from her, trying to hide the emotion in my face. "When I first came to Dumnonia, I was taken in by a fisherwoman who raised me as one of her own. But the people who had destroyed my home also came to these shores and murdered my adopted family. I managed to escape and eventually I was accepted as a warrior by the Pendragon clan. They have been my family these past years and now it looks as though once again I will be alone. It seems that the gods have willed this and wherever I go, disaster and misery follows."

The girl looked at me with compassion. "Forgive me, I would never have asked had I known the answer would be so sad. I can be a little insensitive at times."

I forced a smile. "Don't worry, you were not to know. So I have given my name and story, what of yours?"

The girl let out a bashful little laugh. "I'm sorry, I am forgetting my manners again. My name is Meinwen. My brother is the king and for most of my life, this is all I have ever known," she swept a slender arm out to indicate the palace and the gardens. "It is not very often that I get to talk to someone from outside of the city."

I remembered Lord Drustan mentioning a Princess Meinwen when I had first sat at his table many years ago. I cleared my throat and adopted a more respectful tone. "My lady, do you think it is possible for you to persuade your brother to allow us to leave?"

"Please, call me Meinwen," she said. "I'm afraid my little brother has very little say in what actually goes on, despite his title. My mother, Quintinia and the priest,

Awstin hold the real power in Dumnonia. And they squabble over it like dogs with a hare. But they are agreed on one thing. You and your companion will not leave Caer Isca. As you have probably surmised, they have no intention of getting a message to Julianus, but fortunately for you, I have despatched a rider of my own to Caer Cadwy. My mother would love to see the Pendragon fall as she still hates Lord Drustan for taking my father's life. And now his grandson has walked willingly into her lair and my mother cannot believe her good fortune. But I cannot wait to see her face when Julianus turns up."

I stood and hurled the handful of stones at the statue in frustration. "I thank you for that my lady, but this is nonsense. My comrades are fighting and dying and I am stuck here at the whim of a child and his overindulgent mother. Let me see her face to face and tell her in no uncertain terms what will happen if she does not release my friend and I immediately."

Meinwen put a hand on my arm. "Please, my mother would have no qualms about having you executed immediately if you make a nuisance of yourself. She keeps you here for her own amusement, because she can. This very moment, they are discussing what they should do with you. If I can, I will do my best to persuade them that it is in their best interests to let you and your friend live."

"I very much doubt they will allow that my lady," I said, looking around at the high walls surrounding the gardens. "But why would you aid the Pendragon? What are you getting from this?"

"Because despite the fact that she is my mother, there is little love between us," the girl's face twisted into a bitter, hateful scowl. "She has devoted her life to my precious crippled brother and has never had any time for me. I am merely a convenient playing piece in her game, to be married off to any warlord powerful enough to bring prestige to our family name. If the Pendragon fall, Gorlois becomes the greatest power in the West and my mother would have me marry him, which is something I am loathe to do." Princess Meinwen's lip twisted into a sneer. "There is something about the man that I do not like. I have met him several times and I find him boorish and lecherous. My mother however has fallen for his charms as most people seem to. She is so blinded by ambition that she cannot see beyond his good looks and she cannot understand why I cannot bear him. There is a darkness to his soul which I find disturbing."

I nodded in response, but I was growing restless and impatient. I fought to control my frustration, clenching my fists tightly. "How long until Julianus gets here?"

"All going well, he should be here before sundown."

"And then there will be more talking while my friends are dying. I thank you my lady for having the foresight to send your own messenger, but If Caer Dor falls, your mother will be as much to blame as King Vortigern."

Meinwen glanced around fearfully at the silent guards that stood either side of the narrow path and replied in a whisper. "You must be careful what you say. There are ears everywhere in Caer Isca, as you have found out. It is time you left now."

I nodded silently in response. "Thank you, my lady," I said before rising from the stone seat and striding away, leaving Meinwen alone in the gardens.

Chapter 4

The Duke of Cerniw

It was the middle of the night when Julianus finally arrived with his entourage. Outside, a ferocious storm had swept in from the west, battering the shutters of the windows and threatening to tear the thatched roof from the palace.

A knock on the door of our chamber awoke me from a disturbed sleep. I arose groggily to answer it.

A nervous looking young woman was standing before me, holding a gourd with a tallow candle stuck in the top. I looked down the dim, torchlit passageway either side but the guards had gone. "My lady Meinwen has sent me to tell you that Duke Julianus of Durotrigia has arrived," she said quietly. "You must hurry before the guards return."

I thanked the girl and Geraint and I got dressed, pulling on our freshly polished mail shirts and strapping on our thick sword belts before allowing the girl to escort us to the King's hall.

At the doorway leading into the hall, two leather clad guards crossed their spears in front of us, barring our way.

"The Pendragon warriors are not permitted to enter the hall," one of them said. The girl suddenly adopted a tone of authority. "Princess Meinwen gives her permission for them to enter. Please step aside."

The guard shook his head. "Lady Quintinia expressly forbade these two from entering."

"And who will one day be a queen?" Another female voice said from behind us. "A queen who will remember fondly those who served her faithfully and not so favourably those who stood against her?"

I turned to see Meinwen standing there, her face lit by the candle she was holding. She spoke with the confident ease of someone who was used to being obeyed and her expression was stern and unyielding.

The guard immediately backed down. "I'm sorry my lady," he said, stepping to one side.

We entered the torchlit hall where a long table had been placed in front of the King's throne. A number of people were sitting at the table, most of whom were Erbin's advisers, priests and nobles, but at the far end stood Julianus and his entourage.

He was a large, imposing man; lean, with dark, greying hair, short and brushed forwards in the style of the old Roman emperors, clean shaven with narrow, chiselled features and a large beak of a nose. He was wearing a suit of white enamelled scale armour with bands of gold trimmed white leather protecting his broad shoulders over which he wore a scarlet cloak which dripped rain droplets onto the smooth floor. On the table before him was a polished helmet studded with rubies with a large crest of red horsehair that ran from front to back. The man seemed to radiate an air of power and was in his own way as much a warrior as Drustan Pendragon, though of a very different sort. This was a man who knew how to command respect without having to resort to cruelty or barbarism. Either side of him stood a group of similarly clad warriors, though none wore armour as ornate as Julianus'.

Quintinia, who was seated at the table nearest to King Erbin looked up as we walked in. She looked flustered and shaken, her forehead sheened with sweat. "Who permitted these men in here?" She demanded, standing up and glaring furiously at the guards at the door.

"I did, mother," Meinwen said calmly. "Is there a problem with that? After all, as warriors of the Pendragon this discussion concerns them as well, does it not?"

Quintinia's cheeks puffed indignantly. "If their mission was so urgent, why is it that they were found blind drunk in a nearby tavern?"

I fixed Quintinia with an icy stare. "Uther's mount became lame and we had to stop to enquire as to where we could find another. We had been riding all through the night and much of the previous day and we were not drunk," I took a deep breath to calm my anger and compose myself before continuing. "If you do not believe us, then why is Duke Julianus here?" I said. "You knew very well that we had an important message to deliver regarding the fate of the Duke's wife and to deliver Uther to his safety and you have prevented us from doing that, Quintinia. And why were we not invited to this discussion? Maybe so that you could tell the story as you saw fit?"

Quintinia's face grew red with rage. "How dare you speak to me like that. I am mother to the king of Dumnonia and with a word I could have you flayed alive and fed to the hounds."

For the first time, Julianus spoke and his powerful, stern voice echoed in the torchlit hall. "And I am the Battle Duke of Durotrigia and I say these men should be heard. If these two men have news that concerns Uther's mother, why is it being kept from me, Quintinia? And where is my son?" His voice was deep and powerful, bearing traces of an accent that I could not place.

Quintinia's jowls began to quiver as she forced a smile. "My Lord Duke, your son is resting and be assured that no one is trying to keep you in the dark. But we require clear minds here and these two are too belligerent for their own good. They will contribute nothing useful to our discussion."

"Of course they are belligerent, Quintinia, they are warriors," Julianus said with a hint of contempt. A ripple of mutters ran through the assembly and I saw Quintinia's face flush once again. "They would not be much good as warriors if they weren't would they? Let them speak."

Julianus turned and looked at me with dark eyes that bore the intensity of a bird of prey. He nodded at me to indicate that he wished for me to speak.

I cleared my throat nervously. "My Lord Duke, we were sent from Caer Dor to ensure Uther reached your stronghold and with a request for aid. Lady Branwen is in grave danger. Caer Dor is being besieged by the armies of King Vortigern under the command of his son, Prince Vortimer, who has also employed Irish and Saxon mercenaries as well as some clan chiefs who were once loyal to Drustan Pendragon. We have reason to believe that Duke Gorlois is working with Vortigern as he was using his ships to prevent any escape by sea."

"You have no proof of that," Quintinia butted in, raising her voice so all could hear.

Awstin, the elderly priest tapped his staff on the flagstone floor once for attention. "It is also common knowledge that the Pendragon stole the Holy Chalice from

Ynys Wytryn and burned down the church there. Maybe what we are seeing is divine retribution," he looked at me with narrowed, hostile eyes and I felt my lip curl into a sneer.

"A convenient excuse to attack, wouldn't you say, Father?" The Duke replied.

A man standing next to Julianus spoke up. He too was clad in enamelled scale armour and was obviously a relation of the Duke as he bore the same nose and stony features, although he was younger and his eyes were blue. "It may be that Gorlois wishes to see an end to Pendragon power and I may add, with good reason," he gave me a steely accusatory look. "But his loyalty to King Erbin and Dumnonia is unquestioned, whereas the loyalty of the Pendragon is shaky to say the least."

Julianus ignored him and directed his questions towards me. "What is the strength of his army? How long do you think Caer Dor will hold out?"

It was the sort of question I would expect from a soldier. "I estimate that they were close to two thousand strong, my lord. They also had Roman siege weapons, catapultae, ballistae, that sort of thing. When I left, we were holding out well enough as Caer Dor's defences are quite strong, but we are heavily outnumbered and I don't think we could hold out for more than a few days," I reached into the pouch at my belt and produced the dragon adorned ring. "My Lady Branwen Pendragon told me to give you this as proof that I speak the truth."

I strode forwards and handed the ring to Julianus. He held it between thumb and forefinger, his expression unreadable as he turned the golden ring in the torchlight. "That is the ring I gave to Branwen on our wedding day," he said. His jaw tightened noticeably, the only outward sign that he was controlling a deep emotion. He stood suddenly, addressing the assembly. "We must act immediately. I will return to Caer Cadwy and ready my forces for a counter attack. We have already lost too much valuable time and Uther's mother is in danger."

"But what of Gorlois?" the boy king said in his fluting voice. "He has been summoned to this meeting as well. Perhaps he can also offer assistance."

Julianus took a deep breath and addressed King Erbin. "Your majesty, too much time has been lost already, thanks to your advisers preventing these men from doing their duty. We must act immediately otherwise Caer Dor will surely fall."

"My Lord Duke, do not be too hasty to rush into battle," Awstin, the elderly priest said. "If we act rashly then it could be disastrous. Have you considered that maybe Vortigern is expecting you to react in such a way? If your army is defeated as well as the Pendragon, then Dumnonia is doomed."

Julianus ignored the priest and picked up his shining cavalry officer's helmet. "Your majesty, ready your forces. We will rendezvous with you at sunrise outside of the city and march on to Caer Dor."

"My Lord Duke, will you not take the two Pendragon warriors with you?" Princess Meinwen asked. She caught my eye and I saw the hint of a smile cross her lips.

Julianus nodded as he put on his helmet and tightened the leather strap. "Very well. They are serving little purpose being kept here. With your permission, majesty?"

King Erbin assented with a bored wave of his hand. "Return their weapons and let them go," he said officiously. "Let Uther Pendragon go with his father."

I looked over at Quintinia and she shot me a glance of pure vitriol as I bowed politely towards her.

As Geraint and I strapped on our weapons, I caught the princess's eye again and smiled at her gratefully. When we were out of sight of her mother, she came over and I thanked her for her assistance.

"It was nothing," she replied with a grin. "I was impressed by the way you stood up to my mother and besides, I relish any chance to demean her authority. It lets her know exactly who is in charge around here."

"I hope you forgive me for being so rude to you yesterday, my lady," I said. "I just felt so helpless being stuck here when I should be helping my comrades."

Meinwen smiled sweetly. "Don't be silly. Of course I know why you reacted in that way. And I told you before, call me Meinwen."

"Thank you...Meinwen."

Julianus and his son, the one who had spoken earlier came over to us. He gave a respectful bow to Meinwen. "A pleasure to see you again, princess."

"Uncle Julianus, it is good to see you again. And you Constans."

Julianus' son took the princess' small hand in his and kissed it. "A pleasure as always, your highness," he said charmingly before turning his attention to Geraint and I. His charm melted as he regarded us with a surly look. "So what are we going to do with these two, father?"

"For now they ride with us. Hopefully we can return them to Branwen later, but for now they are part of our army. I hope you do not object to that?"

"No, Lord Duke," I said. "I am just glad that we will have a chance to strike back at our enemies again. We would be honoured to ride with you."

Julianus nodded, satisfied by my answer. "What are your names, men?"

"I am Fergus mac Fiontan, originally of the Deisi. My companion here is Geraint of Powys."

"You are a Gael then?" Julianus asked, his eyes narrowing. Constans gave a derisive snort and muttered something derogatory under his breath.

I nodded. "Yes sir. But I was driven from my homeland by Fiachu, one of the sons of King Niall."

"Niall Noigiallach," Julianus mused. "I remember him well. Fought his band of pirates and murderers many times. And it would seem his sons have taken after him. You choose your enemies well, Fergus mac Fiontan."

Behind me, King Erbin's advisors were bickering amongst themselves, Quintinia's face still flushed with outrage as she glared every now and then towards Geraint and I. We were escorted by Erbin's guards to the stables where Julianus and his entourage had their horses and as the mounts were made ready to ride, Julianus introduced us to his other son.

"Ambrosius, come here," he barked. A young man around my age who had been talking with a group of Julianus' soldiers strolled over, pulling on a pair of thick leather gauntlets. Unlike his father and older brother he was of fair complexion, with wiry golden hair cropped short and pale eyebrows that were almost white, framing intelligent but serious blue eyes. He wore a shirt of polished mail with bronze shoulder pauldrons. The helmet he carried was also in the style of the Roman military, highly polished with broad cheek plates and a bristly crest of red horsehair on the top running front to back.

"Against my better judgement, I am putting these men under your command. Try not to get them killed like the last ones," Julianus said sharply to his younger son before turning to Geraint and I. "This is Ambrosius, my other son. You will remain under his command until we can return you to Lady Branwen, is that clear?"

Geraint and I both spoke in unison. "Yes, Lord Duke."

Julianus sighed and gave his fair haired son a disapproving stare. "Assuming my son can keep you alive that long." He turned on his heel and strode back to his men.

Ambrosius waited for his father to depart and then looked us up and down with a critical eye and a sour scowl on his face. "You fight for the Pendragon?" he asked. We both nodded in unison.

"You will find things very different with my father. We expect our troops to be disciplined, able to follow orders without question. I hear the Pendragon are an ill disciplined rabble."

Geraint bridled at the remark. "We fight well enough though, Lord. Disciplined or not, they all go down with the thrust of a sword."

Ambrosius regarded Geraint with a cool stare and a look of distaste. "Well we will know soon enough, won't we? Saddle up and stay close to me."

We rode out of Caer Isca with Julianus' entourage into the cold spring evening. The storm had passed, although there was still a strong wind and the sky was clear and the moon lit our way along the decrepit Roman road that took us north and then east through fertile, sparsely wooded countryside. There were around two dozen fully armed men with Julianus, all clad in long coats of scale armour and high bronze helmets of curious design crested with plumes of horsehair, with dark blue cloaks and large oval shields that bore the bull's head emblem of Julianus superimposed over the Chi-Rho runes of Christ. There was something peculiar about the men, something in their wide, swarthy faces and dark, glittering eyes that hinted that their origins were far from this land. Geraint and I rode near the back, either side of Ambrosius, who proved to be sullen and uncommunicative. His mouth was puckered and downturned, as though he had a bad taste in his mouth and his brow seemed to be permanently furrowed.

"I have heard tales of these men," Geraint said quietly, leaning towards me in his saddle. "They came with the Romans long ago, from lands far to the east. They are magnificent horsemen and can fight with spear and bow from the back of a horse better than most men can on foot. It is also said that they breed with their horses."

I nodded as I looked at the strange, foreign faces of the horsemen surrounding us. "Who are they?" I asked.

"Sarmatians," Ambrosius said brusquely, overhearing our conversation. The name of these strange horsemen meant nothing to me and I waited for him to elaborate, but instead he fell silent.

For a while we rode on, listening to the jangle of the bronze and bone trinkets on the Sarmatian's bridles. Eventually I attempted to engage the Duke's son in friendly conversation. "Thank you for coming so quickly, lord," I said awkwardly. "I hope we can get back to Caer Dor in time."

"I doubt we will," Ambrosius said brusquely.

We rode on in silence before I tried again. "I couldn't help noticing that Princess Meinwen referred to the Duke as uncle. Are you related to King Erbin?"

Ambrosius sighed with irritation. "We share blood through our grandfather, Flavius Claudius Constantinus, who was proclaimed Emperor by his troops on this very island. My father, Julianus is his son and King Custennin is the son of

Flavius' brother, King Aldrien of Armorica."

"So King Erbin and Princess Meinwen are your distant cousins?" I said.

Ambrosius gave me a withering look. "How very perceptive of you. Yes, we are related in a way."

I waited for Ambrosius to elaborate, but once again he lapsed into sullen silence. A little further on, Ambrosius' brother, Constans, who had been riding at the front of the column with his father, slowed his steed until he came level with us. He was flanked on either side by two warriors around his own age.

"Ah, little brother. How are things with your new pets?" He spoke loudly enough for Geraint and I to hear. Geraint muttered an insult under his breath but Constans did not hear.

"I know nothing about them," Ambrosius said, looking ahead with a frown.

"Naturally. Don't want to get too close after what happened last time do we?" Constans suggested. He turned his attention to me, looking me up and down with a critical eye. "You there. I heard you tell my father that you are a Gael?"

"Yes, my lord," I replied guardedly.

"I hear the Gaels are wild and uncivilised. I think you may prove too much for my little brother to control," Constans said casually. "You see, my little brother is somewhat of a virgin, in more than one sense of the word. My father recently gave him command of a dozen men, all of whom are now dead due to his lack of experience and tactical know how, isn't that right, Ambrosius? All those wasted years you spent studying the battles of Caesar and Alexander, moving your little soldiers around the floor in mock battles when other lads your age were out rutting servant girls. All seems so pointless now, doesn't it?"

"We were ambushed, you know that, Constans," Ambrosius muttered bitterly, the scowl on his face deepening.

"Ambushed, of course. And who had to save you from the nasty Saxons? Who found you hiding in the woods trembling and sobbing like a baby? Do you think Alexander cried and wet his breeches like that at Trebia?"

"Alexander didn't fight at Trebia," Ambrosius corrected sourly. "You mean Gaugamela."

Constans shook his head with a frustrated expression. "Who cares? The point is, you will never be another Alexander. You'd be hard pressed to clean out the stables properly."

Constans' companions laughed uproariously at this comment, but I could see by his face that Ambrosius was haunted by this particular memory. It was an event that was obviously very painful and I felt sorry for him. I had seen my share of bullies and I knew immediately what Constans was.

"Every warrior has been in a similar situation at some point," I said. "Just because your courage deserts you one day does not make you a coward for the rest of your life. Perhaps with a little more battle experience yourself, you will come to realise that, my lord."

Constans glared at me and I saw the flicker of a sneer on his lips, but he lacked the courage for a direct confrontation with me, instead directing his vitriol once again towards his younger brother. "Once again it seems that people are fighting your battles for you, Ambrosius," his tone became more vindictive. "That is why you ride at the back of the column. Our father is ashamed of you. You are an embarrassment to him," he turned his spiteful gaze towards Geraint and I. "Try not to get your new pets killed, won't you?" with that, he spurred his horse back up to the front of the column with his two companions in tow, laughing and joking with one another.

I looked at Ambrosius, whose pale face was contorted with bitterness. "Why does he speak to you like that?" I said quietly. "Who does he think he is?"

"He is the heir to Caer Cadwy and the kingdom of Durotrigia," Ambrosius said tartly, his voice trembling with anger. "And you would do well to remember your place, Gael. I am perfectly capable of fighting my own battles and if I need your help or your opinions, I will ask for them."

He kicked his heels into the flanks of his horse and spurred ahead of us, leaving Geraint and I to exchange weary glances.

It was the early hours of the morning when we first saw the specks of orange torchlight on the large hill that marked the location of Caer Cadwy. We were riding along a well maintained road that took us through farmland, past little sleeping settlements and up the hill. Even in the moonlight, Caer Cadwy was an impressive sight. It was huge, more like a small town than a fortress, with neat stone walls on top of a steep bank of earth, ringed by a deep moat filled with lethal looking wooden spikes. A well-made wooden palisade ran along the top of the stone wall with watch towers positioned at regular intervals. Guards bearing flickering torches patrolled the walls and as we approached, a cornicern sounded from one of the towers, its harsh note echoing across the countryside.

Our horses clattered across a wooden bridge that spanned the moat and the thick wooden gates studded with iron swung open to allow us access. Beyond the gate were rows of wooden buildings, evenly spaced either side of a main street that ran into a wide open space large enough to contain an army.

A soldier clad in mail and a crested helmet ran up to Julianus, slamming his right fist against his breast and thrusting his arm out in salute.

"Rally the troops immediately, Camillus. We ride to battle," Julianus said, climbing from his horse as a stable boy took the reins of his steed.

The soldier gave a brusque nod and jogged off, shouting for the trumpeter to wake the men. Within minutes, the peaceful tranquillity of Caer Cadwy was transformed into a hive of noise and activity. Trumpets and cornicerns sounded, their harsh, braying notes summoning men who poured from their barracks and houses, strapping on armour, helmets and weapons. Commanders shouted at their soldiers, cajoling them into position. Horses were harnessed and led from the stables and soon the large open parade area in the centre of Caer Cadwy was filled with rank upon rank of armed men, clad in identical banded leather armour and bronze helmets. I was fascinated. Never before had I seen a group of men move in such a disciplined way and it was an impressive sight to see several hundred men assemble so quickly. Within half an hour they were ready to move out as priests moved amongst the ranks bestowing the blessings of Christ upon the warriors. Geraint and I dismounted, knelt and made the sign of the cross as a young priest came over, gently placed a hand on our heads and blessed us.

Ambrosius came over to us. "We are to ride ahead with the cavalry. My father is riding with the infantry. You will follow my orders to the letter, understand?" Geraint and I nodded in response.

"Good. Please don't embarrass me any further." Ambrosius returned to his mount and leapt nimbly into the saddle.

"That lad needs a good woman. Perhaps we should introduce him to the lovely Gwenda back in that tavern?" I muttered.

"Either that or a spear up the backside," Geraint retorted.

We rode out once more at the head of Julianus' army amongst the ranks of his cavalry, which numbered around one hundred and fifty men. By the time the sky was lightening in the east, we had reached the outskirts of Caer Isca once again where we were met by King Erbin's commander, a gruff old soldier by the name of Ofydd, who was at the head of a pitiful looking band of horsemen. Constans rode forwards to meet him and the two men clasped one another's arms in greeting.

"Hail Lord Constans," Ofydd said. "I'm afraid this was all we could assemble in the short amount of time given," he gave an apologetic nod towards his sixty or so assembled warriors, many of whom resembled little more than farmers with spears and very little in the way of armour. "I was forbidden from taking any more men. Lady Quintinia said the rest were needed for the defence of the city in case we are besieged."

"They will have to do," Constans said airily. "Hopefully we can overcome this little issue without the need for further bloodshed, unless of course my father has other ideas."

Ofydd gave a noncommittal grunt in reply. "If it's any consolation, the Duke Gorlois arrived not long ago," he pointed a thick finger across the mist enshrouded meadow to where a small band of horsemen were approaching bearing Gorlois' banner of sky blue with the seahorse emblazoned in white in the middle. The horsemen wore shining helms, highly polished with plumes of peacock feathers spilling out from the pointed crest. Their bronze scale armour which reached down to mid-thigh was also highly polished and their deep blue cloaks billowed out behind them as they rode. The lead rider, however, wore a silver cavalry mask that covered his face completely, its exquisite features moulded into the likeness of a Roman god. He also wore a breastplate of silver, crafted to resemble the muscular torso of an athlete.

"Gorlois of Cerniw," Geraint snarled under his breath. "I swear if he comes too close to me, he'll have to wear that mask permanently, because I'll tear his bastard face off."

I placed a hand on Geraint's arm. "Steady on, Geraint. Our time will come."

Gorlois cantered forwards, raising a gauntleted hand in salute, his pale blue eyes blazing behind the disconcertingly impassive mask. He swung a long leg over the back of his white stallion and dismounted with an athletic jump.

We rode forwards alongside Ambrosius with Constans, Ofydd and a handful of personal guards.

Constans dismounted and removed his helmet, his arms held out to embrace the Duke of Cerniw. Gorlois removed his ornate helmet and tossed it nonchalantly to one of his men.

"Hail Constans, well met my friend." He hugged Constans and slapped him on the back. Constans was tall, but Gorlois was even taller. He was lean and athletic, around the same age as Constans, with a handsome face and dark, tightly curled and oiled shoulder length hair. His close cropped beard was neatly trimmed and his teeth were a brilliant white when he smiled. He looked more like a pampered king of ancient Greece than a Cornovii warlord.

"What do you think of the armour?" He asked, taking a step back so that Constans could admire his breastplate. "Byzantine, as is the helmet," he added. "I traded a ship full of Irish slaves in Constantinople to buy weapons and armour for my men. I think it was worth it, don't they look marvellous?"

Constans nodded. "They certainly do my friend. How have you been?"

Gorlois sighed dramatically and shook his head. "My coasts are forever plagued by Irish raiders and now the Saxons have moved westwards as well. Every merchant ship I send out now has to be accompanied by a war galley because of them, at great expense I may add and internally it's not much better. Border raids from the neighbours and constant rebellions by the miners means that tin production is down, all very tedious. Fortunately though, Din Tagel remains impregnable as always," He grinned exposing his pearlescent teeth and placed an arm around Constans' shoulder. "Talking of which, it has been a while since you have visited my home. I have several amphorae of the best Byzantine wine waiting for you, as well as some beautiful slave girls from Parthia."

"I miss our times together, Gorlois," Constans replied wistfully, grinning from ear to ear.

The Duke turned his attention to Ambrosius. "And how is the little brother? Found yourself a good woman yet, Ambrosius?"

Before Ambrosius could respond, Constans replied for him. "He still hankers after that little tart in the nunnery. I think he's saving himself for her." The two friends burst into sniggering laughter.

"I've heard a lot about her," Gorlois said. "Apparently she's quite a beauty. I may have to seek her out myself sometime. But in the meantime Ambrosius, you should come to visit me in Din Tagel. I have a multitude of beautiful girls you can choose from, don't go wasting your life pining over a nun."

Ambrosius' pale face was bright red and he gave Gorlois an awkward smile. "She is a lay sister and not yet a nun as she is yet to take her solemn vows, but I think we have more pressing matters than girls and fancy armour, Gorlois," he said quietly.

The duke swaggered over and placed a hand on Ambrosius' knee. "What could possibly be more pressing than pretty girls, Ambrosius?"

"Well, the fact that Prince Vortimer marched an entire army through your lands apparently unnoticed. And the fact that the Pendragon stronghold, Caer Dor could fall at any moment."

Gorlois' face showed concerned disbelief. "I know. Believe me, it came as a surprise to me as well to find out an entire army had marched through my lands unchallenged. Alas, by the time I arrived with my men, it was all but over."

Ambrosius frowned. "Caer Dor has fallen?"

Gorlois shrugged apologetically and nodded. "When news reached me, I rallied my army and sailed with all haste to Caer Dor, but alas I was too late. Lady Branwen's fortress was in flames and her army all but beaten." He sighed and shook his head with a downwards glance. "However, I was able to negotiate a deal."

"What sort of deal?" Geraint barked.

Gorlois looked up, his eyes blazing with outrage. He let out an incredulous chuckle. "Who is this who addresses a Duke as an equal?"

"Please forgive them, Gorlois," Ambrosius said. "These two men are Pendragon warriors. They were in the battle and delivered the plea for help to my father." Gorlois looked us up and down with contempt. "Looking at the way they are dressed, I should have known. Almost mistook them for Saxon barbarians." He turned away from us and continued talking with Ambrosius. "Anyway, back to this deal I struck. By the time I had landed, Caer Dor had fallen, but Vortimer was obviously not expecting another army to turn up so quickly and upon seeing my formidable force, he agreed to parley. I ordered him to leave Dumnonia immediately or face the consequences, to which he replied he would leave, on the condition that he could take Branwen Pendragon as a hostage. I was forced to agree to these terms in order to avoid further bloodshed."

"How convenient for you, Gorlois," Geraint exclaimed with venom, giving voice to the anger that we both felt. "So now you are in sole control of Eastern Dumnonia, just as you always wanted. What else did you get out of your little deal with Vortimer I wonder?"

Gorlois' expression changed to one of fury as his pale eyes bored into Geraint. "I don't know who you are, but one more word out of turn from you and I will see that you are suitably punished, cur. Be mindful of who you are talking to."

Constans turned to his bodyguard. "Take this insolent dog away and have him flogged. If my brother is too weak to control his men, I will damned well do it for him."

Three men dismounted and approached Geraint, but he pulled his sword from its scabbard and pointed it threateningly towards them. "Do you not know a traitor when you see one?" Geraint yelled. "He will not stop until he has all of Dumnonia kneeling before him."

"Sheath your weapon or I will see that you hang from the highest tree," Constans shouted.

Geraint looked at me and I shook my head to try to dissuade him from his rash course of action. He sheathed his sword with a grin, arms outspread in supplication as the soldiers came over, one of them slamming him in the stomach with his gloved fist. Geraint doubled over with a grunt but was soon upright again and still grinning, his wild eyes fixed murderously on Gorlois. The soldier pulled Geraint's helmet off and backhanded him across the face, splitting his lip. Geraint responded by spitting blood into the soldier's face and almost immediately he went down under a hail of heavy blows and kicks from the other men.

I could not sit and watch my friend being beaten to a pulp and so I went for my sword, but Ambrosius placed a hand on my elbow.

"You will only make this worse for him," he said quietly. "Let him take his punishment."

Ambrosius raised his voice for the benefit of all present. "Twenty lashes for subordinance."

"Make that fifty for luck," Constans added as Geraint's semi-conscious body was dragged away.

They stripped him to the waist and tied him to the trunk of a nearby oak, splashing water over his face until he regained consciousness. The soldier who had first punched him produced a brutal looking rawhide whip from the pack on his horse and gave it a few cracks in the early morning air.

Gorlois sauntered up to the man. "If I may?" he asked politely. The soldier nodded and handed him the whip and Gorlois carefully removed his embroidered blue cloak, folding it neatly and handing it to one of his men. He gave the whip a few test swings before taking a run up and lashing out as hard as he could. The rawhide cord whistled through the air and cracked across Geraint's muscular back. Immediately a welt of red appeared on his pale skin and I saw his body go taut with pain, but he did not cry out as I had seen many men do before.

Again and again the blows rained down across his back and shoulders until the skin hung from his back in scarlet shreds but still he did not cry out.

"You've got to stop this, he's going to kill him," I said to Ambrosius, my voice trembling with barely restrained anger. "He's had his twenty lashes."

"I believe I had upped that to fifty," Constans said, overhearing me speaking to Ambrosius.

"Fifty will kill him and you know it," I snapped back.

Constans shrugged. "Perhaps you would like to join him, Irishman?"

Blind fury overtook me and I lunged towards Constans, but Ambrosius grabbed me and pulled me back with surprising strength.

"Enough!" He yelled. "Release the prisoner."

Gorlois turned and looked indignantly at Ambrosius, breathing heavily with the effort of punishing Geraint. "But I'm only half done and I believe he was about to apologise," he said. "What does your older brother say?"

"My older brother has no say in this," Ambrosius responded firmly. "He is my man and I say he has had enough. Release him now."

Gorlois shrugged and handed the bloody whip back to the soldier. Geraint was untied and his limp, bleeding body was hauled away by two of Constans' bodyguards.

"I will see to it that he receives the best treatment," Ambrosius said, almost apologetically.

I turned away from him, too angry to speak, watching with barely restrained fury as the two soldiers dragged Geraint over to a stream and threw him in.

My anger was diverted by the blare of trumpets from the gentle hills to the east and I looked up to see the bull's head standard of Ambrosius' father, carried at the head of a vast column of armoured men. Julianus had arrived with the infantry and he rode over to us, flanked on either side by his Sarmatian guards. He greeted Gorlois formally before getting down to the business in hand. Gorlois broke the news to him regarding the fate of Caer Dor and he glared at him stonily. "What of Branwen? What has happened to her?"

"Vortimer assured me that she would not be harmed and that she would be well treated," Gorlois replied a little nervously. "He is not stupid, Julianus. He knows that you will not act while he holds the mother of your son."

"Then he is wrong," Julianus said. "I am assuming that he now makes his way back to where his boats are. If we can send our cavalry ahead, we can destroy his boats and trap his army on our shores. Then together we can destroy him. Presumably you know by now where his boats are moored?"

Gorlois fumbled for an answer. "Well, I...no, Julianus. I'm sorry, I don't know."

Julianus' jaw clenched with irritation. "How long ago did they leave Caer Dor? I assume you at least know that."

"Just before I was requested by the King. They are at least a day's march ahead of us, it would be far easier to just let them go."

Julianus fixed Gorlois with a deadly stare, his tone of voice when he spoke was measured and dangerous. "The easy option will not get Uther's mother back. We will send our cavalry ahead, both yours and mine and we will find where they have moored their boats and we will destroy them. Once we have them at our mercy, then we will negotiate terms with them and have Branwen returned."

Gorlois, lost for words merely shrugged and nodded, trying to hide the shame and resentment on his face. As Julianus stormed off, Gorlois peevishly pushed one of his own soldiers to the ground and lashed out at him with a kick. Constans tried to console him, but he shook him off like a petulant child.

Constans turned with a sour look on his face as he strode back to his horse. "Ready the men," he snapped at Ambrosius. "We ride out immediately."

Chapter 5

Ambrosius

It was not difficult to follow the route of Vortimer's army. We galloped in a north westward direction across country until we saw black plumes of smoke on the horizon. Every village and settlement before them had been put to the torch, where the inhabitants had either fled into the surrounding countryside or had been slaughtered.

We came across one pitiful group who had fled, led by an elderly miller.

"Horsemen came first, but they didn't stop," he said, his voice trembling. "When they passed through, we thought we'd be alright, but then came the Saxons and the Irish." The old miller shook his head and closed his eyes against the awfulness of the memories. "They killed everyone they came across, burned everything. They had a woman with them, a prisoner."

"What happened to her?" Constans asked.

"Take a look for yourself."

The old man led us back to the smoking ruins of his village. Corpses lay scattered on the ground, men, women and children, some half burned, some naked. Only the stone buildings of the village remained, a grain store, a tithe barn and a small chapel.

"In there," the miller said, nodding towards the smashed doors of the chapel, his hands shaking.

Constans swallowed nervously and turned to his younger brother. "Ambrosius, take a look."

Without a word Ambrosius dismounted and nodded for me to do the same. Together we approached the ruined chapel with swords drawn and pushed aside the splintered remains of the doors.

We stepped over the eviscerated and headless body of a priest and went inside. The chapel stank of the sickly smell of stale blood and was lit only by weak sunlight that streamed through the high window slits. It had been completely ransacked, but it was light enough for us to see the macabre sight before our eyes. Ambrosius was the first to see it. Something dripped on his face from above and as he looked up, he gave a horrified gasp and stumbled backwards. I looked up into the high gables of the chapel where Ambrosius was now looking with an expression of terror and revulsion.

A figure was floating in the air above us and for a terrifying moment I thought that it was the angel of death that Father Demetrios had told me about in the past. It was female, naked and streaked with blood, staring at us sightlessly with dark, empty eye sockets, white teeth exposed in a death grin, its long red hair was ragged and clotted with gore and filth, its breasts had been removed, leaving two gaping red wounds and it had what looked like dark red wings sprouting from its back.

"What in the name of Christ is that?" Ambrosius hissed, visibly shaken.

With dawning revulsion and horror I realised who it was. Even though they had gouged out her eyes and cut off her lips, turning her once noble face into a grinning, sightless mockery, there was no mistaking the long red hair of Lady Branwen.

Hengest the Saxon leader had made good his threat. This was the infamous Blood Eagle that he had mentioned. They had hacked Branwen's ribs from her backbone and tore her ribcage apart, pulling out her lungs so that they resembled a pair of bloody wings before hoisting her ravaged, dripping corpse into the rafters of the chapel.

I turned away, feeling my gorge rise, leaning against the cool stone wall for support.

I saw Constans standing at the entrance, his face pale and horror struck, his white pommelled cavalry sword held limply in his hand. He quickly turned and left and I could hear the sound of him retching outside.

I stumbled out of the chapel, numb with horror and sat heavily on the ground with my back leaning against the wall, barely noticing the warmth of the spring sun on my face. I hoped desperately that Lady Branwen's death was quick, but I knew that it had been anything but. The Saxons had a deserved reputation for barbaric cruelty and I knew that they would have made her suffer in unimaginable ways and that she would have been alive and conscious when they were hacking her ribs from her back. I wondered what had become of my friends, whether any of them had survived and how poor Uther would react over his mother's awful death when he found out.

At that moment I was vaguely aware of someone standing near me and I looked up to see young Uther, looking apprehensively towards the ruined chapel door.

"Uther, what are you doing here?" I said, my voice trembling, unable to hide the horror and surprise that I felt.

"I wanted to ride ahead with you," he said in a bewildered tone.

"Does your father know you're here?" I asked, my mind still reeling with the horrific sight that I had just seen.

Uther shook his head. "My father is too busy with his warlords to bother with me. Besides, he thinks I am still at Caer Cadwy, but I want to ride ahead with my half-brothers and so I sneaked out." He pointed through the chapel doors. "What is in there?"

"Uther, don't go in there," I said emphatically, but the young lord, impetuous and headstrong was already through the doors before I could stop him. I ran in after him, but it was already too late. I grabbed the boy just as he sank to his knees and the scream that came from the depths of his soul was filled with grief and horror and desolation and I held him tight as he sobbed into my shoulder.

Constans had several of his men cut Branwen's corpse down from the chapel rafters and ordered the miller and the surviving villagers to dig a grave and bury her body.

"My father must not know that we found her like this," he said to Ambrosius and I, still visibly in shock.

We both nodded in agreement, still too stunned to speak. I was still trying to comfort Uther, my arm around his shoulder as he trembled and sobbed.

"What sort of animals would do this?" Ambrosius said finally as we watched the miller and three other villagers start to hack at the ground with shovels and picks.

"I failed her," I muttered, half to myself. "I swore that I would lay down my life to protect her and her son and I have failed. Again I am a wanderer. I have no one."

I barely felt Ambrosius place a sympathetic hand on my shoulder and I turned away and mounted my horse, eager to leave that place that reeked of death, overcome with guilt and grief.

We followed the trail of destruction northward, knowing that Vortimer's forces would be moving a lot slower than ours as the majority of them were on foot and towing siege weapons. Constans sent Ambrosius and I, along with three other lightly armed but capable warriors to scout ahead to see if we could find where they had moored their ships.

We were riding hard through sparse woodland when one of the warriors with us reined his horse in and stopped suddenly.

"What is the problem, Gruffud?" Ambrosius demanded.

The man pointed back the way we had come. "We are being followed."

We all turned and drew our swords, aware of the distant sound of galloping hooves. Soon a rider appeared on a brown horse, his cloak billowing out behind him, bent over his steed's neck and kicking its flanks with his heels.

As the rider drew closer, I saw that it was a young boy and I felt anger rise within me.

"Uther!" I exclaimed.

Ambrosius looked at me with a frown. "I thought Constans had sent him back to Caer Cadwy with an escort?"

I shook my head with frustration. "Uther does not do what Uther does not want to do," I replied caustically.

I cantered forwards, seething with anger as Uther reined his steed to a halt in front of us, yanking the reigns hard and causing the horse to rear up and whinny in protest.

"What the hell are you doing here?" I yelled.

Uther returned my stare defiantly. "I want to kill Saxons."

"We are a scouting party, we are not going to kill anyone," I shouted back. "You are going straight back to Constans."

The young lord shook his head stubbornly, his face twisted with bitter grief, his pale blue eyes glassy with unshed tears. "I want to come with you, Fergus."

I sighed and turned to Ambrosius. Uther insisted on coming with us and Ambrosius was forced to relent, partly out of pity. After all, our primary goal was to find out where the enemy had moored their ships and to avoid any engagements. If their ships were lightly defended, we could send news back to Constans who could then sweep down upon them with his cavalry and destroy them before the main army got there. We would then have Vortimer trapped on our shores and at the mercy of Julianus' foot soldiers. Uther was probably safer with us than with Constan's men.

As luck would have it, we encountered a lone shepherd boy out on the hills who told us exactly where Vortimer's boats were moored. He led us up over a bluff and pointed down into a sandy cove a short distance below.

There were around fifty large, broad keeled boats moored up on or near the beach, their masts giving the impression of a forest sprouting from the sea. A dozen or so leather tents had been pitched nearby and I could see men milling around campfires and patrolling up and down the sandy cove.

There was something familiar about the boats. They were built in the style of Roman trade vessels and although they flew no distinguishing pennants, I recognised the distinctive carved figureheads on several of the ships, having seen them sail up and down the wide channel that divided Dumnonia from Dyfed from the cliffs above Penglyn.

"Those are Gorlois' ships," I muttered quietly to Ambrosius.

"How can you be sure?" He hissed back.

I nodded towards the distant boats. "We used to see them from the cliff tops above my village. I recognise the decorated prows."

Ambrosius shook his head sceptically. "Many boats have prows decorated in such a way. You cannot be sure of that."

"Those boats belong to Gorlois," I insisted. "He is playing your father for a fool."

Ambrosius ignored me and crept forwards for a better view. "About one hundred men I would say," he whispered as he lay flat on his belly amongst the long grass of the bluff. "If we can surprise them, we will have a huge advantage. We'll return to my brother and inform him."

We mounted our horses and rode back the way we had come.

"Quicker to take the deer trail through the forest," the shepherd boy shouted, pointing with his crook towards the nearby woodland.

Ambrosius thanked the boy and tossed him a small bronze coin. He caught it and held it up to the sunlight with a wondrous smile on his face. "A real coin? For me? Thank you sir, Thank you so much."

The shepherd boy waved us off as we spurred our mounts on and galloped down the narrow forest path as fast as we dared, eager to get back to Constans and the rest of the cavalry with our news.

We had not gone far when a peculiar feeling overcame me. It was a feeling that I had felt before, a sense of foreboding, a buzzing in the back of my skull and a metallic taste in my mouth. I had felt it just before Drustan was ambushed and killed and at my sister's wedding to Fiachu years before.

"Ambrosius, wait!" I shouted. He had galloped ahead with two other riders and turned in his saddle at the sound of his name, pulling on his reins and slowing his mount slightly.

It was just enough to prevent him from riding full speed into the net that had suddenly appeared across the path, a net that had ensnared the other two riders and their horses.

The forest erupted into a cacophony of whoops and cries as painted, bare chested figures armed with spears and axes emerged from behind bushes and trees.

"Ambush!" I shouted, drawing my sword and silently cursing the shepherd boy for leading us into a trap. "Uther, stay close!"

The two riders who had been ensnared were quickly slaughtered under a violent rain of axe blows as our assailants emerged for the kill. My blood ran cold at the familiar sound of the cries and the sight of wiry, muscular torsos covered in swirling blue markings.

"Picts," I muttered to myself as two wild eyed barbarians ran towards me with spears held ready. One of them gave a powerful thrust, but the blade of his spear caught in my limewood shield and I hacked down, cutting his weapon in half. I wheeled my steed around and kicked out, catching the man under his chin with my booted foot, knocking him out cold.

The other Pict had pulled his weapon back ready to deliver a deadly thrust, but I quickly spurred forwards and gave an underarm swing of my sword, slicing the keen blade across his undefended, naked midriff. The blade bit deeply into his abdomen, tearing through flesh and muscle and spilling his innards onto the forest floor.

"Fergus, help me!" I turned in my saddle to see Uther being pulled from the saddle of his horse by two more Picts and I tried to get to him, but another two men wielding spears and axes appeared out of the trees between me and Uther, preventing me from getting near to him.

I heard another cry for help and turned to see that three Picts had succeeded in pulling Ambrosius from his saddle. Two were trying to pin him down, while the third was standing by with an axe, ready to deliver the killing blow, his arm raised ready.

I charged forwards with a yell and swung my blade, taking the Pict's arm off just below the shoulder. He fell sideways with a shriek and I pulled hard on my reins, causing my horse to rear up and flail its front legs, its lethal hooves driving the other two Picts away from Ambrosius and giving him time to get to his feet and draw his broad bladed cavalry sword.

His own horse had been fatally injured by a spear thrust to its chest and it lay there screaming piteously, its legs kicking in mid-air.

The other soldier who was with us was also dead as I could see a Masraighe warrior hacking mercilessly at his head and face with a gore spattered axe.

I heard Uther call out again and I yelled back, catching a fleeting glance of the young lord being dragged through the bushes. More Irishmen and Picts were charging towards us from the woods and I knew that in moments we would be overwhelmed and slaughtered.

"Get on my horse," I shouted to Ambrosius, but the young nobleman seemed to be in a daze. His helmet had been knocked to one side and there was a large bleeding gash on his forehead. He turned groggily, his sword held unsteadily in his right hand.

"Ambrosius, to me!" I yelled more insistently, but he was too dazed to respond properly. I spurred forwards, forcing the two Picts further back and grabbed the back of his cloak and pulled him towards me.

An arrow whizzed past my ear and I kept my horse moving in a tight circle so as to present a more difficult target and to scout for a gap in the rapidly approaching enemy.

Ambrosius pulled himself onto the back of my horse with difficulty, wrapping both arms tightly about my waist and I galloped down a steep wooded slope as most of our assailants were running downhill to give momentum to their charge and few were coming up the slope. A couple of Masraighe warriors converged on me with spears held ready, but I avoided them easily enough, ducking low over my horse's neck to avoid the remorseless whip of twigs and branches as we charged through the forest.

"Ambrosius, are you alright?" I asked when we were clear of the ambush.

"I'm fine," he replied vaguely.

My horse reared up and whinnied nervously at the edge of a narrow ravine, several paces wide but deep and treacherous, plunging down to a fast flowing stream below. Behind us we could hear the howls and cries of our pursuers relishing the hunt, closing on us rapidly. I cantered up and down at the edge of the ravine, looking for a spot opposite that the horse could jump to safely. Finally I found a clear patch of flat ground, though whether the horse could make such a jump with two armoured men on its back, I was not sure.

I rode back a short distance and wheeled around, getting my mount into position.

"Are you mad?" Ambrosius protested as he realised my intention. "We'll never make it, not with both of us."

The wild shouts from close behind convinced me that we had no choice.

"You're a Christian, Ambrosius?" I asked.

"Of course I am," came the agitated reply.

"Then start praying now."

I kicked my heels into the horse's flanks and we galloped forwards, bending low as the horse leaped across the deadly gap, landing heavily on the opposite side and stumbling awkwardly, throwing us both free onto the soft, springy grass.

I struggled to my feet, slightly winded but otherwise unhurt and was relieved to see Ambrosius was also free from injury. My steed however was not so lucky and it lay on its side whinnying pathetically, its front left leg flailing limply.

"Fergus, your horse," Ambrosius began and I nodded grimly. I knew what had to be done and I felt pity for the noble animal that had borne me for several days over rough terrain. It was a good horse and I felt reluctant to do what I had to do as it had served me well, but I could not bear to see the wretched creature suffer. I drew my short bladed knife and walked over to the injured horse, talking gently and stroking its sleek muzzle.

The horse looked up at me, its large black eyes filled with pain and fear and I kissed its head gently before drawing the sharp blade across its throat. The horse thrashed momentarily as great gouts of dark blood pumped from the wound and then it lay still.

A chorus of jeers from the other side of the ravine caused me to look up. About a dozen or so Masraighe and Pictish warriors stood at the ravines edge, shouting taunts and glaring at me murderously.

"Come and get us then, you sons of whores," I taunted them in Gaelic, sword in hand, my arms spread provocatively. They shouted back furiously, insulting me and my mother in my native tongue.

One of the warriors barged his way to the front, half of his face covered by the crescent marking adopted by his tribe. He stared at me with the cold grey eyes of a merciless killer and with a jolt I realised who it was.

"Fiachu mac Niall," I snarled, feeling both fear and hatred.

His eyes narrowed at the mention of his name and he frowned as he struggled to recall who I was, which was hardly surprising. It had been many years since he had last seen me and then I was a frightened boy on the run and even though I was now a man and a capable warrior in my own right, that callous stare still made part of me feel like a scared child again.

I untied the rawhide cord that held the cheek plates of my helmet together under my chin and cast it aside.

It took a while but then Fiachu grinned as realisation dawned. "Well, by the tits of Danu, if it isn't Fiontan's youngest son." The grin turned into a sneer. "I've been looking for you for years, boy. Sinusa needs your blood."

"Come over and get it then you gutless bastard." I retorted.

"I see you've grown some balls since we last met, Fergus." Fiachu was the same as I remembered in my nightmares, except now he looked more stocky and muscular, his face more hardened and grizzled, but the soulless grey eyes however were the same.

"Oh, I'll get you boy. Don't you worry about that. Sinusa knew you were alive, she knew you were here somewhere, she could sense it. Crom Cruach gave her signs, led us over here. Her body is growing more and more frail and she needs a new one, but only one of Tuatha de Danann blood will do. That is where you and your precious sister come in. Your blood, her body."

"My sister is dead," I lied. "Our curragh capsized and she drowned along with Dorbalos."

Fiachu chuckled. "Nice try. But do not underestimate Sinusa's powers. Your sister lives boy and we will find her and Sinusa will have her new body and you will be rotting in the ground."

Fiachu's eyes flicked furtively to one side and I noticed movement on the periphery of my vision on Fiachu's side of the ravine. While we had been talking, some of his men had broken off, trying to find a crossing point further downstream.

"I will kill you, Fiachu mac Niall. I swear this by the spirits of my father and brother and I swear it by the Morrigan, the hag of war and death. I will come for you soon and I will make you pay." I started to back away slowly until I was level with Ambrosius.

"Let's settle it here and now, boy," Fiachu called out. "I'll make you a deal. If you kill me, my men will let you go and will not trouble you or your sister again."

"I know how your deals work, Fiachu," I called back, still backing away. "I will not negotiate with you. I will not strike any bargains. Ever. But I will kill you. And I will choose where and when." I patted Ambrosius on the shoulder and we both turned and ran down the grassy slope, leaving Fiachu to yell empty insults in our wake.

"What was said between you? Your native tongue is unknown to me," Ambrosius asked as we negotiated a particularly rocky incline. We had been speaking in Gaelic and he had not understood a word.

"Old enemies. Old scores to settle," I replied. "We're going to have to keep moving, they won't be far behind. It won't take them long to find a way over that gap and they are relentless in their pursuit of their quarry."

"What are Picts doing this far south?" Ambrosius asked as we jogged down into wooded country.

"They are Fiachu's bondsmen," I replied. "When his father exiled him to Caledonia, he gained a loyal following of Pictish warriors. Later, when he returned to Eire after his father died, his band of Picts helped him to carve a name for himself."

"What about the others, the ones with the crescents on their faces?"

"They are the Masraighe, Fiachu's adopted tribe. He is their clan chief and together they killed my family and destroyed my home."

We could hear the baying of Fiachu's wolf hounds in the distance and ran through a swift flowing stream in an attempt to break our scent. Ambrosius was flagging and stumbling due to his head wound, which leaked a steady flow of blood that stained his mail coat and I was forced to help him to his feet after he fell several times. We headed in what we assumed was a southerly direction, in the hope that we would run into Constans and the bulk of the cavalry, but we knew that they were at least a mile behind us. Fiachu would also be aware that we were outriders for a much larger force, and so we would now lose our element of surprise. Worst still, it was possible that Constans and the others would now be ambushed by Fiachu's men. As for what had happened to Uther, I could only guess and hope that he had come to no harm.

Ambrosius collapsed to his knees again, soaked and exhausted and breathing heavily.

"Ambrosius, we can't stop. The Picts are as swift as hares, they will soon be upon us."

The young lord shook his head, pulling off his helmet, throwing it aside, exposing his thick mop of wavy, golden hair now dark with sweat and blood and flattened to his scalp. "It's no good, I can't go on. Leave me here, tell my father and my brother...tell them I died fighting."

"I won't leave you to the mercy of those bastards. You saw what they did to Branwen, you think you will be treated any different?"

"I will kill myself," he muttered.

"Then do it now," I said, pulling my knife from my belt and throwing it at his feet. "I will not leave until I see you do it."

Ambrosius looked up at me with weary, pale blue eyes and I stared back at him resolutely. He picked up the knife and looked at the thin but wickedly sharp blade, holding it against his throat with a trembling hand.

In the distance came the howl of a wolf hound. "They're getting closer. Do it now or we are both dead."

He squeezed his eyes shut, his hand shaking uncontrollably as he tried to hold the blade against the pale flesh of his throat. A single tear rolled down his cheek and he threw the knife aside, collapsing to his hands.

"I can't do it," he sobbed.

I walked over and grabbed him by the back of his cloak and hauled him to his feet. "I know. Not that easy is it? Next time you threaten to kill yourself, don't waste my damned time."

I hauled Ambrosius to his feet and we ran on alongside the stream, with me clinging on to the back of his cloak in an attempt to keep him upright, shouting at him to keep moving. We had been running hard for about an hour with no signs of Constan's cavalry force, spurred on by fear and desperation, but now our reserves of energy were running low.

The sound of voices nearby forced us to slide down the slippery bank to hide amongst the reeds growing at the riverside. We crouched down so that only our heads were above the freezing water, covering our faces with slimy, stinking mud to disguise ourselves.

Through the tangle of reeds we saw several Picts jog past where we had been moments before, their patterned bodies slick with sweat.

We held our breath as more of them ran past, along with their Masraighe allies, shouting to one another as they went. We shivered in the cold water, hearing the snuffling of a hound nearby. Carefully and slowly, I pulled Conmor's' knife from its scabbard, waiting for the wolfhound to appear through the reeds, but it never did. Its master called to it and the hound loped off.

When we were certain the last of them had passed, we moved slowly upstream and then struck out through the woods in an easterly direction, taking us well away from the Picts and Irish.

We walked on for several hours before finally turning south, shivering in our sodden clothes, eventually coming to an abandoned cattle byre.

"It'll be dark soon, we're going to have to bed down for the night," I said. "I think we'll be safe here."

There was dry straw lying around which we could use for bedding and to get a small fire going and the four cobble stone walls provided enough protection from the biting wind even if the thatched roof was ragged and full of holes.

After a while, as the sun was sinking in the west and the sky had turned a deep blue, I had a small fire going and we huddled around it, trying to absorb its warmth into our bones.

I dressed Ambrosius' head wound with a piece of rag torn from the hem of his tunic and he produced a chunk of hard cheese and some dried apple from a pouch at his belt which he shared with me.

"I'm sorry about your friend," he said. He had lost the surly manner with which he had greeted Geraint and I and now his tone was quiet and humble.

I looked at him quizzically.

"Gerrynt?" He said with a frown.

"Geraint," I corrected.

Ambrosius shrugged. "I'm sorry I had him flogged. I'm sorry as well for being..."

"Rude? Arrogant?" I finished for him. "Forget it. I'm sure Geraint is man enough to get over it. Gorlois is the one he hates, not you."

Ambrosius considered this for a while as he chewed on a handful of dried apple. "What do you think has happened to Uther?" he asked.

I shook my head, not wanting to think about the boy's fate, especially after what had happened to his mother. Ambrosius put his head in his hands. "What is my father going to say?"

"It was Constans' fault, not yours," I replied, trying to console him. "He should have sent him back with a bigger escort."

"Do you think we'll ever find Constans?" he asked. He was still trembling and his pale face was drawn and tired. He was obviously still in shock following our encounter with Fiachu's men.

I nodded as I chewed on the cheese. "Tomorrow we will find them, we may even run into your father. We were lucky to get away from Fiachu."

"Do you still think Gorlois is with the enemy?" Ambrosius enquired.

I poked at the fire with a stick until bright orange flames leapt back into life. "I know that he hired Fiachu's Picts to kill Drustan Pendragon and I know that he sat and watched as Caer Dor fell. And I'm sure those were his boats," I said bitterly.

"It will be difficult to convince Constans of that. He and Gorlois have been close friends since childhood," Ambrosius said.

"Yes, I noticed," I replied caustically.

I noticed that I still had half a skin of wine slung over my shoulder and we drank it together as we stared into the flames, each lost in our own thoughts.

"Tell me more about this Fiachu mac Niall," Ambrosius said after a while. There was something behind the serious scowl that seemed to beset the young man's face permanently. There was an earnestness and integrity in his expression that made me think this was a person that I could trust.

I told him everything. Of Fiachu's marriage to my sister, of his betrayal and how we had fled across Eire and finally came to Britannia. I told him about the Masraighe's terrible god, Crom Cruach and the sacrifice of the innocents to this ancient demon. I told him about my life in Penglyn with Rhawn and Father Demetrios and how Fiachu had destroyed that village as well and how this event eventually led me to the druid, Myrddin and how in turn I had come to be one of Drustan Pendragon's spearmen. I told him of the battles I had fought in the name of clan Pendragon and I spoke of Nivian, for the first time in ages. And as I remembered her deep green eyes and jet black hair and her perfect body as white as milk, I felt my throat tighten and my voice falter and I felt the warm sting of tears behind my eyes.

"It sounds like you loved her very much," Ambrosius said when I had finally finished and I could see that he was lost in his own thoughts about someone close to him.

I nodded, swallowing hard at the lump in my throat and poking absently at the fire. "What of you?" I said, changing the subject. "What is your story, Ambrosius?"

He shrugged as he gazed at the stars through the ruined roof of the byre.

"Very different from yours," he said. "I have been raised as a Roman, in the belief that one day the Empire shall return to these islands and deliver us from the heathen that has beset this land on all sides. My father always told us that we must keep the light of civilisation burning bright, that we must never give up the hope of a better life for all. But when I see what men are capable of, what terrible atrocities are committed simply because someone else is of a different clan or tribe or has sworn loyalty to a different overlord, I find myself doubting my father's words."

"Your father sounds like quite a visionary," I said. "It is good to have hope. Sometimes that is all we have to keep us going."

Ambrosius lay on his back and looked up at the stars through the holes in the roof. "My father came here at the request of King Custennin, and he brought with him his best troops. After the Romans had left there were years of unrest. Barbarians flooded across the borders and came from across the sea. Petty kings and chieftains with ancestral claims going back to the days of the ancients came forth to try and forge kingdoms of their own. For a while, it looked as though the light of civilisation would be extinguished forever. But my father is a brilliant soldier and tactician. He recruited the Sarmatians, brilliant horsemen from the east who had been serving the Empire along the Great Northern Wall, but who had decided to stay after the Romans left. With these new troops to boost his cavalry force and with the addition of Votadini horsemen, he defeated the Durotriges and as thanks for his service, Custennin gave him their country. But instead of plundering the towns and villages as others would have done, my father was magnanimous in victory and so won the hearts of the people. He set about repairing roads and bridges and encouraging trade between towns. He set up a fair taxation system, a tithe that ensured that all villages and towns would pay what they could afford and that any village in need would be given what they needed to survive. Also, every able bodied man would undergo training and serve a set amount of time in our army, which means that we can always call upon a disciplined, well trained fighting force."

I held up a hand to stop him. "That's all very interesting Ambrosius, but I asked about your story, not the story of your father's kingdom."

Ambrosius frowned and he gazed blankly at the guttering flames for a while. "My mother, Aurelia, died when I was young," he said quietly. "I can't remember her face very clearly, but I remember that she was beautiful and sometimes I can still remember the sound of her voice, especially when she would sing around our family villa. She had a very sweet voice," he paused, his pale eyes glazed with a wistful smile on his lips.

"What of your father?" I asked.

"I didn't see a lot of him when I was young. He was far too busy campaigning and trying to run a kingdom. After my mother died, he sent Constans and I to Rome to be educated. It was there that I learned about the tactics of Scipio and Caesar and Alexander and I excelled in my classes, whereas Constans was continually beaten for not showing an interest. After a few years we returned and began our military training."

"That would explain why Constans feels the need to put you down all the time," I said.

Ambrosius shrugged. "Perhaps. Not that it seems to matter to my father. In his eyes, Constans can do no wrong and I am the one who is seen as the disappointment."

"So tell me about this girl. The nun I heard them mention."

Ambrosius' face flushed bright red and I could tell that he was more at home discussing Roman military tactics than he was talking about the far more complicated subject of women. I grinned at his obvious discomfort as he stammered over his answer.

"We found her wandering when we were out on patrol several years ago. Turned out she was an escaped slave who had wandered all the way from Dyfed to escape a cruel master and she was emaciated and close to death, although she bore no markings or brandings to indicate that she was a slave. We took her back to Caer Cadwy, fed her, looked after her and I visited her every day to see how she was. My father put her to work in the kitchens of our villa and we became friends despite the fact that she couldn't speak a word of my language and so I took it upon myself to teach her both Latin and Brittonic," he smiled at the memory, but soon his smile was clouded by a deeper emotion. "Anyway, eventually my father became aware of our close friendship and he did not approve. After all, a noble born Roman boy friends with an escaped female slave? It was unheard of. So he decided to send Igrainne to the nunnery, away from temptation and kept me busy with military duties." Ambrosius' bitter scowl returned as he tossed husks of straw into the fire.

"What does she look like, this Igrainne?" I asked.

He shrugged. "Dark hair, slim, bluish eyes," he said in a matter of fact way.

I laughed at his lacklustre description and he gave me an offended look. "You will never make a bard, Ambrosius. You are supposed to say her eyes are as blue as the ocean under the summer sun, her skin is as smooth and translucent as the finest marble, her face would rival Aphrodite herself."

Ambrosius gave an awkward smirk. "I am not a natural poet like you Celts. Poetry has always eluded me, I'm afraid. But she is all of those things to me and more."

"So was that it between you and Igrainne?" I asked.

He shook his head emphatically. "Oh, no. Despite my father's warnings, I sometimes still get to see her as she is a lay Sister, which means she can leave the monastery when she is running errands. She has yet to take her solemn vows, so she is still able to leave the monastery permanently at the end of two years. No one knows this, but we are to be wed when her two years novitiate are finished, in another month's time."

"Your secret will be safe with me," I said. "So you are in love with this Igrainne?"

"Of course I am," Ambrosius replied with a sheepish smile. "I loved her ever since I set eyes upon her. She means everything to me and no one, not the nunnery or my father or the war will keep us apart. When her time in the nunnery is finished, we will simply leave together, build ourselves a new life overseas in Armorica and leave this land of tears behind forever."

We rested as best we could, taking turns to keep a look out, but sleep eluded us as we remained cold and damp and the chill of the night air made us shiver despite the meagre warmth of the fire.

As the sky began to lighten in the east, we heard the faint but unmistakable metallic chinking of harnesses and bridles and the distant thunder of many hooves, causing us both to look up in alarm. I quickly dampened the fire with my cloak, easing my sword from its scabbard and stood to one side of the wide, doorless entrance. Ambrosius took up a position opposite, sword in hand. Cautiously, I peered around the edge of the doorway and could see a multitude of dark figures on horseback headed towards us.

"Is it Constans?" Ambrosius whispered.

"I don't know until they get closer."

We stood frozen in the entrance of the byre as the horsemen galloped past, close enough for us to hear the snorting and heavy breathing of their mounts.

Two riders stopped nearby and I listened intently to their mumbled conversation. "Do you think he'll live?" said one, in the Briton's tongue.

"With a wound like that? I very much doubt it. Even if we get him back to Caer Cadwy I doubt he'll survive," came the reply.

The mention of Caer Cadwy was enough to convince us that these men were on our side. We sheathed our weapons and emerged from hiding.

The two riders were surprised at our sudden appearance and before we knew it, we were both facing the points of their spears.

"Who goes there?" One of the soldiers asked.

"Ambrosius, son of Julianus." The spears dropped immediately.

"We thought you were dead, lord," one of the soldiers said, obviously relieved.

"We were ambushed by Picts, but we managed to escape," Ambrosius said.

"Where is my brother?"

The two horsemen looked at one another uneasily.

"We too were ambushed," the soldier began. "We were heading north, through a narrow valley when we were attacked on all sides by Picts, Irish and Saxons. I have never before heard of them working together like that. If it wasn't for Gorlois and his horsemen turning up just in time, we would all have been dead."

So Gorlois was now the hero of the hour, I thought to myself. "Did Gorlois and his men get involved in the fighting?" I asked.

The soldier shook his head. "No, not directly. When they appeared they formed up and sounded a charge that echoed through the valley like the horns of Jericho and that was enough to frighten the barbarians off. They made an impressive sight though. All glittering armour and bright war banners, it would have been enough to frighten Caesar himself. We owe Gorlois our lives," the soldier's expression changed as he looked awkwardly at Ambrosius. "However your brother was badly injured during the fighting, my lord."

"Where is he? You must take me to him." Ambrosius spoke with desperation in his voice.

"He is in good hands lord," the soldier said. "Your father's physician tends him." We were given a couple of spare horses and rode with the cavalry to a temporary camp that had been hurriedly set up in the hills a mile or so away to treat the injured from the battle. We were led past rows of leather tents and men sitting around campfires to a large tent near the centre of the camp. The agonised groans emanating from the tent gave us cause to hesitate before entering, but when we did we found several priests and a physician standing around with grim and ashen faces. The tent was warm, the air infused with sage that was being burned in a small brazier to disguise the odour of fresh blood and was lit by a number of tallow lanterns. Constans lay on a pile of furs near the back, writhing and moaning in agony. The elderly physician was berating a couple of young monks as they tried to hold Constans still. As we entered, the physician turned to face us. He was holding a pair of iron forceps and a small, sharp knife and his apron was spattered and stained with Constans' blood.

"It is not good, lord," he said wearily to Ambrosius. "An arrow has struck him just below the left eye and has buried itself deep in his skull. If we try to pull it out, it could kill him."

"But surely Mercurius, if the arrow stays in, he will definitely die." Ambrosius replied.

The old physician nodded and his jowls shook. "The head of the arrow is partly protruding from the roof of his mouth. If we can force it through, we could possibly extract it that way, but the pain alone could kill him, let alone the infection that is bound to follow."

"Do what you have to do, Mercurius," Ambrosius muttered. I looked over at Constans and could see the shaft of the arrow protruding from his cheek, just below his left eye which had swollen shut. His head was resting on blood stained rags and he shook and wept like a small child, his pain so intense that he was unaware of our presence.

Ambrosius closed his eyes and turned away. "Does my father know?"

"We despatched messengers as soon as we found out," Mercurius said. "His infantry are on their way but are several miles behind us."

Constans gave a pain wracked scream and the monks struggled to hold him down as his limbs thrashed on his blood soaked bed.

"Hold him still," Mercurius shouted, turning his attention back to Constans. "Cadwgan, prepare more henbane and juice of the poppy."

Ambrosius rushed to his older brother's side and crouched next to him, holding one of his hands between both of his.

"I'll have one more try at working it loose," Mercurius said. "Hold his head still." As soon as the physicians forceps clamped around the bloody stump of the arrow, Constans shrieked, trying to turn his head away as one of the monks held him firmly with both hands.

I turned away and left the surgeon's tent, unable to bear the noise or watch any longer. Nearby I could see about a dozen bodies lined up neatly in a row, naked except for their loin cloths, streaked with blood and dirt. A short distance away, a group of soldiers were silently digging a large grave.

Eventually, Mercurius appeared wiping his hands on a blood soaked rag, his face pale and covered with a sheen of sweat. He looked at me and shook his head.

"The arrow is stuck fast. The only option now is to try to force it through, but the arrowhead is tight up against his back teeth which I will have to remove before we even think about trying. It will cause a lot of damage, but if we can force the arrowhead through the roof of his mouth and through his cheek I may be able to do it."

I winced at the thought of what the physician was proposing. "Do you still have the arrow's fletching?" I asked.

"Yes, we cut off the other end and it's in there on the floor."

I went into the tent and retrieved the fletched end of the arrow. The feathers were black with red tips, confirming my worst suspicions. I went back out to Mercurius and handed him the shaft.

"The only thing you can do for him is try to ease his pain until he passes over."

The physician looked at me with weary eyes. "What makes you so sure?"

"This is a Masraighe arrow. The same sort that took my brother's life. It is poisoned."

Chapter 6

The Reunion

Julianus arrived with his personal guard some time before midday and rushed to the surgeon's tent where Constans was. Ambrosius and I could not sleep and instead sat with several other men around one of the fires. Constans' fevered ramblings and moans mingled with the sobs and cries of injured men from the other tents. I turned my face away as a man emerged from one of the tents carrying a dripping bucket of severed limbs, his forearms slick with blood.

"They hit us hard from both sides of the valley," a stout, one eyed soldier by the name of Folant said. "Showered us with arrows and sling shots and blocked both ends of the valley with boulders and tree trunks. We lost a lot of men and horses," he spat a mouthful of ale bitterly into the fire. "I don't mean to disrespect your brother, Lord Ambrosius, but he should never have led us down that valley. It was a death trap. Any fool could see that."

"My father should never have let him take command of the cavalry," Ambrosius said, his tone harsh and unforgiving.

Folant nodded in agreement. "They came screaming down the sides of the valley. Saxons on one side, Picts and Gaels on the other side. We were forced to dismount and form up in a shield wall, in a circle with the horses in the centre. It would have been an absolute blood bath if Duke Gorlois had not showed up when he did."

"So we've heard," I said, not wishing to hear of Gorlois' moment of glory again. He had arrived in camp about half an hour before Julianus to a fanfare of trumpets and cheers from the men, claiming that he had pursued the enemy into the forest but dared not proceed any further as the risk of ambush was too great. After paying a brief visit to Constans, he had then retired to his large tent with several members of his entourage and a number of barrels of wine and ale.

After a while, our presence was requested by Julianus and Ambrosius and I walked through the camp to his father's tent, where his banner bearing the bull's head of Mithras and the Chi-Rho initials of Christ stood either side of the command tent's wide entrance.

Julianus' narrow, strong boned face looked drawn and haggard, his dark eyes had lost their sparkle. He sat behind an oak table where a hastily drawn map had been placed. He dismissed the two generals that were with him with a wave of his hand and closed his eyes wearily.

"What went wrong, Ambrosius?" He spoke slowly but precisely and I could see Ambrosius' face beginning to flush red.

"We were sent ahead to scout the enemy position, father" he replied. "We saw their ships and were on our way back to Constans when we were ambushed and Fergus and I were the only survivors. We tried to make our way back to the main force but we were pursued and we became lost. Constans therefore walked right into their trap."

"We also have reason to believe that the ships we saw belonged to Duke Gorlois," I added.

Julianus glared at me intensely. "Nonsense. Gorlois would never betray Dumnonia in such a way. His loyalty to King Erbin is as unshakeable as my own. I will hear no more of this treasonous talk."

I opened my mouth to protest, but Julianus raised a hand to silence me. "No more, or else you will feel my wrath, man."

I clenched my jaw shut and fought down my internal frustration. I had no doubts that Julianus would have no qualms about punishing me severely if he needed to dampen my defiance.

Julianus pinched the bridge of his nose between thumb and forefinger and I could see the strain in his face. "Constans should have sent out a second scouting party, but instead he was impatient and sought glory. Now look where it has got him. All my life I have tried to teach you both how to lead men and armies in the vain hope that some day you could follow my lead. Why were you ambushed, Ambrosius? And more importantly, where in God's holy name is Uther?" He looked up, his dark eyes hard and unforgiving.

Ambrosius swallowed hard. "We were betrayed by a shepherd who directed us into a trap. We took the forest path where the enemy was waiting. I regret to report that Uther was taken prisoner by the Picts."

Julianus stood and slammed both hands on the table making us both jump. "You were led into a trap by a shepherd? And now my youngest son is a hostage? Am I hearing this correctly?" He was shouting furiously, his face a mask of rage. "What sort of fool are you, Ambrosius? You allowed yourself to get ambushed and as a consequence, my eldest son lies dying with an arrow in his face, my youngest son is at the mercy of northern barbarians and scores of my men are now dead and injured. Not only that, we have now lost the element of surprise and allowed

Vortimer's army to slip through our fingers." His mouth twisted with contempt for his son. "I was right about you. I knew you would never amount to anything, that you were nothing more than a milksop who should have been strangled at birth. You are not fit to command a herd of pigs, let alone men. When we return to Caer Cadwy, I am sending you to the northern frontier of our Votadini allies in Guotodin where I will see to it that you have some sense knocked into you."

"Yes father," Ambrosius said flatly.

"Now get out of my sight and take that Irishman with you."

As we walked from the command tent, I turned to Ambrosius who was brooding silently.

"That was harsh. It was not your fault. Constans should never have gone ahead without sending out more scouts."

"It doesn't matter now does it?" Ambrosius shot back acerbically. "He wants me out of his sight and where better to send me than to the Wall?"

"The Wall?" I enquired.

"Guotodin is a god forsaken, freezing hell hole whose inhabitants, the Votadini are no better than the Picts that they stop from pouring into Britannia. He's sending me to the end of the civilised world to patrol the Great Northern Wall that keeps the Picts at bay, so that he can forget that he ever had another son."

We returned to Caer Cadwy the next day. A grey drizzle fell from the sky, reflecting the mood of the returning cavalry. There had been no great victory as we had expected, but the majority of the men were relieved to be coming back at all. We rode into the central parade ground, weary and deprived of sleep, handing our steeds over to the stable hands.

It was the first time that I had seen Caer Cadwy by daylight and I was impressed by what I saw. It was a hive of activity, with blacksmiths, farriers and leather workers labouring away, the ring of hammers on anvils mingling with the cries of street hawkers selling fruit and bread. Although it was primarily a large military camp, it was more like a small town where civilians mingled with soldiers. There were no beggars or vagabonds in Caer Cadwy, each and every person had a task to carry out and knew what was expected of them and they did so with diligence. The air was filled with smells from a variety of sources, the bakery, the brewery the stables and the tanners all added their particular odour to the mix.

"Anyone who has something to offer is welcome in Caer Cadwy," Ambrosius said as we made our way to the tavern. "Everyone except me, it seems." He added glumly. He had barely spoken a word on the journey back to the fortress. Constans had been rushed back to the Duke's hall on the litter that he had been carried back on and Ambrosius had been refused permission to see him. Indeed his father had decreed that no one, save himself, his physician and a handful of surgeons and priests should be allowed to see Constans in his final, agonised hours.

Ambrosius was wracked with guilt and grief so I suggested something that all warriors turn to at such times of reflection. Ale and wine. At first he had been reluctant to do so, claiming that to get drunk was unbecoming of a Roman of noble birth, but eventually I talked him into it. We entered a rowdy tavern full of drunk soldiers singing bawdy songs who fell silent upon seeing Ambrosius enter.

The young lord looked decidedly uncomfortable as we made our way over to a dark corner and sat at a table. I ordered two jugs of mead from a pretty young serving wench and the soldiers soon forgot about Ambrosius' presence and resumed their song about the exploits of a bored housewife whose husband had gone to war.

Ambrosius downed his pitcher of mead surprisingly quickly and poured himself another. "Two years," he mused bitterly. "I can't believe he's sending me away for two whole years."

I nodded sympathetically. Julianus had requested our presence briefly in his hall as soon as we had returned, where he informed us of his decision. He had also found out about the death of Branwen, but thankfully had been spared the awful details. Ambrosius was to be sent to Guotodin to serve under King Cadlew of the Votadini. Cadlew was an ally of Julianus and kept him supplied with many good horsemen and in return, Julianus sent him trained troops to man the Wall. As Geraint and I were now homeless and without a liege, we had taken on the role of Ambrosius' personal guard and as we did not wish to return to a Caer Dor under the control of our enemy Gorlois, we too agreed to accompany Ambrosius to the northern frontier in the hope that maybe we could find employment with King Cadlew. It was a decision that did not sit well with Ambrosius, whose hopes of marrying his young nun were now scuppered.

"On the bright side it could be a month before we hear from King Cadlew," I said, trying to ease his pain. "Which means that at least you will have a bit of time with her."

Ambrosius gave me one of his withering stares. "Did you not listen to a thing I told you? She is still part of the monastery for another month. When she is finally released, I will be on my way to Guotodin."

"Then we must find a way of getting you to her and you can explain what has happened and if she truly loves you, then she will wait for you."

Ambrosius was inconsolable and so we drank until we could no longer stand, tumbling out of the tavern in the early hours. Ambrosius insisted on taking me to his family home which lay a short ride northeast of Caer Cadwy and so we woke a rather irate stable hand and hired a couple of horses.

Ambrosius' home was huge, impressive even by the light of the moon, a sprawling villa surrounded by lush, arable farmland and pastures for horses and cattle. The villa itself had been built by Julianus and was named Villa Aurelianus in honour of his late wife's family name. It was enclosed by a whitewashed stone wall, twice the height of a man, with guards at the gates who nodded at Ambrosius as he passed and looked at me with a mixture of curiosity and suspicion.

"Have you ever had a bath, Fergus?" Ambrosius slurred, placing a clumsy arm around my shoulder.

I shook my head. "No, never."

"Then you are in for a treat."

We came to the double oak doors and Ambrosius hammered on them loudly until a thin, middle aged woman with a stern face opened them.

"Master Ambrosius, where have you been? You smell of drink young man, it's a good thing your father isn't here."

"Don't worry yourself Elena. I won't be here for much longer. My father has decided he no longer requires my services and is sending me as far north as possible," he replied sourly.

We walked into a spacious hallway lined with marble statues on plinths and woven wall hangings, the colours of the mosaic floor reflecting the light from the numerous torches ensconced on the walls.

"We are going to bathe, Elena. Can you see to it that the hypocausts are fired?" Ambrosius announced grandly.

The housemaid gave me a hostile look as though I were responsible for getting her young master in such a state. "The only place you're going to is bed young man," she chastised, shooting me a thunderous glare as I snorted drunkenly, amused at her outburst.

"And who is this?" She added, pointing a thin finger at me.

Ambrosius put his arm around my shoulders again. "This man saved my life, that's who this is," he said, swaying unsteadily. "And tomorrow we're going to rescue Igrainne from the nunnery."

"You will do no such thing, your father would skin you alive," Elena replied sternly.

"My father wishes it was me dying with an arrow in my face and not Constans," Ambrosius slurred bitterly. "My father, the great Battle Duke of Durotrigia hates the ground I walk upon."

"Nonsense," Elena replied as she took Ambrosius' cloak. "A good night's rest is what you need, young master. I will have a room readied for your friend. I very much doubt you will want to be woken early."

I awoke late in the morning to bright sunlight streaming through a large window and the sound of chickens clucking and scratching outside in the courtyard. I was in a cosy little room in the most comfortable bed I had ever slept in. I lay there for a while, my head pounding horribly until there was a knock at my door and a voice announcing that breakfast was served. I arose groggily and made my way down a wide hallway with frescoed walls depicting the Seven Labours of Hercules which I knew from the tales of Father Demetrios. As I walked into the spacious dining room with its ornate mosaic floor, I received some odd looks from the servants until I realised I was still wearing my coat of mail and had slept in it all night.

"Good to see that you have brought your rustic manners to the Duke's household," Elena said frostily.

I mumbled an apology and sat on a padded couch at a low table that had been laid out with breads, cheeses, cold meats and fruit. Ambrosius sat opposite looking as bad as I felt, his pale eyes glazed and unfocused.

We ate a hearty breakfast before retiring to the baths, an experience which I found to be refreshing and invigorating, having never before sampled the delights of submerging myself in hot water. I luxuriated in the sensation as a slave poured a jug of hot water over my back. We had been discussing how we intended to get a message through to his beloved Igrainne. Upon the strict instructions of the duke, the Abbess had forbade any contact between Igrainne and Ambrosius, threatening to tell his father if she saw him near the monastery again. She also knew all of Ambrosius' servants by sight, so sending one of them was not an option. We decided that I would go, disguised as a beggar.

"I can get you some clothes and rags from the slave's quarters," Ambrosius said enthusiastically. "Then we'll ride to within sight of the monastery and you will continue on foot. Igrainne usually works with the beggars, giving alms to the poor, so I'm hoping you will see her. You can then give her my message."

"I don't even know what she looks like, but I'll see what I can do." I said.

"Just look for the prettiest nun there and hand it to her. I taught her how to read and she has a basic grasp of Latin, so she should be able to understand it." Ambrosius replied with a smirk.

After we had submerged ourselves in the cold waters of the adjoining frigidarium, we dressed and left the villa, taking the two horses we had hired. Ambrosius had managed to get some particularly filthy looking rags that smelled as bad as they looked, presenting them to me in the stables.

"Which grave did you find these in?" I protested, wrinkling my nose in disgust as I pulled on the ragged, threadbare hessian tunic.

"You are doing me a great service my friend," Ambrosius replied. "For the second time, I owe you a lot." He reached down, scooped up a handful of horse manure and before I could react, smeared it over my face and hair.

"What the hell are you doing?" I yelled, gagging at the pungent stench.

"Making you a more convincing beggar," Ambrosius said in a matter of fact way.

"Beggars don't smear themselves with horse shit," I replied, wiping the mess out of my eyes.

Ambrosius shrugged. "You can bathe again when you return."

By the time Ambrosius had finished with me, I was transformed from a Pendragon warrior into a sorry looking wretch who had fallen upon hard times. We rode for a couple of miles until we came to a collection of wooden huts surrounded by a low palisade down in a lush little valley with a river passing nearby.

"That's the monastery," Ambrosius said, indicating the buildings with a nod. "I will wait here. Find Igrainne and hand her the message. The hypocausts have been fired back home, so the baths will be nice and hot."

"Thank you so much, my lord," I muttered sarcastically as I dismounted my steed and picked up my staff.

Ambrosius handed me a small wax tablet no larger than the palm of my hand, wrapped carefully in linen and sealed with a blob of beeswax and I set off down the narrow, cobbled road that wound its way down to the nunnery.

I hobbled up to the open gate, leaning heavily on my staff. Two bored looking guards leaning on spears stepped forwards to enquire as to my business.

"I am starving sir, I haven't eaten for days," I said in the most pathetic voice I could muster.

"You look well fed to me," one of the guards snarled. He was overweight with lank, greasy hair that hung from under a leather cap.

"Sir, please have pity. I used to be a soldier like you, but a Saxon spear in my thigh ended my career. I have not been able to work since."

The guard glanced nervously through the gate. "You can go through, but I must warn you. A lot of those poor sods in there are carrying the plague and have come not for food but for a blessing before they die. If I were you, friend, I'd go elsewhere for a free bowl of gruel."

I looked beyond the guard at the collection of ragged, miserable people gathered in the courtyard. "Plague?" I repeated.

The soldier gave a fearful nod. "Seems it started in Ynys Wytryn. Swept through the monastery and more or less wiped out every Christian soul. Some say it's God's punishment on the Abbot for losing the Holy Chalice, others say it was the curse of the druids, who he tried to wipe out. Whatever the cause, it's spreading fast."

I felt the hairs on my arms rise as I remembered Myrddin's curse, when he had called down the wrath of Cailleach, the hag of death and disease upon Abbot Neirin and Lord Glaesten's men on Ynys Wytryn.

"What about the Abbot?" I asked.

The fat guard shrugged. "He still lives and has fled the monastery, or so I've heard, though many of his monks are now dead. If I were you though, I would turn around and forget that I ever saw this place."

"I'm desperately hungry," I insisted. "I will take my chances."

"Have you ever seen someone dying from the plague?" the other guard suddenly said, his eyes glistening salaciously. He continued before I had finished shaking my head, eager to tell me the horrible details.

"They're covered in great weeping boils that gather under the arms and between the legs and leak stinking pus. You start to cough up blood and black bile and then finally die, burning from the inside out. Is that what you want, friend?"

"I just want food," I replied humbly.

The guard gave a disinterested sigh and stepped aside, allowing me to pass. I grovelled and thanked him as I limped through the gate into the courtyard beyond. It was crowded with people, young and old, men and women. All were filthy and tired looking, some sat despondently with their backs against the log fence, slurping at wooden bowls of watery, grey gruel.

A number of sisters, conspicuous in their clean white habits, moved amongst the weary people, sorting the sick from the healthy and guiding them to a long wooden building, presumably where they could die coughing up their guts in a little comfort with the blessing of Christ. There was very little chatter, just coughs, moans and weeping and no one gave me a second glance as I entered.

I pushed through the crowd, past a woman singing softly to a dead baby in her arms whose lips and hands had turned black and joined a line of people waiting to be served gruel from a large black cauldron at the end of the courtyard, scanning the faces of the nuns moving quietly amongst the wretched men and women, offering words of comfort, looking for one that matched Ambrosius' description of his beloved Igrainne.

"Are you sick my friend?" A serene, female voice spoke beside me. I turned to see a plump faced young nun with a look of concern on her face.

"No, but I was wondering," I began. "I have a message for someone."

The girl gave a knowing smile and I knew immediately that she could see through my disguise. "Igrainne?"

I nodded self-consciously and the sister pointed to the long, wooden building housing the sick and dying and her smile rapidly vanished. "In the infirmary. But unless you're sick yourself, I wouldn't go in there. I could pass on the message for you."

"Thank you sister, but I promised someone that I would do this personally."

"Christ be with you, child," she said as I pushed my way through to the infirmary. The first thing that struck me as I walked through the door was the smell. It was the sickly stench of death and it hung in the air like an invisible mist, causing me to gag.

The infirmary was lit with tallow candles and high, narrow windows that let in small shafts of sunlight that fell upon rows and rows of sleeping pallets padded with straw and rough blankets. Every pallet was occupied by sick and dying people, their moans and sobs filling the fetid air. Some screamed out incoherently as delirium gripped them whilst other coughed and spewed black bile into wooden bowls at their bedside.

I wondered whether Myrddin was aware of the terrible sickness that he had unleashed upon the land and I felt more than a little ashamed to be in such a place on false pretences, delivering a love letter amongst so much death and misery. I wandered amongst the rows of wretched souls, trying to get a glimpse of the faces of the nuns who were tending to them.

One old man near the back of the infirmary was coughing the last dregs of his life into a mucous filled bowl held by a slender sister who was trying to comfort the man in his final moments. Finally the old man fell back, his thin body wracked with convulsions, his ragged tunic stained with the black filth that had spewed from his lungs. After a brief moment, he was still, his yellowing, bloodshot eyes staring lifelessly up at the rafters.

The sister let out a weary sigh and muttered a prayer, making the sign of the cross over the old man's twisted body before looking up and catching my eye.

The first thing that struck me was the girl's beauty. Despite wearing the unflattering wimple and habit of a lay sister, the girl's outstanding beauty shone through. Her lips were full and red in contrast to her pale, marble like skin, her face was heart shaped, with fine, high cheekbones and a pointed chin. But it was her eyes that were most captivating. They were a deep blue, almost violet like my own, flecked with a rim of gold about the iris. They were eyes that I knew immediately and when I saw her I laughed aloud with sheer, ludicrous joy.

Igrainne was none other than my own sister and I realised then the similarity in the name that had not occurred to me earlier. Igrainne was the Briton's version of the name Ygerna and I laughed even louder.

Ygerna frowned at me with puzzlement and concern. "Can I help you at all?" She said, her voice sounding strange in the tongue of the Britons.

"You already have," I replied, feeling tears fill my eyes as I beamed from ear to ear.

"I'm sorry, I don't understand," she began and she took a shocked step back as I placed my hands around her slender arms.

"Don't you know your own brother?"

Ygerna hesitated. "But both of my brothers died," she paused as she looked into my eyes and recognition dawned on her face. "Fergus?" she muttered, hardly more than a whisper of disbelief.

I nodded, still smiling, unable to speak for the lump in my throat.

Ygerna let out a little sob and flung her arms around me. We stood embracing one another amongst the dead and the dying. All those years that I had assumed my sister had drowned and yet here she was, just as Brighid, the mysterious woman in my visions had told me.

Ygerna took a step back, still holding both of my hands, hands that had been hardened over the years from hours of practice with sword and spear. She cast a wary glance at a large set, ferocious looking senior sister and pulled me to one side, behind a wattle screen where we could not be seen.

"How can this be?" she whispered through her tears. "I truly thought you had drowned. Where have you been, brother?" She touched my face gently, running her fingers over the stubble on my cheek.

"It's a long story," I said, wiping a tear from her soft cheek with the back of my finger. "But one that I will be able to share with you soon. What of Dorbalos? Does he still live?"

Ygerna looked down and shook her head. "He made sure I was safe, but the cold was too much for him. He clung to the curragh for as long as possible, but in the end his strength failed him and he offered a prayer to Manannan mac Lir to take his life in exchange for mine. He let go of the curragh and sank beneath the waves."

I put my arms around her once again as she wept bitterly. "So what happened then?" I prompted gently.

"The curragh washed up on a shingle beach at night and I walked for hours, not knowing where I was or where to go. By morning, I was cold and hungry, wandering over bleak moors where I was accosted by a group of bandits. They took me to their camp, but as luck would have it, one of the Duke's patrols were passing by and after a brief fight, the bandits fled. I was frightened and I ran too, but was later found by the Duke's son."

"Ambrosius?" I said with a smile.

"How did you know that?" her eyes widened with wonder.

I handed her the wax tablet with a gentle smile. "Because he sent me to give you this."

"You know Lord Ambrosius?"

I nodded. "He and I have been through a lot together recently and have become quite good friends over the past few days. He seems like a good man."

Ygerna smiled. "He is, Fergus. He is kind and gentle and caring. He looked after me when we returned to Caer Cadwy, made sure I was safe and secure. He was a little shy at first, but we became good friends. I do miss him so."

"He misses you too," I said. "And I will miss you as well."

She blinked at me. "What do you mean?"

"In about a month's time we are to be sent to Guotodin in the north, for two years. That is why Ambrosius had to get a message through to you, to let you know that the marriage would have to be delayed."

Ygerna let out a little laugh. "Marriage? He never mentioned marriage to me."

"But Ambrosius told me you were to be wed. That you were going to leave the Sisterhood and marry him."

Ygerna took a quick furtive glance around the wattle screen before resuming the conversation. "It is true that I will not be taking my solemn vows and will be free to leave at the new moon, but marriage? Ambrosius is sweet and kind, but I have never considered marrying him. Besides, his father would never allow it," she looked down at the ground with a morose expression. "Not only that, you forget that I am already married."

I nodded wordlessly. It was a memory neither of us wanted to share.

"So what do I tell him?" I asked, scratching at the uncomfortable sackcloth tunic chafing against my skin.

"Just tell him I received the message. He does not need to know about this conversation. The last thing I would ever want to do is hurt him in any way."

I smiled at her reassuringly. "Very well, sister. I must return now. I will see you at the new moon. I won't tell Ambrosius just yet that we are related. I want to see his face when he finds out that we are brother and sister."

Ygerna laughed and embraced me one more time. "Farewell my brother. Wait for me if you can."

"I have waited years already," I said, stroking her hand. "One more month is nothing."

I kissed her on her cheek and then made my way through the stinking infirmary to the fresh spring air outside, determined to get my sister away from that place of disease and death.

Chapter 7

Villa Aurelianus

Two days later the news came through that Constans had died. The arrow in his face had festered, poisoning his blood beyond any hope of redemption. Physicians were replaced by priests who had given him the last rights as he lay sobbing and weeping like a newborn, delirious in his agony up until the moment his soul left his body.

We had been summoned to the Great Hall of Caer Cadwy where Constans was being treated and we knew that the news was bad. As we approached the huge hall of split oak logs, I noticed the collection of crows on the roof and I knew then that Morrigan, the Phantom Queen had come to claim his soul.

Julianus looked tired and drawn, his eyes red and sunken as he stood before the assembled crowd in the hall and announced the death of his eldest son.

Constans was buried three days later, next to his mother with his feet towards the rising sun so that he would be facing Christ on the day of judgement. Dorbalos had always told me that we buried our dead in a similar way so that Belenos the sun god would smile down upon us. I preferred Dorbalos' explanation. There was no judgement or guilt associated with the Old Gods.

After the funeral, a feast was held in the Great Hall in honour of Constans.

Julianus occupied the top table on a raised dais so that he was above everyone else present, with Gorlois seated on his right. Ambrosius had been relegated to one of the lower tables and as his personal guard, I sat next to him, all too aware that his father had purposefully snubbed him in favour of the Duke of Cerniw.

Halfway through the feast, Gorlois stood and gave a long and sycophantic speech, praising the prowess and fortitude of Julianus and placing emphasis on his lifelong friendship with Constans and how he regarded him as a brother. Julianus in turn thanked the Duke of Cerniw for saving his cavalry from destruction at the hands of the Saxons and Irish and praised Gorlois' timely arrival and subsequent routing of the barbarians. Later on, as the wine began to flow more freely, Julianus announced that although he had lost a dear son in Constans, he had gained another son in Gorlois and the two men embraced to the raucous applause of the assembled guests. I noticed that one of those standing and applauding the loudest was Quintinia, who had been sent to the funeral to represent the young King Erbin. She had been accompanied by Princess Meinwen and the pair were seated at Julianus' table. Meinwen smiled when she caught my eye and I gave her a wink of acknowledgement.

"I think I need some air," Ambrosius said sourly, rising from the bench and making his way through the hall.

I followed him outside into the crisp spring evening, sensing that he needed some company. He was sat on an empty barrel, staring up into the dark blue sky at the first stars appearing.

"Don't take it to heart, Ambrosius," I said, sitting on a barrel next to him. It had been a clear, sunny day, unseasonably warm and the heat of the day could still be felt.

"I am an embarrassment to him," he muttered. "All my life I have tried to do the right thing, to be the son he wanted, but I was never good enough."

"I know how you feel," I said, remembering how my own father had doted upon my older half-brother. The difference was, Conmor had been a friend and protector to me, whereas Constans had been nothing more than a spiteful bully to his younger sibling. "My father was the same. But deep down, he still loves you. You are his son and that has to count for something. All of that with Gorlois is just drunken posturing, nothing more. Pay it no heed, Ambrosius."

"I thought I was doing the right thing when we rode through that forest," he said, staring down at his hands. "My only thought was to get back to Constans as quickly as possible and I vowed to myself that this time I would do it right, but when it came to it, when the attack happened, I froze, just like I did before."

"What do you mean?" I enquired.

"I mean I became ineffective," Ambrosius snapped bitterly. "With fear. I didn't know what to do and if it hadn't been for you, I would be dead. Probably better if you had let me die to be honest. I am no leader of men and I never will be. I can't even lead a scouting party without getting them killed. You can study the great generals inside out, but if you don't have the qualities of leadership then it is all meaningless. My father can see that and that is why he is sending me far away out of his sight. I am nothing to him and rightly so."

I looked at Ambrosius and could see the torment in his pale eyes, the permanent scowl on his face. "Don't be so hard on yourself, Ambrosius. I have a feeling inside that you are destined for greatness and one day you will be a great leader of men and your father will be proud of you, of that I am sure. You have an inner strength which I have not seen in others and that is why I saved your life in that forest rather than abandoning you to your fate."

Ambrosius gave a humourless chuckle. "I do not mean any disrespect Fergus, but your experience of leaders has been limited to petty warlords and chieftains of desolate hill tribes. I was taught to aspire to the likes of Caesar and Philip of Macedon, men who led great armies into battle."

"And one day you shall," I said with conviction.

"Don't be despondent, Ambrosius," A loud voice said from behind us. We both turned to see Gorlois standing there with a goblet of mead in his hand. He was immaculately dressed, with a white tunic bordered with gold thread and a cloak of ermine about his broad shoulders. His short cropped beard and shoulder length hair had been perfumed and oiled and hung down in tight ringlets. He placed his arm around Ambrosius' shoulders and crouched down beside him like some kindly uncle about to give advice.

"Your father is a good man and a good judge of character," he said with a look of feigned sincerity on his face. "But I fear in your case, he has treated you unfairly. You did what you thought was best and that is commendable. You were not to know that an ambush was awaiting you, which incidentally is exactly why I did not send my cavalry into the forest in pursuit of the barbarians. With hindsight, it was an obvious place for an ambush."

"So what would you have done. Gorlois?" I enquired, unable to keep the hostility from my voice.

The Duke shrugged arrogantly. "I would have retraced my steps along the route that I knew was safe. It's obvious really."

"Hindsight is a great thing," I said. "Exactly how many barbarians did you kill on that day, Duke?"

Gorlois frowned thoughtfully. "Hard to tell really. Enough to make them run for their lives though and save Julianus' cavalry from being wiped out."

"I hear that the barbarians fled before you even had a chance to charge. There was no great massacre, you let them get away."

Gorlois glared at me and I could see the intense dislike in his eyes. "Be careful what you say, Gael. Just because you are the personal guard of Julianus' son, do not let your new position go to your head. You were not there, you did not see what happened. The barbarians fled into the forest and to pursue them would have been suicide. Any idiot knows that, isn't that right Ambrosius?"

Ambrosius did not answer, but his pale face flushed red with anger and humiliation.

"Never mind, Ambrosius, we all make mistakes" he said finally, giving the Duke's son a patronising pat on the back. "We can catch up again soon, we have plenty of time. Your father has invited me back to discuss the division of the Pendragon lands," he looked at me and smiled and gave a wink. "I shall probably be here to see you off when you go. Where is it you're going again?"

"Guotodin," Ambrosius answered flatly.

The Duke of Cerniw smiled, exposing his perfect white teeth. "Ah yes, the realm of the Votadini. Your Gael barbarian should fit in nicely there. Cold, damp, grey...dour, uncivilised with no redeeming features, a lot like your homeland." He gave me a slight bow with a smirk on his face.

Gorlois stood and gazed at the first stars appearing in the evening sky and sighed deeply. "You know, I have a good feeling about the future," he said before patting Ambrosius on the back once more and returning to the hall.

Over the next few months the weather stayed unseasonably warm. It was between the time of Imbolc, when winter starts to lose its icy grip and the ewes are fat with their unborn lambs and before the early summer festival of Beltane, or Calan Mai as the Britons called it, when need fires were lit and people would drive their cattle between them to ward off disease and ensure fertility. The forests and meadows bloomed with new life and Geraint and I were officially sworn in as Ambrosius' personal guard, at his own request in his father's Great Hall in Caer Cadwy. We knelt before Ambrosius amongst an assembly of priests and warriors, with our swords planted on the ground before us and swore before almighty God that we would protect Ambrosius with our lives and swore our allegiance to the young lord.

As the bodyguard of the Duke's son, we were given lodgings in a small room in one of the wings of Villa Aurelianus and spent most of those warm days practicing with sword and spear in the courtyard. Sometimes Julianus himself would come to the villa to watch us practice in the courtyard, his gaze critical and impassive. He would sometimes discuss techniques with us, showing us variations on swings, parries and lunges and was particularly keen that we should learn to fight from horseback. It was a welcome diversion for him, but he was particularly critical of his son, berating him publicly when he made mistakes or failed to live up to his expectations.

Ambrosius was far from a natural fighter as he lacked the aggression and killer instinct that Geraint had, but he had good technique and he made up for his shortfalls with a dogged determination to succeed, especially under his father's critical eye. Geraint, still angry at the lashing he had received, seemed to delight in knocking the wind out of Ambrosius and planting him on his backside after beating him black and blue with the wooden practice weapons, but Ambrosius would climb to his feet, bruised but undefeated and return for more punishment, hoping in vain for some recognition from his father.

One day, news reached us that Julianus was departing for Din Tagel to meet with Duke Gorlois to discuss the division of the Pendragon lands, but before he left he introduced us to Cletus, the captain of his guard. Cletus was a Sarmatian, one of a group of about two dozen of his kind who had been tasked with passing on their considerable skills of horsemanship to the cavalry of Caer Cadwy. As wide as he was tall, Cletus had a hard looking, flat face with a scant, mousey coloured beard and small eyes that glistened like black marbles. Cletus was fiercely proud of his origins, his ancestors hailing from the great, barren plains that stretched endlessly to the east of the Roman Empire. It was a wild and lawless land of vast, green steppes, peopled by warring bands of horsemen who learned to ride before they could walk. According to Ambrosius, Cletus and his comrades were the descendants of an auxiliary unit of Sarmatians known as the 6th Victrix, who had been stationed up near the Wall by the Roman army and who had decided to stay when the other legions left the islands forever. They generally kept themselves separate from the other soldiers of Julianus' army, preferring to sing their own songs and marry their own women and tell tales of their own ancestors around their hearth fires. They shunned the worship of Christ, preferring instead to pray to the open sky whilst kneeling before a sword thrust into the ground and they treated their horses better than they treated their own women.

Cletus, like the other Sarmatians in his band wore a long coat of bronze scaled armour that reached past his knees, with a high, pointed helm, crested by a horsehair plume. The Sarmatians carried slender, curved swords and two handed lances which they wielded with deadly efficiency from the backs of their horses and everywhere they went, they proudly carried their dragon standard before them, a curious banner that howled like a wolf when the wind was right, topped by a ferocious looking golden dragon head with red silk that spilled from its gaping mouth and flailed out behind it in the wind like tongues of flame. But it was their demonstration of horse archery that impressed us the most. They were able to hit a target at full gallop, with short, curved bows that took the strength of two normal men to draw to their full extent, hitting them dead centre every time.

"I will teach you to fight from a horse, like us Sarmatians," Cletus told us in his gruff, curiously accented voice. "A Sarmatian never leaves his horse. Your horse is your best weapon. There is no honour to be found fighting on the ground. You must tower over your enemy and knock him aside like wheat before the scythe. You must become as one with your horse, be aware of its every twitch and movement as it must become aware of yours. You must enter the mind of your horse and read its thoughts and bend it to your will with just a flex of your knee or a press of your heel."

Cletus trained us relentlessly, showing us how to strike a target with a two handed spear grip at full gallop whilst using our knees to guide our horses and remain in our saddle and how to effectively wield a sword from the backs of our mounts. We trained until our palms bled and our thighs were chaffed from the hours spent in the saddle and we would limp back to our quarters at the end of the day stinking of horse sweat and nursing bruises that we had gained from falling from the backs of our steeds.

Now that Ambrosius was in effect master of Villa Aurelianus in his father's absence, Geraint and I had more or less free reign of the villa and its grounds. We got to know and became friendly with the servants and slaves of the household and the surrounding farmstead. Elena, the maid of the house, despite our initial frosty meeting actually grew to like me and I her. She reminded me in a lot of ways of Rhawn, the fisherwoman who had taken me in and raised her as her own back in Penglyn. She was straight talking and down to earth and the other slaves and servants respected and feared her. She also turned a blind eye to my dalliances with Hefina, a sweet young kitchen girl who had taken a particular shine to me. Whenever possible, we would rush off to some secluded area of the farmstead, to the warmth and silence of a barn or a hidden hay bale while Geraint did the same with Hefina's older and far less attractive sister.

A week before we were due to depart, a herald returned from Guotodin with a message from King Cadlew. Apparently, the king's soothsayer had read the entrails of a sacrificial sheep and foretold that the arrival of a prince from the south before Beltane would spell King Cadlew's downfall and so he decided that it would be better to delay Ambrosius' departure until after Beltane. This was welcome news to both myself and Ambrosius, as we would be able to spend precious time with Ygerna who was soon to leave the sisterhood.

When the time came, Ambrosius, Geraint and I rode to the monastery to meet Ygerna. Geraint was in a foul mood as we had given up meat and wine for Lent and were reminded every day of Christ's self-denial in the wilderness and how he had resisted the three temptations of Satan by father Porcius, Julianus' austere and humourless priest who insisted that we were to attend mass every morning and evening in the small family chapel. We had another week to wait until the feast of the Paschal Triduum, which celebrated the death, burial and resurrection of Christ and which more importantly spelled the end of our period of enforced abstinence. "I'm going to hell anyway, so what will it matter to the Almighty if I have a swig of wine now and then?" Geraint grumbled as we rode down the dusty, cobbled road.

"It's all about self-sacrifice and discipline," Ambrosius said over his shoulder, his tone irritable. "It helps to fortify the soul."

Geraint huffed dismissively. "Life's miserable enough as it is, so why do these priests insist on taking away the few pleasures that we have?"

"To remind you that life is not one endless pursuit of pleasure, that there is more to life than drinking and women and fighting," Ambrosius retorted.

"That's all my life consists of," Geraint muttered, looking at me with a mischievous grin and a wink.

Ambrosius reined his horse to a halt and dismounted silently.

A slender girl was walking up the road towards us wearing a grey woollen shawl over a plain linen dress and carrying a bindle over her shoulder. I knew immediately from her posture that it was my own beloved sister and I too dismounted and followed Ambrosius who had removed his cavalry helmet and tucked it under his arm.

Ygerna looked up and smiled with joy, casting aside the sack containing her meagre belongings and ran to embrace the Duke's son.

They stood for a long while in one another's arms before Ygerna looked at me with tears of happiness in her violet blue eyes and walked over to me and embraced me as well.

"So my brother is not a beggar after all," she said, admiring my coat of shining mail and the ornate war helm that had once belonged to Eamonn O'Suilleabhain, chieftain of the Eoganachta.

"Brother?" Ambrosius stuttered.

We both turned to him and smiled.

"Igrainne, or Ygerna, is my sister. I knew one day that I would find her."

Ambrosius simply stood open mouthed with a frown on his brow. Slowly the scowl turned into a grin. "So Igrainne was never a slave?"

I shook my head. "We are the children of Fiontan mac Duggan, chief of the Deisi tribe. Ygerna is high born as am I. She used the story of being an escaped slave to cover her true identity."

"To hide from Fiachu mac Niall?" Ambrosius surmised, beginning to make sense of the situation. His eyes flashed with hope. "But this changes everything. If Ygerna is high born, then my father can have no objections to my proposal."

On hearing the name of the son of King Niall, Ygerna stiffened and looked at me fearfully. "Does Fiachu seek me still?"

"He does, but he will have to kill myself and Ambrosius to get to you," I answered, taking her small, pale hand in mine. "Don't worry Ygerna, he will never find you. And we would die rather than let you fall into his hands."

Rather than return to the villa, Ambrosius insisted that we head eastward, following the course of a well maintained Roman road and then striking out across the vast, gently rolling plains of Durotrigia until in the distance we saw a great ring of huge upright stones. A warm wind buffeted us and the fresh scent of early summer filled the air. Herds of stout limbed horses watched by armed men grazed on the lush green grass and Ambrosius explained that this was where the Sarmatian's bred their mounts for his father's army. The stones had been placed long ago by giants, according to the locals and the place used to be sacred to the druids. Ambrosius told us that local chiefs still sometimes met at the stones to discuss matters of importance.

We rode into the stone circle, tethering our horses nearby and marvelling at the construction of the ancient monoliths in silence. I walked over to one of the towering stones and placed my hand upon it, feeling the tingle of its earthly power run through my arm. This was obviously a place of great importance and it was no wonder that the druids had revered it and I found myself wondering briefly about the fate of Myrddin. He had promised that he would help me find Nivian, but after I had lost the Chalice he had abandoned me.

"Do you remember, Igrainne when we used to come here?" Ambrosius said, leaning upon one of the stones.

Ygerna smiled and nodded. "Of course I remember. And in the summer we would bathe in the stream down there and once you slipped on the rocks and knocked me in."

Ambrosius laughed at the memory and I realised how rare it was to see him laugh. "And when it rained so heavily that we had to squeeze into the hollow of that tree for shelter." He nodded to the remains of a thick, hollowed out oak across the stream.

"How could I forget that?" Ygerna replied.

After the laughter subsided there was a long silence broken only by the faint hum of insects and the chattering of birds before Ambrosius plucked up the courage to speak again. He turned to address me, his face red and flustered. "Fergus, as the last remaining male heir of your household, do I have permission to ask for your sister's hand in marriage?"

I grinned and shrugged. "Why not ask her yourself?" I replied.

Ambrosius coughed self-consciously and cleared his throat. "Igrainne, or rather Ygerna...would you do me the honour of marrying me?"

Ygerna let out a little chuckle and gazed thoughtfully over the sun drenched meadows of Durotrigia where the horses were peacefully grazing. Her expression gradually darkened, her light hearted, joyous mood shadowed by something more brooding. Finally she stepped forwards and took both of Ambrosius' hands in hers. "I wish I could, Ambrosius. But I am already married. And the vows were made fast in the names of Danu and Lugh, the Old Gods of my people."

He blinked at her and nodded slowly. "Of course, how foolish of me. You are still married to Fiachu mac Niall." He let out a deep sigh and looked down at the ground, unable to hide his disappointment.

"But if Fiachu mac Niall were to die, you would be free to marry again, with my blessing," I said. "And I intend to find him and kill him."

We returned to Villa Aurelianus where Ambrosius decided he would speak to Father Porcius. We met him in Julianus' study, a cluttered room with shelves and alcoves which were overcrowded with busts of old emperors, rolled up scrolls, vases and old weapons and pieces of armour. A large map of Britannia rendered in ink faded to brown on calf's skin dominated one wall.

The austere Father Porcius sat behind a sturdy desk of oak and listened to the young lord's proposal in silence. He wore white robes that bore the Chi Rho runes of Christ in gold filament. He had a full head of thick, white hair and a pinched, humourless expression and he regarded us all with a reproachful look as Ambrosius had insisted that Ygerna and I accompany him as well.

"I know my father had objections before, but things are different now. Ygerna never was a slave, she is of noble birth," he held before him Ygerna's silver brooch, the one that she wore on her ill-fated wedding day. It was a smaller copy of the one which I had inherited, my father having had it made especially for the wedding. "This is proof of her heritage. Fergus wears a similar brooch, which attests to their high born status."

"Ambrosius, I have no doubts any more that Igrainne...sorry, Ygerna is of noble birth. The problem is that she is already married."

"But surely Father Porcius, you can annul this pagan handfasting. Besides, it was never consummated," Ambrosius protested.

"You only have her word for that," Porcius snapped, giving Ygerna a distasteful look. "The marriage cannot be annulled without the permission of the husband. Pagan or not, it does not matter. In the words of Athenogoras of Athens, second marriage is only a specious adultery."

"And what if someone were to kill her husband?" I put in.

Porcius glared at me for speaking out of turn. "Then I would refer you to the writings of Quintus Tertullianus. One husband in the flesh and another in the spirit. This would be adultery. Joint knowledge of one woman by two men."

"Father Porcius, I too have studied the writings of Tertullianus," Ambrosius said patiently. "And did he not say remarriage was possible if the dissolution of the first marriage had occurred prior to one's conversion to Christianity? Fiachu mac Niall is not a follower of Christ, therefore if he died then remarriage would be possible."

Porcius was lost for words. I saw his face glow red with indignation and I smirked to myself.

"So are you willing to commit the sin of murder so that you can know this woman carnally?" He finally spluttered.

"No, he isn't," I said. "But I would quite happily kill him. Therefore the sin would be mine, father."

"And you could live with that on your conscience?" the priest said with distaste.

"For what he has inflicted upon my sister and I? Quite happily. Believe me father, the world would be a better place without men like Fiachu mac Niall. Besides, I have another reason to seek him out as well."

"And what would that be?"

"He holds captive someone dear to me. I intend to get her back."

Father Porcius sighed. "Very well. If this pagan Irishman were to die, then I see no reason why Ambrosius should not be free to marry the girl, though I am not condoning murder or violence. And apart from the fact that you do not yet have your father's permission, a marriage born of such a sin would be doomed and I for one would not condone such a union. You would have to find someone else to do it, I will have no part in such a sordid affair. Plus your father has Patria Potestas over you, Ambrosius. If you go against his will, his wrath will be terrible."

Ambrosius' jaw clenched with restrained anger. "I am my own man, father and outdated Roman customs do not concern me. If you will not marry us, then I will find a priest who will, with or without the Duke's permission."

He turned and left the study, leaving Ygerna and I staring silently at one another with expressions of bewilderment.

Ambrosius had another fortnight with Ygerna, freed from any responsibilities. It was an idyllic and carefree time, the weather stayed unseasonably warm and the hedgerows were overgrown with hedge parsley and purple foxglove that waved gently in the breeze. When we were not with our women, Geraint and I spent the days training in the villa courtyard and the fields, sometimes on horseback with Cletus and his Sarmatians, sometimes practicing archery. Occasionally Ambrosius would join us for a while, but more often than not he would ride out with Ygerna, and Geraint and I would have to follow dutifully, far enough behind to allow them their privacy. Quite often Geraint and I would be left for hours in a secluded wood, where we would practice our swordplay, surrounded by the heady perfume of bluebells. We would then retire, sweating and exhausted to sup ale and eat bread and cheese and watch the tiny creatures of the forest flit and swoop while Ambrosius and Ygerna disappeared to some secret spot known only to them.

Occasionally we would smuggle Hefina and her sister out of the villa and allow them to accompany us and we would get pleasantly drunk on the wine and ale that they had stolen from the stores and then we would collapse onto the soft forest floor to make love, sometimes returning to the villa in the early hours of the morning. On some days we would go hunting wild boar and deer in the forests around Caer Cadwy, or practice falconry with one of Cletus' birds.

I had noticed a change come over Ambrosius and had put it down to the presence of my sister. He seemed more light hearted and less serious than before. Gone was the bitter scowl that seemed to permanently mar his features. He would now laugh and joke with Geraint and I, whereas before he always seemed to be slightly aloof, as though our bawdy humour was somehow beneath him. My sister too had changed. Apart from growing into a fine young woman, she was happy and content, glad to be able to spend the short time with the people that she loved and cared for.

But as always seems to be the case, these good times were not to last. Indeed now I look back upon that time with bittersweet memories as it seemed to mark the end of an era of innocence and contentment that I would never find again.

It all ended with the premature return of Julianus and the arrival of Gorlois and his entourage one fine, warm day. Geraint and I were just retrieving our arrows from the archery butts when one of the farm hands yelled excitedly, pointing down the straight, cobbled road that led out of the estate, towards a band of brilliantly attired horsemen, their mail coats glittering in the sunlight and their deep blue cloaks billowing out behind them. They carried with them the unmistakable seahorse banner of Gorlois ap Gerdan, Battle Duke of Cerniw alongside the bull's head banner of Julianus and as they drew nearer, a horn blared out from their ranks to signal their arrival at Villa Aurelianus.

We went to the gate of the villa flanked by Cletus on one side and Cornelius Varius on the other. Varius was a short, stocky bull of a man in his fifties but still as fit as any man in Julianus' army, with thick, strong limbs and a battered looking, scarred face. He was the commander of Julianus' foot soldiers and a capable general in his own right, having risen to the rank of tribune in the Roman army in Gaul. He had come out of retirement and crossed the sea to Britannia to serve under Julianus, having once served under his father, the usurper Constantine. It was Varius who had turned the Britons of Durotrigia and Dumnonia into the disciplined warriors that now garrisoned Caer Cadwy and the other fortress towns around the two countries, towns like Lindinis and the port of Durnovaria in the south.

Gorlois raised a gauntleted fist to halt his entourage and dismounted, nodding curtly at Varius.

Julianus also dismounted and walked over to his trusted general, clasping his forearm in greeting.

They exchanged a few words before the duke turned towards Geraint and I.

We bowed with deference towards the duke.

"Where is Ambrosius?" He demanded.

"In the courtyard, Lord Duke," I replied.

Julianus led Gorlois through the gate and into the courtyard of the villa where Ambrosius sat under a blossoming cherry tree with Ygerna. Ambrosius stood and dutifully shook Gorlois' hand in greeting.

"Ambrosius, you are looking well," Gorlois exclaimed, slapping the Duke's son on the shoulder in an overly friendly manner.

Ambrosius, bewildered by the sudden appearance of his father and the Duke of Cerniw, gave a strained smile. "Thank you, Duke," he stammered. "I trust you too are well?"

Gorlois nodded and grinned, showing his pearl white teeth as he handed his ornate cavalry helmet with its silver mask to one of his men.

Geraint and I had entered the courtyard from the field where we had been practicing archery and Gorlois glanced in our direction but did not acknowledge us. Instead his eyes fell upon Ygerna and seemed to linger upon her for a long time.

"And who is the young lady?" he asked, his eyes still fixed on my sister.

"This is Ygerna. I mean to ask my father's permission for her hand in marriage," Ambrosius replied. He gestured at Ygerna and she walked over, bowing gracefully before the duke.

"Ygerna," Gorlois muttered, taking her hand and kissing it gently. "A most enchanting name for a most enchanting young woman."

Ygerna flushed red and she averted her eyes. "Thank you, Duke."

"You have chosen well, Ambrosius. Very well. I would never have thought it of you," Gorlois said, his pale blue eyes still fixed upon Ygerna.

Ambrosius gave a strained smile that was almost a grimace but did not reply.

Julianus glared disapprovingly at his son. "You seek to marry an escaped slave?" he said incredulously, looking at Ygerna with distaste.

"Ygerna is not a slave, father. She is high born, daughter of a Gaelic chieftain.

Fergus here can attest to that, for she is his sister. As the only male left in his family, he has given his blessing to the union," he looked down at the ground awkwardly, wringing his hands. "And now I seek the same from you, father."

Julianus' jaw was clenched with restrained anger. "That girl was sent to the abbey for a reason and you waited until my back was turned to smuggle her back into my home? You and I must have words, Ambrosius. In private."

Ambrosius' face flushed with shame as he stayed staring down at the dusty ground of the courtyard. "Yes, father," he muttered.

Ygerna stepped forward, her hands clasped before her. "My Lord Duke, Ambrosius speaks the truth. I am the daughter of Fiontan mac Duggan, chieftain of the Deisi tuath. I am no slave."

Julianus turned his cool gaze upon my sister. "That may be so, but I will not have my son marrying a landless refugee. He is a Roman of noble birth and I will discuss the matter no further with you," he turned his stern gaze upon his son. "Ambrosius, come to my study in two hours. Alone."

Julianus turned his back on Ygerna and Ambrosius and placed an arm around the Duke of Cerniw's shoulders. "Come, Gorlois. You must be hungry after your journey."

I caught up with Ambrosius a few hours later. Duke Julianus had demanded Ambrosius' presence in his study and after about an hour the young lord emerged red faced and flustered. To our astonishment, Julianus had relented, albeit very reluctantly and after a long and heated debate. Ambrosius would be free to marry only once he had proved to his father that he was a man and that there was no better way to prove your manhood than two years spent fighting alongside the Votadini in Guotodin.

That evening, Julianus held a banquet for his guests complete with dancers and musicians. Gorlois had brought with him several amphorae of Byzantine wine which were being poured into silver goblets and jugs by the household slaves. Also present were Cletus the Sarmatian chieftain, Cornelius Varius and Arwel, lord of Lindinis, a fortified town that lay half a day's ride west of Caer Cadwy. He was a man of middle years, finely dressed in the gaudy colours favoured by British chieftains, with long red hair and a drooping moustache that covered his mouth and gave him a curiously melancholy appearance. He sat with his wife next to Ambrosius and Ygerna, whilst opposite them sat Gorlois and his advisor, Dulius, a jumpy, nervous little man with a balding pate. On the other side of Gorlois was Judoc, one of his warlords, a huge, brutal looking man with jet black hair and beard and dark eyes that glittered like balls of glass and hinted at the violent nature of his character.

They all sat around a huge round table of polished oak inlaid with gold and pearl whilst servants and slaves silently and unobtrusively moved about them filling goblets and removing and replacing dishes of succulent meat and pastries.

Geraint and I stood at the doorway on guard duty, not that any guards were really necessary. It was more for show than anything else. We had been told to polish our mail and helmets to a high standard and don the blue cloaks and shields of Duke Julianus of Caer Cadwy. We were to stand on ceremony whilst the guests enjoyed the Duke's hospitality and so Geraint and I had spent several hours polishing our armour with sand and vinegar until it glistened like fish scales.

"I have to be honest with you, Julianus," Gorlois said, leaning back in his chair and holding out his goblet to be refilled. "The tribes once loyal to Pendragon are proving to be a real thorn in my side. They just refuse to accept me as their ruler. Even though they are now dispersed into the hills and spend more time fighting each other, they still find the time to raid my lands in the east and ambush my patrols. I need help and I don't mind admitting it."

"The Dumnonii hill tribes are fiercely independent and always have been," Julianus replied. "They are an ancient and proud people who will not be easily subdued. The Romans couldn't do it and neither will you. Or I for that matter. I was married to one, I should know what I'm talking about."

There was a ripple of laughter around the table.

"So what is to be done about them?" Gorlois said. "Do I hunt them down like wild boar and wipe them out?"

Julianus shook his head. "You will never beat them in their own territory and they will never accept an outsider as a ruler. There is only one person who holds the true right to rule them and that is my youngest son, Uther."

"But Uther is being held hostage by King Vortigern," Gorlois added. "And while he holds him, he knows that you will not move against him."

"And he also knows that while he holds Uther, the highlands of Dumnonia will be in chaos," Arwel, lord of Lindinis said in a nasally, flat voice. "And when the time is right, when we have been weakened by internal strife he will strike again and take the kingdom for himself."

"Vortigern is a wily old snake for sure," Julianus said. "But I fear he may have bitten off more than he can chew. I have heard reports that his Saxon mercenaries have revolted in the east and have seized land from him as payment for their services. Not only that, if the rumours are to be believed, every day more and more boatloads of Saxon warriors arrive on the shores of this island from overseas."

Dulius, Gorlois' advisor swallowed nervously. "I too have heard these rather alarming rumours from the seafarers who dock at Din Tagel. If this is the case, then Vortigern may become the least of our worries."

Gorlois waved a dismissive hand. "Once Vortigern runs out of gold, they will soon go home. They are mercenaries, they go where the gold is. If Vortigern can no longer pay them, they will go elsewhere."

Julianus shook his head grimly, his expression serious. "You have not seen the refugees pouring across the countryside from the east or heard their awful tales of murder and looting. No, these barbaric animals are here to stay. They see us as squabbling weaklings, ripe for slaughter. They see our fertile lands and our forests teeming with game and they want it for themselves. I fear that Vortigern has unleashed a monster upon us, a terrible monster that every day grows in strength while we fight and bicker amongst ourselves."

"I say let them come," Judoc growled. "Let them throw themselves against our shields and taste the sting of our spears. They will soon realise they are not welcome."

"The only way we can survive is if we are united as a country," Ambrosius said. "Until we get the Dumnonian hill tribes back on our side, we will be floundering. Somehow we must get Uther back, show them that he is safe."

Gorlois threw back his head and laughed. "And how do you propose doing that, Ambrosius? For a start, we don't know where in Vortigern's lands Uther is being held. And even if we did know, do you think we could just march in and seize him? Please, this is not one of your wargames."

Ambrosius flushed red with indignation and I saw Gorlois was once again staring intently at my sister with a half-smile on his lips as he drained his goblet of wine and held it out for another refill. Julianus had grudgingly allowed her to attend the feast following his private meeting with Ambrosius.

"Say what you like, but I have a duty to defend this island," Julianus said. "Many years ago, my father, Flavius Claudius Constantinus was declared emperor by his own troops in this very land. It was my father who stripped Britannia of manpower in his bid for power. He took the legions with him across the sea to Gaul to seize power from the Emperor Honorius, but in so doing he weakened Britannia irreparably. Shortly afterwards the Britons rebelled and cast off the yoke of Rome forever and I bear that shame. Although I was not born here, this is my home and I intend to make amends for what my father did to the people of this land. I will not let it fall to barbarians or usurpers, ever."

"A noble task, Julianus," Gorlois said as he nibbled on a stuffed date. "But a difficult one. The biggest problem is uniting all of the people of this land under a common cause. But to do that you must overcome the ancient tribal enmities that go back centuries. It will never happen."

"It happened under Roman rule," Ambrosius said. "There is no reason why it could not happen again. All it takes is one man, a figurehead to unite the Britons under one rule."

Again Gorlois chuckled dismissively. "And just who will that be, Ambrosius? You?"

"The wielder of the Sword of Kings," said Arwel tentatively.

Gorlois laughed loudly and slapped the table. "The Sword of Kings? Arwel, you should know better than to believe in such folk tales. The legend of the Sword of Kings was a fable, invented to give the Britons hope when the Romans invaded. There is no such thing and even if there were, it is lost forever, probably rusted beyond all recognition at the bottom of some bog."

"I do not know of this legend, Arwel," Julianus said. "Please relate it to us."

Arwel cleared his throat and began to stroke his long moustache. "It was said that long ago, before the Romans first came to our lands, the tribes of Britannia were at war, much as they are now. The druids held a gathering to discuss the crisis. They called upon the Old Gods for their insight and were told to forge a sword, a mighty weapon imbued with the powers of sun and earth. It was to be named Caledfwlch, the Sword of Kings and it was forged on a midsummer's eve in a cave deep underground, a place that existed between the worlds. It was taken and hidden and guarded closely by the druids until the true ruler of Britannia came forwards to claim it. That ruler was Cunobelinus, chief of the Catuvellauni tribe and with the Sword before him, he defeated his enemies and conquered Britannia and when he had finished his conquest, he returned the sword to the druids. But his enemies fled overseas and appealed to the emperor Claudius for aid and that was when the Romans came and conquered these islands. After his death, Caratacus, the son of Cunobelinus tried in vain to find the sword to help him conquer the Romans, but he was eventually captured and sent to Rome. The location of the sword remained a secret, known only to a handful of druids who were awaiting the next great ruler who could wield Caledfwlch and throw off their Roman oppressors. The Sword eventually fell into the hands of Queen Boudicca of the Iceni, albeit briefly."

"And we all know what happened to her," Gorlois quipped with a smirk. "This Sword sounds more of a curse than a blessing."

Arwel continued undeterred. "Boudicca was betrayed by a group of chieftains and druids who had grown jealous of her rise to power. They took the Sword and hid it from her and subsequently her revolt failed. The Sword was taken and returned whence it came, but by then, the druids had all but been destroyed by the Romans, for they attacked and destroyed their stronghold on the Holy Island and hunted the remainder down wherever they found them and the true resting place of the Sword was lost forever. There is however, a prophecy, passed down through the years that goes like this," Arwel cleared his throat and raised his voice.

"From the shadows of an empire, a dragon shall arise,

From western lands, behold.

To rightfully wield the Sword of Kings

And slay the king of old."

I felt the hairs rise on the backs of my arms upon hearing the prophecy again. The last time I had heard it had been in Old Mother Argoel's cave back in the Forest of the Horned One.

The silence that followed was broken by Gorlois' condescending applause. "A nice tale, Arwel. No doubt told around every hearth fire in every petty hovel in the land. But hankering after mythical swords to solve our problems is hardly the solution. But if we were to forge our own sword and claim that it was Caledfwlch..."

"That would never work," Arwel interrupted. "It was said that Caledfwlch burned with the fire of the midsummer sun and sang when it was wielded."

"Of course, how convenient." Gorlois said, his tone heavy with sarcasm. I noticed Lord Arwel's fist clench tight with anger.

"Gorlois is right," Julianus said. "Searching for a mythical sword is not an option. We must prepare our citizens, train them and arm them for war otherwise we will be overrun. We are beset by enemies on all sides and I have always strived to train my men to fight as Romans, for the legions of antiquity were second to none. My father had a dream of toppling the Emperor from his throne and of ruling the Empire himself, but in so doing, he stripped this land bare of the flower of its manhood. The Empire is gone now from these islands and it will never return as it is beset now with other problems. As we speak, the Franks overrun Gaul and the Huns stream over their borders to the east, whilst in the south, the Vandals have taken control of Rome's African territories. We can no longer look to Rome to help us and we must accept the bitter truth that now we stand alone. But I have a dream that we can forge our own empire, an empire that will eventually rival that of Rome here in Britannia."

"An ambitious dream for sure," Gorlois said, smiling at Ygerna. "And if anyone can accomplish this task, it is you, Julianus. It is just such a shame that Constans is not around to inherit your legacy. He would have made a fine ruler."

Julianus nodded in silence.

"The Duke still has Ambrosius to continue his legacy," Arwel said, his eyes flitting from person to person, eventually settling upon Ygerna. "And hopefully someday grandchildren as well."

"Indeed, congratulations are in order I believe," Gorlois said, raising his goblet in salutation to Ambrosius. "Your wife to be is truly the vision of loveliness. Tell us how it was you met, Ambrosius?"

Ambrosius shifted uncomfortably, glancing over at me. "It's a long and rather dull story," he said with a dismissive wave of his hand. "I wouldn't wish to bore you all with the details. Suffice to say Ygerna was one of the many refugees that fled to our land and she was taken into the safety of Caer Cadwy. That was how I met her."

"You said your father was a Gaelic chieftain, my lady?" Gorlois enquired, his eyes boring into my sister's. "How is it you ended up in Britannia?"

My sister smiled politely, but her eyes betrayed the sadness that the memories brought back to her. "We were travelling from Eire to the kingdom of Dyfed, where some of my people settled many years ago. We hit a storm and our ship was wrecked. Myself and my brother were the only survivors." She glanced uneasily at me, as if willing me to affirm her story in case I was questioned, aware that she had omitted the real reason for our flight from our homeland.

"I saw your brother earlier did I not, my lady?" Gorlois enquired. "Where is he now?"

Ygerna nodded towards me. "He stands right behind you, Duke."

Suddenly all eyes were upon me. I remained motionless, my spear clutched in my right hand, my left resting upon the rim of my shield. I stared coldly at Gorlois and I saw the flicker of recognition his eyes. "Ah, Ambrosius' new bodyguard. Yes, we've met before, haven't we?"

I nodded. "We have, Lord Duke. I was in Ambrosius' scouting party when we were chasing Vortimer's army. We also met at Lord Constan's funeral."

"Indeed," he said, raising his goblet to his lips. "You were the one who saved Ambrosius' life after his costly mistake were you not?"

I glanced over at Ambrosius and could see his scowl deepening. "It was an ambush, Duke. Not a mistake. It could have happened to anyone."

"Anyone who takes directions from a shepherd boy, that is," Gorlois retorted with a sly smirk and a wry glance at Julianus.

I ignored his barbed comment and kept my face expressionless.

"And what was your name again, soldier?" He asked.

"Fergus, sir."

"Fergus?" he repeated. "Interesting." He regarded me for a moment with calculating eyes, as though he had heard my name before and was trying to place it in context.

I just hoped that he did not realise that Geraint was the man that he had flogged for insolence before we had set off after Vortimer's army, but fortunately Gorlois did not even glance in Geraint's direction.

The Duke of Cerniw finally gave a brief nod and turned back to the others at the table. The conversation turned to more superficial and mundane matters as Gorlois tried to persuade Ambrosius to visit him at his sea fortress of Din Tagel when he returned from Guotodin. He proceeded to boast of the magnificence of his fortress and the booming trade that he was doing with Greece and Constantinople, despite pirate infested waters. Gorlois' power lay in his ability to trade overseas with his fleet of galleys and merchant ships and Din Tagel was now one of the few safe ports in Britannia that merchants from the continent were willing to dock at. As a consequence, Gorlois controlled much of the precious trade that came from overseas and this was obviously something that he liked to boast about whenever he had a captive audience.

After they had finished eating, Julianus invited his guests into his spacious, mosaic floored lounge. Slaves quickly cleared away all traces of the meal and as the guests made their way through the large double doors at the end of the dining room into the lounge, I noticed Gorlois' hand lingering on my sister's back.

Chapter 8

The Silver Mask Slips

The next day I awoke to the unmistakable ring of steel on steel. I arose from my bunk groggily and opened the shutters that looked out onto the villa's courtyard. Bright morning sunlight streamed into our small chamber and I saw Gorlois in the middle of the courtyard, stripped to the waist, his athletic body glistening with sweat and perfumed oils as he gracefully parried and counterattacked in mock combat with an ornate looking Byzantine sword. He was sparring with his warlord Judoc and three other men of his personal guard in set piece moves that made the exercise look more like a carefully choreographed dance than real combat. As I watched, Judoc lunged forwards with a swing of his blade and Gorlois deftly sidestepped it, spinning lithely to parry two more carefully timed attacks with a clang of metal on metal.

"What does that fool think he's doing?" Geraint growled beside me, his voice still thick with sleep and the aftermath of a skin of wine. "If he tried to pull off anything like that on the field of battle, he'd be dead in no time."

I grunted in agreement.

"Should we go out and join them?" I suggested.

"Best not to. The temptation to accidentally kill him may prove too overwhelming. Still, seems like your sister is enjoying the show." Geraint nodded to the far side of the courtyard, where my sister was sat on the stone bench under the squat cherry tree with two other young housemaids admiring Gorlois' prowess with a blade. After the elaborately planned series of attacks and counterattacks Gorlois turned and grinned at Ygerna, breathing heavily and I saw her face flush as she smiled back sheepishly.

"Seems like the Duke of Cerniw has one admirer at least," Geraint said provocatively.

I ignored his jibe and splashed cold water over my face from a bowl on the table and pulled on my undershirt, tunic and heavy mail shirt, buckling my thick sword belt around my waist.

"Come on, we're late," I said. "We've got a gruelling session ahead of us with Cletus today."

We spent the morning training in the field with the Sarmatians, striking straw targets with a lance at full gallop. Ambrosius had joined us as well and later we attempted close formation charging, falling back and regrouping as rapidly as possible to charge again, our battle cries cutting through the peace of the countryside as we thundered towards our targets.

"Where is Ygerna today?" Ambrosius asked me between attacks as we galloped back to our start position to reform. "She usually likes to watch our cavalry training. Have you seen her?"

I avoided his gaze and pretended to adjust my horse's bridle. "No, I haven't seen her today, Ambrosius," I lied. "I'm sure she has some reason for not being here though."

Ambrosius shrugged as we wheeled our mounts around and lined up for another charge and I felt a twinge of guilt as I noticed Geraint's accusatory look.

We spent most of our time training in order to avoid Gorlois, who had a habit of making some barbed comment every time he saw Ambrosius. However, during the evening meals, Ambrosius was forced to endure his company and it was after one such evening meal that I saw a true reflection of the Duke of Cerniw's character.

It was early one fine evening, when Geraint and I were sat in the courtyard under the narrow windows of our quarters sharpening our swords with whetstones and polishing our armour with sand and vinegar. We were chatting idly, having consumed the best part of an amphorae of wine between us, when Gorlois appeared on the other side of the courtyard accompanied by the massive Judoc. Both men seemed quite drunk as they reeled across the courtyard, oblivious to our presence.

One of the housemaids was approaching from the opposite direction, a skinny unobtrusive girl who always had a smile for me whenever I saw her. She was carrying a large amphorae of oil from the kitchens, balanced on her bony shoulder when Gorlois staggered and reeled into her, knocking her sideways and causing her to drop the container of oil to the ground. There was a loud crash as the amphorae shattered, spilling its amber coloured contents everywhere.

Gorlois stumbled back, his dark blue trews and tunic spattered with oil. The girl began to apologise profusely, but Gorlois flew into a rage.

"Do you realise how expensive these clothes are, wench?" He screamed. "This tunic is embroidered with Persian silk and now it is completely ruined thanks to your clumsiness."

The girl continued muttering apologies as she knelt down to gather the ceramic shards.

Gorlois reached down and grabbed a handful of the girls' brown hair, twisting it spitefully. "Stand up when I'm talking to you, bitch," he snarled, pulling the girl to her feet.

He put his face close to hers and whispered something that I could not hear, causing the girl to sob with fright before throwing her to the ground and kicking her hard in the belly.

The girl doubled up in pain as Gorlois unclasped his belt and folded it in two, intending to beat her with it.

Geraint and I stood at the same time. "Enough," I shouted, causing Gorlois to freeze mid strike.

He looked over, incredulous that anyone should dare to give him such a direct order.

"Is that how you address a duke, soldier?"

I walked forwards with Geraint at my side. "That is how I address anyone who is beating the hell out of a young girl," I retorted, my jaw clenched with anger.

"Ah, Ygerna's brother," he said as recognition dawned. "Playing the hero." He wrapped his belt back around his waist and looked down at the servant girl. "Get on your feet, girl. Consider yourself lucky this time."

Geraint went to the girl's side and helped her as she struggled to stand upright, sobbing and clutching her abdomen. Gorlois' eyes narrowed as he looked at Geraint.

"Aren't you the cur that I flogged several weeks ago?" he said, stroking his carefully groomed beard.

Geraint turned and faced the Duke defiantly. "That's right. The very same. And it's a shame for you that you did not kill me, Duke." He spat out the last word with vitriol, his dark eyes becoming glazed like those of a rabid dog.

"There is time enough yet," the Duke threatened. He turned to me, pointing a finger. "Now I know where I've seen you before. You were with this fool when I flogged him. You both fought for Branwen Pendragon did you not?"

"Aye and we are still loyal to the Pendragon," I replied, unable to keep the hostility from my voice. "And I wonder what my sister will make of this when I tell her."

I saw a flicker of apprehension cross the Dukes face. "I don't know what you're talking about," he said with a smirk. "All I saw was a servant girl stumble and fall. How about you, Judoc?"

The glowering warlord glared at me menacingly. "I saw exactly the same, Duke. In fact did you not stop to help her up?"

Gorlois smiled at me, showing his perfect white teeth. "Do you know, Judoc, I believe I did. And anyone who says otherwise could be in for a very difficult time."

The two men strode off, back to their wing of the villa, Judoc's massive shoulder purposely clipping Geraint's as he passed.

One morning, Gorlois came to watch our training, accompanied by the glowering Judoc. He had one of Cletus' falcons perched on his wrist and was idly feeding it hare entrails from a leather pouch.

Soon after their arrival, Ygerna appeared along with a young female slave who Ambrosius had appointed as her handmaiden. She was dressed in the style of a Roman lady, in a cornflower blue dress and a pink shawl held in place with her silver brooch. Her dark hair had been gathered at the back of her head in plaited braids and hung down in ringlets either side of her face, accentuating her slender neck and perfectly proportioned face.

Gorlois was the first to greet her with a bow and a kiss of the hand. "You are looking truly radiant, Lady Ygerna," he said with a smile that verged on lechery. "We were just admiring Ambrosius' prowess with a lance. He really has come on well since we last met, but why he spends all his time training when he could be with you, I'll never know."

"Ambrosius knows that soon he is to depart for Guotodin, a wild and dangerous land. It is important that he hones his battle skills. I'm afraid that duty comes before pleasure, Duke."

Ygerna smiled flirtatiously at the Duke of Cerniw.

"Ah, you see, that is where I go wrong. Pleasure has always come first with me. And if I were Ambrosius, I would make sure I spent every waking hour in your presence my lady, for that would be pleasure enough for any man."

Ygerna laughed, abashed by the Duke's compliments. Geraint and I were close enough to hear the conversation as we rested our horses and soon Ambrosius joined us.

He dismounted from his sweating steed and removed his helmet, his fair, wavy hair plastered to his scalp with sweat from the exertion of training, his cheeks flushed and red. He walked over and kissed Ygerna on the cheek.

"I'm sorry I haven't had time to be with you today, Ygerna," he said breathlessly. "But there are still a few techniques I need to perfect before we leave."

Ygerna shrugged and smiled at him, brushing a sweaty lock from his brow. "You do what you must, my love," she said.

"Why don't you come hunting with us this afternoon, Ambrosius?" Gorlois said, putting an arm around Ambrosius' mailed shoulders.

"I intend to put these fine birds through their paces," he lifted his other arm where the falcon was perched, its tiny head, covered with a decorative hood, twitching this way and that.

Ygerna's face brightened. "A break from training may do you good, my love," she said, smiling sweetly at the young lord.

"Very well, we could do with a rest," Ambrosius decided reluctantly. "We will meet you at noon."

Later that day we met with Gorlois on a hill close to the villa known by the locals as Cama's hill after the river Cama that wound its way through the surrounding countryside.

Gorlois was wearing a purple velvet robe, a mark of his high born status, elaborately patterned with gold thread and high leather riding boots. His curled and oiled hair was held back with a jewelled silver diadem and at his waist he wore his Byzantine cavalry sword. He was accompanied by three other men, one of his personal guard and the brutish looking Judoc, his heavily muscled, bulky frame clad in black leather armour from head to toe. The other man present was no more than a youth, short and wiry with a wide, flat face and mousy hair tied back and I surmised from his appearance and lack of verbosity that he was a Sarmatian, probably Cletus' falcon handler. He obviously knew what he was doing as he was emitting a series of high pitched whistles and was gently stroking a falcon perched on his gauntleted wrist. They were watching another one of the falcons as it hurtled through the sky towards an unfortunate pigeon, seemingly guided by the subtleties of the Sarmatian's shrill whistles.

"Ah, Ambrosius, you have come to join us," Gorlois said jovially as we approached. "Fancy trying your hand at falconry?"

Ambrosius smiled and nodded, making his way over to the Sarmatian lad and greeting him in his own tongue. The two began talking like old friends and Ambrosius took the falcon onto his wrist, chattering to it gently as he did so. The bird twitched its head at the familiar voice and then Ambrosius raised it in the air and pulled off its hood whilst letting out a long, high pitched whistle.

The bird shot off like a loosed arrow, straight towards its target, bringing down the pigeon in a flurry of feathers before the other bird had fully turned.

Gorlois forced a smile. "Well done. You are obviously more of a falconer than a swordsman, Ambrosius."

Ambrosius ignored the Duke's jibe and let out a shrill whistle, recalling his falcon to his wrist.

"I think you'll find I'm fairly good with a sword now as well, Gorlois," he said, replacing the hood over the bird's head and handing it to the Sarmatian boy.

"That sounds very much like a challenge to me," Gorlois replied with a smirk. "Do you wish to try your blade against mine? Show me what you have learned?"

Ambrosius glanced at Ygerna and then back at the Duke. "I think I've had enough of sword play for today," he replied.

"Come on, Ambrosius. No need to be afraid, I will not hurt you. Just your blade against mine, like in the old days with Constans," Gorlois had a sneering grin on his face and he was obviously referring to a time when he and Constans had bullied the younger Ambrosius relentlessly as I saw a muscle clench in his cheek.

"Lord Ambrosius said he doesn't want to fight you, Lord Duke," I said firmly. "Not because he is afraid of you, but because he cannot afford to injure himself before our departure to the north."

Gorlois glared at me with antipathy. He desperately wanted to say something to try and intimidate me, but the presence of my sister prevented him from doing so. "Very well," he replied with a forced smile. "Perhaps then a wager. One of your men against mine, Ambrosius? For, say, an amphorae of Byzantine wine? Your bodyguard seems to enjoy jumping to your defence, I wonder if he can fight as well?"

Ambrosius shook his head. "I cannot, Gorlois. These two men are my personal guard, I dare not risk injuring them."

Gorlois shrugged and turned grinning to Judoc. "Have you ever heard of such a thing, Judoc? Warriors who are afraid to get injured? Obviously their training leaves a lot to be desired, but it is exactly what I expect from ill-disciplined Pendragon rabble who rely solely upon their reputation."

"Let me fight whoever he puts forward, Lord Ambrosius," Geraint said, his eyes fixed on Gorlois.

"No, Geraint it proves nothing," Ambrosius replied. "There will be enough fighting when we go north."

Geraint spat on the ground at the Duke's feet. "And we are supposed to just stand here and let him insult the Pendragon name, when we all know what a treacherous piece of filth he truly is?"

"How dare you speak to a duke in such a manner," Gorlois strode towards Geraint but stopped short at the point of his blade.

"Choose your man, Duke," Geraint snarled.

"Gorlois, this is pointless," Ambrosius began, but Gorlois raised a hand.

"He has insulted my honour. I'm afraid there is now no way back. I will choose my man and you will fight until first blood, understood?" The Duke turned to Judoc and slapped him on his huge shoulder. "I choose Judoc," he said with a swagger. The huge, dark haired Kern stepped forwards and slid his sword from its scabbard. Ambrosius sighed with despondency. "Very well, to first blood."

Gorlois whispered something to Judoc and I saw the flicker of a grin behind the large man's thick black beard. I knew that Gorlois wished Geraint dead from that look.

Ygerna was looking nervously from man to man, her hands raised to her face. "Please Gorlois, this is not necessary," she said, but the Duke merely smiled at her. She turned to me and grasped my arm. "Fergus, can't you do something?"

I shook my head as the two combatants squared up to one another. Geraint's dark eyes had glazed dangerously, the way they always did when violence was imminent and he took up his fighting stance, his sword held out in both hands with the blade facing forwards and bouncing lightly on his feet.

Judoc gave his thick bladed sword a couple of powerful swings causing the blade to hiss through the air audibly. Suddenly and without any warning he lunged forwards, swinging the blade towards Geraint's neck with a bellow.

Geraint ducked under the swing and sidestepped the second which immediately followed. He was nearly a head and a half smaller than his opponent and half his weight, but what Geraint lacked in bulk and size he made up for with speed and aggression. Geraint feared no man, having survived the fighting pits of Viroconium in his youth. He had long ago conquered his fear of death and had never backed down from a fight. He carried with him an insatiable anger that continually simmered beneath the surface, a desire to strike back for all the terrible things that had happened to him when he was younger, but he was my friend and a better, more loyal friend I had never had.

Judoc attacked again, moving forwards as he swung, trying to intimidate his opponent with his superior size and strength, but Geraint did not back away. Instead he stood his ground and parried Judoc's blows easily and as the bigger man thrust his blade forwards in an attempt to impale him, Geraint batted the sword aside and drew his own blade in a slash across Judoc's thick forearm.

The Kern let out an enraged cry and dropped his blade as the flesh in his forearm split open and started to leak blood. He clasped his other hand across the wound to stem the bleeding, his teeth bared, white against his black beard as he glared hatefully at Geraint whose blade was now pointed at his throat.

"First blood," I called. "We win."

I saw Gorlois' mouth twist momentarily with anger, but he forced his charming smile and bowed. "Gentlemen, the wine is yours. I shall have it brought to your quarters when we return."

I noticed from the corner of my eye that Judoc had stooped to retrieve his blade with his good hand and as Geraint turned away, he stood and surged forwards with the sword raised, intending to bring it down on Geraint's head.

"Geraint, behind you!" I yelled.

Expecting treachery, my companion was already one step ahead and dropped to one knee and in one dexterous movement, reversed his own sword and thrust out the blade behind him.

Judoc's momentum took him onto the point of Geraint's sword, which entered just below his breastbone and emerged from his back.

Geraint withdrew his blade and rolled to one side as the huge Kern toppled forwards with one last exhalation of breath, landing face first on the grass.

Ygerna let out a horrified gasp and turned away, but otherwise there was silence. Gorlois' other bodyguard had his hand on the hilt of his sword, ready to draw it at the Duke's command, but Gorlois raised a palm to still him.

He heaved Judoc onto his back with a booted foot, but the Kern lay still, staring lifelessly into the blue sky. "You've murdered him," he said quietly, staring accusingly at Geraint who was casually wiping his sword clean with a rag.

"Wasn't murder, Duke. He tried to kill me, it was self-defence."

Gorlois' face was white and with rage. "By God you will pay for this," he hissed. "All of you," he pointed a trembling finger at Ambrosius. "It's all your fault. If you had had the guts to fight me, none of this would have happened. You are not a man, you do not deserve Ygerna." He paced back to his horse and mounted it in one agile motion, reining it around to face us. He looked at my sister and then at Ambrosius.

"It's time you chose a man over a boy, my lady."

As Gorlois and his remaining bodyguard rode off down the hill, Ygerna looked on after him, her eyes filled with tears.

"Ygerna, I didn't want this," Ambrosius began, but Ygerna just slowly shook her head. She looked down at the corpse of Judoc in disgust. "There will come a time, Ambrosius, when you cannot rely on others to fight your battles for you. I wanted you to prove him wrong, to show me what you were made of, but you didn't."

Ygerna mounted her own horse and despite Ambrosius' pleas, rode off down the hill after the Duke of Cerniw.

Geraint shrugged nonchalantly as he sheathed his sword and stood beside Ambrosius, placing a hand on his shoulder. "Women. As long as I live, I will never understand them."

When Julianus found out about the incident with Gorlois, he was not pleased. We were summoned to his study that afternoon and stood in silence while he paced up and down in an attempt to calm his anger.

"So please tell me how a duel over an amphorae of wine results in the cold blooded murder of one of my guests?"

"Geraint was defending himself, father," Ambrosius stammered nervously. "The duel was over and Judoc attacked him from behind, meaning to kill him."

"The duel was not over," Gorlois retorted. He was standing on the other side of the study with his bodyguard. It was Gorlois who had made the formal complaint to Julianus, despite being the instigator of the duel. "Judoc had not submitted."

"The duel was to first blood, Gorlois," Ambrosius said, raising his voice slightly. "Your rules. And I have four other witnesses who will back me up on that."

The Duke of Cerniw glared at Geraint who stood with his hands behind his back staring up at the oak beams with a bored expression. Gorlois gestured at him. "My Lord Duke, this was not over an amphorae of wine as has been suggested by your son. This barbarian cur insulted my honour for a second time, suggesting that somehow I was complicit in the downfall of Caer Dor and the death of Uther's mother, an implication that I find outrageous and distasteful. Judoc meant to teach this whelp a lesson as he was a loyal friend to me who found this man's slurs on my character as hurtful as I do and now he lies dead, murdered by an ill disciplined son of a sow."

Geraint turned to face the Duke of Cerniw, his eyes glittering dangerously. "Still your treacherous tongue you dog or I will pull it from your head."

"Silence!" Julianus yelled, his face burning with indignation as he glared at the Powysian warrior. "You have no right to speak to my guests in such a manner, let alone a duke. Consider yourself lucky that I do not hang you from the nearest tree." Julianus took a deep breath and regained some composure. "Ambrosius, it is obvious to me that there has been tension building between your men and Duke Gorlois and so I intend to take action. You are to be billeted in Caer Cadwy where you will undertake basic drill training under commander Varius for your last couple of weeks here. Ygerna will be confined to her wing of the villa until you are gone. Gorlois, you are welcome to remain here for as long as you feel is necessary. We must plan our moves against Vortigern and we must do it soon," he turned his steely gaze on Geraint. "As for you, if you ever insult one of my guests again, I will have the insolence lashed out of you, do you understand?"

Geraint nodded, but his hazel eyes still burned with defiance. "Yes, Lord Duke."

Julianus sat heavily at his desk and let out a loud, irritated sigh. "Now get out of my sight, all of you."

That night the dreams returned. I was used to disturbed nights, waking in the dead of night in a cold sweat after facing the shades of the men that I had killed, seeing the same faces night after night, contorted in the agony of their final moments. It was the reason why warriors drank to excess, because it made it easier to come to terms with what you had done and if you drank enough, you would have at least one night when you would not be faced with the accusatory faces of the dead. But it had been a long time since I had dreamt of the events of my childhood.

I dreamed again that I was back in Eire. Once again I was a child in the hall of my father, surrounded by the familiar faces of my Tuath, but this time there were new faces as well. Ambrosius, Geraint and Brynmor were present as well as Father Demetrios, Rhawn and Bron, all sat at one of the long feasting benches talking together. But on the raised dais at the end of the hall, where my father's table was, sitting next to my old mentor Dorbalos, there sat Julianus, though sometimes when I looked he was my father, Fiontan mac Duggan. I could see that Dorbalos was trying to say something to me and judging by the earnest and desperate expression on his face, to warn me about something, but his voice was lost in the general commotion of the hall.

Suddenly the great oak doors flew open with a gust of icy wind and everyone in the hall turned towards them.

Fiachu mac Niall was standing there, the dark crescent on his face giving him a sinister appearance. He was flanked on either side by the skull headed Malbach, the dark druid in his robe of crow feathers and on the other side by the wizened and bent form of Sinusa, her head covered by her black hood.

As I looked on in terror, all three began to chant, a menacing, monotonous drone that drowned out all other sound and I noticed that everyone around me began to break out in huge, weeping boils, their flesh becoming clammy and pallid, like the unfortunate souls that I had seen in the little religious commune where I had found Ygerna.

I tried to cry out, but fear had constricted my throat and my eyes were drawn to the sinister figure of Sinusa as she reached up with gnarled, claw like hands and drew back her hood. But instead of the harsh, ancient face of the blind witch, there was Nivian, staring back at me with a mocking expression, her lips moving as she continued chanting.

Suddenly there was a flurry of black, shrieking objects flying through the doors, past the three menacing figures and into the hall.

I raised my arms to my face as the multitude of crows swept towards me, sharp claws and beaks bared to tear at my flesh and I awoke suddenly, sitting bolt upright in my bunk, covered in a sheen of sweat and breathing heavily.

All was silent except for the steady, rhythmic snoring of Geraint in the bunk above me.

Silver moonlight streamed through the small, narrow window of our chamber and I raised myself from my bed, my legs trembling as I walked over to the window to breathe in the chilly night air.

I looked out onto the courtyard, bathed in the silver blue light of the spring moon and breathed deeply, smelling the scent of the basil bush just outside of our window. I estimated from the moon's position that it was the early hours before dawn and as I looked up at the bright scattering of stars and the misty band known by my people as Lugh's Chain, a movement in the courtyard brought my eyes back down.

A figure, wearing a long white dress was furtively making its way across the courtyard, its head covered by a white shawl. For a brief moment, my heart seemed to stop as I thought it may be a Banshee, a sinister female spirit that prowled the hills of my homeland and whose appearance was a portent of death. But then I saw a second taller figure rush out from the opposite wing to meet the first.

The two met in the shadows of the gabled walkway that ran around the perimeter of the courtyard and embraced one another passionately. The taller of the two was unmistakably Gorlois, but I could still not make out the identity of the smaller female as her face was still covered.

But as Gorlois kissed her, the shawl slipped from her head and to my astonishment I saw that it was my sister, Ygerna.

Chapter 9

Londinium

That morning, with the rising of the sun, we prepared for our departure to Caer Cadwy.

Ambrosius was dour and short tempered and I agonized over whether I should tell him about what I had seen earlier before sunrise. I knew that the knowledge would destroy him as he loved my sister very much, but another part of me felt that he had a right to know what was going on. I decided that I would leave it, to let events play out as they must. Soon we would be leaving for an entire year and a lot could change in that time.

I said my goodbyes to Hefina, and hugged her as her pretty blue eyes filled with tears at my departure, promising that I would return, though in my heart I did not know what my future held. I had heard many tales of the Northern Frontier and knew that it had claimed the lives of many men. I knew first-hand about the ferocity and cruelty of the Picts, or the Cruithne as they called themselves and I knew from bitter experience that they were a foe not to be taken lightly. We would be in their territory, near the great forest that covered Caledonia, beyond the Wall. As I tightened my horse's bridle and checked its packs, I noticed my sister and Ambrosius across the courtyard and I caught her eye.

She kissed Ambrosius lightly on the cheek and then came over to me, her eyes brimming with tears.

"I can't believe after all these years that I found you only to lose you again, brother."

I shrugged, unable to meet her gaze. "I'll be back in a couple of years and so will Ambrosius. Wait for us and we will return."

There was a long pause as Ygerna struggled to find her next words.

"Fergus I...I don't know if I can marry him," she said in a tearful, hushed voice.

"Then you must tell him," I said, rather harshly. "Don't make him hold on for nothing."

Tears streamed down her cheeks. "I couldn't do that to him, but I don't think..."

"You don't love him?" I shrugged. "How many people in our position marry for love, Ygerna? We have a chance here to restore our position, to ally ourselves to one of the most powerful families in Britannia. We could eventually raise an army of our own and go back to Eire and reclaim our homeland. Surely that has to be worth something?"

"We can never return to Eire, Fergus. Remember that we still bear the curse of Crom Cruach. You will die if you do."

"Then we will forge ourselves a kingdom here and call our people to us. But we cannot do this if you do not marry Ambrosius. He is a good man, Ygerna. He has honour and integrity and he loves you very much. Please, for the sake of our people, do as I ask."

Ygerna gave a wan smile and nodded. "Very well, brother."

I kissed her on her cheek and embraced her. "Wait for us, sister. We will return."

We left Villa Aurelianus in the early morning sunlight. The air was filled with the heady scent of early summer and humming insects and Julianus came to watch his son depart near the front gates of the villa.

Ambrosius turned in his saddle and slammed his right hand against his armoured chest and extended it outwards in a Roman salute. His highly polished mail and iron greaves and helmet shone brilliantly in the early morning light as did ours. His father did the same in return, his stony face betraying no emotion. "Go with my blessing, son," Julianus said.

Ambrosius nodded once and turned back, spurring his horse forwards with Geraint and I following and so we left Villa Aurelianus behind us and took the cobbled road that ran between fields of grazing cattle towards the fortress of Caer Cadwy. I turned one last time to see the whitewashed villa with its red tiled buildings nestled amongst the fertile fields and wondered if I would ever return. I had only spent a short time at Villa Aurelianus, but they had been happy times and I smiled to myself as I thought of Hefina with her pretty, round face and curvaceous body. She was a sweet girl, of sturdy peasant stock and I would remember our carefree, lustful times in the hay barn with fondness during the cold nights to come.

"Don't worry, there's more where she came from," Geraint said, seeming to read my thoughts. "I wonder what Votadini women are like?" He added.

"I hear they're little different to the Picts," I said. "The only difference is, they are our allies and it is only their men folk and the Wall that keep the Picts from pouring into Britannia."

We arrived in Caer Cadwy after a short ride and were escorted to our barracks by Camillus, the same soldier who had welcomed Julianus when we had first arrived weeks ago. He led us through the fort bustling with workers and soldiers, past workshops producing armour and weapons for Julianus' army until we reached a collection of long wooden huts on the other side of the wide parade ground where groups of soldiers marched in unison whilst others practiced with sword and spear against battered striking posts, the sounds of their blades striking the wood echoing continuously around the open space.

"This will be your new home for the next few weeks, gentlemen," Camillus said, leading us into a small dingy room in one of the huts with four bunks. It smelled strongly of unwashed bodies. "Once you have settled in, commander Varius will come for you. Make sure you are ready."

After a short while, commander Varius appeared at our door. I had met Cornelius Varius briefly before at Villa Aurelianus when Gorlois had first arrived. He was squat and powerfully built with pale, emotionless eyes and a scar that ran diagonally across his face, ravaging his grizzled features. "Your training begins from this moment in," he growled. "Follow me."

We were taken back out onto the parade ground where we joined a group of two dozen awkward looking recruits, taken from the cantrefs and villages and hamlets around Dumnonia and Durotrigia. Most of them came from a background of farming, fishing or herding and had little military experience, which automatically gave us an advantage. Ambrosius had explained to me before that all able bodied men were required by command of the king to undergo military training which was how Julianus managed to field such a large and well equipped army to protect his lands and the lands of King Erbin.

"These men will eventually be under your command, Ambrosius," Varius said, eyeing the nervous young men. "So it is my job to turn you from a spoiled rich boy into a soldier that your father will be proud of and for the sake of these poor bastards here. I hear from your father that you led your men into an ambush and that you're lucky to be alive. Believe me, by the time I've finished with you, you'll wish those Pictish dung flies had killed you."

Cornelius Varius proved true to his word. He was harsh and uncompromising, yelling in our faces at the slightest mistake or striking us with a rod of hazel every time we made a wrong turn or were too slow in forming up into a shield wall. Ambrosius was not treated with any favour, despite his high born status and Varius seemed to single him out for particularly harsh treatment. He told us that we had spent far too long on horseback and that we needed some proper infantry training before we could be considered soldiers. We learned how to turn and advance as one unit at the sound of a cornicern and to fall into formation at a moment's notice. We learned to advance in the Testudo formation, completely protected on all sides and above by a wall of shields while local boys were called in to pelt us with rocks and stones. We were taught other formations as well, like the Wedge, a triangular formation used for breaking the enemy's shield wall and the Orb, a defensive ring of shields to be used in the dire event of being completely surrounded. Eventually we were able to fall into these formations instinctively, and to fall back, advance or regroup whenever we heard the relevant command or series of notes on the cornicern.

"Soon some of you lucky sons of bitches will be accompanying me north to the Wall," Varius told us one day as we stood to attention on the parade ground in the driving rain. "There we will encounter the Picts, the most contemptible race of bastards ever to tumble out of a dog's arse. You will soon come to realise why I have treated you all so harshly. For if you mess up out there, it will not be a hazel rod across the knuckles. If you mess up out there and the Picts get their filthy hands on you, you will wish your whore of a mother had never spread her legs to beget you. For if the Picts get hold of you they will make you suffer until the fires of hell will seem like a welcome break. There is one thing that separates us from the Picts, Saxons and Irish. It is the one advantage that the legions of Rome had over their adversaries and it is this; discipline. They may be ferocious and be able to put up a bloody good fight individually, but that is all they can do. They are a rabble, they do not act as a unit, but we do and that gives us an advantage. Our strength lies in our discipline, never forget that. And one more thing. Get used to this weather, boys. For this is what it is like all the time up there."

At the end of each day we limped back to the barracks to collapse on our hard bunks until the day came when we were to leave Caer Cadwy for the long journey into what many of the Britons referred to as Hen Ogledd, the Old North. There were three dozen of us mounted on horseback and my steed was a sturdy dapple grey mare from Julianus' stables which I had named Bebba. She had proved a little timid at first, but as she grew to trust me, she had turned into a fine warhorse. We were followed by our baggage train of five heavily laden mules led by three handlers and Julianus' priest insisted that we were accompanied by half a dozen monks who were travelling north as missionaries to spread the light of Christ amongst the heathen tribes of Caledonia. They too were mounted on mules as their religion forbade them from riding on horseback.

When we set out from Caer Cadwy not long after the summer feast of Calan Mai, or Beltane as it was known by my people, a small crowd had gathered to watch us depart. It was a misty morning the day that we set off and the air was still heavy with the smoke from the Beltane fires of the previous night and as Varius barked his orders, our small detachment of troops rode out in unison through the great oak gates of Caer Cadwy to the cheers and applause of the surrounding crowd and the dolorous chanting of the monks.

We rode eastwards, following the Roman road which took us past the Great Stones where Ambrosius had proposed to my sister and I saw him gazing wistfully at the stone circle in the distance. The monks sang for most of the journey and occasionally we too joined in and by late morning, we had reached the border, a small river little more than a brook that marked the boundary between Durotrigia and Atrebatia, a large kingdom whose ruler, King Elaf held an uneasy truce with us but who also recognised Vortigern as High King.

We were met by a contingent of his troops on horseback who eyed us warily, but the presence of the monks and the fact that we had our shields slung on our backs and flew the pennants of Durotrigia on our lances indicated that we came in peace and so they reluctantly agreed to escort us through their land.

Their leader, a stout, bearded man with no front teeth wore a suit of bulky leather armour and a leather helmet and despite the warmth of the day, wore a cloak of wolf fur about his broad shoulders. His name was Aeron and he proved to be amiable enough when he was convinced that we were no threat, engaging Ambrosius in conversation soon after our meeting.

"So where is it you're headed, lad?" He asked as he and his men rode alongside our troops.

"Londinium," Ambrosius replied. "From there we will take a boat northward to Guotodin."

Aeron snorted. "Rather you than me. Cold, miserable shithole. You will be lucky if you ever get there in one piece, the seas are crawling with Saxon pirates. Why the hell would you want to go there anyway?"

"It's a long standing alliance between us and the Votadini. They sent men to aid us when we needed them and they keep us supplied with trained horses and so we supply them with soldiers to train their men and help keep the Picts at bay."

Aeron adjusted the strap of his leather helmet. "It's not the Picts you should be worrying about. Or the Irish. They raid, take what they want and bugger off. But the Saxons..." he shook his head with a grim expression. "Those bastards are here to stay. Take a look around you," he pointed to a villa in the distance, its windows shuttered and its fields lying fallow and overgrown with weeds. "It's the same everywhere. Those who can afford to are leaving, abandoning their homes and fleeing westward, or across the sea to Armorica."

"I know," Ambrosius replied. "Many refugees pass through our land and the number seems to be increasing day by day."

"Aye, but do you know why? Because the Saxons are on the move. They are creeping steadily westward and driving all before them with fire and sword. I hear tell that Vortigern had some kind of dispute with Hengest, the Saxon leader and now Hengest is taking what he thinks Vortigern owes him and more besides."

Ambrosius idly patted his horse's neck to calm it as a bee hummed past. "I hear that Vortigern took the kingdom of Cantia from King Gwyrangon and simply gave it to Hengest. Is that not payment enough?"

Cantia was a small kingdom in the far south east of Britannia and Vortigern's betrayal of King Gwyrangon was well known.

"That is not all," Aeron said, leaning forwards in his saddle. "It is said that Vortigern has fallen madly in love with Rowenna, Hengest's daughter and that he is so besotted by her that he is subject to her every whim. He dare not raise a finger against Hengest for fear of upsetting his daughter."

"So Hengest is taking whatever land he wishes and Vortigern turns a blind eye?" Ambrosius speculated.

Aeron nodded and spat on the ground. "Hengest's desire for territory seems insatiable. Every day more boatloads of Saxon warriors arrive on our shores as Hengest has sent word back across the sea that we are easy pickings and some are even bringing their families. They are here to stay, I tell you and word is that Vortigern has lost control of them."

"So what is the future for Atrebatia?" Ambrosius asked.

Aeron shrugged and shook his head disconsolately. "Who knows? What is the future for any of us? Regia to the east has already fallen to the Saxons, but that is no surprise as they couldn't even muster a pot to piss in between them. But now the Saxons are at our borders and we know it's no good appealing to Vortigern for help and our forces are overstretched as it is. Whichever way you look at it, it does not bode well."

"What we need is an effective ruler, a high king who can unite all of the kingdoms under one banner, not one who merely pursues his own greed and self-interest," Ambrosius said.

Aeron sighed and nodded in agreement. "That we do lad, that we do."

"We must trust in the judgement of the Lord," said brother Carwyn piously. He was the senior brother amongst the group of monks accompanying us and his pompous, judgemental attitude sat poorly with the rest of the men, especially Geraint who had a low opinion of the clergy anyway. Ambrosius however tolerated their presence as he was a devout, God fearing Christian.

"Amen, brother Carwyn," he agreed. "And with God's help, we will one day find that king."

For the next two days we travelled through Atrebatia, along a neglected and uneven Roman road, passing many abandoned or ruined villas and farmsteads. On the first day, we camped near a small hamlet and bartered with the locals for bread, cheese and beer before setting off again early the next morning. Occasionally we would come across bands of hungry, ragged people travelling the other way, the dispossessed who were fleeing from the Saxon hordes at the borders, each with their own horrifying tales of rape, pillage and murder. The monks helped them whenever they could, handing out bread and dried fish from their satchels and offering their blessings until they had nothing more to give. Eventually we came to a wide green valley crested with trees.

"This is as far as we go," Aeron said. He nodded at a distant line of beech trees. "Beyond those trees you are in Lundein. Follow the River Tamesis and you will eventually reach Londinium, though most of it is in ruins now. Good luck."

We thanked Aeron and his men and said our farewells before descending into the lush, green valley where a wide river meandered slowly through the countryside. After half a day's travel, we saw the stone walls of Londinium in the distance. It was a huge place, dwarfing even Caer Isca in Dumnonia and Ambrosius told me that once it had been the Roman administrative and trade capital of Britannia, but as we drew nearer I could see the ruined roofs of its red tiled buildings and places where the city walls were beginning to crumble through years of neglect.

We were met at the gates by a group of guards in rusting Roman helmets armed with spears and shields. After paying a tithe of silver carried in our mule's baggage train, the gates were opened and we were escorted into the city.

The streets were empty and overgrown with weeds, overlooked by uninhabited, crumbling buildings whose roofs had collapsed and were home only to packs of pathetic, starving dogs and cats. Crows, pigeons and gulls nested in the rotting gables and every now and then their forlorn cries would echo through the ghostly streets.

We rode further into the city, towards the port and soon there were signs that the place was not completely deserted. Several buildings had been repaired, their tiled roofs replaced with thatch and tendrils of smoke could be seen twisting upwards into the summer air. The smell of wood smoke and sewage indicated a human presence and it grew stronger the further we travelled. Soon we could see people, peddlers selling their wares, old women sat outside of houses once occupied by noble Roman families and unkempt children playing in the pools of stagnant, stinking water that had gathered at the roadsides. They all stopped and stared as we rode past, three dozen armed and armoured men on horseback causing more than a little consternation.

"I've heard stories about Londinium, but I never expected this," Geraint said as he rode at my side. "It's even worse than Caer Isca."

"We won't be staying lad, don't worry," Varius said, overhearing him. "Once we have found Captain Jalmarr and we have our ships, we'll be leaving for Guotodin."

"Captain Jalmarr?" Geraint enquired, looking up at the dark, empty windows of the buildings either side of a narrow street that we were travelling down.

Varius nodded. "He's a foreigner, as is his crew, but he can be trusted."

As we wound our way down to the docks, the city became more lively and populous. Tall masted ships were moored in the wide river Tamesis and the wooden jetties that projected into the river were a hive of activity as fishermen and sailors loaded and unloaded boats of all sizes. The smell of rotten fish and effluent of all sorts wafted up to us and I saw Ambrosius wrinkle his nose in disgust.

"This place stinks," one of our men muttered as we passed a thriving market, causing the crowds of people to part before us as we rode through them.

We found quarters in a nearby fort with spacious stables, paying the commander of the fort in bars of silver to allow us to stay overnight. The monks segregated themselves from the other men, sleeping in separate barracks and when the men had settled, Varius took Ambrosius, Geraint and I to find captain Jalmarr. Brother Carwyn insisted on accompanying us, much to our disappointment, but Varius reluctantly agreed to let him tag along.

We walked down streets that were so narrow that the gables of the buildings were nearly touching those opposite. Duckboards had been placed over the pools of stinking filth that swilled around at the edge roads, but in places they were broken or non-existent and we were forced to wade through the ankle deep, noxious liquid. Beggars called out to us pathetically from the dark shadows of the alleys and from the shelter of the overhanging roofs, but we ignored them, apart from brother Carwyn who would stop by each one and make the sign of the cross above their heads and offer a muttered blessing.

"If he's going to bless every beggar in Londinium, this is going to take forever," Geraint moaned as he turned away from a filthy woman trying to sell him rotten, discoloured berries.

Varius strode over and seized brother Carwyn by his scrawny upper arm and dragged him away from an old man with twisted, malformed legs.

"Come along, brother," he said gruffly. "We don't have time for this."

"But there is always time for God's work, commander," he protested indignantly, but Varius ignored him, dragging him along the stinking street in his vice like grip.

Eventually, we came to a tavern, tucked away down a narrow, rat infested alley not far from the docks.

Varius looked up at a weather beaten sign above the door that showed a crude picture of two gulls facing one another.

"This is the place," he grunted. "Watch yourselves in here, it can get a little rough."

As if to underline his statement, a man came crashing through the door backwards, his face covered in blood, rebounding off of the alley wall opposite and collapsing in a senseless heap at our feet.

"Looks like my sort of place," Geraint said with a feral grin.

Inside, the low roofed, dingy tavern stank of sweat and stale beer. We pushed our way past groups of drunken sailors and fishermen towards the keeper of the tavern, a scrawny, one eyed midget pouring ale from a barrel into a leather pitcher. Varius spoke with him briefly and the dwarf nodded towards a dark corner where a raucous band of men were seated. They were singing and shouting in a language that I did not understand, but their straw coloured hair, greased and tied back and shaved close to the head around the face, along with their fair complexions marked them out as foreigners, probably Saxons.

As we approached them with Varius taking the lead, the men grew silent and glared at us with barely disguised contemptuous suspicion.

"Which of you is Jalmarr?" Varius snapped.

"Who wishes to know?" said a huge man with braided hair and beard, his deep voice heavily accented and dripping with menace.

"I am commander Varius of Caer Cadwy in Durotrigia. I am here under the orders of Julianus, Battle Duke of Durotrigia and eastern Dumnonia. I seek passage for a number of men to Guotodin in the north."

"Do you have gold?" the huge foreigner asked.

"We have more than enough to pay for your services," Varius replied. If he was intimidated by the fierce looking foreigners, he did not show it in any way.

"I am Jalmarr," one of the men said. He was older than the rest, seated at the far end of the long table, a pitcher of ale in his hand. His fair hair was plaited and had been bleached nearly white by constant exposure to sun, wind and rain and his lined face was the colour of copper out of which peered two pale blue eyes. Like many of the other foreigners present, he wore a hammer pendant around his neck on a leather cord and a rough spun, armless tunic. "And if you have the gold, I have the ships," he smiled, showing a mouthful of white teeth, some of which were missing.

"We have the gold," Varius said. "And we wish to leave soon."

Jalmarr shrugged and took a deep draft of ale. "We'll be ready for you at sunrise. But it will be a cramped five day journey and it is one I do not like to make too often. Too many risks."

"Saxons?" Varius enquired.

Jalmarr grinned again, casting a sidelong glance at one of his men.

"Saxons, Angles, Jutes, Frisians, they're all out there, just waiting to plunder and rob any ship foolish enough to stray too far from the coast. Most of the time though, we are left alone. I am known in these waters and my kinsmen leave me to my own devices." Jalmarr's gravelly voice was curiously accented, making his speech difficult to understand.

"You are a Saxon?" Ambrosius asked.

Jalmarr looked at him shrewdly. "Ah, you must be Julianus' son. Ambrosius, isn't it? I could fetch a high price for you, boy. I expect your father would pay dearly to get his son back from a band of Anglii pirates, wouldn't he?"

Ambrosius was lost for words. If it were known that Julianus' son were in our warband, then we would all be at risk as every enemy of Durotrigia would be seeking us.

"I...I don't know what you're talking about. My name is Livianus."

Jalmarr chuckled and several of his men joined in. "Very well, Livianus. My contacts must have been wrong then. But regardless of who you are, when you hire my ships, you also hire my loyalty. I will not betray you, even if you are wealas."

"Wealas?" Ambrosius repeated.

"It is our word for you Britons. It means foreigner and slave. My people make no distinction between the two."

"You are the foreigner in these lands, Saxon," Varius growled, his bull like body tensing with anger.

Jalmarr leaned forwards and glared intently at the aging commander of our troops. "I am not a Saxon, old man. I am Anglii. My crew is made up of Saxons, Franks, Jutes, Frisians, Angles and even some Britons, most of whom were born in these lands as was I. My father and his father before him were invited over here by the Romans to fight the Picts and Irish as foederati and in return they were allowed to settle here. My family has been here for two generations. This land is my home. Now if you'd prefer to travel with a crew of Britons, I'd wager you'd get as far as the mouth of the Tamesis before my kinsmen plundered your ships and left your corpses floating in the water, but that is your choice."

"Very well, consider yourself hired," Varius said reluctantly. He placed his large hands on the table and leaned forwards until his battered face was inches away from Jalmarr's. "But do not even consider double crossing us, Angle. Because if you do, you and your crew will end up feeding the fish, do you understand me?" Jalmarr held his gaze for a moment before grinning again, his pale eyes twinkling. "Then we have an understanding, wealas. I will meet you and your men at the docks tomorrow at sunrise."

Chapter 10

The Votadini

The next morning a grey mist hung over the docks as our men assembled to disembark, many of them nursing hangovers from an evening of overindulgence. Varius had allowed them to try the local taverns and brothels as it could well be the last chance they had and now they stood to attention, pale and bleary eyed, awaiting further orders from their austere commander. Varius was in a foul mood as two men had vanished, having either deserted, been killed in a drunken brawl or were still sleeping in the arms of some cheap whore.

He paced in front of the men with his sword drawn, ranting about how the Romans would have punished desertion by hanging the man by his arms and breaking his body with mallets, or worse still, decimation, where every tenth man would be taken and executed in place of the deserter. No one dared to speak as we knew that Varius had a predilection for sudden violence and even Geraint had the sense to hold his tongue whilst the old soldier vented his spleen.

He was stopped in his tracks by the appearance of Jalmarr and his huge first mate. "Problems with your men, commander?" Jalmarr enquired with a grin.

Varius whirled around to face him, his face scarlet with rage. "It'll make your life easier," he said with disgust in his voice, looking the Anglii seaman up and down. "We're two men short."

Jalmarr let out a sudden laugh and clapped Varius on the shoulder. "At least two of your men had some sense then. Come now, my crew will help you aboard."

Jalmarr had two boats ready for us. They were sleek and long, made of oak timbers that had somehow been bent to follow the curve of the hull, with twin prows that curved up at the ends and a broad keel with several dozen rowing benches. Each ship had a tall mast to house a square sail which was furled and tied on the cross mast. Our men busied themselves by unloading the baggage mules onto the boats, only too glad to be out of Varius' line of fire for the time being.

I climbed aboard one of the boats along with Ambrosius and Geraint. We would be sharing the boat with brother Carwyn and his six monks along with a dozen of our men. Varius took the remainder of the men aboard the other boat after paying the mule handlers to take our horses back to Caer Cadwy.

Jalmarr placed a hand on my shoulder as I walked down the slippery gangplank to board the ship. "Welcome aboard the Brimwulf," he said with a grin. "That's a fine coat of mail you have there. You will notice none of my crew wear armour. You know why?"

I shook my head as Jalmarr fingered the rings of my mail coat. "Because if you fall in there," he said pointing overboard at the murky waters of the Tamesis. "Nothing will kill you quicker than a fine suit of mail my friend. You will sink straight to the bottom."

Jalmarr patted my shoulder and then busied himself shouting orders to his crew in his incomprehensible barbarian tongue as they secured our baggage with ropes and seated themselves at their rowing benches.

Soon the Brimwulf was gliding gently down the Tamesis through the early morning mist, propelled by two dozen oars. Thirty crewmen bent forwards and pulled back in unison, singing a song to the stroke of the oars, their deep voices filling the morning air as we glided past cattle grazing and slaves toiling in the fields. A little way behind us came the other boat, the Deopnaedre, which Jalmarr said meant snake of the deep. Our boat, the Brimwulf translated as she-wolf of the sea.

Eventually we reached the wide estuary of the river and the boat began to lurch up and down as the waters of the river met the undulating waves of the sea and I could taste the spray of salt water on my cracked lips.

Jalmarr shouted an order and as one, his men lifted their dripping oars from the sea, raising them like spears before pulling them in and stowing them beneath their rowing benches. Several other men busied themselves untying the thick ropes that held the sail in place and then it unfurled with a sound like distant thunder as the wind filled it and the boat lurched forwards.

We followed the coast eastward, sailing into the bright summer sunlight before turning north, making sure that the land was still visible on our portside. Jalmarr poured out a horn of ale from one of the barrels, holding it aloft and offering it to one of his heathen gods before tipping it over the side of the longboat. As he did so, the rest of his crew gave a brief cheer, happy to have appeased the gods.

In response, brother Carwyn and his monks began to pray loudly, obviously unhappy with the pagan ritual that they had just witnessed. Carwyn stood, swaying unsteadily on the deck, with his thin arms raised to the heavens, praying for the souls of the heathens and calling upon the Lord to lead them towards His truth and the kingdom of heaven.

Ambrosius stood at the stern of the boat, holding on to the richly decorated prow that had been carved with intricate, interlacing serpents and stared back across the flat fen lands in the far distance, his mood still dark.

"The year will pass quickly, don't worry," I said, moving up beside him. "There will be no time to brood where we are going, I'm sure."

"I'm afraid that I am losing her, Fergus," he replied flatly, his gaze still fixed on the distant, featureless coastline. "And if I do, then everything will seem meaningless."

"There is more to life than women," I said, trying to sound light hearted.

He shook his head and looked down at the surf lapping at the timber hull. "If I return after this year, will she be there for me? I felt like she was...drifting away."

I looked down at my gauntleted hands awkwardly, feeling my grip tighten on the boats gunwales. "She promised me she would wait for you," I muttered, scarcely believing it myself. I wondered whether I should tell him about Gorlois, but instead remained silent.

"There's something you're not telling me," Ambrosius said eventually, trying to catch my eye. "Has she said anything to you?"

I shook my head.

"I know she is fond of Gorlois, I'm not blind," he said, his jaw clenching with suppressed emotion.

"She has promised herself to you, Ambrosius," I replied, placing a hand on his shoulder. "She has promised herself to you because she knows the type of man you are. You are noble, virtuous and honourable. You are all the things Gorlois is not. She will see through his veneer soon enough, don't worry. I know my sister and I know that it will not take her long to work out what sort of man Gorlois is."

Ambrosius however seemed satisfied by my answer. He nodded once and then changed the subject. "Why is my father doing this? It's just insanity," he mused, turning to look at the Deopnaedre following in our wake and cutting through the waves with its sleek prow, its billowed sail bearing a representation of a snake curled around a warhammer.

"Your father has his reasons," I sighed. "He wants to make a warrior of you and he thinks that sending you beyond the Wall is the way to do it."

Ambrosius wiped his face as a sheet of spray struck us. "I fear the fight may soon be coming to Caer Cadwy," he said. "Vortigern has been too quiet for too long. He must be planning his next move."

"It seems to me that Vortigern has his hands full with rebellious Saxons at the moment," I said. "I doubt he'll be in a position to launch a full scale assault any time soon. I think your father has to look closer to home and to fully open his eyes to see his true enemies. And I think this particular person had a hand in encouraging your exile."

"Gorlois?" Ambrosius said, glancing at me sideways.

I nodded in response.

We stood silently for a while, feeling the lurch of the Brimwulf and looking out across the deep green sea until Jalmarr came to the stern of the ship. He communicated something to the captain of the Deopnaedre, who was standing at the prow of his craft, through a series of complicated hand gestures, before turning to us.

"Ulfhere says he has seen Saxon longboats in the distance," he said to us with a mischievous grin. "If we try to outrun them, they will give chase as they will think we have something worth running for. Alternatively, if we let them gain on us it could also present a whole different set of problems."

"I thought you said your kinsmen would leave you alone?" Ambrosius replied.

Jalmarr shrugged. "Normally, yes. I have been sailing these waters for over forty years, but I have never seen so many ships coming from across the sea as I have recently. Many of them will not know of me and will see me as fair game, even if they are kinsmen. I told you before, these waters are far from safe."

"Why are so many ships coming?" I asked.

Jalmarr looked me straight in the eye. "It's an invasion. The Anglecynn come with the intention of staying for good. I have heard them talking in the mead halls and the taverns. Hengest has sent word back that Britannia has a weak king and is ripe for plucking. The Britons squabble amongst themselves, the Irish are taking territory in the west and the Picts cross the Wall unchecked. Your land is doomed my friends."

Ambrosius ignored the seaman's provocations, but his irritation was evident. "Can you not outrun them? With all your years of sailing expertise?"

"For a day, yes. Maybe two. But look at our ships," he pointed over at the Deopnaedre. "These two boats are designed for carrying cargo. See how the hull bulges out like a pregnant sow? Those boats in the distance will be dracabatas," he frowned as he sought a translation. "Dragonboats. Narrow in the bow, sleek and fast, carrying only the crew and their weapons and whatever else they can stow beneath their rowing benches. You may as well be racing a pregnant cow against a thoroughbred stallion. They will catch us if they intend to."

"You will continue to sail north at full sail. That is an order," Ambrosius said tartly.

Jalmarr's gaze turned icy. "Do not order me around on my own ship, boy. I know who you are and more importantly, I know what you are worth to certain people. You would do well to remember that." Jalmarr spat overboard before striding off over the slippery deck between the rowing benches and shouting to his men in his barbarian tongue.

After a further half days travel, three sails were clearly visible on the horizon, three tiny off white squares standing out against the blue of the sky. Many of our men, including Ambrosius and Geraint had succumbed to seasickness and were constantly heaving their guts up over the edge of the ship to much derisive laughter from the mixed race crew of Saxons, Angles and Britons.

Jalmarr kept the coast in view to the port side, but I noticed that more and more frequently he would go to the back of the boat and squint at the distant dragonboats and I also noticed the concerned whispers and looks of apprehension amongst his crew. By the time the sun was sinking down behind coastline to the west, it was obvious that the three dragonboats were pursuing us as they were now much closer and it was possible to make out the emblems on their sails. The Deopnaedre was sailing alongside us now, just off our starboard bow and was close enough for the captains of both ships to shout to one another comfortably, which they did frequently.

"Ulfhere tells me he does not recognise the emblems on the sails of the ships following us, which means it seems we have three choices," Jalmarr said to Ambrosius as his men prepared a brazier to cook some fish. "We continue to run, which would be futile. We head for the coast and leave the boats moored on a beach, which I am loathe to do. Or we heave to and let them catch up with us and put our faith in the Sisters of Wyrd."

"Sisters of who?" Ambrosius enquired.

"Wyrd. Fate. My people believe that our destinies are woven together by the Three Sisters at the foot of Eormensyll, the tree whose roots permeate the underworld and whose branches reach up to Heofenrice. But now is not the time to speak of that. There are more pressing matters to hand."

Ambrosius' brow furrowed and the familiar scowl returned as he thought. He looked towards the darkening horizon at the three distant ships. "How many men do those dragonboats carry?"

Jalmarr grimaced. "Anywhere between thirty and fifty men."

"Moor the ships on the nearest beach, captain," Ambrosius said decisively. "Can your men fight?"

Jalmarr's pale eyes glistened as he replied. "Our people are born warriors, lord. Warriors first and seamen second."

We moored the Brimwulf and the Deopnaedre on a shingle beach in a small cove on the coast, hauling the boats up the beach and over a small rise with ropes before preparing our weapons and armour. The crews of the two boats pulled spears, axes and swords from the chests beneath their rowing benches and shields that hung on the sides of the boats.

Ambrosius and Varius coordinated our defences, with our men in the centre and the two crews positioned on either flank.

"My men are ready," Jalmarr said to Ambrosius and Varius. "I hope you know what you are doing. It's likely that they will outnumber us."

"We don't tell you how to sail your boats, captain," Varius snapped. "All you have to do is look like warriors. Leave the rest to us."

We waited nervously as the three dragonboats drew closer. In the twilight I could now clearly see the emblems on the sails. One bore two dragons heads facing one another, another had a serpent entwined around a warhammer, whilst the third bore the snarling head of a wolf. Every one carried a full crew, their bearded faces becoming clearer as the warships approached, their round, painted shields lining the lengths of the hulls on either side.

We stood silently on the beach, Angle, Saxon and Briton, shoulder to shoulder, each man lost in his own private thoughts.

"Do you think we can trust them?" Geraint asked as he looked past the shields of our own men at the Saxon and Angle crew assembled on our flanks. He had taken his position to my right, as he always did, so that his shield was protecting the right side of my body.

"I don't know. If they decide to throw in their lot with their kinsmen and turn on us, then we're surely dead. But I think they intend to defend their ships, kinsmen or not."

The first of the dragonboats, the one with the serpent entwined around the hammer, ploughed into the shingle like an arrow striking a target, throwing up a shower of pebbles and spray as it did so. Before the boat had even stopped, the crew were leaping over the sides, spears, axes and shields in hand. I estimated that there were around fifty of them, with another two boat loads close behind.

"Men of Durotrigia," Varius bellowed. "Shieldwall!"

As one, with a single shout, our men formed a line of identical shields, our spears held forwards ready to strike.

The Saxons before us scurried around trying to form up their own shieldwall, their leader screaming at them in their guttural tongue as he paced up and down their line, sword in hand. He wore a coat of highly polished mail and an elaborate helmet with eyepieces that hid half his face, with a golden dragon running along the crest. His straw coloured beard was plaited into two forks and he turned towards us and snarled a challenge.

"Jalmarr, we need you," Ambrosius called.

The Anglii captain jogged over, a wickedly sharpened axe held in his right hand. He too had donned a helmet, a riveted cone of iron with a long nasal protector.

"Ask him what he wants," Ambrosius said to the sea captain.

"Is that not obvious?" Jalmarr replied. The other two boats ground into the shingle, the crews of both leaping over the sides into the breaking waves.

"Just ask him," Ambrosius shot back irritably.

Jalmarr barked something in his barbarian tongue and the foreigner's reply caused the men opposite to laugh and whoop and hammer their shields.

Jalmarr turned back to Ambrosius. "He says he has come from across the waves as he hears that the Britons are geldings and their wives and daughters are in need of real men."

Ambrosius stared back at the barbarian leader with a steely gaze. "Tell him that he has two options. One, that he and his men stay and fight us now, in which case their blood will stain British sand and turn the sea red, or two, that he face me here and now in single combat. If he wins, he may take what he wants of ours. If I win, his crew leave all their weapons, get back in their boats and sail back from whence they came."

I could not believe what I was hearing. Ambrosius offering single combat against a Saxon chieftain would kill him as surely as falling upon his own sword.

As Jalmarr began to shout his translation to the Saxon chieftain, Varius walked over to Ambrosius, his expression grim. "What in the name of Christ and all the apostles do you think you're up to, lad?" He hissed in his ear. "This is not the way we do things. If you get yourself killed, your father will string me up by my balls. At least let me fight in your stead."

Ambrosius shook his head stubbornly. "No, Varius, I must learn to fight my own battles. Is that not one of the reasons my father sent me away? To learn to fight? I have to do this."

Varius began to protest, but a great cheer from the Saxons opposite drowned him out.

"He accepts your challenge," Jalmarr said simply.

The Saxon leader took several bold steps forwards, giving his broad bladed sword a couple of test swings. He seemed relaxed and arrogantly confident as he paced before his men. Ambrosius removed his helmet and knelt before brother Carwyn, who placed his right hand on the young lord's curly golden hair whilst praying for his victory.

"He's lost his damned mind," Geraint whispered. "There are other ways to impress your sister, you know."

"Yes and Gorlois seems to know them all," I quipped bitterly. "I think you may be right though. That day when Gorlois challenged him and he backed down. I think it's been nagging in the back of his mind ever since. This is his way of making amends."

"Damned idiot," Geraint responded. "And now he's going to die because of it."

The Saxon leader shouted out to Ambrosius, throwing his shield to one side and spreading his arms wide, awaiting his opponent.

"He says his name is Octha, son of Hengest and that he admires your bravery and will grant you a hero's death with a sword in your hand so that you may sit with his ancestors in Wealhall, the Hall of Woden the Allfather," Jalmarr translated. Ambrosius quietly made the sign of the cross upon his mailed chest before standing and turning to face his opponent.

"Tell him he faces Ambrosius Aurelianus Constantinus, descendent of Roman emperors and that it is he who will be greeting his pagan ancestors on this day, in the bowels of hell. Tell him also that if I win, his men must kneel before the one true god and accept Christ as their saviour. For I have god upon my side and therefore cannot fail in this task."

Jalmarr hesitated, looking at Ambrosius as though he were mad, before eventually giving a shrug of resignation and translating Ambrosius' words for the Saxon leader.

A great burst of raucous laughter came from their ranks. The Saxons knew their leader could not lose. I looked at Octha and could see the resemblance to his father, Hengest, whom I had confronted outside of Caer Dor alongside Lady Branwen. He was tall and broad, like his father, but less well set, with long, plaited hair the colour of straw and the same cold, pale eyes. He gave his reply in between bouts of laughter and Jalmarr again translated.

"He says a Saxon would never submit to a god of lambs. We are the wolves who are now loose in the lamb pen. Let the slaughter begin."

One of Octha's men tossed him a curved war axe which he caught in his left hand. His leather boots crunched in the shingle as he strode forwards, swinging both sword and axe with a flourish, the steel blades of the weapons catching the orange light of the setting sun as he advanced, his cold eyes fixed on Ambrosius.

The son of Julianus Constantinus muttered a prayer as silence fell over friend and foe alike. Somewhere overhead, a couple of gulls circled, their keening cries breaking the ominous silence.

Octha gave a slight nod towards his opponent and Ambrosius did likewise in response.

Octha's attack, when it came, was sudden, swift and brutal. He gave no indication of what was to come, no war cry or grimace or bearing of teeth, just complete passivity on his face as he launched forwards in a blur of steel.

Ambrosius staggered backwards under the ferocity of the attack, catching the axe blow on his shield and parrying the sword swing with his own blade, more through luck than judgement. Octha did not let up, but continued in his forward assault, raining down blow after blow which Ambrosius struggled to block.

I could feel my jaw clenched tightly, waiting for the inevitable strike that would end Ambrosius' life. Next to me, Geraint was muttering under his breath. "Attack, you fool. Take the fight to him."

Somehow, Ambrosius had managed to survive Octha's initial assault, but was breathing heavily with the exertion, whilst the barbarian leader grinned contemptuously and casually turned to his men with his arms spread wide. The Saxons responded with laughter and derisive jeers as Ambrosius counterattacked with a series of well executed blows that Octha parried and sidestepped with ease. He hooked the blade of his axe over Ambrosius' shield and pulled him forwards, throwing him off balance and butting him in the face with the brow of his helmet.

Ambrosius staggered backwards and fell on his backside in the wet shingle, his nose and mouth streaming with blood. Fortunately, his own helmet had absorbed much of the blow, but he was still momentarily stunned.

Octha swung his axe down, but Ambrosius swung wildly with his sword, managing to knock the axe aside before it buried itself in his skull. He staggered to his feet and turned just in time as Octha attacked again, but this time Ambrosius was forced to defend himself without his shield, which lay discarded on the beach a short distance away.

Steel rang on steel as the two men fought on, but I could see that exhaustion was beginning to take its toll on Ambrosius. His counterattacks were wild and uncoordinated and he was swaying on his feet, whereas Octha still seemed fresh and sharp. His men jeered and hammered their spear shafts against their shields and laughed as Octha easily sidestepped Ambrosius' attacks, not even bothering to raise his weapons to defend himself. He was playing with Ambrosius, like a cat with a mouse, making sure his humiliation was complete before he grew tired of the game and finished him for good.

I saw Varius sigh and look away and beside me, Geraint was still cursing silently. Brother Carwyn and the other monks began to chant in Latin, their deep voices in sharp contrast to the jeers and insults of the Saxons opposite.

As though strengthened by the monks chant, Ambrosius gave a yell and lunged forwards, stabbing out at Octha's midriff. The Saxon leader struck Ambrosius' forearm with the shaft of his axe, causing him to drop his sword onto the shingle. He followed it up with a kick to the groin which caused the young lord to double over in pain.

The Saxons laughed hysterically as Octha casually barged Ambrosius onto his back with his shoulder, grinning as he watched him writhe in pain on the beach. He cast his sword aside and hefted his axe in both hands, preparing to bring its curved blade down into his opponent's chest.

Ambrosius turned onto his front and tried to crawl away but Octha stepped forwards between his legs with his axe raised, ready to deliver the killing blow. Ambrosius fumbled at his belt and turned suddenly, lashing out at Octha's legs with his broad bladed Roman dagger. The Saxon let out a growl of rage and pain as the blade slashed through his calf and then Ambrosius pushed himself up with both arms and twisted his body, trapping Octha's legs between his own, one behind his ankles, the other leg coming up over his thighs. He continued to turn, mustering all the power he could into twisting his body around, flipping the barbarian leader to the ground as he did so. Octha fell heavily onto his back, discarding his axe as he hit the shingle. He was stunned momentarily, but it was all the time Ambrosius needed to throw himself onto the Saxon chieftain. A brief and desperate struggle ensued before Ambrosius managed to get the point of his blade at Octha's throat.

"Submit or die!" he shouted breathlessly. There was no need for a translation. Octha knew exactly what he meant.

The barbarian glared back at Ambrosius defiantly, his pale eyes burning with outrage and humiliation. He growled something back in his guttural tongue and Ambrosius pushed the tip of the dagger into his flesh, drawing blood, forcing Octha to bellow his submission.

"Jalmarr, tell him all his men are to lay down their weapons and return to their boats. Octha must swear upon his heathen gods that he shall never return to these islands or raise a sword against us again. Tell him also that unless he complies with my demands, he will die here and now, without a sword in his hand, so he shall not sit with his ancestors in the next life."

We knew that for a Saxon to die without a weapon in his hand meant that he could never enter the hall of his ancestors in the Otherworld. Instead he would be damned for an eternity to wander the freezing wastes of the Saxon hell.

Jalmarr stepped forwards and translated Ambrosius' demands. Octha snarled with contempt and spat in the Ambrosius' eye. In response, Ambrosius slashed the dagger down one side of Octha's face and pressed the blade against his throat. Octha winced with pain but did not cry out. Instead he replied in his harsh language, his voice full of bitterness.

"He says that he will abide by your terms. But neither he nor his men will ever kneel before your nailed god. They would rather die than accept your god as their own," Jalmarr said, speaking as though Octha's words were his own.

"But those were lord Ambrosius' terms," brother Carwyn protested in a shrill voice, walking forwards. "If the heathens do not accept the word of the Lord, then they must die."

"We cannot demand too much of them, brother," Ambrosius replied. "It is enough that they are willing to lay down their weapons and go home."

Brother Carwyn began to protest, but Jalmarr shouted him down. "Your lord has spoken and the terms are fair. If you demand too much, there will be a bloodbath."

Octha barked out a command to his men and the Saxons reluctantly laid their weapons upon the shingle, their eyes filled with murderous resentment. Our men began to cheer and beat their weapons upon their shields and Jalmarr's crew joined in as well. Slowly the Saxons began to make their way back to their boats whilst Ambrosius pulled Octha to a sitting position with his dagger still firmly pressed against his throat.

Something caught his eye and with his free hand he reached at a silver chain around Octha's neck and pulled free a strangely shaped medallion which I could not quite make out.

"Where did you get this?" He demanded.

Octha's regarded the young lord with impertinence while Jalmarr translated for him. The Saxon leader spat out a terse reply.

"It is payment for your head," Jalmarr said.

With a jerk, Ambrosius tore the medallion from the Saxon's neck and stared at it, his face contorting and reddening with rage.

Ambrosius kicked Octha forwards onto the shingle and turned to Jalmarr. "Tell him to never befoul our land again and that if he does, we shall be waiting for him."

Jalmarr translated as Octha climbed to his feet, his hand pressed against the cut on his cheek in an attempt to stem the flow of blood which was leaking between his fingers, his pale eyes fixed on Ambrosius. He spat on the beach and started to limp back away towards his boat.

When the Saxons had reboarded their boats, Varius ordered our men to collect the discarded spears, axes, seaxes and swords lying on the beach.

Octha waded thigh deep into the waves and then turned, his face contorted with defiant hatred and shouted back to us in his barbaric tongue.

"He says that you have not heard the last of him," Jalmarr said. "That he shits on you and your god and that he will return with five times as many warriors and will lay your lands to waste. He will seek you out and make sure you suffer the agony of the blood eagle after burning your family alive."

"A heathen Saxon cannot be trusted," brother Carwyn hissed into Ambrosius' ear. "I told you, you should have killed the dog."

Ambrosius ignored the monk and dabbed at the blood leaking from his nose with the back of his hand. Our men jeered and shouted insults as the three dragonboats rode over the waves, their oars rising and falling in unison as the Saxons rowed into the distance with Octha standing at the prow of the lead ship.

Varius stood beside Ambrosius and watched the boats vanish into the twilight until only their sails were visible against the darkening horizon. Our men began to chant Ambrosius' name over and over, emphasising the chant by bashing the shaft of their weapons against their shields. The chant was taken up by Jalmarr's crew until we were all shouting Ambrosius' name in exultation of his victory.

Ambrosius picked up Octha's ornate sword and held it aloft for all to see and we all cheered in unison. Although his actions had been rash and foolhardy, there was no doubt that Ambrosius had saved us all from terrible bloodshed and now everyone, both Briton and Saxon, showed their appreciation of that fact.

Varius ordered us to gather the weapons of the raiders and place them in a pile, taking whatever we required. Despite the elation felt by everyone else, his mood was dark and at one point he took Ambrosius to one side and admonished him over his rash actions. We listened intently to the heated debate going on behind a high sand dune. Varius was furious that Ambrosius had risked his life in single combat and also I suspected, a little envious over the respect that his actions had earned him amongst the men.

We made camp on the beach, gathering driftwood for fire and cooking a fish broth from Jalmarr's provisions of salted herring. Despite what we had been through, Jalmarr's Saxon crew did not sit with us, preferring to sit around their own fires and sing their own songs a short distance away. I sat with Ambrosius, Geraint and half a dozen of our men. A short distance away, the monks were gathered in a circle, offering their thanks to God for granting us a relatively bloodless victory.

"Don't worry about what he says," Geraint said, nodding towards Varius. "You spared a lot of bloodshed, although your fighting technique still leaves a lot to be desired and to be honest, I was quite looking forward to cleaving a few Saxon skulls."

Ambrosius ignored him and stared into the writhing orange flames, pulling his cloak tighter as a cool evening breeze blew from across the sea. He was clearly shaken from his encounter with Octha and I noticed that his hand was trembling when he poked at the fire with a discarded arrow.

"Where did you learn that move? The one where you flipped him onto his arse," Geraint persisted. "I've never seen that done before."

Ambrosius sighed, as though the effort to reply was too much. "My brother used to study wrestling techniques of antiquity. He was fond of trying them out on me. I suppose, somewhere along the line, I must have picked up one or two of the moves myself."

Geraint grinned wolfishly, his dark eyes glittering in the firelight. "You're full of surprises Ambrosius, I'll give you that."

We slept on the beach and awoke to a chilly drizzle as the sky began to lighten in the east.

Jalmarr and his crew were already awake and were towing their boats back into the sea.

The captain swaggered over, giving Ambrosius an appreciative grin. He slapped him on the shoulder amiably with a hand as course as dried leather.

"My men respect your bravery, lord. They wish for me to convey their thanks."

Ambrosius' face flushed red and he bowed modestly. "I only did what I felt had to be done."

Jalmarr nodded. "Some are saying that maybe the blood of Wodin flows through your veins. In their experience, you wealas are seldom that brave." He winked mischievously.

"How about your new blade?" He said, pointing at the Saxon sword at Ambrosius' waist. "Can I take a look?"

Ambrosius shrugged and drew the barbarian sword from its fleece lined, leather scabbard. A couple of the men gasped with awe as he drew it and held it before him. It was a fine weapon, broad bladed and razor sharp, with a delicate, interlacing pattern somehow embedded within the steel that seemed to shimmer like the skin of an adder in the grey early morning light. Jalmarr balanced it on a thick finger, near the hilt. "Perfectly weighted," he muttered with reverence. "This is a fine blade, worthy of Weland the Smith himself. Worth several boatloads of warriors, I'd warrant." He held the hilt closer to his face and squinted at runes engraved upon the swords wide, silver plated pommel. "Octha's claw," he muttered, translating the illegible but intricate collection of lines and slashes. Reverently he handed the weapon back to Ambrosius.

"I shall rename it for him," Ambrosius said with a grim smile. "From now on it will be known as Octha's Ruin."

Jalmarr stared out over the seaward horizon, taking a deep breath of brine filled air. "He will come back, you know," he muttered. "What you did was worse than death for him. You humiliated him in front of his shield-brothers. His reputation and his honour have been besmirched and he will not rest until he finds you."

Ambrosius shrugged. "When he comes, I shall be ready for him."

Jalmarr turned and fixed Ambrosius with a cold stare. "I hope you are, boy. For your own sake and for the sake of your people."

As we boarded the boats once again, I noticed that Ambrosius was still holding Octha's medallion in his right hand.

"What was that you tore from Octha's neck?" I enquired as I helped Ambrosius aboard the Brimwulf.

In reply he opened his hand and I saw that the medallion was wrought in the shape of a delicate seahorse, the unmistakable emblem of Gorlois ap Gerdan.

We sailed northwards for several more days before finally sighting the rugged coastline of Guotodin. Despite it still being summer, the air this far north was noticeably cooler and the sky was a relentless grey from which squalls of rain blew every now and then, soaking us to the skin. The stench of stale vomit had become overwhelming and we were all cold, wet and miserable and desperate for the sea journey to end.

Jalmarr stood at the rising and dipping prow of the Brimwulf, holding on with one hand, riding the waves with the confident ease of one who has spent his entire life at sea. He pointed westward beyond the coast towards a great chunk of jagged, black rock that jutted from the surrounding countryside beside a wide loch. At the summit of the flat topped mountain of stone we could make out buildings surrounded by a palisade of wood. "Behold, the fortress of Din Eidyn. Home to King Cadlew of the Votadini. That is where you are headed. We will put you ashore on that spar of sand and that is where we shall part company my friends. The Votadini are no friends of my people and I do not wish to tarry longer than I have to. May your gods walk with you."

"There is but one god, captain," brother Carwyn corrected him, but the Anglii seafarer ignored him.

The two boats ground ashore on a beach of fine sand and the crew helped us to off load our equipment. Jalmarr wished us luck before ordering the boats to be heaved back into sea.

We watched in silence as the Saxon crews rowed the Deopnaedre and the Brimwulf back out into deeper waters, grunting in unison with each pull of the oars.

Varius yelled at us to fall into column formation and we did, our shields held at our sides with the monks walking out in front, their cowls pulled over their heads, chanting one of the psalms as we made our way off the beach and marched towards the distant spur of black rock that rose from the surrounding mist like some monstrous beast rising from the sea.

It was not long before we were met by a band of a dozen or so horsemen wielding short spears and carrying curious, small rectangular shields. They seemed to appear soundlessly out of the mist, like phantoms on stout limbed ponies, many of them bare chested and sporting swirling blue designs, similar to those of the Cruithne. Those not wearing helmets wore their hair and moustaches long and stiffened with lime. Many of them wore chequered woollen cloaks, with torcs of bronze or silver around their necks and decorative bracers around sinewy arms.

I felt myself tense at the sight of these wild looking men, so similar to Picts as to be indistinguishable to my eye. Varius ordered us to halt and strode forwards to meet the intimidating strangers, his hand held cautiously on the hilt of his sword.

The horsemen fanned out and began to circle us menacingly, weighing us up with pale, soulless eyes like wolves circling their prey. Our men began to fidget nervously as they stood motionless, their heads darting left and right, trying to follow the movements of the horsemen.

"Eyes front!" Varius barked suddenly and all movement within our ranks ceased. Three of the riders came forwards until they were within striking distance of Varius. One of them was an old man in his fifties, but powerfully built with a face that looked as if it had been roughly hacked from stone. His chest and arms were bare but covered in the patterns of his tribe, with a thick woollen cloak slung over his wide shoulders fastened with an ornate golden pin. His thick arms were heavy with bands of gold and silver and across his rugged face ran a diagonal scar that had also taken one of his eyes, which was now nothing more than a shrunken white orb that had fallen back into its socket. I noticed that one of the three riders was a red haired youth of no more than fifteen years who regarded us with an aloof arrogance. His face was red with acne, but I saw that he wore a man's sword at his side.

Varius went down on one knee and turned to nod to Ambrosius, who strode forwards and did the same. He lowered his head and spoke respectfully to the man on horseback.

"Hail, King Cadlew of the Votadini, ruler of Guotodin. We have been sent by Duke Julianus of Durotrigia and Dumnonia to aid you in your ongoing war against the tribes of the north."

The older man ignored him and instead rode around us, casting a critical eye upon our ranks with the youth following.

"Damn, Varius. I ask Julianus for men and he sends boys," he growled in a deep and gravelly voice. He stopped before brother Carwyn and the monks. "And what purpose are you going to serve here in the Old North?"

Carwyn dropped to one knee and bowed his head. "To spread the word of the Lord to the heathen, my Lord King."

The Votadini king looked at the monks and began to chuckle, his laughter quickly spreading to his men and the youth at his side. "They have come to preach to the heathen," he echoed sarcastically. "What do you think we should do with them, Lot? I'll be buggered if I'm letting them eat my meat and drink my ale, depriving good warriors of food."

The youth shrugged, a half smile on his spotty face. "I'd say if they're keen to spread the word of God to the Cruithne, then the least we can do is escort them to the Forest of Celidon, father. Let the Cruithne feed them and warm them by their fires."

King Cadlew laughed aloud. "You are wise beyond your years, son," he said, clapping the boy on the back and nearly knocking him from his horse. He turned to one of his warriors. "Take the monks to the edge of the Great Forest. We'll see how kindly the Cruithne take to being preached at by the likes of them."

The warrior nodded and grunted at Carwyn and the other monks to follow him. Brother Carwyn looked around hesitantly. "But we were to escort the Lord Ambrosius," he began, but was cut short by a barked command from the Votadini warrior.

"Go brother," Ambrosius said quietly. "And may God walk with you."

Brother Carwyn gave one last despairing look at Ambrosius, like a man approaching the gallows before the warrior behind him gave him an unfriendly kick to the small of his back to get him moving.

We watched in silence as the half dozen monks were unceremoniously escorted away by three Votadini warriors.

"So you are Ambrosius, son of Julianus?" King Cadlew said, looking him up and down with a disapproving expression.

Ambrosius gave a slight bow of his head. "I am, lord King."

Cadlew gave a derisive snort. "You look nothing like your father. Are you sure you're not a changeling?"

"He takes after his mother, Lord King," Varius said quickly. "In more ways than one."

"Can he fight, Varius?" the King asked.

The stocky commander shrugged. "Well enough, lord King. He defeated a Saxon chieftain named Octha in single combat. Despite his appearance, he has a warrior's heart."

"A warrior's heart will not be enough to survive up here," King Cadlew said, raising his voice so that we could all hear. "The Cruithne feast upon warrior's hearts and wean their young upon their blood. To survive here you must be cunning like the fox, and alert like the hare. Ever alert. For you will be patrolling the land beyond the Wall, close to the highlands and the Forest of Celidon, home of the Cruithne, the painted people whom you know as the Picts. Many of you will not see another summer. If you are lucky, your death will be a quick one. If you are unlucky and the Cruithne will take you alive, you will beg for the release of death," King Cadlew grinned at us as a cold wind blew down the mist enshrouded valley. "Welcome, gentlemen, to the Old North."

Chapter 11

The Old North

If we had found life harsh for those last few weeks in Caer Cadwy, it was doubly so in Guotodin.

We took a narrow and precipitous path up the mountain of basalt to the impregnable fortress that sat at its summit. Din Eidyn was enclosed by a thick stone wall upon which stood a palisade of wooden stakes, three times as high as a man and each as thick as a man's thigh, made even more intimidating by the collection of rotten grey heads impaled upon spears at regular intervals.

Beyond the oak gates were buildings of stone, wood and wattle of various sizes and functions, penned areas where shaggy haired, long horned cattle grazed peacefully and sheep wandered freely around the compound. All of the buildings were dwarfed by the mighty oak beamed hall of King Cadlew of the Votadini and whilst the rest of the men were shown to the stone round houses where they would spend the night, Ambrosius and Varius were invited to the King's hall and as we were Ambrosius' personal guard, Geraint and I were required to go as well, to feast with the Votadini warriors.

The feast proved to be a raucous affair, with plenty of sour tasting but potent ale to swill down the wild boar roasted over long cooking pits. Slaves and serving girls rushed amongst the warriors of King Cadlew, carrying great pitchers of ale and platters of steaming meat, trying to avoid the lustful, prying hands that grabbed at their breasts or buttocks.

Several captured Cruithne were forced to fight to the death with daggers for our amusement, bound to one another by the neck with a thick iron collar and a yard of chain so that they could not back away from one another. Bets were placed by the baying Votadini warriors; spearheads, daggers, bronze armbands and rings of iron as well as one or two more valuable items like amulets of gold or silver changed hands as the wiry Cruithne warriors, naked from the waist up, whirled and slashed at one another with their short blades. Geraint was amongst the baying crowd, having wagered a silver brooch on one of the unfortunate combatants.

As guests of the King, we sat at a lower table, but within shouting distance of him and I watched him as he tore at a rib of roasted boar that dripped herb laden honey and wild garlic down his red beard. Beside him sat his precocious young son, Lot, whose eyes shone with something akin to lust as he watched the two Cruithne warriors fighting for their lives. On the other side of him was his right hand man, a tall, wiry fellow with sharp features and a face as mean as a starved sewer rat who never seemed to smile and next to him was a stern faced woman with long, straw coloured hair tied in two immaculate plaits whom I presumed was the Queen.

"Do you not approve of my entertainment, Roman boy?" King Cadlew shouted at Ambrosius above the din of his men. Ambrosius had chosen to ignore the Picts fighting a short distance away, especially after a jet of blood had spattered his face after the first round of combat and instead concentrated on eating his meal. I knew that he did not approve and that his high born Roman sensibilities would be offended at such a spectacle, but he looked up at the King and smiled politely.

"On the contrary, your highness. It is not the first time that I have seen men die a pointless death. It's just that I find my food far more interesting."

The king stared at Ambrosius with a look of cold contempt. His attention was momentarily diverted as a yell went up as one of the Cruithne, a boy not much older than the king's son, plunged his dagger into the ribs of his opponent, a man twice his age and twice his size. His opponent crumpled to the earthen floor, convulsing and coughing up blood before lying still. The Cruithne boy looked around dazed at the cheering Votadini warriors, his arms hung limply at his side as the men slapped him on his back and raised him on their shoulders in triumph. They placed the boy on his feet before the king, who nodded to his son. Lot grinned like a child given a new plaything and he rose from the bench and swaggered down until he was level with the Cruithne boy.

"Looks like we have an unlikely champion in our midst," the boy prince shouted over the din. The other Votadini laughed and cheered. "In other circumstances, you would have won your freedom," Lot said, his face inches away from the terrified Cruithne boy. "But unfortunately, you are the sworn enemy of my people. And to let you run back to your own people would be folly."

The prince drew an ornate looking dagger from his belt and two burly Votadini grabbed the boy's thin arms and pinned them behind him. He stared at the prince defiantly and said something in a language that I did not understand.

"You people are no better than animals," Lot snarled and with one quick thrust, he plunged the dagger through the Cruithne boy's eye, right up to the hilt and twisted it into his brain. The boy did not even have time to cry out, but merely gave a loud, shuddering gasp as the blade took his life with brutal efficiency.

The Votadini gave another even louder cheer as the prince withdrew the dagger and wiped it off on his fur cloak with a wide grin, allowing the young Cruithne boy's corpse to crumple to the hard ground. The men began to sing and thump their flagons of ale on tables as the lifeless Pictish corpses were dragged off by slaves.

Lot bowed to his father, who looked on with pride, whilst his mother, the queen excused herself from the table with an expression of disgust.

King Cadlew smirked as he looked back over at Ambrosius who seemed visibly shaken by what he had just witnessed. "You see, my young Roman lord. That is the lesson that your father has sent you here to learn. And if you do not learn it well, that is what will kill you. Up here in the Old North you will learn to love killing. The Cruithne are cruel and show no mercy to those they capture and so we do the same. And then we decorate our walls with their heads and feed their corpses to the dogs."

"You must do with your prisoners as you see fit, Lord King," Ambrosius said diplomatically, taking a deep swig of ale from his goblet, his hand trembling.

"Aye and on the morrow we will get some more of the bastards," Cadlew retorted. "Not far from here lies the Forest of Celidon that marks the boundaries of our lands. It is home to the Venicones and come morning you shall ride forth with us and we will strike deep into their territory and bloody their noses."

"Who are the Venicones your highness?" Varius enquired between mouthfuls of succulent pork.

The King held out his goblet to be refilled by a passing serving girl. "The Cruithne or Picts as you southerners call them are made up of many tribes, each with their own gods, languages, customs and lineages. To the north and west of us are the Venicones and the Epidii. North of them are the Vacomagi, the Caledonii and the Creones and beyond them are the Carnonacae, Decantae and the Smertai, the dwellers at the end of the world with nothing beyond them but rocks and grey sea. One thing they all have in common is that their women are revered and are just as ferocious and feral as the men. They trace their lineage not through the father's side but through their mother's. They are like the wolves of the forest, untameable and savage, worthy only to be wiped from the face of the Earth. And if it wasn't for us, they would pour across that crumbling wall and lay waste to all the lands from here to the southern coast."

"Do your men still patrol the Wall?" Ambrosius asked.

The King looked up at the smoke blackened rafters of his hall thoughtfully. "For centuries my people have been keeping the Cruithne at bay, at first because our forefathers wanted to gain favour with the Romans, but now?" the king shrugged and let out a loud sigh. "We fight for our very survival. The Romans have gone, abandoned their Wall and abandoned these islands, but we fight on because it is what we have always done. The Cruithne are the enemies of our blood. We have never known any different. And there is another reason why we keep the Wall manned," his expression turned bitter as he spat a shred of gristle onto his wooden platter. "King Vortigern has my youngest son hostage. And while he has little Uriens, I will not dare to raise a finger against him. He demands that we continue to man the Wall, to stop the Cruithne from pouring into his kingdom. This also serves to tie my men down, but we struggle to keep the Wall manned."

"I'm sorry, Lord King, I did not know." Ambrosius said. "He holds my younger half-brother as well, which is why my father too cannot move against him."

"I look forward to the day when his flayed skin and the skins of his cursed sons adorn my walls. And then I will feed him, skinless and screaming, to my hounds and laugh as they tear the bastard to red shreds."

"It would be no less than he deserves, Lord King," Varius growled, his mouth full of bread and meat.

"But why does my father send men to man the Wall when he bears no love for Vortigern?" Ambrosius said. "It makes no sense. Surely it would be to our advantage to just let the Picts ravage his lands?"

"You forget your history Ambrosius," King Cadlew replied. "In your grandfather's time, the Picts once breached the Wall. They launched a coordinated attack with the Saxons and the Irish and damned near overrun the place from here to the south sea. It is in no one's interest to let the Cruithne breach the Wall again."

Ambrosius nodded with understanding. "And now Vortigern holds my father's leash as well."

The king grunted and took a swig of ale, most of which poured down his beard. "It is even worse for my brother, Cunedda. Vortigern has all of his children and has forced him into servitude. He has been forced to take his entire warband to serve Vortigern in Gwynedd. He tried to resist once, but Vortigern sent him one of his daughter's ears to remind him that he still has the upper hand. Since then, Cunedda has decided that it's better to act like a whipped hound." The king of the Votadini threw a half-eaten rib aside, where it was quickly snatched by one of the large hounds under his table. "The bastard holds all our leashes. You don't become high king without a certain measure of ruthlessness you know."

"Ruthlessness and cruelty will not keep you in power," Ambrosius said. "A king needs the respect of his subjects as well. His laws must apply to all, both high born and low born, or else you are building your fortress on foundations of sand."

King Cadlew let out a sudden, loud laugh. "You sound like your father even if you don't look like him, lad."

We rode out early the next morning. Varius stayed behind to organise our men as they were preparing to march to one of the many border forts stationed along the old Roman wall that stretched cross country from the Irish Sea, known by my people as the Muir Eireann in the west, to the German sea in the east. Ambrosius, Geraint and I were given stout limbed horses by the king as we were to ride with his warband into Cruithne territory. Many of them were now armoured and helmeted as we would be riding to battle. My head throbbed from the excess of ale from the night before and my mouth tasted sour. Geraint too looked bleary eyed and pale and my stomach rolled with nausea and nervousness. Ambrosius was struggling to keep his black stallion under control, much to the amusement of King Cadlew and his retinue.

"The Votadini are born horsemen," he shouted to us through the cold morning mist. "We'd give your father's Sarmatians a run for their money, I can tell you. In fact, we have some Sarmatians amongst us," he nodded at several of his men in close fitting coats of scale armour and high, pointed helms with horsehair plumes and I was instantly reminded of Cletus and the other Sarmatians back at Caer Cadwy.

"A legion of them used to man the Wall during the times of the Romans," King Cadlew explained. "When they left, some of the Sarmatians stayed. Some joined us, some went south to join your father. Most now bend their knee to Vortigern," he spat on the ground, as though the very mention of the High King left a sour taste in his mouth.

Lot, the King's son was also riding with us. He was checking the edge of one of his spears with his thumb and was laughing and joking confidently with the men around him. Despite his age, he showed no signs of apprehension at riding into battle, only an eager excitement at the prospect of shedding Cruithne blood.

The oak gates swung open and a horn blared out and two score mounted warriors rode forth from Din Eidyn with a cheer. Soon we had left the fortress on its impenetrable plinth of rock and were riding through a rugged, wild landscape of rolling hills and deep, rock strewn valleys, past farmsteads with low, thatched roofs and round houses of stone that seemed to float on the surface of dark watered lochs that reminded me of the crannogs back in my native land. Farmhands herding their long horned, long haired cattle knelt as we passed, all of them familiar with the banner bearing a black raven on a purple background that was carried before us by a proud warrior, the sigil of King Cadlew of the Votadini.

As we rode, the king told us of all the battles that the Votadini had fought against the Cruithne, pointing out hills and rivers where his ancestors had fallen or won glory for their people. Eventually we came to a deep, fast flowing river in a steep sided valley that marked the edge of Votadini territory and followed it until we came to a fording point of flat rocks just below the surface of the water.

We splashed across in single file until we were all on the other side, riding up the opposite side of the valley until we reached the top. On the other side, the landscape sloped gently down to the edge of a huge pine forest that stretched as far as the eye could see.

"The Forest of Celidon," Prince Lot said with a grin. He was wearing an oversize helmet and a coat of iron scales sewn onto leather, like many of the other Votadini, his thin but wiry arms barely filling the sleeves. "One of our scouts discovered a Cruithne settlement nearby. They don't know we're coming," he unsheathed the sword at his side halfway, his eyes glinting with the prospect of slaughter.

"I thought we were fighting warriors, not women and children," I said.

The Prince frowned at me. "Cruithne women fight like men, believe me. Do not make the mistake of thinking any of them are innocent, my friend. When the Cruithne capture their enemies, they hand them over to their women and children to torture them. If you have seen what they are capable of, your mercy will soon vanish, southerner."

"I am no southerner, Lord Prince, I am a Gael. And I have seen first-hand what these people are capable of. I have no illusions about the ferocity of these people."

Prince Lot grinned again. "Good. Then we are agreed. No mercy."

He pulled at the reins of his steed and cantered away.

"He can't be more than fourteen summers, but he acts like a man of thirty," Geraint muttered at my side. "I wonder if he was ever a child."

"We were all children once, Geraint," I replied. "I was younger than him when my family were slaughtered. You were younger than him when you were taken from your family. We learn to grow up quickly in this world or else we die."

We rode down the valley and into the dark forest, following a small group that had been sent ahead to scout for the enemy. The ground was soft, carpeted with many years of pine needles and the only sound was the chink and jangle of harness and armour, occasionally punctuated by the snort of a horse. A wary apprehension had descended upon all of us, as we were all well aware that we were now in hostile territory and that the Cruithne were notoriously adept at setting ambushes. Ambrosius had told me that long ago, the Romans had lost an entire legion in these very woods, five thousand men vanished without a trace, never to be seen again and looking around at the pockets of shadow and the densely packed, tall, thick trunked trees, I could well believe it. Although it was very different in appearance, the place had the same feel as the forest of the Horned One, where I had fled when Penglyn had been burned to the ground. I could feel the eyes of hostile spirits upon me, forest gods, ancient beyond reckoning, peering maliciously from the bows and the shadows, cursing the outsiders that dared to enter their domain.

"I hate forests," Geraint muttered, his eyes warily scanning the surrounding pine trees that towered around us. "You could hide an entire army here and ride right past them without knowing."

One of the Votadini turned in his saddle and gave a harsh hiss, prompting Geraint into silence. After a while the scouts returned with a bulging sack which they gave to their king. Cadlew chuckled to himself and dismounted from his horse, walking over to Ambrosius with the stained sack held in one hand.

"It seems we share something in common with the Cruithne," he said, emptying the sack in front of Ambrosius' horse. His steed snorted nervously and he fought to stop it from backing away from the contents of the sack which rolled near its hooves.

On the ground lay half a dozen human heads, their grey flesh streaked red and their hair clotted with congealed blood. Their eyes had been gouged out and the expressions frozen on their lifeless faces were testament to the agonies that they had suffered before they had been allowed to die. What shocked me the most however was that they were familiar to me. The heads belonged to brother Carwyn and his monks.

"Seems we both share a dislike of the clergy," King Cadlew said merrily, chuckling to himself as he turned to walk back to his horse.

Ambrosius crossed himself with a trembling hand and Prince Lot laughed, unable to contain his amusement. "Get used to it, Lord Ambrosius," he said. "If you can laugh about it, life becomes easier."

"There is nothing funny about the slaughter of pious men, Lord Prince," Ambrosius shot back angrily. "We must take time to give them a decent burial."

Lot looked at him as though he had lost his mind. "If we do that, we will lose the element of surprise. Besides, if we are spotted, it will give the Cruithne time to rally themselves and attack us."

"My son speaks sense," King Cadlew said. "We will collect them on the way back. Their bodies are strung up in the trees a short distance from here."

Just as the king had said, a little further on, six pale, headless corpses hung naked by their feet from the trees. Their genitals had been removed and all bore the marks of torture.

"Why would they do this to men of God?" Ambrosius whispered.

"Damned fools should have known to come here unarmed was certain death," Geraint added.

"The Cruithne make no distinction between man, woman or child, or warrior, peasant or monk for that matter," I said. Memories of the pile of heads that I had seen in Penglyn came back to me, villagers whom I had grown up with and I turned away from the gently swaying bodies in the trees, fighting the rising tide of revulsion and allowing anger to fill my soul.

By the time we reached the settlement of roundhouses nestled in a hollow and virtually hidden by the trees, I was ready for slaughter.

We approached silently, splitting into four groups so that we could attack from all sides at once, fanning out and awaiting the horn blast that would signal our attack. Below us, the people in the settlement were completely unaware of our presence. Dogs and filthy children ran between the squat round houses, women carried pitchers of water or milked goat and cattle whilst the few men present chopped wood or stood guard, idly leaning on spears.

Immediately before the attack, I was given a lit brand of brushwood and told we were going in with fire and sword. I put all feelings of pity out of my mind, instead focusing on what these people had done to the unfortunate monks and what their brothers had done to my friends and family in the past.

Geraint grinned at me from behind the cheek plates of his helmet, his eyes glittering with the prospect of spilling blood. I nodded at him and turned to Ambrosius, who was fidgeting nervously with the strap of his helmet. "Stay close to us," I said. "We're here to protect you and if we fail, your father will have our hides."

Ambrosius nodded in response. "I can handle myself, don't worry about me," he said impatiently.

When the blast of the horn sounded a single mournful note, I yelled at the top of my voice along with the others as we spurred our horses down the wooded incline towards the clearing below.

The people in the little village were caught completely unawares. Forty armed horsemen thundered out of the forest from all directions, screaming like banshees, brandishing deadly flame and steel.

A small child ran directly in front of my horse and I trampled over it without a shred of remorse, swinging my sword at the fleeing mother and taking the top of her head off. A Cruithne warrior ran at me from a nearby hut brandishing a spear, but I blocked his thrust and shoved the burning torch into his face. He fell back screaming, clutching at his seared face, giving me time to cleave him from collar to breastbone with a single downward swing. I thrust my flaming brand into the thatch of the hut that he had run from and could hear children and women screaming inside.

All around me was carnage and death. Picts were running in panic in all directions, but the fury of battle was upon me and I showed no mercy to any I encountered, young or old, male or female. All that I felt was the exhilaration of vengeance.

"Where's Ambrosius?" Geraint shouted over the screaming and the clash of weapons. His mail shirt was spattered with blood and his blade was red all the way to the hilt.

I shook my head and tried to find him amongst the chaos, but everything and everyone were moving too quickly.

"I'll find him," Geraint said and pulled at the reins of his horse, turning away and galloping off into the smoke.

A band of Cruithne warriors came running out of a burning hall wielding spears and axes. I spurred my horse towards them, along with several Votadini horsemen with a ferocious battle cry, sword held before me, pointed towards the enemy. We ploughed into them in a maelstrom of hooves and steel, hacking and swinging at the Cruithne around us. Soon the enemy were either dead or scattered and I looked around, dripping sword in hand, for my next victim. Through the smoke of burning thatch, I saw someone darting into the forest, having somehow avoided detection until now. I kicked my horse's flanks and galloped towards the tree line where the person had disappeared. A Cruithne warrior ran at me from behind a tree, screaming insanely, axe raised to strike. I swung my sword and caught him in the side of the face, severing his lower jaw in a spray of blood and bone shards. I wheeled my horse around, trying to find the person who I had seen earlier and spurred off in the direction I thought they had gone, over a rise and down a gentle slope until I saw her up ahead.

She was a young girl, no more than fifteen or sixteen summers old, thin but wiry, with long dark hair tied back. She had come to a precipice that fell away to a river below with no obvious way down and she hesitated, not knowing which way to go. She turned fearfully when she heard the jangle of my horse's harness and gasped with terror at the sight of me. I must have presented a terrible sight. A warrior in his prime, in a coat of knee length mail spattered with blood and gore, face enclosed in a steel helmet with its bronze brow ridges and plume of red horsehair, sword dripping with the blood of her kin.

She stared at me with dark eyes like those of a hunted doe, breathing heavily and holding a small knife in her right hand. There was something about this wild girl that reminded me of Nivian, all those years ago, though she did not have the same beauty. I stared back at her, feeling the elation of battle beginning to subside, to be replaced with a growing feeling of remorse and pity.

I swung my leg over and dismounted from my horse, my eyes still fixed on the girl and hers on mine. As I approached, she ran first right, then left along the edge of the precipice with a whimper of fear, before turning to face me again, holding the knife out in front of her, dropping into a crouch, her dark eyes suddenly burning with wild ferocity.

"Drop the knife," I commanded, but she appeared to not understand.

Not far behind me, I could still hear the screams of the villagers as they were slaughtered by the Votadini. I sheathed my sword and walked towards her with my right hand held out. "I won't hurt you, drop the knife."

She appeared to relax slightly, but then moved with surprising speed, slashing out with the knife at my midriff, the blade skittering harmlessly against the iron links of my mail coat. I caught her thin wrist on the backswing and twisted, causing her to drop the knife with a squeal whilst grabbing a handful of hair with my other hand. She clawed feebly at my gauntleted fist, whimpering something in her native tongue. I let go of her hair and instead grabbed her by the upper arm, so thin that my fingers met and led my horse by the reins with the other hand back the way I had come.

She jabbered at me in her native language, pleading, sobbing and cursing by turn until we reached the outskirts of the burning village.

By the time I got back, it was all but over. The air was filled with the acrid stench of burning thatch and the sobs of the survivors, a small band of young females that had been herded together, their clothes torn and in rags. Corpses littered the ground, men, women and children, their limbs twisted where they had fallen. Somewhere a woman screamed continuously and in the midst of it all stood King Cadlew, face streaked with red, grinning like a god of death, sword in one hand, curved axe in the other. He bellowed triumphantly to his men brandishing his weapons in the air, and in response they did the same.

Geraint emerged from a burning hut, his white teeth glinting between the cheek plates of his helmet as he spied me and grinned. He was holding two heads in his left hand, one male and one female and he lifted them for me to see. He was in his element, amongst death and carnage and I walked over to him, leading the trembling girl by the arm, trying not to dwell upon the grisly trophies that he held.

"They didn't even know we were coming," he said, his voice full of mirth. "It was beautiful. Like slaughtering pigs."

I ignored his comment. "Where's Ambrosius?" I asked.

Geraint shrugged. "Couldn't find him. I'll wager he's nearby though, hiding in the trees. The King's right about him. Doesn't have the stomach for killing, that lad."

I turned away from him and walked through the ruined village, dragging the girl with me and calling Ambrosius' name. Nearby, between a sheep pen and a pig shed, Prince Lot and one of his men were raping a couple of Cruithne girls, their pale buttocks thrusting rhythmically at their captives as they lay spread eagled across a pile of firewood, sobbing and pleading, whilst several companions looked on shouting encouragement.

I walked past them until I found Ambrosius sat on a pile of logs in front of a dead dog. He had removed his helmet and cast it aside and was staring listlessly at the corpse of the animal before him, his face pallid and glistening with sweat. An elderly man lay face down nearby, his expression peaceful in death.

"Ambrosius," I said as I walked over to him. "I wondered where you were."

The young lord appeared not to hear me, but continued staring at the scrawny black dog at his feet.

"I killed him," he muttered dreamily. "He ran at me with a staff and I killed him and then I killed his dog."

I looked again at the old man and his little dog and thought how pitiful the sight was. "We've all killed this day, Ambrosius," I said.

He looked up and I could see his eyes were clouded with tears as he appeared to notice the girl for the first time.

"We came to fight against the Picts, not slaughter dogs and old men and little girls. This is not how it is meant to be," he placed his head in his hands, his torment obvious.

"These people tortured and killed brother Carwyn and his monks. Do not waste your pity on them, Ambrosius," I replied, barely believing the words that came from my mouth.

"Do you think God sees it that way, Fergus?" he spat accusingly, his eyes red rimmed. "Do you think the Almighty sees this as a good thing?"

I frowned, unable to answer, wondering what Father Demetrios would have said if he could see me now. "You think too much," I said. "It's the worst thing that you can do in these situations. I remember my first time, with Lord Drustan. We'd rode out before dawn to raid a Cornovii village..."

Ambrosius stood and cut me short. "Save your stories for your grandchildren, Fergus," he said bitterly, retrieving his helmet and striding away. "I'm sure your father and brother would have been proud of you."

We rode back to Din Eidyn, taking with us the spoils of our conquest, a ragged, pathetic huddle of weeping prisoners, a handful of sheep and cattle and a couple of cart loads of grain, wool, dried meat and ale. We stopped to bury brother Carwyn and the other monks at Ambrosius' insistence and stood in silence as he led a prayer for their pious souls before King Cadlew lost his patience and urged us onwards again.

The girl I had captured stumbled along behind my horse on the end of a length of rope tied around her neck with her hands tied in front of her, like all of the other prisoners.

"What have you got her for?" Geraint enquired with a nod towards my captive. "Bit scrawny isn't she?"

I glanced around at the girl staggering along behind me, her face sullen and defiant. "She may have her uses," I replied. "Cooking, cleaning, weaving. I may even be able to sell her."

"Not much good for fucking though," Geraint quipped. "No meat on her. No tits, no arse, just skin and bone."

"There's more to life than fucking and killing, Geraint," I said, finding his presence irritating.

The Powysian shrugged philosophically. "Drinking and feasting come high on my list as well," he replied with a grin.

We returned to Din Eidyn as conquering heroes. Workers in the fields cheered our return as we rode past, with King Cadlew's raven banner fluttering in the breeze. Two score horsemen had rode out and two score horsemen had returned, bearing slaves and plunder.

That evening, we celebrated our success in the King's hall. A bard played at the foot of the King's table, composing a tune about the brave exploits of our warband, but conveniently leaving out any mention of children burned alive in their homes. The bard had travelled from Eire, the king had told us and it took a while before realisation dawned. It was none other than Oengus, son of Ruadainn, the hostel owner who had offered us protection when Fiachu mac Niall had driven us from our home and pursued us relentlessly across the country. After he had finished playing, I excused myself and made my way over to him.

"It would seem that I never repaid you for the kindness you showed me my friend," I said in my native Gaelic as he attempted to pack his lyre into a lambskin bag whilst simultaneously quaffing ale from a drinking horn.

Oengus looked up, a quizzical expression on his broad, flat face. Time had changed him little over the seven or so years it had been since I had seen him last. He was a little heavier, his face a little redder from excess, but his eyes still twinkled with humour and his hair and curled moustache and neat triangular beard bore no traces of grey.

"Well, I suppose you could get me a drink, but I'm sorry, my friend, do I know you?" he said, gently placing his lyre on a bench. I noticed his right hand moving unobtrusively towards a small seax at his belt.

"I am Fergus mac Fiontan of the Deisi and you helped save my life. I owe you and I have never repaid you."

Oengus frowned as he scrutinised my face and then smiled warmly, placing both hands on my shoulders. "Little Fergus? The boy who was running from Fiachu mac Niall? You survived?" He laughed heartily. "It's good to see you lad, it really is."

After exchanging embraces, we sat together in a quiet corner of the hall, away from boisterous, carousing Votadini warriors. Oengus drained two leather pitchers of ale before I had even touched mine and his merry face was flushed crimson. I told him all about my escape across the sea, how Ygerna and I were split up and thought one another dead and about the death of Dorbalos.

His eyes lost their lustre at that point and he stared down at the dark liquid in his pitcher.

"When I returned to the hostel, it had been burned to the ground by Fiachu. I found my father and sisters amongst the blackened timbers," he swallowed hard and downed half of his ale before continuing. "They had been bound hand and foot and burned alive inside the hostel. When I found them, they were nothing more than charred skeletons." He closed his eyes and took a deep breath to fight the rising emotion within him. "After that, I had nowhere to go. I took my harp and began to travel, listening to the gossip in chieftain's halls and selling information to their enemies for the price of a meal and a bed. I decided that my skills would be best used elsewhere, so then I crossed the sea and came to this land, where I have been ever since. I have sung in the halls of Saxons, Britons and Cruithne. All confide in me and all think me a friend," he winked at me with a mischievous smirk. "They tell me their deepest secrets, which I then sell to their enemies. There is nothing that goes on in these islands that I don't know about."

"Then you'll know that Fiachu is fighting for King Vortigern and that the King has taken Uther Pendragon captive?" I said, taking a mouthful of sour ale.

Oengus winked again and tapped the side of his nose. "I know too that Fiachu has a stronghold far to the north and west, on a remote mountain known as Beinn Mhor amongst his Cruithne friends."

I leaned forwards, my interest growing. "You know where he is?"

Oengus nodded and smiled at a passing serving girl. "Of course I know where the bastard is. I've followed his movements closely since the death of my father and sisters, I've even sang for him, ingratiated myself within his inner circle if you will."

"Then you could lead me to him?" I whispered enthusiastically.

"I'd do so gladly if it wouldn't mean certain death for you. Fiachu mac Niall will not be an easy man to kill if that's what you're planning. He has that Masraighe witch with him constantly. She frightens the shite out of me. It's like she can see inside your soul with those sightless eyes of hers. She has...powers." Oengus suppressed a shudder and took another swig of ale.

"All I'd need is to get close enough to him to stick a blade in his neck," I said.

Oengus nodded thoughtfully. "Last I heard he had crossed back over the sea to Eire to fight for his brother, Loegaire, who now sits on the High King's throne in Tara. How long he'll be gone is anyone's guess."

I cursed under my breath. I knew that to cross the sea would mean certain death for me.

Oengus reached over and placed a hand on my shoulder. "There is nothing I would desire more than to see that callous whore-son rotting in the ground. But if you are set on this, then bide your time for a little longer, friend. When he returns, I will seek you out and I promise you, I will get you close enough for you to do what you must do. Maybe I can also find out where this young Lord Uther is being held."

I clasped his hand in mine in gratitude. "Thank you, Oengus son of Ruadainn. How can I ever repay you?"

Oengus shrugged and nodded at the thin Cruithne girl who was crouched against the timber wall with her head resting on bony knees. She wore a slave's iron collar now, which the King's blacksmith had placed around her neck for the price of a keg of ale.

"You want her?" I said with disbelief.

Oengus shrugged, still grinning. I whistled and the girl got to her feet and came over, her large dark eyes full of resentment towards me.

"What's her name?" Oengus asked taking her thin face in one hand and turning it left to right as he scrutinised her.

I shrugged. "Probably something unpronounceable," I replied. "Seems too surly for my liking."

Oengus addressed her in her own melodious language and the girl replied in a quiet voice.

"Brida."

The bard spoke gently, stroking the girl's hair and I saw a faltering smile cross her face which vanished just as quickly.

"I think she likes you," I said.

"Everyone likes Oengus mac Ruadainn," he said and I knew that it was true. I just hoped that he would honour his word and get me within striking distance of Fiachu mac Niall.

Chapter 12

The Forest of Celidon

"Riders approaching from the north," the sentry said, letting a blast of icy wind blow in through the open door of the guard house. He was virtually buried in a bearskin cloak, only his eyes and the top of his helmet visible.

His hands, enclosed in thick woollen mittens, held the shaft of his spear.

"I'll meet them," I said groggily, rising from my hard bunk and rubbing my hands over the dying flames of the brazier. "You get some rest, Morgus."

The soldier nodded gratefully and placed his spear in the wooden rack against the wall, cursing the northern weather. I donned my cloak and helmet and pulled my sheepskin gauntlets on before stepping out into a biting flurry of snow. I walked along the top of the thick stone Roman wall, careful to avoid the patches of black ice. It was crumbling badly in places and missing entirely in other areas, where it had been crudely repaired with timber gangplanks that spanned across the gaps.

I nodded a greeting to the other sentry who stood with a burning torch in his hand, looking out across the barren stretch of white land to the north that gleamed in the moonlight where I could see three distant riders approaching.

I pulled my fur cloak tighter around me and could hear my teeth chattering. We had been here in the north for nearly a year and a half with no word from the outside world. Once a month, if we were lucky, a cart of grain and dried meat and ale would arrive from Din Eidyn, but more often than not it would be ambushed by the Cruithne and we would be forced to survive on whatever we could hunt or fish from the rivers. The men grumbled constantly about returning home, but we received no news of home. They were sick of the lack of food, ale and women, but most of all they had learned what it was to fear the Cruithne. We all had. Of the three dozen men who had marched out from Caer Cadwy a lifetime ago, only a score remained. Three had deserted, five had died from sickness and the remainder had died at the hands of the Cruithne. They were as elusive and devious as they were savage, preferring to attack at night, moving with stealth and silence in small groups that would scale the Wall and slash the throats of our sentries, sometimes eviscerating them and leaving their insides scattered in the snow. On a couple of occasions they had taken our comrades alive and tortured them overnight, their terrible screams and pleas for mercy still haunted our restless dreams.

Once they broke into the barracks of our small fort and killed one man, leaving the rest of us unscathed. They had beheaded him, castrated him and strung him from the rafters right under our noses and vanished back over the Wall before we knew what had happened. It was a warning that they could take our lives whenever they wished and from that night on, no one slept in peace. On moonless nights they would crawl close to the wall and make noises all night, howling demonically and raining curses upon us in their own tongue. We knew that they were toying with us, tormenting us for their own amusement and that they could destroy us on a whim. Come first light, we would open the gates and send out a patrol on horseback to hunt them down, but more often than not we would be chasing shadows. On the occasions when we caught them however, we showed them no mercy and the Cruithne heads that peered sightlessly from lances on our wall were mute testament to our hatred of them. We looked forwards to the times when a Votadini warband would arrive so that we could ride out with them and deliver our retribution upon the Cruithne. More often than not it would be reprisal attacks upon one of their camps or settlements, or cattle raids, but on a few occasions, we had encountered an entire Pictish warband and the result had been a bloody but brief struggle in which we had emerged victorious.

One of the riders swung his torch twice to the left and once right and I yelled down to the gatekeeper. "Open the gates."

The men below removed the heavy oak beam that barred the thick gate shut and it creaked open ponderously as the riders approached. I descended the precarious wooden steps and raised a hand to the riders who were swathed in furs from head to foot.

One of them swung his leg over his steed and leaped from his saddle, still holding the reins of his horse. "We bear a message for Lord Ambrosius," the rider said, his breath escaping in plumes of white frost.

"Go wake him," I said to one of the sentries as the others took the reins of the rider's horses and guided them to the stables.

Moments later Ambrosius emerged from the barracks, his thick black cloak wrapped around his shoulders. Life on the northern frontier had changed him. His face was no longer cherubic but had hardened and become more gaunt and chiselled, his chin now covered with a reddish blonde scant beard. His scowl had become permanent, marking his face with hard lines and his eyes had become cold and distant. Ambrosius the boy had gone forever. Ambrosius the man had been born in the cold wastes of the Old North.

He nodded at the Votadini horsemen who gave him the Roman salute, thumping their right hand to their chests and extending their arms outwards.

"Lord Ambrosius, I come bearing ill tidings from the south," the lead rider said.

"Go on," Ambrosius prompted, his voice betraying no emotion.

"A deadly plague has swept through your homeland and killed many, but there is worse I'm afraid. I regret to inform you that your father, Duke Julianus is dead."

Ambrosius stood and stared at the man in silence, the only reaction was a flexing of a jaw muscle in his cheek. "Who now rules Caer Cadwy?" he asked finally.

The rider shook his head. "I do not know, my lord," he paused before continuing. "The King demands your presence tomorrow. We must leave at first light."

Ambrosius nodded in response. "Thank you comrade," he said. "We have room in our barracks for you to stay. I'll have someone fetch you some warm soup."

The riders thanked him and followed one of the sentries to the barracks, leaving Ambrosius staring blankly into the cold night sky. I walked over to him and placed a compassionate hand on his shoulder.

"My father is gone," he muttered flatly. "What becomes of us now?"

"You become the ruler of Durotrigia and Caer Cadwy," I replied.

Ambrosius shook his head. "I'm not ready to rule. How do I follow in my father's footsteps? He was a great general, a ruler of men, a seasoned veteran of many battles. I do not even have the blood of kings in my veins."

"No, but you have something better. You have the blood of Roman emperors within your veins. You have Geraint, Varius and I who will aid you to the bitter end. When the time comes, you will rise to the occasion Ambrosius. You will become a leader of men, a great leader."

Ambrosius turned and gave me a bitter smile. "I wish I had your confidence in my abilities, Fergus."

The next morning the sky was a flat grey and the ground was thick with virgin snow as we saddled up and rode out through the gate, away from the old Roman fort for good. Varius saluted us as we left with the three Votadini warriors and Ambrosius turned in his saddle to face the old veteran. "Tell the men, Varius. We may be going home very soon."

The old bull grinned, showing a mouth that was missing teeth and I realised what a rare sight it was to see him smile with genuine happiness.

We rode most of the day through a bleak white landscape until we finally saw the great black outcrop of rock in the distance next to the dark watered loch, winding our way up a narrow path where a couple of men could hold an entire warband at bay until we came to the large oak gates of Din Eidyn.

Ambrosius, Geraint and I were led into the King's hall, where he sat on a throne of carved stone between two blazing fire pits. King Cadlew wore a thick cloak of deep blue chased with gold thread and a golden crown on his wide brow. Ambrosius knelt before him and we did the same, removing our helmets and holding them under our arms.

"Arise, Lord Ambrosius," the King said. "You have served me well and I think your father would have been proud of the man you have become."

He paused momentarily before continuing. "I am sorry for your loss. Julianus was a great man and without him, Vortigern's lust for power and domination will go unchecked. You are the only one who can rightfully take his place as ruler of

Durotrigia and lord of Caer Cadwy. Therefore, I release you from my service. Go forth with my blessing, Ambrosius son of Julianus."

We stood as one before the king of the Votadini. "Is there any other news from my homeland, Lord King?" Ambrosius asked.

The King rose from his throne with a grunt and walked over to Ambrosius, placing an arm around his shoulder. "Walk with me a while and we shall talk."

The King escorted Ambrosius through the great doors of his hall and out into the frigid afternoon air, followed by Geraint and I and two of his own personal guard to stroll around the grounds of Din Eidyn.

"I am told that a terrible plague swept through Dumnonia and Durotrigia, killing many," the King said, breathing onto his hands and rubbing them for warmth. "But your father did not die of the plague. I've been informed that he was invited to a peace conference in Caer Baddon, to discuss terms for getting his son back. However it would seem that he was betrayed and murdered during the conference. I do not know all of the details, suffice to say that King Vortigern was behind it."

Ambrosius looked down at the ground, his jaw clenching with suppressed anger, his gauntleted fist closing tightly around the hilt of Octha's Ruin.

"Who now rules Durotrigia?" he asked, his voice strained with emotion.

"The western Battle Duke, Gorlois now rules Durotrigia, with the blessing of King Erbin though from what I hear, whoever holds Erbin's strings is the true ruler."

I noticed Ambrosius' lip curl with hatred. "Was there any news of anyone else?" Ambrosius asked hopefully. I knew he was concerned for the wellbeing of my sister, Ygerna as was I.

The King shook his head with a grim expression. "I suggest you speak to the bard, Oengus. It is he who brought me the news. Feel free to stay in Din Eidyn as long as you wish, as my guest."

Ambrosius gave a slight bow. "You are too kind, Lord King, though my men are eager to return home. We will stay tonight and enjoy your hospitality and leave for home in the morning."

"Whatever you wish. Though I have something for you before you leave," King Cadlew gestured towards a low roofed shack with an open front where a thickset blacksmith hammered away at a white hot length of iron with a heavy hammer. He looked up as the king approached, his bearded face streaked with soot and sheened with perspiration, immediately dropping to one knee when he saw his liege.

King Cadlew waved impatiently at the man to get to his feet. "Wynfar has something for you, in gratitude for your service."

The smith moved quickly to a shelf at the back of his workshop and produced three bundles of oil soaked rags, handing them reverently to his King with a bow. King Cadlew handed one to each of us and we unwrapped them carefully.

They were three seaxes, slender, single bladed knives, longer than a dagger though shorter than a sword, the blades being as long as a man's forearm in scabbards of finely worked red leather that bore the curious, swirling patterns peculiar to the Votadini and Cruithne. The blades were flawless and razor sharp, the hilt bound with calfskin. Ambrosius' was more ornate, with emeralds set in the pommel. We thanked the King profusely for the gifts.

He grunted in reply and took my seax, turning it in his hand so that the flawless blade reflected the weak winter daylight. "Never underestimate the usefulness of the seax in the shieldwall. Swords are too cumbersome, but these," he mimed an overhand thrust on me. "These can mean the difference between life and death. It's why the Saxons use them. Lethal in close combat. Remember that."

He handed the seax back to me hilt first.

"Lord King, before we go I would like to speak with the bard, Oengus." I said.

King Cadlew shrugged. "He'll be entertaining in my hall tonight if he's sober enough."

As we wandered back to the King's hall, I drew the seax halfway from its decorative scabbard and marvelled at the perfection of the blade and somewhere I heard the harsh cry of a raven.

That evening, as we sat drinking in the King's hall before a roaring hearth fire, I put forth my plan to Ambrosius.

"I mean to find and kill Fiachu mac Niall and rescue Nivian. Oengus can help me do that."

I could see that Ambrosius was not keen on my plan. "Tomorrow I must leave for Caer Cadwy to find Ygerna and to muster men still loyal to my father," he said. "For all I know, she could have perished in the plague as well. I need to find out if she is safe or not. Besides, to go after Fiachu mac Niall alone would be suicide. I cannot allow it, Fergus. You are sworn to my service and I will need you now more than ever."

I fought to keep a lid on my anger. "My lord, I have to do this," I said, using his formal title. "I'll be back with you in Caer Cadwy within the month. Besides, you have Geraint to protect you."

We both looked over at Geraint who was reeling drunk and fondling a plump serving girl on his knee. He looked up at us bleary eyed. "What?" he slurred. Ambrosius shook his head in despair. Geraint shrugged and went back to burying his face in the girl's ample bosom. "Geraint is like a savage dog who only listens to you," Ambrosius said. "I'm not sure he even likes me."

"Believe me, you'd know it if he didn't," I said and Ambrosius grinned, knowing I spoke the truth.

Oengus, who had been regaling the Votadini with the exploits of Cuchulainn, the warrior hero of my people whilst strumming his lyre, concluded his tale to much uproarious applause and was given a large pitcher of spiced ale. I caught his eye and beckoned him over and the little man swaggered to our corner of the hall. I greeted him warmly and introduced him to Ambrosius.

He sat next to him, opposite me and placed his leather pitcher on the stained oak table.

"I have news about our mutual friend," he said in slurred, hushed tones as he leaned towards me. I reeled back from the fumes of stale ale on his breath. "He has returned from Eire, having successfully fought his brother's enemies. Loegaire, his brother, has rewarded him with more men, so now he has a force to be reckoned with. His retinue has expanded from a warband to a small army made up of Cruithne and Masraighe and other Gaels who have joined his cause. Soon, with the coming of spring, he will be on the move again and I hear he'll be heading south, to fight Vortigern's enemies." He glanced significantly at Ambrosius.

"If he were to die, would the army still hold?" Ambrosius asked.

Oengus smirked and took a gulp of ale. "Fiachu mac Niall may be a brutal, merciless son of a whore, but he is charismatic and generous to his followers. His men would crawl naked through a pit of hot coals for him, though if he were to die, his army would more than likely melt away like snow in the summer." Ambrosius sighed thoughtfully and tapped the stained oak table with his fingertips. "I cannot go with you, Fergus. I have to find out what has happened to Ygerna. I have to take my men home and I have to pick up the pieces of what remains of my father's legacy. But I fear that if I allow you to go, we will never meet again in this world. I have no wish to let Fiachu mac Niall live, but I do not want to let you go to your certain death either."

"With all due respect my lord, I am a fully grown man capable of following my own destiny," I said, my patience wearing thin. "I will serve you unto death, but all I ask is that I be allowed to avenge the death of my father and my brother and all the others of my clan who perished at the hands of this man."

Ambrosius finally relented. He turned to Oengus. "Are you sure you can get near Fiachu mac Niall without arousing suspicion?"

The bard winked and raised his pitcher of ale. "I can get closer to him than his own mother could, Lord. Soon it will be Imbolc and Fiachu and his men will be in need of entertainment for their feast."

"Very well. Take Geraint with you. You will need him more than I will. And if you succeed, return with all haste to Caer Cadwy."

I smiled and nodded. "Don't worry, my Lord. I intend to return and when I do I will be carrying Fiachu mac Niall's head." I turned back to the bard. "What news of Uther?"

Oengus leaned forwards and lowered his voice. "From what I have gathered, he is being held hostage by King Vortigern in his great tower, Dinas Ffaraon, somewhere in the realm of Gwynedd. The tower is solid stone, huge and impregnable. King Vortigern sits there like a great grey spider in his web, directing his sons, Vortimer, Catigern and Pascent to fight his battles and to do his bidding. Ever since his Saxon mercenaries rebelled against him, he has holed himself up within his tower, growing ever more distrustful and paranoid, believing that everyone is conspiring against him. If you ask me, he is losing his grip on his kingdoms as well as losing his mind."

I glanced significantly at Ambrosius whose brow was furrowed in thought. "I will return home, raise an army and march upon Vortigern's tower. I will rescue Uther. I owe that much to my father."

I looked at Ambrosius as though he had lost his mind. "You will march into Vortigern's lands and rescue Uther from an impregnable stronghold? My lord, that would be nothing short of suicide."

Ambrosius folded his arms and glared back at me stubbornly. "No more suicidal than your mission to kill Fiachu mac Niall. My father's men were the finest warriors in Britannia and they will rally to my banner."

"What of Gorlois?" I asked. "Do you really think he will relinquish his hold upon Caer Cadwy when you return? Do you think that he will meekly creep back to Din Tagel and hand you back the kingdom of Durotrigia?"

Ambrosius raised his head, his mouth fixed in its characteristic grim scowl. "I shall deal with Gorlois first, however is necessary. As I said before, my father's men will flock to my banner, not his. I have no doubts that Gorlois was behind the murder of my father, just as he had paid Octha for my head. He will pay for his treachery with his life."

I nodded slowly as I stared down at my leather pitcher of ale. Ambrosius' mind was made up, his will set upon this course of action and there was nothing anyone could do to dissuade him.

The next morning was cold, but the sky was clear and we rode out from Din Eidyn with the blessing of King Cadlew. Oengus was with us and he had with him Brida, the Cruithne girl whom I had captured during our first raid with the Votadini over a year and a half ago. She had grown and filled out considerably and was not unattractive, her dark hair now hung in braids decorated with beads of coloured glass and she wore a knee length woollen tunic over a pair of leather trews and a chequered cloak with a slender knife at her waist, but when she saw me her dark brown eyes flashed with hatred.

"Is she coming with us?" I asked, nodding towards the girl.

Oengus nodded. "Of course. Brida has proved a most loyal travelling companion. I have been teaching her the ways of the bard and she is learning quickly. She likes her new life, despite what you may think."

I looked at the girl doubtfully. "I hope she can be trusted."

King Cadlew had sent a couple of riders with us as an escort and by midday we had met up with Varius and our remaining comrades. King Cadlew had provided them with horses to take them to the border of Guotodin and Strathclyde to the south.

I looked at our men and realised how much they had all changed. All were now seasoned warriors and it showed in the grim expression on their faces and the hardness in their eyes. Many wore furs over their leather armour, or thick Votadini cloaks with their distinctive chequered patterns. Many of them now carried short Votadini spears and a few had the small square shields used by the northerners and Cruithne alike.

Varius brought the men to a halt and saluted Ambrosius. With the death of Julianus, Varius was now under the command of Ambrosius and I had no doubt that this hard bitten, stout warrior would prove as loyal to Julianus' son as he had been towards the Duke himself.

"The men are pleased to be going home, lord," he said. "Though what we are returning to is anyone's guess."

"Indeed, Varius. We must be prepared for any eventuality," Ambrosius replied. He turned to face me in his saddle. "This is where our paths diverge my friend."

I clasped his forearm with my right hand in the Roman style of greeting and farewell.

"Give my love to Ygerna. Tell her I will be back with the first shoots of spring."

Ambrosius nodded. "May God be with you, brother."

"Which route will you take home?" I asked.

Ambrosius stared up with eyes that matched the colour of the sky. "We will travel south until we pick up the old Roman road that will take us to the city of Eboracum. From there, we will go south through Rheged where we will get a boat back to Dumnonia."

"That will take you dangerously close to Vortigern's territory," I said.

"That is a risk we will have to take. King Ceneu of Rheged bends his knee to Vortigern, though he bears no love for him. I think we will be granted safe passage through his lands."

"I hope you are right my lord," I said, feeling the chill of the northern winter seeping into my fingers through my leather gauntlets.

Ambrosius looked at me for a moment with pale blue eyes that had the look of one who had seen too much and had now become immunized to suffering and hardship and again I found myself thinking how much he had changed.

Ambrosius reached down to his thick belt and unstrapped the Saxon sword at his side. "I want you to take this," he said, handing Octha's Ruin over to me hilt first. "It deserves an owner who can wield it properly. Please take it."

Tentatively I took Octha's Ruin from his grasp, not knowing what to say. I drew it from its scabbard, feeling how finely balanced it felt in my hand and marvelling at the twisting pattern that snaked up the razor sharp blade.

"Thank you my lord," I said humbly, turning the blade in my hand and watching how the weak sunlight seemed to dance across its polished surface. The hilt was bound with shark skin that seemed to cling to the palm and the cross guard was decorated with intertwined golden dragons and serpents. Whoever had forged this blade was both an artisan and a skilled blacksmith as I had never seen its like before.

Ambrosius trotted over to Geraint and patted him on the shoulder and the stocky Powysian acknowledged him with a respectful nod. "Look after yourself, lord," he said. "And don't worry about him. I'll make sure he gets back safely."

Ambrosius smiled and turned his steed around, riding back to Varius and the waiting men. One of the men gave a single blast on his war horn and the soldiers moved as one, riding south over the snow covered land. We watched in silence as they crested a white hill and Ambrosius turned in his saddle and raised his hand in salute for a moment before disappearing over the hill's summit.

I looked northwards, towards the bleak hills where we would soon be travelling. Not far beyond those hills were the lands of the Cruithne and I felt a knot of apprehension in my stomach at the thought of travelling through these lands. Beyond the Great Forest of Celidon were the highlands, a wild, rugged area of rocky hills, lakes and mountains, a cruel and hard place which had given birth to the Cruithne people and shaped their character. It was no accident that these people had remained unconquered by the Romans. Only the hardiest of folk could possibly survive in such an unforgiving place.

"So this is it then," Geraint said at my side. "What's the plan?"

I shrugged with uncertainty. "We find Fiachu and kill him and rescue Nivian. I'll work on the details along the way."

"Ingenious," Geraint said drily. "Bet it took a long time to come up with that one."

Oengus was speaking quietly with Brida and then looked up. "Brida can guide us safely through the Great Forest," he said. "Though we may have to make you two look more Pictish."

That would not prove too difficult. We already wore the chequered woollen cloaks favoured by both Pict and Votadini and were now carrying the small square shields and short spears of the northern clans. The only thing we lacked were the tribal markings on our skin that every Pict wore.

We rode northwards until by mid-afternoon we came to the banks of a long, narrow loch and Oengus insisted we stop. The sun was already beginning to dip below the hills to the west and the air had become bitterly cold. Brida collected firewood from a nearby copse of pine trees and soon had a fire going while Oengus collected water from the loch in a small iron pot and produced some dried leaves from a leather pouch, tearing them into shreds and sprinkling them into the boiling water. Soon we were all huddled around the fire drawing our cloaks tighter around us in an attempt to keep out the biting cold whilst watching Oengus take the boiled leaves and transfer them into a small clay bowl which he then started to mash with a stone pestle until they had been reduced to a blue paste. He then handed the bowl to Brida and muttered something to her. The girl took the bowl and sat cross legged in front of me and I could feel the antipathy radiating from her.

She placed a finger into the bowl and scooped out a blob of blue paste, lifting it to my face. I flinched back involuntarily and she slapped me hard with her left hand. "Be still," she snapped.

Oengus chuckled at my startled reaction as he opened a skin of ale. "Let her do what she must. Don't worry, it's only woad. It's what her people use to paint themselves with. Of course, it would be better if we could do it with a needle, but I very much doubt that you would want to look like a Pict for the rest of your days," He laughed to himself and lifted the goatskin full of ale to his lips.

Brida began to croon softly as she worked, using her delicate fingers to trace spirals and dots of blue over my face.

"Why do you people do this? Paint yourself with woad I mean."

Brida looked up at me, her dark eyes wide and glittering with dislike. For a while she did not answer but carried on with what she was doing. I wondered whether she had understood me and then she muttered quietly. "We paint ourselves so that the gods notice us. Woad holds the essence of the Earth Goddess within it and protects us from harm," she looked at me accusingly. "At least, that is what I used to believe."

I felt a pang of guilt and wondered whether the girl felt the same about me as I felt about Fiachu mac Niall. She continued her work in silence, moving on to Geraint when she had finished.

Oengus laughed at my painted face. "That's much better, though I fear you're a little too tall and a little too pale to pass as a true Cruithne. Geraint here is far more convincing. He has the same swarthy look, short, brutal and ugly..."

"Careful, bard," Geraint warned. "Or I'll make myself look even more convincing by adding your head to my belt."

Oengus laughed heartily and tossed the ale skin to Geraint who caught it and grinned reluctantly as he removed the stopper and drank from it.

Oengus stood with a grunt and walked over to his horse, producing furs and woollen blankets from his saddle bags and tossed them to us. "We must try to get some sleep, we have a long and arduous journey ahead of us tomorrow." He then produced his lyre from its sheepskin bag and began to strum it gently as we stared into the flickering, dancing flames of our fire. As warmth began to return to my body, I grew drowsy. All of my apprehensions about the future drifted away as Oengus sang a song of doomed love between a mortal man and a shee maiden in my native Gaelic and I soon found myself lulled into sleep by the haunting ballad and the bard's gentle, melodious voice.

That evening I dreamed of Carnun, the Horned God. A rustling sound, like the noise made by an animal passing through undergrowth caused me to look up. The moon was high in the sky, making the snow glow a ghostly white and causing the frost on the pines to dance with tiny speckles of light. Our fire had died down to a deep red glow and I was aware of my three companions huddled in furs around me, deep in sleep.

I looked up at the tree line and there he stood, bathed in shadow, taller by half than any mortal man with huge, sweeping antlers that jutted out from either side of his head, his hunting spear held before him.

I froze, transfixed by the green glow of his eyes that gazed upon me impassively, like twin stars against a black void. I felt my breath catch in my chest and my hands begin to tremble with fright and then the Otherwordly phantom turned and strode silently into the blackness of the forest with great, silent strides.

Without knowing why, I rose to my feet and followed, my mind screaming for me to turn and go back, but my body seemed to be under the control of another. I walked through the dark forest of frosted pine trees, glimpsing the cold light of the moon between the tangle of their branches, aware that the Horned One was not far ahead of me.

The forest floor eventually sloped down to a fast flowing river. I looked around, but could not see the Horned One anywhere, but it was then that I heard a woman singing softly. A shaft of moonlight shone down upon a tattered looking figure hunched at the riverside, busily washing something and as I approached I saw that it was a woman, washing a coat of bloody mail in the freezing waters of the river. As she heard my approach she looked up and to my astonishment I saw that it was Old Mother Argoel from the Coedwig Dyn Bannog, the Forest of the Horned One near Penglyn.

"Danger lies ahead," she muttered, her voice croaking and ancient. She looked older than I remembered, if that was even possible, her eyes more sunken, her long grey hair even thinner, her face almost skeletal. For one terrifying moment, her face became that of Sinusa, the Masraighe priestess, but then changed again as a cloud passed the moon and I realised with a chill that I was in the presence of Macha, the Maiden of Death.

"Whose armour is that?" I asked, watching as she scrubbed at the gore encrusted links of iron.

"Maybe yours, maybe the son of Niall's," she said enigmatically. "Between you both you have been keeping me very busy." She pointed a gnarled finger to the opposite bank of the river.

Dozens of people swathed in shadow stood on the other side watching me in complete silence and I wondered how I had not seen them before. As I looked back at them, I saw that they all bore some kind of mortal wound, some with deep red slashes across face or abdomen, some missing limbs.

"Who are they?" I whispered.

"Look closer," the old woman said harshly. "Do you not know?"

I looked again and realised who they were. There were Picts, Gaels, Britons and Saxons, mostly men, but also some women and children, all staring at me with awful dead eyes, silently accusing me of what I had done, their dark red wounds glistening in the moonlight. I saw several faces I knew from the past, deathly pale, blood spattered but recognisable nonetheless. I saw Eber, the first boy I had killed back in Caer Dor many years ago, a great gaping wound in his neck, loops of glistening intestine hanging from the gash in his belly. I saw the harsh faced Brithru, champion of Eamonn o' Suilleabhain, lord of the Eoganachta, his mail shirt punctured by a bloody wound in his abdomen and behind him was Corryn, wearing a blood stained monks habit, his face and body covered with deep cuts, glaring at me hatefully. Near the front of the group was the Pictish woman and her child who I had killed during our first raid with the Votadini. The top of her head had been sheared off and I could see the moist glint of gore and brain in amongst her matted hair as she and her son stared at me with dead, accusatory eyes.

I could feel their anger and despair engulf me like a black tide and I turned away, unable to look any further, trembling and sobbing for breath.

"They wait for you on the other side," Macha said. "All those whose lives you have ended prematurely and those whom you are responsible for either directly or indirectly."

"Why do you show me this?" I stammered, feeling the strength draining from my legs.

"Whether or not you join them is down to you." She reached into the river and pulled out three flat stones which she lay before me. Each had a symbol carved upon its surface. One bore a triple spiral, one the Chi Rho rune of Christ and the third bore a symbol that I took to be a sword.

"Which path will you choose, Tuan?"

I reached out and instinctively picked up the triple spiral and Macha rocked back and forth on her heels. "The Old Gods," she muttered. "Just as I thought. But beware, Tuan. We are the playthings of the gods. They rejoice in our happiness but they also betray us and laugh at our tears. It is all the same thing to them. Seek out this symbol and you will find aid, but it will come at a price."

I looked down at the stone in my hand, worn smooth by countless years of water running over its surface and felt a warmth radiating from it. The interlocking triple spiral began to glow a deep blue and started to throb in my hand and then I felt as though I were falling backwards.

I awoke with a start, lying curled around the remains of the fire, still bundled in thick furs. Brida looked up with a gasp at my violent awakening. She had been gathering sticks and had built a small pyramid over the embers of the previous evening's fire which collapsed as she jumped back startled.

She regained her composure and curled her lip into a sneer. She said something in Pictish to Oengus who was nearby, stroking the muzzle of his horse. He gave a terse reply before addressing me with a grin. "Did you sleep well?"

I shook my head. My body ached all over and my joints were stiff with the cold that had penetrated through the furs. Geraint coughed violently and spat a great gob of phlegm to one side, cursing quietly. The sky had clouded over again and tiny, wisp like flakes of snow fell gently.

When Brida had the fire going she boiled a handful of oats in water and added a pinch of salt and we ate a meagre meal of porridge before striking camp and preparing to leave.

"We must move on now," Oengus said, his breath rising in a great cloud around him as he rose to his feet. "We have a long journey ahead of us."

Geraint stood with a grunt and trampled over the remains of the fire, kicking the ashes into the snow. He reached down and gave me his hand to help me up and as I stood, I felt something hard roll from the confines of my cloak. Looking down I saw a smooth, palm sized pebble which I picked up. Turning it over in my hand, I saw that one side was deeply engraved with a symbol that caused my heart to jump. It was an interconnected triple spiral

Chapter 13

In the Lands of the Cruithne

By mid-morning we had reached the great forest of Celidon, following a well-worn deer path that took us deep amongst the towering evergreens, each step taking us further into wild Cruithne territory. We rode in silence, following Brida who stayed a short distance ahead, jumping at the slightest rustle of a branch or the sudden flapping of a bird's wings. My hand rested uneasily upon the hilt of Octha's Ruin and I noticed that Geraint was the same, the tension in his posture was obvious.

The forest showed few signs of human habitation, but occasionally we would encounter signs that others had been or were still present. We passed a few stones, no more than knee high, covered with moss and lichen, but bearing strange symbols interlaced with crude pictures of people and animals. Soon we found a small pond around which a number of clay pots and bowls of grain and berries had been laid. The branches of the surrounding trees were hung with small scraps of cloth and strings of bird bones.

"What's this?" Geraint whispered as he rode up next to the Pict girl.

Brida turned her narrow, painted face towards him, her eyes cold. "Offerings to the spirits of the forest. They watch our every move, just as they watched you when you destroyed my village." she yanked on her horse's reins and rode away.

I had the uneasy feeling again that malevolent eyes were watching me from the deep green shadows, but put the sensation to the back of my mind and told myself there was no point in fretting over the unknown when there were so many other physical dangers to face.

As we rode on, the forest became denser and more tangled, the path barely discernible amongst the twisted roots that reached up through the sparse layer of snow that had managed to settle on the forest floor. The feeling of being watched intensified the further we went and Geraint stopped suddenly once or twice with his hand raised to silence us, his face intense as he strained to hear some distant sound.

"What is it?" I whispered.

He shook his head. "Not sure. I thought I could hear movement over there," he nodded discreetly to his left. "I think we're being stalked."

Oengus nodded in agreement as he came closer, his eyes wide with fear. "I think you may be right. I say we keep moving, pretend we haven't noticed."

Geraint and I both muttered our agreement and we moved on, watching for the slightest movement.

Geraint came up beside me and leaned over in his saddle. "How do we know your little Pict isn't leading us into a trap?"

"We don't. But I think Oengus can be trusted and she seems to like him, so I doubt she'll betray him."

Geraint gave a derisive snort. "You forget one thing. She's a Pict and we destroyed her village and probably killed her family as well. These people cannot be trusted at the best of times. They have no sense of honour or loyalty, we know that first hand. This is a mistake, Fergus. We're riding to our deaths."

"This is my choice, Geraint. I never asked you to come with me. Perhaps you should have stayed with Ambrosius."

Geraint shook his head in frustration. "If you're going to get yourself killed, I want to be around to smash a few heads before you go to your grave my friend."

I laughed despite myself at Geraint's sheer pig headed stubbornness.

"What's funny?" he asked, with an offended look.

"If ever I reach a ripe old age and I have land and a hall of my own, I shall sit before my hearth fire and I shall have a loyal hound curled at my feet and that hound's name will be Geraint, in honour of you, my friend."

The stocky Powysian failed to see the funny side. He snorted derisively. "You'll never live that long."

We followed the course of a rapidly flowing river upstream. The ground was rising steadily, becoming more rocky and uneven as we progressed.

A movement amongst the trees caught my eye, quick and furtive and I pulled back on my horse's reins, scanning the treeline.

"They're over there as well," Geraint said, looking in the opposite direction. He had drawn his sword halfway from his scabbard, but I placed a hand on his arm to still his movement.

"We must keep moving," Oengus said with desperation in his voice. "They're trying to surround us."

"He's right," Geraint agreed. "We must ride with all speed to outmanoeuvre them."

We kicked our heels into the flanks of our mounts and spurred them onwards into a gallop. Suddenly the forest around us erupted into a cacophony of animal noises, hoots and whistles. Our hunters no longer made any attempt to hide their movements and I could now see pale figures amongst the trees, sprinting through the woods trying to keep up with us.

Brida was up ahead, but we were catching up with her. Without warning, her horse reared up and she toppled off of it backwards, landing awkwardly. As I drew closer, I saw the length of twine strung between two trees that had caused her to fall from her steed. I reached down to help her to her feet and saw that she was in obvious pain and clutching her left shoulder. At that moment, a number of men came swinging down from the trees, their pale bodies painted with the tribal patterns of the Cruithne.

I shouted a warning to Oengus and Geraint and drew Octha's Ruin from its scabbard, pulling the girl away with my other hand.

The Cruithne began to fan out cautiously, their dark eyes fixed on me intently as they moved with spears and axes held ready. Geraint came up beside me, sword and shield in hand, shouting challenges to the Picts who were now surrounding us. More were coming up, sprinting through the woods to join their comrades for the kill, whooping and howling as they came. Oengus was muttering prayers to Danu and Lugh as dozens of Picts appeared as if from nowhere.

One of them made a lunge for Geraint's horse with his spear, but the Powysian blocked the thrust with his sword and swung the blade backhanded across his assailant's throat in a movement so quick, I had not realised what had happened until the Pict fell back squirting blood from his severed arteries. Another took advantage of the situation and charged forwards, but Geraint split his skull down to the jaw before he could even get close.

"Come on, you painted sons of bitches," he yelled, holding his gore spattered blade aloft. "Come and taste Powysian steel!"

The other Cruithne were more cautious, though they kept their eyes fixed on Geraint's every move.

"You should have gone with Ambrosius like I said," I muttered to Geraint as the Cruithne began to close their ranks, stopping any chance of escape. There was no way that we could charge through them as we did not have enough room to build up any momentum and our horses would be impaled by their short spears even before we were.

"I wasn't going to leave you to die alone, Irishman," Geraint replied, wheeling his horse around, his blade held ready to strike. "This whole thing was a stupid idea, but if we die, we die fighting. Together."

"We could just surrender," Oengus offered hopefully. "I am not a fighter. My skills lie in word and song, not smashing skulls."

"Well, you can't sing your way out of this one, bard," Geraint replied sarcastically.

"Surrender is not an option, Oengus," I said grimly. "We have seen what these people do to captives. You could not imagine in your worst nightmares the suffering that you will endure at their hands. It is better we die sword in hand." Oengus ignored me and shouted a few sentences in Pictish, but was greeted with jeers and aggressive shouts. Our horses whinnied nervously and became skittish as though sensing our fear and I struggled to control my mount as it twisted around and started moving sideways.

Brida screamed as one of the Picts lunged forwards and grabbed her, pulling her back into their ranks by her hair. I moved forwards to try and save her, but my horse reared up with a cry as it tried to avoid a half dozen spear points thrust in our direction.

The stone bearing the triple spiral rolled out of the pouch on my belt and landed face up before the Picts.

One of them yelled out to the others, stooping down to retrieve the stone and then held it up for all to see.

Silence descended upon the Cruithne as all eyes were fixed upon the stone. One of them sounded a hunting horn several times, its brash tone reverberating amongst the frozen trees.

"What's going on?" Geraint whispered.

I shook my head, as puzzled as he was, still expecting the Picts to attack at any moment.

The Cruithne ranks began to part as a single tall figure strode towards us, carrying a long staff and wearing a headdress of antlers over hooded green robes. As he passed, they bowed their heads respectfully, some even dropping to one knee before the mysterious figure. He stopped next to the Pict holding the stone and exchanged a few words with him before raising his voice to address the others in terse, monosyllabic tones.

Immediately, all spears were withdrawn and the tall man in the headdress strode forwards, pulling back his hood with one hand and regarding us with eyes of pale blue.

Although his face was painted with the swirls and patterns of the Picts, the long, bony profile, the tawny beard and the huge beak nose were immediately identifiable.

"Myrddin," I cried in disbelief.

The druid looked at me with a thin smile, inspecting me from top to toe. "Our paths have been brought together yet again. I have been expecting you, Fergus mac Fiontan."

The fire from the small central fire pit gave a welcome warmth in the cramped, dimly lit stone house. It reminded me of Old Mother Argoel's home, cluttered with all kinds of objects; skulls and bones, both animal and human crowded shelves that also held clay bowls and small glass bottles. Shrunken heads preserved in cedar oil hung from the rafters, their sightless, empty eye sockets and mouths sewn shut so that their spirits could not escape, as well as various charms and herbs that all added to the curious odour of the place. We huddled around the glowing fire as a slender Pict girl, a servant of Myrddin's, silently ladled stew into wooden bowls and handed them around to us along with a chunk of hard black bread. Outside came the steady beat of drums and singing as the Cruithne danced around a huge bonfire that had been lit especially for the coming of Imbolc and which now burned in the centre of the small hamlet of turf roofed stone hovels. Already the light was beginning to fail and I was only too glad that I did not have to spend another night outside.

Myrddin came over and joined us, sitting on one of the upturned logs that acted as stools around the fire, accepting a bowl of stew from the girl without a word. He had reset Brida's dislocated shoulder, smearing it with a paste made from comfrey leaves, which the folk of Penglyn used to call knitbone and then he gave her a herbal concoction of willow bark and henbane for the pain and the girl lay drowsily on a pile of furs nearby. As we ate Myrddin stared at me with a half-smile that made me feel a little uneasy. "So what brings you this far north Fergus mac Fiontan? Is it the desire for vengeance or love or maybe both?"

"You know the answer to that so why ask?" I replied a little sourly. "I could ask you the same question. What are you doing here amongst these animals?"

"The Cruithne are some of the few peoples left in these islands who still honour the Old Gods and the Old Ways," the druid replied defensively. "They may seem cruel and harsh to outsiders, but I feel at home amongst them. After your monk friend ran off with Bran's cauldron, I searched high and low to find it, but it is hidden from me. My travels eventually brought me here and this is where I've remained ever since. The Cruithne are what the people of these islands used to be, before the coming of Rome. They are hardy, resourceful, independent and they respect the land they live in and revere the spirits of wood and mountain and stream. They have not lost the connection with the land like the rest of you." He glared at us with a thinly veiled contempt.

The Pict girl who had served us our mutton broth now returned with a jug of spiced ale. She poured some into a wooden bowl and handed it to me with the hint of a shy smile on her face. She was a little younger than me, with tanned skin, long, slender legs and large dark eyes that stared out of a well formed, narrow face, which, like Brida's was painted with swirls of tiny blue dots. She was topless and I found my eyes drifting towards her pert, painted breasts as she leaned forwards to give me the drink. I felt my pulse quicken at her proximity and the earthy perfume of her body, but forced myself to turn to Myrddin. The druid was suppressing a smirk, as though he knew exactly what had been going through my mind.

"You promised me you would help me find Nivian and Fiachu mac Niall, but you never kept your side of the bargain," I said accusingly.

"You promised me the Chalice and you lost it," Myrddin retorted with an icy stare. "Your clumsy attempt to acquire it brought doom to the last of the druids and now a great plague ravages the land as you have angered both the Old Gods and the new. You allowed your half-witted monk friend to vanish with one of the great treasures of Prydein, an artefact that could have restored us to our former glory and now you expect me to help you?"

I felt anger begin to rise within me and I placed my bowl of spiced ale aside, spilling some of it as I did so. "You were the one who unleashed the plague upon Abbott Neirin and Lord Glaesten, not me. I did exactly what you asked in the knowledge that you would help. If you don't want to help me, that's fine. I piss on you and your gods." I pulled at the bronze triple spiral necklace that I wore, snapping it free of its rawhide cord and threw it at the druid's feet.

Myrddin calmly reached down and picked up the bronze emblem, turning it over in his bony fingers. A curious expression crossed his face as he examined the trinket and for a moment he seemed lost in deep thought. "I did not say that I wouldn't help you," he said slowly, as if talking to a child. "I asked why I should. And quite rightly, you pointed out that I gave my word. And the word of a druid is all important. We alone know the true power of words, is that not right Oengus?"

The little bard started as though woken from a sleep. "Oh...yes, definitely. Words hold great power, in speech, curses, songs and incantations. The power of the word is far greater than the power of the sword." Oengus gave me a sideways look and dropped his gaze towards the fire.

Myrddin nodded and smiled his thin smile. "The gods have brought us together again for a purpose, Fergus. I know that, for I have foreseen it. I will offer you whatever aid you require to find Nivian, though I have foreseen something more troubling."

"What is that?" I asked.

Myrddin leaned forwards, his thin face lit eerily by the flickering orange glow of the fire. "Uther must be the one to unite the Britons. If he dies without an heir, Britannia will surely fall. Vortigern is losing his grip on power. Each day that passes, it slips further from his grasp and he knows it. He also knows of the prophecy that a son of the House of Constantine shall one day become High King. He has been told this by Sinusa, the Masraighe sorceress. This places Uther and his half-brother Ambrosius in great danger, especially now that Duke Julianus is dead. Vortigern now has nothing to fear and as we speak, his agents scour the land looking for Ambrosius. He plans to have both of them ritually killed. He thinks that by doing this, he will ensure his unrivalled claim to the throne, but he is wrong. His kingdoms will fragment and the land will fall to the invader and all will be lost. But the son of Julianus is riding into a trap. Two people will betray him and this will lead to his downfall."

I stared into the flickering flames unsure as to what to do. My mind told me that I should seek Ambrosius and warn him as not only was he my friend, he was also my liege lord and I had sworn to defend him with my life, but my heart told me to seek out and slay Fiachu mac Niall and to rescue Nivian.

"What should I do?" I said quietly.

"That is for you to decide," Myrddin said. "It is time that you and I went on a journey."

"A journey where?"

"Into the realm that exists between the worlds. You have travelled there before, so I need not warn you of the perils we may face. There you may find the answers that you seek."

I nodded with acceptance. "What must I do to enter this realm?"

"Tuela will prepare a concoction that will help to loosen your spirit from its earthly shackles. Stay with me and do not stray from my side." The druid turned to the Pict girl and muttered something to her. She nodded and turned away into the shadows near the far wall and began to take various clay bowls down from a shelf which she emptied into a larger stone vessel.

"Fiachu is protected by powerful magic," Myrddin said, drawing my attention back to him. "The sorceress Sinusa draws upon the power of her dark god. She has been guiding the son of Niall through omens and portents, advising him when and where he should fight his battles, telling him what moves his enemies were making before they actually made them. She probably knows already that you are on your way to kill him."

"Is there anything we can do?" I asked.

Myrddin looked down at his long hands thoughtfully. "I can make us invisible to her second sight and disguise our true intentions for a short while. But the Crooked

One is powerful and grows stronger each day with every innocent soul that is fed to him. In return, he grants part of that power to his vassals in this world, namely Sinusa and her dark druids. I seek guidance and aid from the Old Gods, but I fear their power in this world is waning."

Tuela returned with two bowls of green liquid and handed one to me and one to the druid. Oengus, Geraint and Brida watched in silence as we put the bowls to our lips and drained them in one gulp.

The liquid had a bitter, earthy taste and reminded me instantly of the time I had found my spirit name in the forest of Coedwig dyn Bannog many years ago. I tried hard not to gag at the vile taste, but managed to keep the foul liquid down. Tuela took the bowl gently from my grasp as Myrddin sprinkled some aromatic dried herbs onto the fire which burned brightly for a brief moment before vanishing in a puff of pungent blue smoke. He began to chant quietly in the Sacred Tongue, reaching over and taking my right hand in his left.

"Stare into the flames," he muttered between verses. "And take this for protection," he handed my bronze triple spiral back to me and I held it tightly in my hand as I gazed into the dancing flames.

Myrddin resumed his chant in time with the muffled beat of Pictish drums outside beyond the wattle door of the hut. My head began to spin and I felt as though I were being dragged towards the fire and with a jolt I felt myself falling forwards towards the glowing hot embers, but never reached them.

Suddenly I was flying, soaring over rugged white hills and rock strewn valleys in the icy grip of winter, swooping over fast flowing rivers and a great rift that tore the land in two. My senses seemed heightened, my vision and hearing far sharper than ever before. In front of me was a bird, a falcon that soared gracefully upon the cold winds and I knew that this bird was Myrddin, or rather Myrddin's spirit form. Down below I noticed a line of tiny figures trudging through the snow and as we swooped down towards them I could see that they were soldiers, swathed in thick furs and carrying spears and shields. There were around a score of them, two of which were on horseback and as we flew directly over their heads, I realised who they were. One of the figures on horseback looked up and with my enhanced vision I saw the familiar scarlet plume and the enamelled scale armour under the furs. It was Ambrosius, with Varius and the men on their arduous journey home. Further to the south I could make out another group of men on horseback, approaching Ambrosius' small force. There were perhaps three dozen of them and I saw that they were flying the seahorse banner of Gorlois, the Duke of Cerniw. As I watched, the group split, obviously meaning to intercept Ambrosius' band from two sides.

We circled them several times and I tried to shout down to Ambrosius, to warn him that he was in danger, but instead I let out a piercing shriek which caused some of the other men to look up.

The bird ahead of me let out a cry and glided northwards, away from Ambrosius and the others and I followed, reluctant to leave my lord to his uncertain fate. I turned to see the horsemen charging into the line of Ambrosius' men from both sides, catching them completely unawares and I tried desperately to fly back towards my lord but seemed to be drawn northwards against my will, as though I were trying to swim against the current of a fast flowing river. Abandoning my futile attempts to get back to Ambrosius, I followed Myrddin's spirit form and we flew over the Wall, a great ribbon of stone that cut across the white landscape as far as the eye could see in either direction, following the contours of the land, separating the realm of the Cruithne from the rest of Britannia. We glided over the Great Forest of Celidon, a huge blanket of deep, frosted green draped over the snowbound countryside and continued, ever northwards, eventually coming to the outskirts of the vast forest and traversing wild, inhospitable terrain for many leagues, over dark, fathomless lochs and great boulder fields until we came to a range of mountains, hostile and brooding beneath a veil of grey cloud.

Myrddin banked to the left and I followed, feeling the icy blast of the wind buffet against my face and body. We swooped down between the peaks of two great hulks of snow covered rock towards a stone fortress perched precariously on the side of one of the mountains. It was growing dark and the fortress was lit from within by tiny sparks of orange light. As we drew closer we could see spearmen manning the wooden palisade that surrounded the thatch roofed stone hall and a single narrow path that wound its way down the mountainside from the fortress. Myrddin swooped down and perched upon the roof of a wooden watchtower that overlooked the narrow, precipitous road and I did the same. The spearmen patrolling the palisade ignored us and Myrddin then glided over the open compound to land on the thatched roof of the stone hall, near to the smoke hole. I followed and the druid eased his small, feathery spirit form through the hole with me close behind.

We perched on a smoke blackened rafter amongst thick cobwebs within the hall, looking down upon a multitude of people below. Bands of warriors sat at several long tables eating and drinking and I noticed that they were marked with the tribal patterns of both Cruithne and Masraighe, the Gaelic Masraighe sporting the dark blue crescent around one eye. One man was striding up and down the length of the hall speaking to the others and immediately I recalled the self-assured swagger of Fiachu mac Niall. Although I could not make out what he was saying, his words were met by rapturous applause, cheering and thumping of tables from the throngs of wild looking, painted warriors.

Fiachu stepped onto a bench and leapt lithely onto one of the long tables so that all could see him, raising both hands for silence so that he could be heard by all.

I struggled to hear what was being said, as though I were listening to him speak from under water, his voice seeming muffled and indistinct.

After Fiachu had delivered his speech, the hall erupted once more and the throngs of warriors began to chant Fiachu's name over and over, their voices gradually becoming clearer to my ears. No one seemed to notice the two small falcons perched within the shadows of the rafters and I wondered whether we were visible to them at all.

An oak door near the back of the hall swung open and a group of seven dark robed figures entered, one of whom was being carried on a wooden litter.

A respectful silence fell as the curious group entered, one of them being a small girl with raven black hair and striking green eyes, no more than five or six years old, holding the hand of another who I presumed was her mother. She too had eyes of emerald green, accentuated with black kohl and the crescent marking of the Masraighe, with straight black hair that hung down to her slender waist, held back from her beautiful face by a circlet of silver. For a brief moment I did not recognise her, but then I looked closer at the wide, pale face, the pouting red lips and the magnificent, slanting green eyes and I realised that this cold, regal looking lady was Nivian. She was standing next to another person from my past whose presence sent a chill down my spine. The hairless, skull like head, the lecherous, leering expression and the hunched, carrion crow body was that of Malbach, dark druid and betrayer of my people. He was whispering something to Nivian, the way he used to whisper poison into the ear of my father and I fought the urge to swoop down and claw his eyes out.

As the group entered, Fiachu made his way over to Nivian and took her hands in his and she smiled at him as he gently kissed her on both cheeks.

The four acolytes carrying the litter laid it down on the flagstone floor and I knew immediately who the figure was hidden amongst the folds of the grey robes before she had even drawn her hood back with her wizened, skeletal hands. It was Sinusa, High Priestess of the Masraighe and the sight of her froze the blood in my veins. She looked like a corpse that had dried and withered, her white, sightless eyes had sunk deep into their orbits and what remained of her lank white hair hung in straggling wisps from her pale skull. She whispered something to Malbach, her voice hoarse and faint, her scrawny neck barely able to support the weight of her own head.

Could it possibly be that the small girl was my own daughter, the offspring of myself and Nivian? She was definitely around the right age and my mind returned to the words of Brighid, the goddess who had come to me when I had been close to death.

My mind whirled with unanswered questions, some of which I did not wish to know the answers to. Anger, grief, betrayal and confusion all assailed me at once.

I was suddenly overcome by another sensation, a feeling of malevolent dread and my eyes were drawn to the skeletal figure on the litter and it was then that I noticed that Sinusa had turned her sunken blind eyes directly towards me. Her hideous, ancient face had twisted into a mask of triumphant hatred and the sense of sheer malevolence was almost a physical presence which threatened to overwhelm me. She could see me.

Suddenly, the hall began to spin and I felt myself falling from the rafters, dropping into a thick black smoke that engulfed me completely.

For a moment, I felt weightless, suspended in the darkness and then the smoke began to clear and I found myself outside in the light of the full moon, perched atop a standing stone and looking down upon a ritual being enacted before me. About a dozen black robed priests bearing torches were leading Nivian and the small girl whom I assumed to be my daughter forwards towards an altar stone on the top of a snow covered, barren hill.

A prone, motionless figure lay upon the stone, pale and naked in the moonlight, a man of around my own age and build. Before him stood Malbach, his dark eyes glistening with a feral intensity, a silver knife held in his left hand.

At the head of the altar, flanked by two other druids, was Sinusa, her face covered by the hood of her shawl.

One of the druids held a silver bowl near the head of the altar and as I watched, a dreadful realisation struck me. The victim on the altar was me.

I watched with horror, unable to move or speak as Sinusa let her robe fall to the ground to expose her hideously shrivelled, emaciated naked body beneath. The small girl was also stripped of her robe and she too stood shivering in the moonlight as Malbach raised the silver dagger high and chanted in the Sacred Tongue.

The other druids stood motionless as he brought the knife down and sliced it across the victim's throat. The man on the altar bucked several times as blood pumped from the wound in his throat, running down channels carved into the surface of the altar to be collected in the silver bowl held by one of the druids. The steaming bowl was handed to Sinusa who lapped at it greedily before passing it to the small girl.

I became aware of a distant, pulsating rumble and an overwhelming sense of terror overtook me. I flew into the freezing night air, forgetting Myrddin's advice and carried on going, my one overwhelming desire to put distance between myself and the awful ritual that I had just witnessed. The rumbling sound grew steadily louder and I turned briefly to see a great black, boiling mass, like thunderclouds but far darker, rolling towards me over the mountains, filling the night sky as far as I could see. I flew faster in an attempt to get away from the vast, seething blackness that surged towards me, aware that if it caught me, I would be consumed and destroyed forever. It seemed to me that this thing was alive, summoned from the depths of Cythraul to seek me out and devour my soul. I knew that this thing pursuing me was none other than the Crooked One himself, Crom Cruach, God of the Mound, the Bloody Worm, ancient beyond reckoning, older than time itself. Tendrils of blackness, like the tentacles of some monstrosity from the lightless abyss began to overtake me as the thing loomed ever closer, pulsating and growling as it came.

I flew harder, letting out a long, piercing cry of sheer terror. Myrddin was nowhere to be seen and I had nearly lost all hope when somewhere up ahead, a brilliant globe of blue light appeared. I heard a female voice in my head, telling me to fly for the light and I did, thrusting myself forwards with all my might, plunging into a world of impossibly bright light, aware that the malevolent blackness behind me was retreating back to whatever hellish void had spawned it, before finding myself falling and spiralling downwards.

Chapter 14

The Fomoiri

I awoke gasping for breath, vomiting up bitter green liquid onto the packed earthen floor, confused and disorientated. I was vaguely aware of Geraint and Oengus crouching over me, offering words of comfort. Geraint helped me back up into a sitting position and offered me a bowl of ale, but I shook my head, wiping vomit and mucus from my beard.

I was trembling all over and my breath came in ragged gasps. The memory of that boiling black mass was like the worst nightmare that I had ever had. To know that something that dark and evil existed and was looking for me was enough to drive me to the brink of insanity.

Opposite me, Myrddin still sat bolt upright, his eyes closed serenely, his breathing steady and even.

Suddenly his eyes snapped open and he took a sharp intake of breath. His glazed, blue eyes focused and he looked pale and shaken.

"She has summoned the Crooked One. His minions are coming for us," he said, his voice nothing more than a whisper.

"What did you see?" Oengus asked fervently.

I looked at him and then at Geraint. "Ambrosius is in great danger. Gorlois has found him."

"Ambrosius will be leagues away by now," Geraint frowned at me as Tuela draped a woollen blanket around my shoulders. "We'd never get to him in time to be of any use."

"Then we must save my daughter," I added.

Geraint blinked at me. "Your daughter?"

"I have a daughter. I saw her, with Nivian."

"So this girl of yours, this Nivian, she still lives then?" Geraint asked. "But how do you know that any of what you saw was real? All I saw was you lying there twitching and drooling like a madman. You haven't moved from that spot for several hours, as Oengus is my witness."

"It was a journey of the spirit," Myrddin said impatiently. "Have you been listening to nothing that we've said? And what your friend saw was very real indeed. He speaks the truth. Sinusa has seen him and we are all now in great danger."

"Nivian has joined the enemy," I said flatly. "She has become an acolyte of the priests of Crom Cruach. And I know that the girl is our daughter. She is about the right age and they intend to drive her soul from her body so that Sinusa can use it. Only one of Tuatha de Danann heritage will do and there are only two other people left in this world in whose veins flows the blood of the Tuatha de Danann. One of them is me, the other is my sister. But Ygerna is no longer of any use to them, as she is no longer pure."

"And so they have chosen your daughter instead," Oengus added with dawning comprehension.

I nodded with a grim expression and picked up the bowl of spiced ale, taking a deep gulp. The drink refreshed me somewhat and I looked at Geraint. "I cannot let this happen."

"So what's our next move?" Geraint asked as he watched Tuela disappear back into the shadows.

"Sinusa must be stopped at any cost. Fergus and I must face the minions of Crom Cruach alone," Myrddin said, climbing to his feet and leaning heavily on his staff.

"I will come with you, I can fight," Geraint said, placing a hand on the hilt of his sword.

"You cannot fight beings summoned from the black depths of Cythraul, fool," Myrddin snapped contemptuously. "These are not creatures that can be killed with iron or steel. We must draw them to us and choose our battleground."

"So what must be done?" I asked, feeling cold fear grip my bowels.

"After the ritual, Fiachu's army will be moving south with the renewed power of Sinusa to aid them," Myrddin said. "Come morning we must depart with all haste. Fiachu mac Niall's stronghold is in the territory of the Creones, a particularly warlike clan of the Cruithne, many of whom have now joined his cause."

"But how do we get into his stronghold without getting caught?" Geraint asked. "And if we do manage to get in and kill Fiachu mac Niall and this high priestess and rescue Fergus' long lost lover and new found daughter, how the hell do we get out again in one piece? I'm not one to shy away from a fight, Fergus will tell you that, but I draw the line at outright suicide."

Myrddin walked over to the workbench against the wall and took several phials down from the shelf. "There are other methods that we can use besides brute force you know. As I said before, I can make our true intentions invisible to Sinusa's second sight so we will not be seen as a threat. Oengus is well known to Fiachu and can gain us entry into the stronghold easily enough. You two will play the part of his Pictish bodyguards. Oengus' companion has done a good job with the clan markings, but Tuela will make you look indistinguishable from one of the Creones. By the time she has finished with you, your own mothers will not recognise you. I will find my own way in and once we are all in place, I shall find the stores," he held up a crystal phial of black, viscous liquid. "A few drops of this in each barrel of mead or ale will render his entire army insensible for several hours. I will attempt to divert Sinusa's attention from the rest of you. Once they are incapacitated, we will do what we must do."

"But not all of them will be incapacitated," Geraint put in. "What do we do about them?"

"We will cross these bridges one at a time. For now we shall eat and rest fully, for our journey ahead will be difficult. Tuela will prepare something for us."

We huddled around the hearth and ate a tasty mutton stew heavily laced with herbs and spices, swilled down with bitter tasting Cruithne ale and thick slices of black bread. Afterwards, Oengus produced his lyre and began to strum a gentle, soothing tune and soon I felt myself becoming drowsy.

Myrddin showed me to a partitioned area of the cluttered stone hut, divided from the rest of the house by a heavy, embroidered curtain, where a small, fur covered bed sat against the cobbled wall. I stripped off my armour and weapons before climbing in, ensuring by habit that my sword and seax were within reach. I slept with the seax at my side, with my right hand resting on the hilt. I found it comforting to know that it was there and it is a habit which I continue until this very day. Sleep quickly took me and I wondered briefly whether Tuela had laced the food with something to aid our rest.

I was awoken several hours later by a movement next to my bed. Instinctively I pulled the seax from its scabbard and sat bolt upright, wide awake within an instant, my senses screaming and my heart thumping. In the gloom I could make out a dark figure standing over me and I drew my arm back to strike, but a small hand gently pressed against my shoulder and eased me backwards with a soothing whisper.

The smell of pine resin and musky, earthy perfume assailed my senses and I realised who the unseen figure was. At first I had taken it to be Tuela, Myrddin's servant, but I was mistaken. Carefully, Brida pulled back the sheepskin that covered me and climbed into the bed beside me, pressing her soft, feminine curves against my battle hardened body.

She was whispering something breathlessly in her native tongue as she started to kiss my neck and face and I was overcome by a sudden surge of desire as I grabbed her slim waist and pulled her on top of me. Long suppressed instincts took over and we made love quietly but passionately in the darkness.

Afterwards, we both lay in one another's arms in silence, a Gael and a Pict, two strangers who should have been enemies but who had instead found simple pleasure with one another.

That night as I lay listening to the monotonous beat of the Pictish drums, feeling the warmth of Brida's body against mine, I slept deeply and peacefully for the first time in over a year.

The next morning we set off from the small Cruithne settlement as the winter sun crept up over the distant hills, spreading yellow shafts of light that reflected off of the white of the snow. We were escorted by a dozen Pictish warriors who had agreed to take us as far as the river that marked the boundary of their territory. The other Picts stood silently and watched us leave, their wild, painted faces making me feel more than slightly uneasy. For the past year and a half these people had been our bitter enemies and now here we were amongst them, relying upon their protection.

We rode up into the hills with Oengus and Brida up ahead. The Cruithne girl gave no hint of what had happened the night before and had gone back to giving me sullen looks and short, one word answers to my questions. Myrddin, swathed in thick furs like the rest of us, rode a nut brown Cruithne pony carrying supplies of dried meat, ale and extra furs and blankets. His mousy beard was braided and his face was adorned with a series of blue dots that formed a spiral on either cheek and forehead. On his head he wore his ceremonial leather cap with the antlers and on his shoulder was perched a small sparrow hawk whose head twitched continuously from side to side.

By midday we had reached the river and crossed it over a fording point composed of a series of large, flat slabs of black rock. Our Pictish escort turned back and headed home and I looked northwards towards our destination with a growing sense of dread. Angry black mountains brooded against a slate grey sky, their summits lost in swathes of thick cloud. How anyone could exist in such a hostile land was beyond my comprehension and it was no wonder that it had given birth to such a hardy and tenacious people as the Picts.

Myrddin made an offering to the gods of the land, pouring a small quantity of ale and meat into a hole that he had dug in the snow as a libation and then called upon Arianrhod, the goddess of retribution, Keeper of the Silver Wheel of the Stars, to guide us safely through the mountains.

As we progressed into the foothills through knee deep drifts of snow, I wondered whether Arianrhod had heeded his prayers as the weather suddenly turned against us.

Dark clouds rolled down the mountainside towards us and soon we were fighting our way blindly through a ferocious blizzard, unable to see an arm's length in front of us.

Eventually after struggling for several hours through the blinding storm we were forced to seek shelter in a cramped cave in the mountainside. We sat despondently around a small fire, listening to the wind howling down from the mountain's summit and watching the snow swirl and cavort, countless millions of wind driven flakes that stung the face and obscured the vision.

"We're never going to get there at this rate," Geraint complained, warming his hands over the small fire. I barely recognised him as Tuela had spiked his hair with lime and improved the tribal markings on his face so that now he was indistinguishable from a Pictish warrior. She had done the same to me and I knew that I too would be equally unrecognisable to him. "Why would anyone want to live in a place like this?"

"In the summer it is beautiful," Brida said defensively, cradling her injured left arm against her thin body, her dark eyes lingering upon me longer than usual. "The hills are full of game and covered with purple heather. And when the sun sets behind the mountains, the sky turns colours that you have never seen before. We are the Cruithne and this is my home and we learn to accept the short summers and the harsh winters which would kill the likes of you, southerner. The spirits of this land do not welcome you."

Geraint stared back at the girl, his dark eyes glazing the way they did before violence was imminent. "I was raised in the valleys and mountains of Powys, girl. Not much different to this landscape. Harsh winters or your spirits do not frighten me."

Brida held his gaze. "Then maybe you should fear the Cruithne. My people do not take kindly to strangers in their lands."

"And no doubt you intend to sell us out to Fiachu mac Niall, you little bitch." Geraint tried to get to his feet, his hand falling to the hilt of his seax, but I placed a firm hand on his shoulder to keep him down.

"Come now, please let's try not to kill one another," Oengus said calmly. "I can assure you that Brida has no such intentions. Her clan were no friends to Fiachu mac Niall. They hate him and the Creones as much as they hate the Votadini."

"The Creones?" I asked, remembering the name mentioned by Myrddin and King Cadlew.

"The Creones are the clan that have allied themselves with Fiachu and the Masraighe. Brida's people are the Venicones, sworn enemies of the Creones," Oengus explained. "There is only one thing the Cruithne hate more than one another and that's outsiders."

"We know that," I replied, glancing at Geraint who was now silently fuming and still glaring at the Pict girl.

"Fortunately for us," Oengus continued, pointing at me with a small eating knife that he produced from a pouch on his belt. "We now have Myrddin as a companion."

I turned and looked at the druid who was sat bolt upright breathing deeply with his eyes closed and his head tilted forwards slightly, the antlers from his headdress casting eerie shadows against the cave wall opposite. We knew better than to disturb him in such a state as he was probably walking between the worlds seeking guidance and answers from the spirits of the land. A short time before we had found the cave, he had been whispering intimately to his sparrow hawk before releasing it with a flurry of wings, the tiny creature vanishing almost instantly into the white storm.

I hunched into my fur lined cloak and shuffled closer to the fire, my mind in turmoil, mirroring the snow storm outside. I found my thoughts drifting constantly to Nivian, trying to make sense of what I had seen on my spirit journey. Had she willingly become a worshipper of that foul and ancient god or had she been forced into their degenerate cult? I refused to believe that she would willingly sacrifice our daughter, if that was who the small girl was, to their vile deity.

Oengus began to sing a song from our homeland, a lament about a prince's unrequited love for a Shee maiden from the Otherworld. His voice was rich and profoundly emotional and even Geraint sat in thoughtful silence gazing into the flames. Brida joined in as well, her voice sweet and harmonious, her tones interweaving with Oengus' to produce a sound the likes of which I had never heard before.

The song, though beautiful, helped only to add weight to my already sinking mood and by the time the bard and his Pictish companion were finished, Geraint and I were both deeply lost in our own private thoughts, listening to the howling storm just outside the cave.

"What will you do when you find her?" Geraint asked at last, breaking the silence.

"Who?"

"This Nivian. What will you do if she has become one of them?"

I sighed and shook my head. "I don't know. But if she has made her choice then so be it. I will at least give her the chance to come back with me. I owe her that much."

"Why not just forget her?" Geraint suggested. "Kill Fiachu, rescue your daughter, leave her to her fate. There are plenty of other women out there."

"Not like her," I responded with a wistful smile. "Not one day has passed where I have not thought about her, even after all these years. Wondering whether she is alive or dead, who she's with, what she looks like now."

"You said you owe her," Brida suddenly interjected, unable to disguise the bitterness in her voice. "What do you owe her?"

I looked over the fire at the young Pict girl, the blue markings on her face seemingly had a life of their own as the flames cast jumping shadows and were reflected in her large dark eyes. If her shoulder was hurting her, which I assumed it was, she showed no outwards signs. Her eyes bored into mine and I could read jealousy in her expression.

I swallowed hard as the memories came streaming back. "Several years ago, my village was attacked by Fiachu and his Picts. They burned it down and slaughtered everyone, but I ran into the forest to hide and heard screaming. I followed the sound and found Nivian. She was..." I trailed off, my voice becoming heavy, my throat constricted. I cleared my throat and continued. "She was being ravaged by three Picts. I was only young, not much older than you, there was nothing I could do. I took one down with a slingstone, but the others turned on me. I panicked and ran, abandoning her to her fate. Every day I revisit those events in my mind, wondering if there was anything else I could have done to save her, but instead I ran and saved myself and the guilt of that decision has been with me ever since." I looked down at my hands in their worn leather gauntlets, fighting the emotions arising within me.

"And so you come to my land, slaughter my people, kill our children and rape our women," Brida said bitterly, her painted face contorting into a mask of hate. "Does that make you feel better? Does that make your guilt go away?"

I shook my head solemnly, unable to meet the girl's ferocious gaze.

"We are all victims of fate and we all do things we regret," Oengus said, placing another pine branch on the fire which sizzled and popped. "Sometimes it is better to just let go. This guilt and pain and anger that you carry will only lead to your destruction my friend. I have seen it happen many times before," he shook his head sadly and reached for his goatskin of wine. "As for me, I find my solace in this." He pulled out the stopper with a mischievous smirk and started to gulp at the rich red liquid and then smacked his lips, wiping his mouth with the back of his hand before continuing.

"When Fiachu killed my father and sisters and destroyed our hostel, I can't pretend that I wasn't bitter. But on the other hand, if I had been with them, I would be dead as well. Rather than dwell on their deaths and let desire for vengeance guide my actions, I count every day as a blessing. The gods have spared me, for what reason I do not know, but I am alive and that is all that counts." Oengus winked at me with a broad grin on his face and tossed the skin of wine over.

Geraint poked at the fire with a stick, his demeanour sour. "Sometimes the desire for revenge is all you have," he muttered. "Many times I have found strength in my anger. Without it I would have died as surely as a man in a desert without water. It has kept me going, driven me onwards, made me better, faster, stronger than my enemies. It is part of me and I have no intention of letting go of it."

Oengus shrugged. "For a warrior, maybe that's not such a bad thing. But an angry bard is no good to anyone."

Geraint chuckled and I laughed too. Soon all three of us were laughing and the sound of our laughter echoed against the damp stone walls of the cave.

Suddenly Myrddin gasped and his eyes snapped open. He looked at us with momentary confusion, as though waking from a deep and drunken sleep, but then he fixed his pale eyes upon me.

"They have found us," he gasped and I felt my blood run cold. "We must go to the top of the mountain. You and I."

After two hours of hard and precipitous climbing, we reached the summit of the mountain. Several times my foot slipped on the ice and I would surely have plunged to my death had Myrddin not caught hold of me at the last moment. He was as sure footed as a mountain goat and as swift as a hare and I struggled to keep up with him as he strode from rock to snow covered rock. We climbed in near complete darkness, for which I was grateful as it meant that I could not see the plunging chasm below me. Myrddin climbed ahead of me, tying a rope to rocky outcrops and dropping it down to me. I looped the rope around my chest and under my arms so that I would be suspended if I fell and climbed ever upwards, my hands numb with the cold despite my thick leather gauntlets, my face stinging from the constant barrage of wind borne snowflakes that bit like thousands of tiny insects.

Eventually the druid hauled me bodily over a lip of rock, placing one hand around my sword belt and heaving me over into the snow where I lay gazing up at the black sky breathing heavily and watching my breath condense into clouds of vapour before my eyes.

When I had recovered my composure I struggled to my numb feet and squinted through the ferocious storm towards the tall figure of the druid, his robes whipping out around him as he strode through knee deep snow towards a single large standing stone, leaning heavily on his staff.

The stone was half again as high as a man, wider at the top and tapering slightly towards the base, covered in the now familiar swirls and crude animals favoured by the Picts. It leaned over at a precarious angle, looking as though it would topple at any moment.

Myrddin traced the outline of a spoked wheel in the snow by pouring the remains of the ale from his goatskin onto the ground and stood before the stone, his staff held aloft in both hands. "Taranis, Lord of Storms, hear me now. We are but humble travellers through this realm and are not worthy of your wrath. Lift this storm that we may proceed unhindered as we go to face a far darker enemy, a foe of all living things. Aid us in our quest, Great Thunderer I beseech thee."

The druid then planted his staff in the deep snow and knelt before it, singing a keening song in the Sacred Tongue.

As I stood shivering, my head buried in the confines of my furs, I noticed a slight shift in the storms intensity. The wind dropped, its shriek now becoming a moan, the stinging flecks of snow becoming less intense. I looked up at the black, tumultuous sky above and noticed shafts of weak blue moonlight fighting its way through breaks in the cloud. Taranis, known to my people as Tuireann, the Great God of Storms and Thunder had heard his prayers and I found my frozen fingers fumbling at the bronze triple spiral around my neck as I muttered my own prayer of thanks.

As I looked back towards the stone monolith, something caught my eye. Something was moving just beyond the boundary of my vision and I squinted through the dying blizzard to try and make out what it was. As I looked, there was another movement near the periphery of my vision and in the dim shafts of intermittent moonlight I could see dark figures moving stealthily, as though attempting to surround us.

"Myrddin," I shouted insistently.

"I know," the druid replied. "Get into the circle that I inscribed and whatever you do, do not set foot outside of it."

I thought I heard something behind me, a sinister whispering that was quickly stolen by the wind and I drew my sword and seax and whirled around to confront whoever was there, but I could see nothing.

"That will do you no good," Myrddin said, grabbing me by the shoulder. "Get into the circle and stay there."

I wondered how anyone could have followed us up the mountain without us knowing before realising with a chill that whoever was out there was not of our world. I stood next to Myrddin in the circle and watched the ill-defined shadows moving in the darkness, whispering and hissing as they circled us like wolves circling their prey.

"Who are they?" I whispered, my sword and seax still held in my hands. "What are they?"

"Sinusa has summoned the Fomoiri to her bidding. They are the demons that dwell beneath the dark waters of the seas and lakes of the world. She has grown powerful indeed, this is exactly what I had feared."

The very word Fomoiri seized my heart with dread. As a child, I had heard tales of these fearsome creatures around the hearth of my father's hall on dark winters evenings, about their battles with the Fir Bolg and the Cessair, the ancient peoples who had inhabited my island home before the coming of the Tuatha de Danann and the sons of Mil.

"How do we fight them?" I whispered, unable to disguise the fear in my voice.

"We don't," Myrddin replied. "If we set foot outside of this circle they will tear us apart. We must delay them, force them to wait until daybreak. They have no power in daylight and must return to the dark waters from which they came. If we can survive until then, I can banish them for good."

The figures circled us, their forms amorphous and indistinct, whispering maliciously. It was impossible to estimate their numbers as they seemed to merge and reform continuously, sometimes taking vague animal or human forms, sometimes mere patches of darkness that slithered over the snow. I heard them whisper my name several times and felt my breath catch in my throat. I tightened my grip on my weapons, which although I knew were useless against these demons gave me comfort nonetheless.

A woman's voice called from the darkness, a cry for help from someone in obvious distress, a voice which called my name from the past and which I knew immediately, despite not having heard it for many years.

It was Nivian's voice.

She was calling for me, pleading for me to come to her and help her, sounding so convincing that I took a step forwards to leave the wheel inscribed in the snow. Myrddin grabbed my cloak and pulled me back with surprising strength.

"No," he shouted harshly. "They're trying to lure you out. It is not Nivian that you are hearing."

"But I heard her," I protested. "She's out there."

"Use your sense, lad," Myrddin chided. "How could she possibly be here? They will use every trick possible to lure you out and when you do they will tear your soul from your body and take it back to Sinusa."

The things in the shadows hissed malevolently when they saw that they had failed to entice me and began to whirl around in the gale like shoals of dark, formless fish in black waters.

Another voice came from out of the darkness, this time a male voice, its tone harsh and commanding. "You broke your oath Fergus," it said accusingly. "You were sworn to protect me and instead you abandoned me in favour of going after your long lost love. Now my men are dead and I have been taken by the enemy. It is all your fault, oath breaker."

The voice was unmistakably that of Ambrosius, voicing the doubts that had been playing on my mind since we went our separate ways.

"You could have abandoned your futile quest for revenge and fulfilled your duty, as a man of honour would have done," the voice that sounded like Ambrosius continued. "But instead you have chosen the path of vengeance and lust over duty. You are not a man. You are not a warrior. You are nothing."

"Be silent!" I yelled into the biting wind, raising my sword in a gesture of violence, my face flushed with shame and guilt.

"Do not listen," Myrddin said, grabbing me by the shoulders and shaking me. "They know your doubts and fears and they mix them with half-truths and use them against you. Do not listen."

"I should have gone to Ambrosius and Varius and the others. They needed my help and I wasn't there," I lowered my sword and looked down at my feet.

"Your lord is more than capable of fending for himself," Myrddin said softly. "This path you have chosen is no less important than that one. You are letting your doubts and emotions cloud your judgement and that is what they are relying upon."

The wind began to pick up pace, pelting us with tiny flecks of snow and ice that stung the face. The shadows began to move more swiftly now, some coalescing into vaguely human forms. One of them came forwards and stood before me, about a dozen yards from the circle. Although the face was enshrouded in shadow, there was no mistaking the short, stocky silhouette with its spiked hair.

"You have come all this way to kill me boy?" the familiar calm, cold voice said. "Then here I am, standing before you, unarmed. Kill me."

I tightened my grip on my sword and seax and fought the urge to charge out of the circle and strike Fiachu mac Niall down once and for all.

"What are you waiting for? Come and kill me, or do you not have the stomach for it?"

"You are not Fiachu mac Niall," I replied. "You do not belong in this world, begone."

The thing before me chuckled insidiously. "You never knew what happened to your little friend, did you?" It said, crouching before me in the snow. "Once all of my men had finished with her, I took her as my own. Apart from her obvious skills in bed, she also proved to have a certain aptitude for the arcane. Sinusa took her under her wing and initiated her into her priesthood. She is content where she is, what makes you think that she would ever want to run away with you? The boy who fled for his life and left her to her fate at the hands of my Cruithne? You are a coward and she despises you, if she ever thinks of you at all, that is."

I felt rage and shame boiling inside of me. "Shut your vile mouth, or by Dagda I'll..."

"You'll what?" the thing impersonating Fiachu said. "You'll kill me? You're not capable. You are powerless, just as you were powerless that day when my men ravaged Nivian over and over again."

I yelled with incoherent fury and charged forwards, slashing my sword with all my might at Fiachu's head. Instead of meeting flesh and bone, my blade slid through his shadowy form like it was cutting through mist.

The thing laughed and dispersed into the darkness and I felt an awful chill as tendrils of blackness began to wrap themselves around my legs and arms, slowing my movements so that it felt like I was moving through water. I tried to lash out, but my blows were slow and ponderous as the darkness crept up my arms and worked its way into me like fingers of ice.

I cried out in panic as I felt myself being dragged inexorably towards the things that waited in the shadows, trying with all my strength to extricate myself from the grip of this demonic creature.

I felt a sharp crack as something heavy hit the back of my head, a bright flash and an explosion of pain before I sank into blackness.

Chapter 15

The Price of the Gods

I awoke shivering in the snow with a splitting headache. Bright sunlight streamed down upon me, hurting my eyes and causing my head to pound even more. Myrddin was crouched over me, his face looked pale and thin, his eyes dull and sunken with exhaustion.

"Do not sit up too fast," he said, placing a hand on my chest. "I did hit you rather hard."

I sat up carefully, feeling pain explode in my head and felt a large lump on the back of my skull.

"Why did you hit me?" I asked, my speech sounding thick and slurred.

"It's a good thing that I did. The Fomoiri had a hold on your mind and they knew what would bring you out of the circle. If I hadn't have hit you when I did, you would have been lost for good."

"Well, thank you then, I suppose," I said unconvincingly, squeezing my eyes shut against the bright sunlight. "What happened to them?"

Myrddin sighed wearily and leaned heavily on his yew staff. "All night I have battled with them. Eventually I was able to summon the spirits of this mountain to aid me and they drove the Fomoiri screaming into the night."

"Will they return?" I asked with a shudder, not wishing to repeat the experience of the previous night.

Myrddin shook his head slowly. "They are gone now, banished to whatever dark depths they came from but I fear that the mountain spirits must now be appeased."

"How?"

"They require a life in place of the ones that they have saved. The Cruithne girl, Brida, must die." The druid gestured towards the slightly tilted monolith.

"But she's innocent," I protested. "If we do that, we're no better than Sinusa and her dark druids. I won't allow it."

"Fool," Myrddin snapped harshly. "This is not about you and what you will or will not allow. This is the realm of spirits we are dealing with, the Otherworld, where vows are not made lightly. If we do not do this, we will anger the spirits and all of us will then be in danger."

I stood unsteadily, feeling my knees crack. I was so cold that I could barely move. "I will have no part in her murder."

"Why the sudden pang of conscience, Tuan? You have been murdering the girl's people for over a year, what difference is one more dead Pict to you? You hate them, don't you?"

"I don't murder innocent girls," I snapped peevishly, picking up my sword and seax and sheathing them in their fleece lined scabbards.

"Do you not?" Myrddin replied doubtfully. "You have sent many souls to the Otherworld, Tuan. Many of whom were innocent."

I thought of the small child that had run into the path of my horse and his mother during our first raid against the Cruithne and how I had let my horse trample the small body into the ground. And how, in my battle lust I had cut down the child's mother without a second thought and the children's screams that I had heard when I had set light to their house. I shook my head angrily and squeezed my eyes shut to clear the awful image in my mind and walked away from the druid, starting the precarious climb down the mountainside.

"Careful, or you will end up killing yourself," he called after me as though berating a child.

"What do you care? Don't pretend you're concerned with my wellbeing, Myrddin. I know that the only reason you are helping me is because you need me as much as I need you at the moment."

My foot slipped on a patch of ice and I tumbled awkwardly down the steep slope. Luckily my fall was broken by a gorse bush and I cursed angrily as I tried to extricate myself from the thorns. Myrddin climbed down to where I was and offered his hand with an exasperated expression.

Reluctantly I took it and he pulled me free. The druid looked on with wry amusement as I pulled thorns from my clothing.

"You are right, Tuan. We do need each other. Fate has woven our paths inextricably together, whether we like it or not. I fear that you and I are woven together more completely than either of us realise at the moment. The threads of our lives forms an interesting pattern."

"Why must you always talk in riddles?" I asked, my mood sour.

"Everything is a riddle, Tuan," Myrddin replied as though he were addressing a small child. "Life and death, love and hate, good and evil. A riddle that is only understood by the gods."

I ignored him and continued my descent more carefully. Myrddin threw me one end of his rope and I took it and looped it around my waist again.

"Do not worry about the girl," Myrddin said as I began to climb down a particularly steep and rocky face. "She is Cruithne. She will give her life gladly as she knows that she will return someday to this world. We all do, Tuan. Death is merely a transition. You of anyone should know that."

"And what if you're wrong, Myrddin?" I called back, feeling for footholds in the rock face with frozen feet. "What if the followers of Christ are right? What happens when no one even remembers the Old Gods? You are the last of the druids, the last one who remembers the Old Ways. When you are gone, their memory will fade until no one will remember them at all."

"And why do you think the land bleeds and drowns in its own tears?" Myrddin called down after me. "Precisely because the people of these lands are turning away from the Old Gods. They have forgotten that they are one with the land. The followers of Christ offer them a paradise after death and sever their links to their ancestors and to the spirits of tree and mountain and lake. Unless the people of this island turn back to the Old Ways, they are doomed. Their nailed god from a distant land will not save them."

"Just like taking the life of an innocent girl will not save us," I shouted back.

By the time we got back to the cave it was mid-morning. We were met by a very irate and cold looking Geraint who emerged from the small cave with sword and seax drawn.

"Where the hell have you two been?" he demanded, his dark eyes glittering dangerously.

"Making sure our passage through these mountains will go unhindered," Myrddin replied, pushing past Geraint and ducking into the cave.

Geraint looked at me and frowned. "What happened to you both? You look terrible."

I shook my head timorously. "I'll tell you some other time," I said as I followed the druid into the cave.

Inside the cramped little cave, Oengus and Brida still sat crouched around the remains of the fire and when he saw me, the little bard smiled with relief.

"Thank Dagda," he said, slapping a cordial hand on my shoulder. "We thought you were both dead. Where have you been?"

I looked at Brida who turned away with a sour scowl and wondered whether it would be better to just let Myrddin sacrifice her to the mountain spirits. She hated Geraint and I and with good reason and I did wonder where her loyalties would lie when the time came. I wondered what had possessed her to lie with me that night and concluded that it was merely the desire for a physical connection, a need to be fulfilled like the scratching of an itch, nothing more.

"We must depart now," Myrddin said, gathering his leather satchel and slinging it over his shoulder. "There is no time to lose. We have been delayed long enough."

The winter sky was a brilliant blue and the day was considerably warmer than it had been. We trudged through knee deep snow, making slow progress towards our destination.

Myrddin's little sparrowhawk returned, perching on his hand and he listened intently as it chirped into his ear before flying off again down the mountainside.

We followed its route, eventually coming to a dark and narrow loch in the valley below, surrounded by pine trees.

Once again, Brida was scouting ahead of us, her injured arm strapped securely against her body. Every now and then she would turn in her saddle and raise her good arm to signal that all was well ahead.

"It will have to be done soon," Myrddin whispered to me, out of earshot of Geraint and Oengus.

"I'm not doing it and I won't allow it." I said firmly, my eyes fixed on the deep loch ahead.

"You would rather invoke the wrath of Arianrhod and the spirits of this land? Then so be it. May the curse be yours and not mine. So shall it be." The druid looked at me with one eye closed and made a curious gesture with his left hand, with two fingers extended.

"Keep your curses to yourself, druid. I have the protection of the goddess Brighid." Myrddin fixed me with an ominous stare. "I hope so, for your sake. I know why it is you are reluctant to take her life. I know that she lay with you and took your seed the other evening in my home. But know this, Tuan. If the gods are not appeased then they will take someone more dear to you."

He yanked on the reigns of his pony and cantered away, leaving me alone with my thoughts.

We travelled on without incident for another two days, through barren, mountainous land, not seeing any sign of another living soul. Occasionally we came across the curious stone markers engraved with strange patterns and on the second day we encountered a more grisly landmark.

We had climbed to the summit of a large hill where we found a line of human skulls that had been placed upon spears spaced at regular intervals and tied with red rags that fluttered in the cold breeze. The skulls had been painted with woad with the swirling patterns of the Picts and we knew that this was a spirit barrier that marked the boundary between the Caledonii and the Creones, two rival Cruithne tribes.

"We must appease the guardians with blood," Myrddin said, pulling out his silver dagger from his belt. My mind went back to when we had crossed into the territory of the Eoganachta many years ago back in Eire, when Ygerna and I were being pursued by Fiachu mac Niall. We had come across a spirit barrier then and Dorbalos had collected several drops of blood from each of us in a silver cup and buried it in the ground to ensure that we could cross into their territory safely.

The irony of the situation was not lost on me. Now here I was, years later, running towards my enemy rather than away from him. I held my palm out to Myrddin, who had produced a bowl from his satchel which had been fashioned from the skull of an unborn infant.

I winced involuntarily as he drew the blade quickly across my palm, catching the small rivulet of blood in the bone bowl. Oengus and Geraint followed my example and then Brida stepped forwards holding her small hand out.

Myrddin took her hand in his, his long, gaunt face expressionless as he looked into the girl's dark eyes. My hand began to stray towards the hilt of my seax as I anticipated the druid making a sudden unexpected move on the girl. Myrddin's pale eyes caught mine however and he paused for a moment before giving Brida a quick cut on the palm and collecting her blood in the tiny bowl of bone.

He then dug a small hole before one of the spirit barriers with his silver dagger and poured the offering into the hole as he shouted out to the guardian spirits to let us pass unhindered.

We set off again, following the shoreline of a deep, narrow loch until we could strike North West again. Brida refused to go too close to the loch for fear of the Fuath, a deadly spirit said to dwell in the dark depths. Oengus tried to convince her that she was safe, that the Fuath would not emerge during the daylight, but still she refused to go too close to the loch.

"In my homeland we called them Kelpies," I said to her and she smiled briefly at me.

"Ceffyl Dwr in my homeland," Geraint added. "I saw one once, when I was out rounding up stray sheep with my brother. Hideous thing it was, sat by the shore eating something, with hair like pondweed and claws as long as daggers. Chased us all the way home it did."

Oengus grinned at the Powysian. "It obviously saw you as a potential mate, Geraint. Though I'm sure you've had far worse in your time. The gods only know what offspring you and a monster like that would produce."

Geraint threw the little bard a sour glance and muttered something derogatory about the Irish under his breath. Oengus winked at me slyly and I chuckled to myself, amused at his playful goading of the Powysian.

We travelled over another range of snowy hills until by mid-day we could see a smudge of grey smoke against the blue sky, rising in a series of snakelike columns.

"There's a settlement up ahead," Brida said breathlessly, pointing towards the tell-tale smoke in the distance. As usual, she had been scouting ahead, sometimes on foot, running back to us when she spotted anything unusual.

As we came to the crest of a large hill, we looked down at a small huddle of turf roofed stone hovels in a deep valley, on the shore of a wide bay. Beyond, in the far distance, a large mountain loomed, dominating the view to the west with another slightly smaller peak just behind it.

"Over there is Beinn Mhor, the Great Mountain," Oengus said, nodding towards the distant, misty peak. "That is where Fiachu mac Niall's fortress is. We'll have to see if we can get the locals to ferry us across the bay."

"What if they're not friendly?" Geraint said, a frown furrowing his brow as he looked down at the small settlement at the foot of the hills.

"Don't you worry about that, my friend," Oengus replied with a wink. "Just let me do the talking and everything will be fine."

We followed a cleft in the hill, formed by a small but fast flowing stream, down to the collection of crude stone buildings. My nostrils picked up the smell of dried fish and smoke from peat fires and I was reminded instantly and painfully of Penglyn and my life with Rhawn and Father Demetrios. A dog barked as we approached and soon several men emerged from the houses clad in thick furs and armed with spears. Their hair and beards were unkempt and they bore the painted faces of their kind and they glared at us with barely disguised hostility as we approached.

Oengus walked forwards and greeted the men like long lost brothers in their own language, turning every now and then to indicate us with a sweep of his arm. Their eyes settled uneasily upon Myrddin, who sat motionless upon his pony and returned their stare impassively, his antlered headdress and the curious necklace of bones, feathers and polished stones evidence that he was some kind of priest or magician of the ancient order.

After a terse conversation, one of the men indicated for us to follow him.

We walked along a muddy path that had been cleared of snow between the low roofed hovels. Down by the shore were a number of boats, curraghs and coracles, many of which had been overturned and pulled up onto the shingle beach to be repaired and to keep vermin out.

We were led to the largest building in the settlement, a large, stone walled roundhouse with a turf roof, where we were introduced to the village elder, a grey haired but sturdy old woman with one leg who surrounded herself with large wolfhounds and who was waited upon by a whole host of daughters and granddaughters. Her home was warm but dingy, with only the glow from a cooking pit and a number of reed torches providing any light in the place. Dried and drying fish hung from the rafters, giving the place an overpowering odour that reminded me of Rhawn's home back in Penglyn. Oengus explained to her that we required passage over the bay and would be willing to sell our mounts for supplies and a small boat. She agreed to Oengus' proposal and to allow her eldest son to take us, on the condition that Myrddin would bless every house and boat and tend to the sick and that Oengus would entertain the people of the village that evening. Oengus acquiesced with a bow and a charming smile. "I shall regale you with tales of heroes and lovers of old and songs that will bring tears and laughter in equal measure," he claimed with a sparkle in his eye.

We were given a bowl of fish broth and oats each and sour Cruithne ale. A little later, the folk of the village began to arrive, crowding into the open space by the fire pit that served as a communal meeting place for the villagers.

Most were suffering from minor ailments that they thought Myrddin would be able to cure and they stepped forwards one at a time as the druid made a great show of battling the unseen malevolent spirits that were causing the villager's problems, whipping them lightly with birch twigs to drive them from the victim's bodies and trapping them in oak balls which miraculously appeared in his hands and which he then cast onto the fire with a great flourish where they exploded in a cloud of bluish smoke that caused the assembled crowd to gasp with astonishment.

This charade continued for several hours before Geraint and I grew bored and left the stuffy, dimly lit roundhouse to get some fresh air.

"I'm glad to be out of there," Geraint grumbled as we sat down on a pile of logs that had been cut for firewood. "The stink of dried fish and Picts was becoming too much to bear," he took a deep breath of crisp winter air and looked out over the bay at the distant mountain, Beinn Mhor and its twin peak before continuing. "Do you think their illnesses are really caused by evil spirits, or is Myrddin just putting on an act?"

I shrugged, remembering back to when I had first seen Myrddin back in Penglyn, when he went under the guise of a travelling mystic. "A bit of both, I think. The people expect a show and that is what he gives them. Whether they are cured or not in the long term is irrelevant. But some of the things I've seen him do, I cannot explain." I thought about the sinister spirits from the previous night and how it all now seemed like a terrible dream and I told my friend all about the Otherworldly encounter.

Geraint looked thoughtful for a moment as he watched two small, ragged looking children pelting snowballs at a three legged dog.

"I saw him bring you back from the dead. Back in Ynys Wytryn, when you were stabbed in the stomach and should have died."

I remembered the moment well, when I had hovered between worlds and met with the Goddess. "That was the power of the Chalice," I replied.

"I wonder where that is now?" Geraint pondered. "Any man who has an object like that would wield a lot of power."

"Which is precisely why it is best hidden away. Best not to give men any more reason to fight and slaughter one another."

Geraint grunted, unconvinced by my argument. "What of the Sword of Kings? Do you believe that exists?"

"I know it exists," I replied. "And I know where to find it."

Geraint's dark eyes flashed with wonder. "You do? Then why not find it and take it for yourself?"

"Because I am not a king," I said simply. "It is a king's sword, meant only to be wielded by the true king of this land."

"And who do you suppose that will be?"

I looked the Powysian in the eye, holding his gaze for a moment. "Uther Pendragon."

Geraint snorted contemptuously. "Uther Pendragon? That unruly little whelp? How could a brat like that hold a kingdom together?"

"He is the only one who can unite all of Dumnonia and Durotrigia. The Dumnonians loyal to the Pendragon will flock to his banner as will the Cornovii in the west and the warlords of Durotrigia in the east. He is our only hope of seizing power from Vortigern and his sons."

Geraint shook his head dismissively. "The Pendragon are fragmented and scattered, those that have not been slaughtered by Gorlois, that is. The Cornovii are stunted, underfed weaklings and Dumnonia is still ruled by King Erbin, a crippled whelp who has only just stopped sucking on his mother's tit. And now Durotrigia will be in pieces after the death of Julianus and every warlord of every cantref for miles around will be trying to seize as much of it as they can. It's going to take more than a spoiled, over indulged child to sort that lot out."

I pulled off my gauntlet, exposing the dragon ring that Drustan Pendragon had given to me after I had sworn my undying loyalty to him and held my fist before Geraint's face.

"Remember this?" I said fiercely. "You bear one as well. A symbol of your loyalty to the name of Pendragon. If Uther is alive, our loyalties are still with him, unto death."

Geraint looked down at the ring on his own stout finger and pulled it off. "I took no such oath. My loyalty was to the man, not the name. I followed Drustan Pendragon because he saved my life, took me under his wing and nurtured me, gave me back the family that I had lost. I swore loyalty to his daughter Branwen out of respect for her. But my service to the Pendragon died with Lady Branwen. There is no way I would ever bend my knee to Uther," he tossed the ring over to where the children were playing and stood and entered the roundhouse again, leaving me alone outside, watching the thin children scrabbling in the snow to retrieve Geraint's ring.

That evening we sat in the crowded roundhouse drinking sour ale and listening to Oengus singing and strumming his lyre. Later on, he produced a bone flute and played haunting melodies that captivated the villagers who listened in awed silence. After a while, he upped the tempo again with some bawdy drinking songs and soon the folk of the small fishing village were dancing and making merry in the crowded roundhouse. The arrival of a bard in any village was cause to celebrate and the Cruithne were no different to anyone else in that respect.

Brida slept nearby, curled up on a sheepskin next to a couple of wolfhounds while Geraint and I sat alone, away from the Cruithne villagers, our demeanour menacing enough to prevent them from bothering us. Myrddin had said that it was best that we did not interact with them, as questions would be asked with regards to our origins when they realised that we did not speak their language.

We spoke in hushed tones over a jug of ale with a single tallow candle burning before us.

Myrddin came over and sat with us, pulling up a stool to the small table.

"The omens are not good," he said ominously. "You have disappointed the gods. You should have let me do what was necessary."

I looked over at Brida sleeping peacefully on the sheepskins. "There will be many others soon enough. Why can you not offer one of our enemies to the gods? Why does it have to be her?"

"They asked for her."

"Well, they're not getting her," I replied, leaning forwards towards the druid. "And if you touch a single hair on her head, I will be sacrificing you to the gods, druid or not."

"You stubborn young fool," Myrddin hissed furiously. "Do you really think that you can prevail without the protection of the gods? Do you have any idea what you are facing?"

"I have more of an idea than you do as I have faced them before. The Goddess is with me, that is all that I need."

The next morning we awoke early and made ready to depart. Outside, down by the shore a curragh was waiting to take us across the bay where we would make the last leg of our journey. Gulls wheeled over the fishing nets gathered at the water's edge, crying out to one another as they sought for a stray fish left by the fishermen.

A broad faced Pict with dark hair tied in braids awaited us silently, standing by the curragh repairing a net. At his feet a pitiful looking black hound lapped at a pile of fish innards. He looked up as we approached with dull disinterest and listened half-heartedly as Oengus spoke to him, finally indicating with a nod and a grunt that we were to board his boat of cowhide and willow. He tied a small leather coracle to the back of the boat and gave a shrill whistle and the black dog jumped in as well, settling itself near the mast of the curragh as its master cast away from the shore towing the little coracle behind it.

Soon the huddle of stone houses receded into the distance as we rode over the waves, the Pictish fisherman guiding his curragh swiftly and skilfully to the opposite shore.

Myrddin's sparrow hawk returned to him while we were in the curragh and again he allowed it to settle on his hand and listened intently as it chirruped away in his ear. Finally he gave the bird a gentle kiss on its head and set it free again, watching it as it winged its way towards the distant mountain.

"Can you really understand what that bird is saying?" Geraint asked sceptically, eyeing the little bird with curiosity.

The druid nodded and looked serenely at the Powysian. "Animals are sometimes far better company than most people I find."

"Does it have a name?" Brida asked.

Myrddin nodded. "Of course he does. Everyone and everything has a name."

"What is it?"

"His name is Lugotrix."

We reached the other shore and jumped off of the boat onto a narrow shingle beach that sloped gently up to jagged black rocks. Oengus spoke briefly with the fisherman who listened and then nodded once before producing an oar crudely carved from driftwood. He then untied the coracle and climbed in it with his dog, scooping at the green water. The little round boat wobbled unsteadily for a moment but soon picked up speed and glided across the water and soon the fisherman and his dog were nothing more than indistinct specs in the distance.

"I had to pay him with all of our horses for this one boat," Oengus told us, patting the leather side of the flimsy looking curragh. "I just hope it's seaworthy."

"If it's not, you'll be feeding the fishes." Geraint added as he removed a boot and poured out a dribble of water.

"If it's not, we'll all be feeding the fishes," Oengus replied with a dark smirk.

We climbed over the slippery, jagged rocks and headed inland, over a white, unspoiled landscape towards the distant twin mountains enshrouded in mist.

"Soon we will have to part ways," Myrddin said, leaning upon his staff. He had removed his antlered ceremonial headdress and now wore a simple grey hood pulled forwards so that his bearded face was barely visible. "I will have to find my own way into Din Mhor, Fiachu's fortress. You will accompany Oengus, acting as his bodyguards. Once you are in Fiachu's hall, listen for Lugotrix's call thricefold. After you hear this, do not eat or drink anything offered to you. Oengus will lull Fiachu's men with gentle songs which coupled with my infusion should render them insensible. Fergus, you will kill Fiachu mac Niall. Geraint, you will seek out and slay Sinusa. I will prepare an escape route for us, so be ready to get away quickly."

"What about Nivian and my daughter?" I said. "You do remember your promise, Myrddin?"

The druid nodded. "I remember my promise to help you find Nivian. I said nothing about helping to rescue her. My priority is seeing that Sinusa is killed, to end the power of their dark god. Anything else and I am afraid you are on your own."

I laughed bitterly. "I should have known you would say that. Maybe Geraint and I will leave you to fend for yourself when it comes to fighting our way out."

"Hopefully it will not come to that," Myrddin replied. He held out the crystal phial containing the thick, black concoction. "This mixture contains henbane and the juice of the poppy, enough to knock out an army. It is the same as the one we used to knock out the monks at Ynys Wytryn."

"And what a great success that was," Geraint added laconically.

Myrddin ignored him and continued. "Tonight is the feast of Imbolc. Fiachu and his men will be celebrating as Imbolc heralds the end of winter and therefore the beginning of the campaigning season will not be far off. All will be celebrating and so with the will of the gods, all will be drinking and eating," once again Myrddin raised the small bottle before concealing it in a pouch on his belt.

Imbolc. I remembered the time back in Penglyn when I had first set eyes on Myrddin, when Nivian had told me about Cailleach, the Hag of Winter and how we had shared our first intimate moment together and then the heartbreak that I had felt when she had shared Myrddin's bed that evening.

I looked at the tall druid with growing resentment. "Just make sure it works," I said. "And once this is all over, you and I are finished."

Myrddin turned his disturbingly pale eyes towards me. "That is not for either of us to decide. That is down to the will of the gods."

After a while we came to a set of evenly spaced boundary stones, knee high, bearing the crescent symbol of the Masraighe.

"This is Fiachu's territory," Oengus said, kneeling by one of the boundary stones. He looked up at the blue sky as though expecting a dragon to swoop down upon him. "I have an uneasy feeling about this," he added ominously.

"His land is protected by powerful magic, I can feel it," Myrddin said as he rummaged in his leather satchel. He produced four small linen pouches on rawhide strings stuffed with pungent herbs and handed one to each of us.

"Wear these next to your skin at all times. It will render you invisible to the witch and offer you protection from her magic."

"Smells like garlic," Geraint noted, holding the odorous ball to his flattened nose.

"Garlic, dill, fennel and other protective herbs," Myrddin replied. "Harvested with a silver sickle during the full moon, thus offering the protection of Arianrhod, Goddess of the Moon. Very powerful indeed, but only while it stays against the flesh."

I tied the pouch of herbs around my neck and pushed it down the front of my filthy tunic underneath my mail shirt. I realised that I had been wearing the same garment for well over a year and it was stained with blood and sweat and crawling with fleas and lice.

"I must be leaving you now," Myrddin said finally. "May the gods go with you and watch over you." He spat on two of his fingers and touched each of us on the forehead before turning to leave.

"Good luck, Myrddin," I called after him, feeling slightly guilty for my earlier outburst.

The druid turned and looked at me, a slight smile on his thin lips. He nodded once and then strode off northwards, across the snowy landscape, swinging his rowan staff as he went.

Geraint nudged me and pointed down at the druid's tracks in the snow. As we watched, the snow seemed to close over them, so that soon there was no trace that he had ever been there at all.

Chapter 16

In the Hall of the Enemy

The only route up to Din Mhor was a single narrow trail that wound precariously up the side of the mountain. It had been cleared of snow, which lay in dirty heaps to one side and crudely paved with slippery cobblestones. We made our way steadily upwards until we could see Din Mhor up ahead, nestled into the side of the mountain, a ring of stone topped with a wooden palisade patrolled by dozens of spearmen. The path wound upwards towards the great oak gate, above which was flying Fiachu mac Niall's banner; the red crescent on an off white background. My pulse quickened at the sight of that banner and I took a couple of deep breaths to calm my nerves.

Brida came jogging back to us, absently rubbing at her injured shoulder. "Warriors are coming," she said, glancing at Geraint and I. One word from her and we could all be dead, I thought, hoping that Oengus was correct in his judgement of her character.

Half a dozen spearmen were approaching down the narrow path on foot. As they came closer I could make out the facial markings of both Cruithne and Masraighe. Fiachu had chosen the location of his fortress well. Like Din Eidyn, the fortress of the Votadini, it was virtually impregnable as the only access to it was up the narrow mountain path, which could easily be held by one man against many.

"Leave this to me," Oengus said under his breath as he bowed politely at the approaching men. He greeted them in their own language and struck up a brief conversation. Some of the men looked over at Geraint and I with suspicion bordering on hostility, but we remained silent, casually leaning on our spears and trying to look bored.

Finally the leader of the band, a large and surly Masraighe warrior with spiked hair relented and indicated for us to follow him.

The path was barely wide enough for two men to walk abreast and as we approached the imposing looking fortress, the leader of the welcoming party raised his spear and waved it at the men on the ramparts.

The oak gates creaked open and we were ushered into an open courtyard with stables, sheep and pig pens and cattle byres alongside thatched longhouses where the warriors ate and slept. Somewhere within the compound came the ringing of a smith's hammer and nearby a number of slaughtered and gutted pigs hung from a large wooden frame by their back legs, their blood staining the ground beneath them. In the centre of the large open area was a huge figure, a crude representation of a man woven from wicker rods that towered above the surrounding buildings. Cruithne and Masraighe went about their business, barely giving us a second glance and we were instructed to wait outside the Great Hall that sat near the rear of the compound, its walls decorated with the emblems and banners of a dozen Cruithne and Gaelic tribes, some of which I had seen before, many of which were unknown to me.

A group of black robed Masraighe druids passed close by walking towards the Great Hall and my blood ran cold at the sight of the lead druid. The crow feathered cloak, hunched back, gleaming bald head and missing right hand were unmistakable.

"Malbach," I muttered under my breath.

Geraint heard me. "That's the one you told me about?" he whispered.

I nodded in affirmation. "If I get the chance, I'm going to kill him too."

Our escort returned from the Great Hall and requested that we follow him in. As we approached the doors of the hall, two Pictish guards came forwards and took our weapons from us before indicating with a nod that we could proceed.

Inside the hall was spacious, lit with many torches ensconced upon the walls. A walkway ran around the inside of the hall, giving access to private chambers above and several large elongated cooking pits glowed with heat as slaves stirred cauldrons and turned spits on which the carcasses of boars and calves sizzled in their own juices.

Half a dozen men, stripped to the waist, were carrying out weapons practice in the open central area of the hall, the clash of steel on steel echoing throughout the building whilst others sat at long tables drinking and offering advice.

The Masraighe druids, led by Malbach, had entered just before us and unobtrusively made their way past the group of warriors to a door at the back of the hall. Upon our arrival, the ringing of blades ceased and one man came forwards, his stocky, muscular body covered with the swirls and decorations of the Picts, but his face bore the crescent of the Masraighe.

A large, red headed man tossed him a stained rag with which he mopped the sheen of sweat from his face and torso before tossing it back. The red headed man eyed us with derisive hostility, his ravaged face was permanently fixed in a half smile due to an old battle scar that ran from the corner of his mouth to his ear and I recalled that he was the bodyguard who had accompanied Fiachu on the day that he had married my sister and murdered my people.

"Oengus mac Ruadainn, to what do we owe this unexpected pleasure?" Fiachu mac Niall's voice was cold and calm as always, but always with an underlying hint of threat. He swaggered forwards and stood before us, his sword held loosely in his right hand, his broad chest rising and falling visibly with the exertion of exercise.

Oengus gave a flourishing bow before the lord of the Masraighe. "Lord Fiachu, the pleasure is all mine. I thought that I would spend Imbolc entertaining my most generous patron as I was travelling close to your lands. Besides, your ale and wine is by far the best for many leagues around."

Fiachu gazed upon the little bard with cold grey eyes. "You drank enough of it last time you were here, bard. My hospitality has its limits you know," he looked towards Geraint, Brida and I, his eyes narrowing with suspicion as he did so. "I know your surly little wench, but who are the other two?"

My heart was racing in my chest as his eyes settled on me. Was it possible that he had seen through my disguise and had recognised me? I held my breath and fought to keep my composure.

"These two men are my bodyguards, lord," Oengus answered quickly. "Venicones from the east. Travelling these isles is a perilous business these days, as you may appreciate."

Fiachu's soulless eyes lingered upon me and for one dreadful moment I thought that it was over, but instead he nodded, satisfied with Oengus' explanation and diverted his gaze back to the bard.

"So what do you have planned for our entertainment, bard?" Fiachu said, raising his voice for all to hear. "I hope for your sake it is good and not the same drunken rambling that you served up before, otherwise I will have to roast you alive like I did with your father and your sisters." The large red headed man and the others around him laughed raucously at his joke and the son of Niall allowed himself a sly smile.

Oengus kept his composure, but I noticed that his hands were trembling. "Oh, I have an evening of entertainment planned for you that you will not forget for many years, my lord."

"Glad to hear it. Now get out of my sight until sundown. I will call for you when I need you."

Oengus bowed again, but Fiachu turned his back on him and returned to his men to resume his exercise.

We left the hall and wandered across the enclosure, past the enormous wicker effigy to a rickety lean-to against the outer stone wall. A brazier glowed next to a pile of logs, surrounded by bales of hay for seating.

Our Pictish escort indicated that we were to wait here until summoned. No one offered us food or ale and so we sat huddled around the brazier for warmth.

"How are we supposed to kill him if they take our weapons?" Geraint asked as he cast a log onto the brazier.

I reached down to my boot and pulled out Conmor's knife that I had carried since childhood. "I'm surprised that you don't carry a concealed weapon, Geraint." Oengus placed a hand on my arm and pushed it down, hushing me with a sharp hiss. "Keep it concealed you fool or else we're all dead."

I looked around the compound but all of the Masraighe and Cruithne were going about their own business, tending livestock, fetching water or carrying firewood. One small group were carrying out weapons practice whilst another herded a sorry looking collection of prisoners to a holding pen opposite, which was already full to bursting with captives, mostly women and children who wept and sobbed pitifully. The sight of them brought back terrible memories of the mass sacrifice of my own people on the barren plains of Mag Sleacht many years ago and I felt an urge to run over and set them all free, but I knew such a move would be suicidal. I turned away and tried to block out their pathetic cries for mercy.

I noticed that Brida was looking over at them with a fearful look on her face and then looking towards the giant wicker figure.

"What's wrong, Brida?" I asked. I placed my hand tenderly on her shoulder and she turned towards me with a start, her thin face pale and frightened.

"The Losgadh Famhair," she muttered, her eyes fixed on the huge effigy. "Those people will burn this night."

I frowned at her, not understanding.

"The Burning Giant," Oengus translated. "A sacrifice to Crom Cruach."

I looked again at the cage full of wretched prisoners and remembered the agonised screams of my own people as they were lowered into the burning pit on the plains of Mag Sleacht many years ago. "We cannot let that happen," I said, my voice thick with emotion.

"What do you mean?" Geraint asked. "Don't tell me you're thinking of setting them free?"

"I'm not leaving them to burn," I replied with conviction. "I can't stand by and watch those people die in agony like I did with my people."

Geraint's dark eyes flashed with anger. "Those people are nothing to us. They're Pictish whores who would eat your still beating heart as soon as look at you. We have spent the last year and a half fighting them so why should we risk our lives to set them free? This is not what we have come here to do."

"Have you ever seen women and children being burned alive, Geraint?" I shot back at him. "Have you ever heard their screams as the flames blacken their flesh? I have and I still hear them in my dreams and it is something that I never wish to hear again."

Geraint stood, still glaring at me and for a brief moment I thought he was going to swing for me. "You are not throwing away my life for them. They are as good as dead and if you want the truth, I couldn't care less whether they lived or died, or indeed how they die," he shot a vitriolic glance at Brida. "The whole stinking race can burn for all I care."

Oengus raised a hand in a placatory gesture. "I hate to say this, but Geraint has a point, though I do not agree with his sentiments. We would be putting ourselves at unnecessary risk if we try to save those people, let alone angering a god. And even if we did set them free, they would have nowhere to go and would only be recaptured again or freeze and starve on the mountainside. We do what we need to do and we get out. Sorry Fergus, but that's the way it has to be."

I spat on the hay strewn ground in disgust and shook my head. Geraint was still glaring at me as if daring me to push the issue further.

"You're right," I conceded reluctantly. "There's nothing we can do."

I placed my arm around Brida's thin shoulders and to my surprise, rather than pulling away, she nestled her head into my chest.

Oengus gave a satisfied nod. "So let's just kill Fiachu mac Niall and get out of here."

"How are we going to even get close enough to kill him?" Geraint continued.

Oengus tapped the side of his nose. "Once Myrddin's potion takes effect, they won't know a highland bullock from their own wives. Fiachu's personal quarters are towards the rear of the hall, on the left. If we can secrete you in there, Fergus, the job is as good as done. It shouldn't be too difficult to get in there with no one noticing. Brida can help you with that. All you do then is wait for him to retire and then cut the bastard's throat," he mimed a blade going across his own throat with a forefinger.

"And what about the witch?" Geraint asked.

"She'll probably be there as well tonight, though she usually retires early," Oengus explained. "The dark druids have their own quarters, behind the Great Hall, usually patrolled by a couple of guards. They shouldn't be too hard to handle, especially if they've drunk some of Myrddin's spiked mead. Sinusa has her own hut, so it should be quite straightforward getting in and sending her black soul to Cythraul."

"You make it sound so straightforward, Oengus," I said, warily watching a couple of black robed Masraighe druids walk by. "I wish I shared your confidence." Oengus smiled serenely. "We can kill him in his sleep and be away before morning. Once the deed is done, there is a stream that runs through this fort that runs down from the mountain," he pointed his finger at a narrow stream of fresh water that bisected the compound and vanished near the far wall. "There is a small grate of iron beneath the wall, just below the water's surface and just wide enough to crawl through. Brida can lead us to it. We leave via that, get off the mountain and sail away." He spread his arms wide with an expression which suggested that this would be the easiest task in the world.

We waited for several hours, feeding the brazier with logs to stay warm and eating from our own provisions, minding our own business. Brida had fallen asleep with her head on my lap and I had placed my cloak over her to keep her warm, absently running my fingers through the dark braided locks of her hair. Geraint and I looked sufficiently threatening to dissuade any curiosity and with our painted faces and hair spiked with lime, we looked indistinguishable from many of the Picts present.

Eventually, as the weak winter sun began to dip towards the horizon, we were summoned. Our escort returned with a young Masraighe druid whose face had been ravaged by pox.

"Lord Fiachu requires your presence," he announced without emotion.

We followed him to the Great Hall and again were required to surrender our weapons at the door. Reluctantly I handed over Octha's Ruin, my Votadini seax and the short bow that had been a gift from Lugubelenus, chief of the Hidden Folk along with a leather quiver of arrows.

Inside, the hall was already crowded with drunken warriors. Tumblers and fire breathers performed in the open central area near the cooking pits as fearful looking slaves rushed around with platters of meat and jugs of ale to feed the insatiable appetites of the warriors and sitting on a high table, reclining on a throne of carved oak was Fiachu mac Niall, flanked on either side by bodyguards and retainers.

I looked along the line of faces sitting at Fiachu's table. At one end was the skeletal, leering face of Malbach, his shrewd eyes scanning the throngs of people. Directly to Fiachu's left sat the red headed giant with the ravaged face, but further along, sat at Fiachu's right hand was a familiar face that caused my heart to jump. Nivian looked exactly as she had during my spirit journey with Myrddin. Her figure was fuller and more womanly, but that only added to her incredible beauty. Her green eyes were still striking and immediately familiar, accentuated with a black paint and by the crescent on one side of her face that made them burn like green coals against her pale skin. Her hair shone like polished jade and had been straightened and pulled back and bound at the top of her head with a circlet of bronze so that it cascaded down her shoulders like a black fountain, crowned with a diadem of jewelled silver. She wore a black satin dress which had been decorated with silver thread and was gathered at the waist with a black leather corset studded with polished bronze studs.

Fiachu leaned over and spoke in her ear and she nodded once and rose from the table. He stood and banged a jewelled silver goblet on his table.

"My woman Nivian shall now dance for us," he announced in Gaelic in a loud voice.

His words struck me like a hammer blow. His woman? So Nivian had well and truly joined the enemy after all. I tried to tell myself that she must have been forced into this partnership, but she looked relaxed and content with Fiachu and had even smiled when he spoke to her.

The fire eaters and tumblers cleared the floor and the small group of musicians in the corner began to play a different tune on their pipes, lyres and drums. Nivian cast aside the black velvet cloak that she had been wearing and began to gyrate and move in time with the music. The Cruithne and Masraighe warriors fell silent as she span and leaped with grace and fluidity. As the tempo of the music increased, the warriors began to hammer goblets and fists against their tables, keeping time with the music as Nivian's dance became more wild and lustful, her lithe body twisting into impossible shapes as she writhed seductively before the assembled warriors, moving between their tables and tempting them with her slender, womanly form.

My heart began to beat faster as she came towards the back of the hall where we were still standing. Soon she was standing before Geraint, close enough to feel his breath on her face, moving her body suggestively in front of him before slipping away from him and dancing in front of Oengus.

I felt my chest tighten with panic as she span away from the bard and stood before me, her green eyes burning with lust the way they had in the sacred cave many years before. For a moment she danced before me with a wanton expression, her pouting red lips slightly parted before a flicker of shocked realisation crossed her face. She came closer and draped her slender, pale arms around my shoulders, placing her mouth close to my ear.

"Why have you come here?" she whispered discreetly.

The heady smell of her exotic perfume, the heat of her breath and the touch of her lips against my ear caused my blood to rise. "I've come for you, Nivian," I stuttered breathlessly.

She smiled enigmatically and span away again, her dance becoming more and more charged with lustful sexuality as she gyrated and bucked on the floor, swinging her head so that her lustrous hair fanned about her as the music reached a crescendo that ended with her falling back and lying prostrate on the floor in apparent exhaustion.

The warriors cheered and applauded and thumped their tables as Nivian skipped to her feet, bowed and retrieved her cloak.

"She recognised you, didn't she?" Oengus whispered.

I nodded with a look of concern.

"If she tells Fiachu we're here, there's going to be trouble," he continued.

Again I nodded. "Our fate rests in her hands," I said quietly.

Nivian took her place at Fiachu's side and I watched her closely to see whether she was about to betray us to her lord, but she sat back down and looked over at me with a slight smile on her lips as Oengus was called forwards with his lyre. He gave a flourishing bow and strode forwards confidently, strumming his instrument and singing in a loud and clear voice.

I looked around for Brida, but the Pict girl was nowhere to be seen and so Geraint and I found a relatively quiet corner of the hall and sat down, near a group of women and low ranking men who were not deemed worthy enough to sit with the warriors. They were the shepherds, millers, brewers and swineherds of the fort along with their women and they glanced at us with fearful suspicion but left us in peace, which was exactly what we wanted. While the warriors dined on choice cuts of meat, we were given a vegetable stew with lumps of fatty mutton and bitter tasting, watery ale, but it was better than nothing.

As Oengus entertained the warriors, my eyes kept straying towards Nivian who turned her head and met my gaze with her emerald eyes every time, her expression enigmatic and unreadable. A movement in the smoke blackened rafters caught my eye and I saw a small, greyish brown bird settle on one of them. It was Lugotrix, Myrddin's sparrowhawk and upon seeing him I nudged Geraint's foot under the table and nodded towards the bird.

Geraint confirmed with a surreptitious nod and kept his eyes on the bird awaiting the signal.

A slave girl dressed in a grey woollen tunic came over with a jug of ale and began to refill our leather beakers.

"The lady Nivian wishes to speak with you privately," she said discreetly as she poured ale into my beaker.

"Where?" I asked.

"Follow me," the girl replied and she walked away from our table towards a side door in the hall.

I rose from the table and followed her at a discreet distance, easing my way past drunken men and trying to look as unobtrusive as possible. Fiachu was engaged in conversation with his red bearded companion and so far had showed no signs that he suspected anything.

I followed the slave girl through the door and down a set of stone steps that led to a cold, stone lined cellar filled with barrels and clay amphorae and sacks of grain, barley, oats and apples as well as slabs of dried meat and fish that hung from hooks in the wooden ceiling. She carried a torch made of rushes soaked in pitch and indicated that I was to follow her behind a stack of crates and barrels. She then handed me the torch and pointed at a figure in black hidden at the far end of the cellar before vanishing discreetly back the way she had come.

As I approached, Nivian threw back her hood and took a couple of steps forward. She was radiant and beautiful, more beautiful than I could ever believe was possible.

"Fergus, why have you come here?" she asked, her emerald eyes sparkling in the light of the torch.

"I told you, I came for you," I replied with a slight tremor in my voice. "And for my daughter."

The mention of my daughter took her off guard and she looked momentarily shaken. "But how can you possibly know about Morgana?"

"Myrddin showed me," I replied, unwilling to elaborate any further. "You named her after my mother?"

Nivian nodded. "It was the least that I could do for you," she said before her tone changed and became bitter. "Myrddin is a fool, always poking his beak into other people's lives. He has no idea what he is messing with here."

I looked into the eyes of the girl who had once been both friend and lover to me. "Why did you join them, Nivian?"

She glared at me defiantly. "I had no choice. It was either join them or live the life of a slave, or worse and I vowed from a young age that I would not live the life my mother had. When I was captured, I was taken before Fiachu who claimed me as his own, thus saving me from being degraded any further by his men." Her green eyes flashed with anger at the memory and her full red lips curled into a sneer. "Fiachu flew into a rage when he found out what had happened to me and he made me watch as he tied the men responsible to a stake, cut off their manhood and let them bleed to death. That was when I realised what he was capable of. Luckily, Sinusa saw that I had a gift, something that would grow if nurtured and so she took me under her wing and showed me the power that could be gained if I were to follow Crom Cruach, the Crooked One," her sneer turned to a smile of triumph.

"Fiachu and Sinusa killed my people and the people of Penglyn," I snarled bitterly. "They deserve to die."

"So you have come with vengeance on your mind as well? You intend to kill my lord and my mentor, Sinusa?" She looked at me analytically, her eyes narrowing. "I have dreamed of this moment for years and neither you nor anyone else will stop me now."

Nivian shook her head impatiently. "You have put yourself in great danger by coming here. You have walked unwittingly straight into Sinusa's trap, just as she knew you would. I implore you, Fergus, if the love that you bore for me meant anything, you will leave this place now and forget that you ever saw me."

I laughed bitterly. "You know that I am not going to do that, Nivian. The reason I am here now is because I never forgot you. Every day I have thought about you, wondered where you were, dreamed about you in my sleep. And I have been consumed by guilt ever since that day that I left you to your fate. When I found out from Old Mother Argoel that you still lived and that you had been taken by Fiachu mac Niall I vowed that I would find you, whatever the cost."

Nivian's expression softened and she stepped forwards and took my left hand in both of hers. "Oh, Fergus. Fate separated us on that day for a reason. It was the will of the gods that we were to follow different paths, but by doing this, you are going against the will of the gods and no good can come of it. Please, I implore you, leave tonight and never return. You are in great danger."

"I will leave, but only if you will come with me," I said, looking deep into her haunting eyes. She shook her head slowly.

"I cannot leave. My life is here now, amongst the Masraighe and at Fiachu's side. These are my people now, Fergus. Please let us depart as friends and not as enemies."

I closed my fingers gently on her slender hand, feeling the softness of her skin with my thumb. "Do you love him?"

She looked down at the flagstone floor of the cellar with a troubled expression. "Despite what you think of him, he saved me from the clutches of his men and made me his lady. His strength and reputation are all the protection I need and he treats me well most of the time."

"Most of the time?" I echoed sourly. "By making you dance like a tavern whore for his men?"

She snatched her hand back, the look of defiance returning to her face. "At least Fiachu would never have abandoned me after watching me being raped as you did. Leave now or face the consequences."

I felt my face flush with shame and anger. "I was a boy and there was no way that I could have taken on fully grown warriors. I did what I could, Nivian. I never wanted to abandon you and I have lived with the burden of that guilt every day since then. But if you refuse to come with me, at least let me take my daughter."

"You cannot take her. She belongs here."

"I know what you are planning to do with her," I said, a sense of betrayal growing within me. "I know that you want to make her a vessel for the soul of that vile witch. Do you really think I'm going to leave here knowing that you are going to do that to my daughter?"

She looked at me with contempt. "You don't understand, do you? It is a gift that we are giving her. She will carry the soul of the greatest sorceress that ever lived, it will be an honour for her, the ultimate act of love a mother could carry out for her child. Would you deny her that?"

I looked at her with disbelief. "They really have warped your mind, Nivian. Just like they did with my father. Sinusa is evil and she is willing to let thousands of innocents die so that she can cling to life and increase her dark powers. She has to be stopped once and for all and so does that blasphemy that she worships."

"Be careful of how you speak about the Crooked One," she hissed harshly.

"Crom Cruach is not a god of light. It is a monster, mindless and terrible, a god of the void, of misery and suffering. Dorbalos knew that as did Father Demetrios and Old Mother Argoel and Myrddin. And I know for I have seen it. It will consume and destroy you and I will ask you one more time. Come with me, Nivian. Come away from this place and return with me to Dumnonia."

Nivian let out a condescending chuckle. "You haven't heard a word I've said, have you? This discussion is over. I never wanted to see you die, Fergus, but it looks as though it is now inevitable. I gave you the chance to escape because I loved you once, but you are too stubborn or too stupid to heed my warnings." Nivian tried to walk past me, but I seized her upper arm.

"So what happens now? You go and betray me to your husband? Let the witch know that I'm here?"

She turned and gave me a pitiful look. "She already knows you're here. Weren't you listening to me? I told you that you have walked willingly into her trap. Did you really think you came here of your own free will? Sinusa's will guided you here as you are the only missing piece that she needs. Your blood Fergus. Remember? She needs your blood to complete the ritual, but rather than scour the land looking for you, she has brought you to her instead. The visions that Myrddin had, the prophetic dreams were manipulated by her. She has led that misguided fool here as well, knowing that he would bring you with him." Her lip curled into a desultory sneer. "Myrddin, the last of the great druids. Last of the great fools," she shook her arm free of my grasp and walked off through the cellar. I watched her disappear around the barrels and wondered whether she was speaking the truth. Surely Sinusa had not influenced my decision to come here unless she truly was as powerful as Nivian had implied and as Myrddin had feared. If that was indeed the case, then we were in grave danger and I had to warn the others. Unconsciously, I reached down the front of my mail shirt and tunic and felt the linen ball of protective herbs that Myrddin had given me, resting next to my bronze triple spiral and wondered whether either could protect me against Sinusa's magic.

I extinguished the torch and made my way back through the cellar and took the steps back up to the hall. Nivian had returned to her place next to Fiachu and I walked back over to Geraint who was sitting at the end of the table glowering into his ale.

"They know what we're here for," I whispered across the table.

"How?"

"Sinusa, the Masraighe witch. She's known all along. It's a trap and we've fallen for it."

Geraint leaned forwards on his elbows. "If that's the case, we have to get out of here now."

"Not without my daughter," I replied.

Geraint's face hardened. "Fergus, be realistic about this. There is no way that we are rescuing anyone. We are in a fortress surrounded by our enemies and at any moment they could turn on us. We have no weapons. We are hundreds of miles away from our homeland. You must choose your battles and this is not one that we can possibly win. We leave, now."

"You go then. I will not hold it against you if you leave, my friend. I have to try and find my daughter."

Geraint stood and looked at me, his mouth downturned and grim. "You are a mad, stubborn Irishman. If you stay here, it is certain death. I'm not a coward, you know that more than anyone. But I will not die for nothing. I'm leaving and this is your last chance to come with me. We can go away, rethink our strategy and return another time if needs be."

I shook my head. "If I do not do this now, I will never get the chance again. My daughter is in danger and I have to save her."

"Then may the gods walk with you, friend." Geraint patted my shoulder and made his way to the main doors of the hall, but upon seeing the guards at the door, he diverted his route and vanished into the shadows. As I watched him go, a fluttering caught my attention and my eyes were drawn up to the rafters where Lugotrix still sat. The bird let out three chirps in rapid succession and as I watched, Lugotrix flapped his wings and flew through the smoke hole in the thatched roof.

The mead and ale was flowing well and the men were becoming more rowdy, their mood reflected by the bawdy drinking songs that Oengus was now singing. Some were standing on the tables and a couple of brawls broke out, but were quickly contained by the others. Several men were copulating with slave girls amongst the rushes on the floor and even on the tables whilst Fiachu mac Niall reclined on his throne, regarding his men with an amused smirk on his face.

I got up from the bench and attempted to mingle with the other warriors. As long as I remained anonymous, just another warrior amongst hundreds, I could stay safe and perhaps get close enough to Fiachu mac Niall to slide my blade into his ribs without being seen as he walked amongst his men.

A tugging at the sleeve of my mail shirt gained my attention and I looked round to see Brida looking back at me. She was dressed in the plain roughspun grey tunic of a slave girl.

"The guard has gone. You can get into his chamber. Follow."

She pushed her way unobtrusively through the crowd and I followed at a distance until we came to a wooden door near the back of the hall covered with a heavy curtain embroidered with the Masraighe crescent symbol.

"Quickly, this is your only chance before the guard returns," Brida said in heavily accented Gaelic as she held the curtain aside.

"They know why we're here," I whispered to the Pict girl. "You've got to warn Oengus and get as far away as possible."

Brida shook her head. "Too late. You must do this now. Myrddin has drugged the mead, did you not hear the bird? Find somewhere to hide and strike while he sleeps."

I placed my hand gently against her cheek. "Thank you Brida," I said genuinely. "And if it's any consolation, I am truly sorry for what I did."

The girl placed her own small hand over mine and gave a sad smile. "You will do what you must, Fergus mac Fiontan. You freed me from a life of drudgery and for that I must be grateful."

I leaned forwards and kissed her tenderly on the forehead, but she pushed me away, glancing fearfully to the other end of the hall. The guard, who had left his post to relieve his bladder was now returning, stopping only to grab a horn of mead from a passing servant. Brida made her way over to him and draped an arm around his neck whilst pressing her slender body up against him, distracting him long enough for me to duck behind the curtain into the darkness beyond.

The chamber beyond was lit only by the glowing embers of coals in four bronze braziers spaced evenly around the room. The walls were hung with heavily embroidered tapestries and the shields of Fiachu's allies with their many different clan emblems, surmounted with crossed weapons of all types; swords, seaxes, spears and axes.

A large, fur covered bed took up most of the floor and a strange but not unpleasant smell permeated the room and I noticed the source was a smaller, engraved silver brazier with a plume of pungent blue smoke emanating from it. The smell reminded me immediately of Old Mother Argoel's home back in the forest near Penglyn.

I eased one of the swords from its mounting on the wall and took a seax from another and positioned myself between one of the tapestries and the split log wall. All that I had to do now was to bide my time until Fiachu retired to his chamber. I waited, listening to the muffled sounds of festivities coming from the hall. At some point, Fiachu made a long and rambling speech to his men, but I could not make out the words and after a while, the music and raucous laughter resumed as I waited alone in the darkness, like a deadly spider awaiting its prey.

Eventually, there were sounds of voices and movement outside the door. I held my breath as I heard Fiachu's distinct voice, his speech heavy and slowed with ale and mead, which had hopefully been laced with Myrddin's concoction. There was another voice, a female voice which was unmistakeably Nivian's, the musical sound of her laughter bringing back bittersweet memories. The two of them came into the chamber and collapsed onto the bed and I stood in silence, my fist clenched around the hilt of the seax as I listened to them making love an arm's length away. I fought the urge to leap from cover and kill him there and then, but did not want to run the risk of Nivian raising the alarm and so I waited until her moans of pleasure and his bestial grunts gave way to drunken snores.

After a while, I eased myself from behind the curtain. By the dim orange glow of the brazier I could see them both lying on the large bed, Nivian's pale, slender arm draped over his muscular shoulder. I crept silently around to Fiachu's side of the bed and knelt before him, inches away from his face.

I clapped my hand firmly over his mouth and placed my full weight on top of him, placing my mouth next to his ear.

"This is for my father and my brother and Dorbalos and Rhawn and all the others that you have taken from me," I whispered as I brought up the seax and plunged it beneath his ribs and up into his heart.

Fiachu bucked under my weight as his life ebbed from his body. I felt the wet warmth of his blood against my chest as it spurted out in scarlet torrents. Soon his body became limp and lifeless and I stood, trembling all over as I looked down on his bloodied corpse lying next to the woman that I had loved.

Nivian stirred and her eyes flickered open. Even by the dim light of the braziers I could see the horror on her face as she looked from her dead husband and then to me, standing with a dripping seax in my hand, covered in his blood. She opened her mouth as though to scream and in desperation, coupled with an insane fit of jealousy, I drove the seax with all my force between her bare breasts.

Nivian fell back with a choked cry, as the blade penetrated her chest up to the hilt. I staggered backwards and sank to my knees, unable to take my eyes off of Nivian's lifeless body, feeling nothing but a terrible numbness that overwhelmed all of my senses.

How long I remained there, I do not know, but I know that I sobbed and shook until a noise behind me brought me back to my senses.

The door opened and torchlight flooded the chamber and I reached for the sword that I had taken from the wall and whirled around to face the intruders, my eyes burning with a wild insanity, not caring whether I lived or died.

Five armed men, both Pict and Masraighe entered the room bearing torches and swords and fanned out before me.

I dropped into a fighting stance, knees slightly bent and ready to spring forwards, feeling like a cornered animal. I knew that I would soon die, that I had left it too long to make my escape, but I no longer cared and I was confident that I could take at least one or two of them with me, but the men did not attack. They merely watched me warily, their weapons held at the ready.

A dry and soulless chuckle came from the doorway and a half dozen black robed Masraighe priests entered, led by Malbach who regarded me with malicious, glittering eyes, a sneering, thin smile on his lips.

Four of the priests carried a litter and I knew immediately that the emaciated bundle of rags that sat upon it was Sinusa, the Masraighe sorceress, even before she turned her sightless, sunken eyes towards me. Her toothless mouth hung open and she laughed, a mirthless, rasping noise that chilled my blood.

"To be honest, we did not believe that the son of Fiontan mac Duggan could be so easily influenced to do our bidding," Malbach said with mock wonder, the stump of his right hand hidden in the voluminous sleeves of his robes as he looked past me at the bodies of Fiachu and Nivian.

Sinusa spoke, and her voice was like something from the grave. "We called your name into the void and you came to us like a moth to a flame. Crom Cruach has brought you to us, that we may finish the ritual begun years ago."

I looked at Malbach with bewilderment. "But why would you have me kill your leader? What sense is there in that?"

The dark druid threw back his skull like head and laughed with genuine amusement. "Oh, you truly are a fool. So easily manipulated, so naive, just like your father," he made a gesture towards the doorway and in walked Fiachu mac Niall with a wry smile on his face with Nivian just behind him, her dark hair hanging down to her slender waist.

My face froze in an expression of confused disbelief, much to the amusement of Fiachu. Nivian regarded me with a cold glare, her face betraying no emotion.

"But I killed you," I blurted stupidly.

Fiachu shrugged. "I'm sorry to disappoint you, but you most certainly did not."

"Then who..." I turned to look back at the bed, at the two lifeless, bloodstained corpses lying upon it, their inhuman faces frozen in death, amber eyes staring glassily into the void.

"No!" I exclaimed in shocked disbelief. It was impossible, there was no possible way that I could have mistaken the two things lying there for Fiachu and Nivian, but there they were, their dead eyes staring sightlessly up at the rafters, their hooves bound with twine, two mountain goats lying dead like the results of some obscene practical joke.

The world seemed to spin around me and I felt a wave of nausea as I struggled to make sense of what was happening.

"Of course we couldn't have done it without the help of your friends," Fiachu said, still grinning. He beckoned to someone beyond the doorway and in walked Oengus, his lyre still held in his hand. He looked at me and gave an apologetic shrug. "I'm sorry, Fergus. I did like you, but I'm afraid I can't afford to have any loyalties to anyone, except to myself and Brida."

I looked at Oengus the traitor with disbelief. "How could you do this after what he did to your father and sisters? Why?"

Oengus did not reply but merely looked down at the floor in shame, unable to meet my accusatory glare, until I demanded an answer a second time.

"Lord Fiachu has one of my sisters who still lives," he replied with a tremor in his voice. "He promised to reunite us if I did this one thing for him. I am so sorry, Fergus."

I shook my head, my lip curling in disgust.

"You have no idea of the powers that work against you, boy," Sinusa rasped. "Submit to your destiny now."

"Never!" I yelled and lunged forwards, swinging the blade at her hideous, corpse like face.

With a speed that I never believed possible, Fiachu drew his short sword from its scabbard and checked my blade mid swing in a shower of sparks. He barged me backwards with a powerful thrust of his shoulder and I stumbled back, ducking the swing of one of his men and thrusting my blade into his midriff.

I pulled it free, just in time to block the incoming swipe of another man, sending him sprawling with a savage butt of my forehead that crunched against his nose and despatched him to the Otherworld with a rapid thrust of my sword into his throat.

Fiachu came forwards, his sword and seax a blur of steel as he advanced, forcing me onto my back foot. My leg hit the bed and I stumbled backwards as the son of

King Niall skilfully disarmed me with a flick of his wrist. Before I knew what was happening, my back was against the wall of the chamber with the blade of Fiachu's seax pressed against my cheek.

"You made the biggest mistake of your life coming here, lad," he said calmly. "But at last we can finish what should have been completed years ago."

I looked into his dead, grey eyes which betrayed no emotion and in one swift movement, he sliced the seax across my right cheek, opening the flesh from the corner of my mouth to my ear.

I felt an explosion of pain and felt my mouth fill with warm, metallic blood as I sank forwards onto my knees, choking.

I looked up in time to see one of the Picts stride forwards and swing the butt of his spear towards my head. There was a flash of light before blackness engulfed me and my pain vanished.

Chapter 17

A Reluctant Freedom

When I regained consciousness, I was in a world of pain. Slowly I opened my eyes as I realised I was choking on my own blood and that I was hanging by my wrists from the bars of a wooden cage. The coarse rope dug into my flesh painfully and my arms felt as though they would be torn from their sockets, but that pain was as nothing compared to the wave of agony that assailed me when I coughed and felt as though my face would tear in half.

Through my haze of agony I was aware of a terrible din; drums clashing, horns blaring, people chanting and screaming and also the acrid smell of burning and the feeling of heat upon my exposed torso. I attempted to manoeuvre myself around on my toes to see what was going on and saw dark figures cavorting before a mass of intense orange flame.

Slowly my mind began to make sense of my surroundings. I was outside of Fiachu's hall, in the open compound of Din Mhor, watching some sort of ceremony taking place. The wicker effigy had been set aflame and all of the prisoners that I had seen beforehand had been herded into it to be burned alive before the baying, chanting crowd of Cruithne and Masraighe warriors, their agonised screams mingling with the pounding of drums and the clash of cymbals.

I saw Malbach in his black crow feathered cloak, surrounded by similarly attired priests, his arms upraised to the heavens and his enraptured face lit eerily by the amber glow of the flames as he shouted exultantly to his vile god.

A sharp blow to my exposed stomach knocked the wind out of me and I looked down to see a squat, ugly Masraighe warrior eyeing me belligerently. He struck me again through the bars of the cage with the butt of his spear.

"He wakes, my lord," the man barked with a contemptuous sneer.

I turned my head as best I could to see Fiachu mac Niall walk into view. He held on to the wooden bars of the cage and leaned forwards, examining me as though I were some rare and dangerous animal.

"I've waited many years for this moment," he said softly. "It's a shame that we do not have your sister as well, but your offspring will work well enough," he frowned thoughtfully. "Tell me, what ever happened to the beautiful Ygerna?"

"She drowned," I uttered with difficulty.

Fiachu chuckled icily and looked down at the straw on the floor of the cage. "We both know that's not true. If I had the time, I'd beat the answer from you, but it's irrelevant now. I would like to know where she is though, as I've promised her to my men. No one makes a fool of Fiachu mac Niall and gets away with it."

"You're wasting your time, Fiachu," I repeated adamantly. "My sister is dead."

Fiachu reached through the bars of the cage and grabbed a fistful of my hair, twisting my head painfully. "You lie," he snarled. "And before you die, I will know the whereabouts of your companion and any others who have aided you. Who is the druid that you have been travelling with? The one seen skulking about earlier in our stores?"

I hawked up a glob of bloody phlegm and launched it in his direction. It struck his chequered cloak on the left shoulder and a dangerous sneer crossed his face.

"I'll make sure you die slowly and in great pain, lad. Sinusa only needs a cupful of your blood to complete the ceremony, but she's agreed to let me have you after she's taken what she requires. I'll make sure I extract it all as painfully as possible."

He wiped at the slime on his shoulder and turned away to watch the awful spectacle before him.

Soon the heat, the noise, the stench of charred flesh and the pain and discomfort that I was enduring became too much for me and once again I lapsed into unconsciousness, but before my senses left me completely, I heard the shrill call of a small bird of prey, repeated three times.

By the time I came around again, I felt a brief sensation of falling before landing heavily on the filthy straw strewn floor of the cage. Strong but gentle hands raised me to a sitting position and my eyes flickered open to see two hooded men crouching over me. One had a sword drawn and was looking around furtively whilst the other examined the wound on my face.

The crowd of warriors and priests had gone and the great blazing bonfire had died down to a pile of crackling red coals that still gave off a considerable amount of heat. The smell of burned flesh still filled the air and I was vaguely aware of drums receding into the distance.

"Can you walk?" The hooded man examining my face asked.

"Myrddin," I gasped with gratitude and relief. However my brief elation was overcome by a more sombre emotion that clouded all other thought. "I have failed," I added miserably. "Oengus has betrayed us to Fiachu. I thought that I had killed him, but it was Sinusa's magic, she had clouded my mind. She led us here, it was her all along."

"I realise that now," Myrddin replied as he held my head in his hands, turning it so that he could examine the wound by the moonlight. "They caught me in the stores and I only managed to escape with my life thanks to the timely arrival of our friend here," he nodded towards Geraint.

"Did you manage to get the sleeping draught into the mead?" I asked.

The druid shrugged. "Partially, but not enough, I fear. Events have changed and our plans must change with them," he regarded me with a scowl. "Can you walk?"

I nodded and forced myself upright, my head pounding from the blow I had received. I stood unsteadily for several seconds, bracing myself against the bars of the cage. I noticed three dark heaps on the ground near the door of the cage where Geraint now stood, his hood thrown back, wiping blood from his sword with a rag. He kicked at one of the bodies of the guards and grinned at me, his white teeth gleaming like a feral beast in the moonlight.

"You see what happens to you when I'm not around?" he said, tossing me my sword and seax in their scabbards. He also handed me my bow and quiver of arrows. "That's the last time these bastards will be taking our weapons." He spat on one of the lifeless corpses.

I strapped the weapons around my waist and slung the bow and quiver over my shoulder, feeling weak and nauseous from loss of blood. The deep wound on my cheek had congealed into a ragged black line which leaked every time I exerted myself. From the hall, I could hear the muffled sounds of continued revelry and drunken singing and could see the yellow glow of torchlight seeping out into the darkness from between the timbers.

"Hurry, there may still be time," Myrddin hissed insistently. "The priests have gone up to the mountain's summit to complete the ceremony. We may still be able to prevent it."

"But they need my blood to complete the ceremony," I said, seeing my helmet on one of the corpses and reaching down to retrieve it.

Geraint nodded at the bodies on the ground. "That's what this lot came for. They must have drank some of Myrddin's spiked mead, because when it came to fighting, they couldn't hit a cow's arse with both hands. It was too easy, really." He sheathed his sword with a smirk.

"Where is Fiachu now?" I asked.

Myrddin nodded towards the Great Hall. "He is preparing for the ceremony. They need your blood, so we do not have much time, but if we move quickly, we could get to the top of the mountain, kill Sinusa and get your daughter back. There are no warriors with them and we could be away before Fiachu and his men get there, but we must hurry."

"But I want to kill him," I snarled, closing my hand on the sharkskin hilt of Octha's Ruin.

"If you go in there, you will surely die, they will have your blood and Sinusa will be able to complete her ritual," Myrddin snapped impatiently, pointing a long finger towards the hall. "You will have your chance to face Fiachu another day." Geraint nodded in agreement. "Your woman is up there with that witch. If we can capture her and your daughter as well, then Fiachu will surely follow. We draw him out and choose where and when we face him."

"Very well," I said, loosening my grip on my sword. "Lead the way out of here." Myrddin led us through the shadows to the back of the hall where the small stream flowed down from the mountain. Furtively we ran along it, following its course to the left and stooping low to stay within the shadows and to avoid detection by the handful of men bearing torches and patrolling the palisade. The stream ran rapidly, carving a deep groove in the rocks near the western edge of the fortress. Myrddin plunged into the ice cold water and Geraint and I followed his lead as he waded knee deep towards the thick stone wall of the fortress. At the base of the wall, just beneath the water's surface and virtually invisible was an iron grill, set within a narrow tunnel in the rock, where the water flowed through, just as Oengus had told us.

Myrddin gestured towards it and Geraint waded forwards, crouching into the tunnel and placing the blade of his seax between the rusted grate and the stone. He placed his weight against the hilt of the seax and pushed until the grate broke loose and creaked open.

Myrddin and I crawled through the narrow opening which was barely wide enough for a man to get through, half submerged under the bitterly cold water of the stream.

We emerged on the other side soaked and shivering and helped Geraint through before setting off around the rear of the fortress, careful to stay within the shadow of the palisade and then scrambling up the mountainside in the moonlight.

My face and head throbbed terribly as we climbed the rocky slope of the mountain and I felt breathless and light headed through lack of blood, struggling to keep up with the fleet footed Myrddin as he climbed the slope easily with his long strides. Geraint grabbed my arm and helped me where he could until eventually we approached the summit and Myrddin crouched down behind a boulder and indicated for us to do likewise.

Up ahead we could see a procession of torches winding up a narrow path which had been cleared of snow, towards a large, flat stone at the windswept summit where a group of black robed priests, also bearing torches, waited patiently and I realised with a shudder that this was the place that I had seen during my spirit journey with Myrddin, where I had witnessed my own sacrifice.

"Wait here. I will cause a distraction," Myrddin whispered. "You will know when to strike."

With that he vanished into the moonlight, his dark form blending into the night.

"Can you fight?" Geraint asked quietly.

I nodded with more enthusiasm than I felt.

Geraint squeezed my shoulder reassuringly and nodded once.

The procession of priests took up position in a circle around the altar stone while Malbach walked forwards with Nivian, his handless arm linked with hers. Behind them came four men bearing the litter on which Sinusa was seated, her ancient body enshrouded in black, with only her skeletal hands exposed, gripping the staff that lay across her lap.

The men placed the litter gently down on the frozen ground before the altar and helped Sinusa to rise to her feet. The crone then cast aside her black robes and let them drop in a heap, standing naked in the moonlight, her decrepit body little more than bones covered with loose, sagging skin, her empty breasts hanging like two pendulous sacks.

One of the priests stepped forwards and handed her a silver goblet which she took and drank from greedily and I noticed with disgust the unmistakable stain of blood upon her wizened lips, blood that could only have belonged to one person. Absently, my hand went to my face and I realised with horror that I had been a fool and that my blood had already been collected for the ritual whilst I had been unconscious in the cage.

The priests began to chant rhythmically, a haunting, discordant sound that rose and fell like the mountain wind as a small figure was brought forwards and I recognised her immediately as my own daughter.

Nivian stepped forwards with a motherly smile and took both of her hands, guiding her towards the stone altar under the greedy, sightless eyes of the ancient witch. She too was naked, with jet black, wavy hair that tumbled over her small shoulders, her emerald eyes, so like her mother's were wide and frightened.

The cup of blood was handed from person to person until it reached Nivian, who then crouched before my daughter and handed it to her with a serene smile.

The little girl took the goblet in two tiny hands and hesitantly raised it to her lips. I could not believe that Nivian was allowing this monstrous ceremony to take place and I nearly yelled aloud with outrage, but Geraint placed a restraining hand on my shoulder.

With silent gestures he advised me to ready my bow before sliding off into the shadows, moving quickly across the rugged, icy terrain in a crouch and soon vanishing completely.

Muttering a silent prayer to the Goddess, I slid one of the aspen arrows from my quiver and nocked it on the bow string with trembling fingers, holding my breath and drawing it back to my ear. The aspen arrow would dispel the witches black soul, sending it screaming back to the dark void of Cythraul and I realised in that moment why Lugubelenus had given me these particular arrows. The short yew bow creaked as I drew it back and lined up the steel tip of the arrow with the centre of Sinusa's emaciated chest.

At that moment there was a flash of green light and an explosion of smoke from a short distance away and my night vision was momentarily incapacitated. After a few seconds however, I could make out a tall robed figure with antlers silhouetted against a cloud of billowing green smoke holding a staff aloft and emitting a blood chilling, bestial howl. Although common sense told me this must be Myrddin, the towering figure seemed far too tall, its presence too intense and its glowing green eyes wild like the beasts of the forest and I remembered what the druid had told me years ago about how his body was a vessel for Carnun, the god of wild beasts and in that heart stopping moment I knew that he had spoken the truth.

Immediately everyone present at the ceremony, including Sinusa, turned to face the Otherwordly figure which had appeared out of nowhere and I knew that this was the moment to strike.

I released the string and let my arrow fly towards the ancient Masraighe priestess who had half turned back towards me as though she knew what was happening, but it was too late for her. The aspen arrow struck her in the side of the neck and she staggered backwards a few steps as I slung my bow over my shoulder and charged forwards with Octha's Ruin and my Votadini Seax drawn.

I hacked down two unarmed priests who tried to check my advance before I reached Sinusa who was now staggering towards me with her arms outstretched, her wrinkled face twisted with hatred as she choked on her own blood, the arrow shaft protruding obscenely from her scrawny neck.

The mysterious stag headed apparition vanished as quickly as it had appeared and chaos reigned as the assembled dark druids shouted and screamed in confusion and from the corner of my eye I could see Geraint run from the shadows slashing indiscriminately with his sword at the stunned priests, taking down three of them before the others even realised what was happening.

Sinusa faced me like something from a nightmare, reeling and barely able to stand as she vomited gouts of blood down her bare chest, her hands clawing feebly at me as she stumbled forwards, cackling with derision despite the mortal wound that she had sustained. I thought that she was trying to speak, to call down one final curse upon me, but her words were drowned in blood and came out as an indistinct gargle. Overcome with disgust, I swung my Saxon blade at the obscene thing before me, slicing easily through the thin neck, sending the head spinning to the ground as the decrepit body took a few more faltering steps before collapsing in a heap before me. I felt no elation, no sense of satisfaction over having partially avenged the deaths of my people and my family, only revulsion for the ancient thing lying lifeless at my feet.

My reflections were short lived however as several of the more foolhardy druids attempted to rush me, urged onwards by Malbach who was glaring at me with utter hatred.

One of them swung a torch towards my head, but he was untrained in combat and I ducked it easily, countering with a simple thrust of my seax that slid between the man's ribs a mere finger's length, piercing his heart and killing him instantly.

I killed three more of them with ease, sidestepping their clumsy swings and despatching them with a thrust of my seax or a slash of my sword.

I saw the panic on Malbach's face as the other priests attempted to flee into the night shadows and I strode purposefully towards him, my eyes boring into his, revelling in the terror that he must have felt as I approached like some ancient war god, my hair spiked with lime and my grim face painted with blue woad and streaked with blood and gore.

Malbach held his staff before him as though he were offering it to me, his skull like face rigid with fear as he sank helplessly to his knees.

I stood before him and sheathed Octha's Ruin, my short bladed seax still held in my other hand.

"Stand up," I muttered, feeling hatred coursing through my veins.

Malbach stood falteringly, leaning heavily on his staff with his one good hand. "Fergus mac Fiontan," he said with a trembling smile, his shoulder twitching spasmodically. "This was the will of Crom Cruach. You must understand I never bore you or your family any malice."

"Don't you ever mention my name or my family again," I hissed venomously. "You tricked my father with your lies, you discredited Dorbalos and you laughed as my people died at the hands of your men. I have spent my life running in terror from you, but now the Goddess is with me, as is Carnun, Lord of the Beasts. Now you will meet your precious Crom Cruach."

I pushed the wickedly sharp blade into his midriff and pulled him forwards onto it as I sawed upwards through his abdomen, feeling his hot innards tumble from the deadly gash over my hand and legs to slip in a steaming, glistening pile on the ground between us.

Malbach gasped and choked as I let him fall slowly into the bloody mess and I watched mercilessly as he sobbed and writhed amongst his own guts in agony. He held out his thin hand towards me, his eyes pleading for the mercy of a quick death, but I did not grant him one. Instead I left him to wallow and squirm away his last moments in his own slime and filth.

"Tuan, quickly. We must go now, before the survivors go and get aid." I turned to see Myrddin before me, looking breathless and haggard, his rowan staff held in both hands.

"Where is Nivian and my daughter?" I demanded.

In reply he pointed the gnarled head of his staff towards Geraint who was striding towards us holding a struggling bundle under one arm and his dripping sword in the other hand.

I sheathed my seax and took the tiny wriggling figure wrapped in a priests black cloak, teasing apart the folds to reveal a small, pale wide eyed face staring back at me.

I felt a conflict of emotions staring down at that perfect little face. Love, pity, guilt and sadness all churned inside of me like the ingredients of a cook's cauldron. "Don't be afraid, Morgana," I said softly. "I am your father, I will not hurt you." The little girl's mouth turned downwards and her green eyes filled with tears. "Where's my mummy?"

I looked at Geraint who nodded impatiently at a prone form lying amongst the corpses of the priests. My heart jumped to my throat as I looked at Geraint's bloody sword and I feared the worst. The Powysian seemed to read my thoughts and wiped his blade with a stained linen rag before returning it to its scabbard. "Don't fret, she's not dead. She just refused to cooperate and tried to lay a curse upon me so I lay my own curse upon her in the only way I know," he held up a gauntleted fist. "We've got what we came for, so let's get out of here. Soon this mountain will be swarming with Masraighe and Cruithne howling for our guts." Myrddin crouched over Nivian's motionless body and fumbled at a pouch on his belt, producing a tiny clay bottle which he waved under her nose. I was relieved to see her stir and within a few moments he was helping her to stand.

I walked over to her, holding Morgana close to my chest. On seeing her mother, the little girl began to wail pathetically, holding her arms out towards her.

Nivian stood unsteadily and glared at me with defiance. "How far do you think you will get before he finds you?" she spat vehemently. Her left eye was swollen and discoloured where Geraint had hit her, but her spirit was far from broken.

"We want him to find us," I replied flatly. "We know that he will come looking for you, that is why you are coming with us."

"I'd rather die than go anywhere with you," she said, her striking green eyes burning with anger.

"That can be arranged," Geraint said, half drawing his seax from its scabbard. "Let me do you a favour, Fergus and remove this bitch from your life once and for all." Nivian's eyes sparkled with contempt as she looked at Geraint, her sensual mouth set defiantly.

I grabbed Nivian's delicate jaw and turned her head so that she was facing me. "Geraint, keep your eyes on her. If she tries to get away, you have my permission to kill her. Now let's move."

Geraint placed one hand on Nivian's back, grabbing a handful of her cloak and forcing her into a jog as we followed the narrow, moonlit path down the mountainside. The path wound down to the fortress and in the silver light of the moon I could see several distant figures running towards its gates.

"The priests are going to raise the alarm," I said, pointing at the fleeing druids. "We have to get off the path."

"Too treacherous," Myrddin said. "We have no choice but to go past Din Mhor. The path runs in front of the fort and continues down the mountain. It is the only safe route down."

"You say that the path can be held by one man against many, Myrddin?" Geraint asked.

The druid nodded. "So they say, though I would not like to be the man in that position."

"Then you go on," Geraint replied. "I'll hold them for as long as I can."

I shook my head resolutely. "No Geraint. This is not your fight, this is mine. We stand together or not at all."

"You have your daughter to look after," Geraint objected. "You have to get her to safety or else all this will have been for nothing."

"Myrddin will take her and her mother to safety. I stand with you my friend."

Geraint gave a thoughtful grimace before clasping my right forearm in his strong grip and slapping me on the shoulder. "So be it. We die together."

"Sword in hand, like the heroes of old," I added with a grin that started my face bleeding again. I wondered briefly whether word of my exploits would ever reach my father and Conmor in the Otherworld and whether they would be proud of their youngest son and brother.

Nivian gave a contemptuous snort. "If Fiachu gets hold of you, you will die sobbing and screaming for your mothers."

I felt my blood boil at the mention of his name. "He is welcome to try. There is nothing I would like more than to see the life go out of his eyes as my blade pierces his heart. He no longer has his witch to protect him, remember."

Nivian gave me a frosty look. "Just because Sinusa is gone does not mean that Crom Cruach has abandoned us."

"When did you change Nivian?" I asked. "You are not the girl that I knew back in Penglyn."

She took a step forwards and stroked our daughter's long dark hair. "I changed on that day," she replied, her eyes beginning to brim with tears. "That day that you abandoned me and left me to my fate. Old Mother Argoel's ragged little helper died on that day, along with the rest of Penglyn. But Fiachu and Sinusa gave me my life back and I was reborn and now you have taken that from me and I shall never forgive you."

"I do not seek your forgiveness," I replied bitterly.

"We must hurry," Myrddin interjected as he watched the oak gates of the fortress swing open to allow the fleeing priests access. "They've raised the alarm."

We ran as quickly as we could down the treacherous, icy path towards the fortress, our eyes fixed warily on the torches that moved along the ramparts. The guards would be looking out for us and so we waited until a cloud drifted across the moon to make a dash past the fort's entrance. Geraint had his hand across Nivian's mouth and his seax at her throat as he dragged her along, in case she decided to call out and I still carried my daughter, wrapped in the black cloak and held close to my chest and as I ran past the large oak gates in a crouch I could hear some sort of commotion coming from within the fortress. Voices were raised and one gruff voice in particular was shouting out the same phrase over and over again in Pictish. At that moment, a single note from a horn pierced the winter's night, its harsh, monotonous tone spurring us into action. Throwing all caution to the wind, we ran, no longer concerned whether we were spotted or not.

Nivian took the opportunity to scream for help and an arrow whirred past my head and clattered against the cliff face to my left.

"They've seen us," I called to the others as another arrow skittered across the frosted ground between Myrddin's legs.

Soon the path took us around a bend, out of the sight of the fort and out of range of arrow shot. I handed my daughter to the druid, who took her and placed her within the folds of his robes. She wailed in distress even as he tried to calm her with soothing whispers.

"At least let the child have the comfort of her own mother," Nivian said sourly. Reluctantly, Myrddin handed Morgana to her and the child immediately clung to her mother and buried her face in her silky black hair. Nivian calmed her with a few tender words, even as Geraint dragged her unceremoniously by the scruff of her cloak, forcing her into a jog again.

We rounded another bend so that once again we were visible from the palisade of Din Mhor. I turned to see a number of orange torches streaming out of the gates and snaking down the path in pursuit of us.

"They're coming," I shouted and everyone turned to look at the rapidly approaching procession of flickering lights.

"Keep moving, we'll find somewhere to make our stand," Geraint said as he helped Nivian to her feet. She had slipped on a sheet of ice that covered the path for about a dozen paces and had nearly plummeted over the edge into yawning darkness. We carefully made our way across with our backs pressed against the cliff face until we could feel our feet gripping the rocky path again. The ice was black and all but invisible in the moonlight and the path here sloped upwards slightly and even a fool could see that it was the ideal place to make a stand as it automatically placed anyone on the ice at a severe disadvantage.

"Here is as good a place as any," I said, unslinging my short bow from my shoulder and pulling an arrow from my quiver. "Myrddin, you take Nivian and Morgana to the boat. We'll cover your escape."

The druid took Nivian by the arm gently but firmly. He gave a shrill whistle and Lugotrix appeared, swooping down out of the night sky and settling on his shoulder. "I will send Lugotrix back to let you know when we are safely on the boat. Make your way to the shore if you can."

I nodded once and the druid made a curious hand gesture.

"Morrigan be with you both. Feed her crows well."

"We intend to," I replied and the druid smirked enigmatically before leading Nivian and Morgana away down the mountain path. I watched them briefly until they disappeared around a bend and then turned to Geraint. The Powysian had unstrapped his helmet from his belt and was now fastening the cheek plates under his chin. I did the same, placing on my head the ornate helmet that I had won from the Eoganachta chieftain, Eamonn O'Suilleabhain. It was dented and scarred in places now, but it still bore the ornate bronze work around the nasal flange and brow ridges and I winced as I pulled the cheekplates tight and felt it press against my wounded face. I ignored the pain and fastened the rawhide cord under my chin.

"I wish we had spears to keep them at a distance," Geraint muttered as the guttering light of the torches grew ever closer. We could hear them now, Cruithne and Gael voices baying for our blood, screaming out challenges and insults as they closed the distance between us.

I drew my bowstring back to my cheek as Geraint stood with his arms outspread and bellowed his own challenge, belittling their manhood and cursing their mothers for promiscuous dogs.

The first half dozen warriors sprinted towards us, casting their torches aside and running at us with spears, swords and axes.

I fired at the lead man, a large, bare chested Pict, hitting him square in his ample belly, the shaft sinking into his soft abdomen right up to the feathers. He let out a high pitched squeal as he stumbled backwards and slipped sideways on the ice, tumbling into the blackness. The next one fared no better, slipping face first, allowing me enough time to nock another arrow and shoot it through the top of his skull, killing him instantly. My next arrow hit the next man in the hip and he fell back on the path screaming and cursing, blocking the progress of the others behind him.

Eventually the injured man was pulled aside and the others pressed forwards en masse, intending to overwhelm us with sheer weight of numbers.

I loosed off another three shots, unable to miss at such a close range, until finally the warriors of Din Mhor managed to close the distance between us. I stepped back and let Geraint come forwards as the first of our assailants reached us and the sound of steel ringing on steel filled the night air.

Geraint fought like a wild animal, his blade striking with power and deadly precision, taking the lives of one man after another as he screamed with battle born fury.

I fired my bow over his shoulder, loosing one arrow after the next with lethal accuracy, watching man after man fall back or tumble screaming into the abyss on our left.

Eventually there was a lull in the assault as our assailants realised the futility of their actions and instead brought their own bowmen forwards. Arrows began to whistle dangerously close to our heads and we decided to fall back as best as we could. We ran on until we found a rocky outcrop near a bend and took cover behind it, listening as the Pictish arrows shattered harmlessly against the rock or merely whistled into the darkness.

Soon they resumed their assault and the next wave of warriors charged forwards in an attempt to overwhelm us. The path where we stood was just wide enough for us to fight side by side and the bend and the outcrop of rock offered us protection from their archers.

We fought on as hard as we could, keeping the enemy at bay with their own spears which we had retrieved from the corpses of their dead, but we were slowly giving ground as the men behind the ones in front pelted us with rocks that bounced off of our helmets. Many of our attackers were under the influence of Myrddin's concoction which slowed their wits and clouded their judgement, making them easy prey, but there were many of them, far too many for two men to keep at bay. Geraint took a nasty slash to his mid-thigh but fought on regardless, the wound serving only to infuriate him even more. We took it in turns covering one another's retreat down the mountainside until a familiar voice yelled my name with such hatred that I stopped where I was. I turned to see Fiachu mac Niall, with Geraint blocking his path and watched as the two men fought, both highly skilled fighters locked in a duel to the death, their blades clashing together and sparking against the night sky.

I ran to the aid of my friend, calling his name, my blood seething with the desire for vengeance.

Geraint was breathing heavily when I reached him and I could see that he had taken another wound in his side and that his strength was failing. He backed away from his assailant, his sword and seax held in a defensive position.

"Go Fergus, you cannot best him," he said between gritted teeth, his eyes fixed on the Gael warlord before him. "He will kill you."

Fiachu mac Niall gave a feral grin when he saw me, but there was no humour in that grin, only a deep seated malice.

"Stand aside," Fiachu snarled at Geraint. "He is mine."

"Fergus, I mean it. Run now or he will kill you," Geraint said, holding his ground. He was in obvious pain and I noticed how he was reeling like a drunk man.

"Are you going to let your friend die for you, lad?" Fiachu sneered. He was wielding two short swords as he always did and behind him his men were baying and jeering.

"Don't give him the satisfaction of killing you here," Geraint hissed at me. "Even if you manage to kill him, his men will slaughter you. Go now. Your daughter needs you."

I turned and looked down the mountain path. In the distance I could see the moonlight reflecting off of the sea and wondered whether Myrddin had managed to get Nivian and Morgana to the little curragh. At that moment, I saw the moonlight reflecting off of something else. The steel blades and spear heads of several dozen men streaming up the path towards us. Somehow they had managed cut us off, perhaps by some route that we were unaware of and I realised with horror that we were trapped.

"There is nowhere to go, Geraint," I replied grimly. "We're trapped."

Geraint risked a quick glance over his shoulder to see the men running up the path to seal our fate.

It was all the time Fiachu mac Niall needed. With a lightning quick thrust, his blade pierced Geraint's mail coat and sank into his midriff to protrude a hand's length from his back. The Irishman pivoted around gracefully and smashed the other blade against the side of Geraint's head, knocking him sideways off of the precipitous path into the blackness below.

I screamed out incoherently in fury and despair and lunged at the Irishman, slashing and stabbing wildly, looking for an opening in his defence. His own two swords moved with an equal speed, blocking and deflecting my furious blows with ease. Fiachu gave no ground, but I lunged forwards, intent on killing him, hacking violently at his head, intending to batter him into submission with the strength of my attack.

Fiachu knocked each blow aside effortlessly, letting me tire myself against his impenetrable defence. I attacked again and again, fury and frustration making my strikes less accurate until soon I was breathing heavily and my wild attacks became slower and more obvious.

Behind me, I could hear Fiachu's men approaching, cutting off my escape route.

"Where's my woman, boy?" Fiachu demanded, his voice calm and deadly as always.

"Soon she will be far away from you, where you will never find her," I replied defiantly.

"You will tell me," he insisted. "Do you think I will grant you a quick death? A warrior's death?" he shook his head slowly with an expression of feigned pity, his cold grey eyes glittering maliciously. "I still intend to kill you slowly, to hear you scream for death's release. You do not deserve the death of a warrior. You are nothing, just like your brother and your father before you."

Mention of my family goaded me into action again and I attacked with renewed fury and this time one of my blades found its mark, my seax slicing into Fiachu's bare shoulder.

The Masraighe chief snarled through gritted teeth, his eyes betraying both surprise and anger as he staggered back, dropping one of his swords to the ground.

The realisation that Fiachu mac Niall was not invincible spurred me on and I pressed on with my assault, forcing him backwards, his confidence giving way to desperation as he struggled to defend himself with one blade against my two whilst simultaneously trying to quell the flow of blood from his shoulder with his other hand.

I swung high with my seax and then low with Octha's Ruin, feeling the sword's steel tip bite into the flesh of his thigh.

Fiachu fell heavily against the cliff face, his expression one of outraged disbelief. Never before had he been bested in single combat and I could see this reflected in his eyes.

I swung at him again, eager to end his life once and for all, but Fiachu mac Niall was far from beaten. He counterattacked with the sudden ferocity of a cornered wolf, his sword dancing in his hand with a speed that I barely believed was possible.

I fell back under the ferocity of his assault, feeling my heels on the edge of the mountain path, knowing that one more step back would send me plunging to my death, just as Geraint had done earlier. Desperately I tried to hold my ground, unable to find a gap in the rain of skilful blows that were aimed against me. Fiachu's sword tore across my chest, severing the mail links of my shirt and biting into my flesh. Instinctively I stepped backwards into nothingness and felt the terrible surging sensation of falling, bracing myself for the awful impact I knew must come.

Chapter 18

Into the Night

I fell backwards for what seemed an eternity, finally feeling an incredible thump that knocked the wind from my lungs and then I was tumbling in an uncontrolled flurry of limbs down a steep slope, my fall being mercifully broken by the thick snow that covered the mountainside.

My leg twisted awkwardly beneath me and soon I came to rest, shaken and bruised but otherwise undamaged apart from the deep gash across my chest.

I looked up at the heights from where I had fallen. Mercifully, the drop was not sheer, but rather steeply sloped and I thanked Cailleach, the Hag of Winter, for the blanket of snow that had broken my fall, for otherwise it would have meant certain death.

A shaft of moonlight illuminated my surroundings and I saw Octha's Ruin and my seax lying nearby. My bow, the gift from the Forest Folk of Coedwig dyn Bannog, was snapped in two and useless and so reluctantly I cast it aside. It had served its purpose well, having destroyed a great evil just as Lugubelenus had foresaw.

Far above I could see the twinkle of torches on the mountain path and I knew that Fiachu would be sending men down to retrieve my body.

I stood unsteadily, feeling a lance of pain in my right knee and started down the slope of the mountain, the snow coming up to mid-thigh and impeding my progress. A short distance away I saw a body lying motionless in the snow and I immediately thought of Geraint.

I fought my way towards the immobile figure, calling Geraint's name as I went, barely aware of the throbbing gash on my chest and on my face, both wounds inflicted by my grievous enemy somewhere above. My knee hurt badly, but was not broken and I gritted my teeth against the pain and bore it as best I could. I knew that the corpse before me was Geraint's before I had reached it, even though it lay face down in the snow, as I saw the familiar pattern of his cloak. I knelt down before my friend, grasping his shoulder and rolling him onto his back. Snow had stuck to his short, dark beard and his face was badly bruised and covered in blood, with a large gash across his forehead where I could see the white gleam of bone beneath. I looked down at the wound which had killed him, a neat puncture that had torn through his mail shirt and penetrated his abdomen.

The mountain spirits had taken their sacrifice, just as Myrddin had predicted they would and I let out a feral cry at the moon, a cry of loss and anger that echoed down the mountainside.

I held Geraint's head, my eyes filling with tears, overwhelmed with grief at the loss of my best friend. "I will avenge your death, Geraint. By the Old Gods and the new I will make Fiachu mac Niall pay for this," I reached down and closed his eyelids. "To me, to my house come you all after death," I muttered, saying the ancient prayer of my people, the prayer of Donn, the god of death. "We will meet again, my friend."

I held his bloody head against my mail clad chest and wept, but my grieving was short lived as in the distance I could hear the howling and barking of dogs and I cursed inwardly, remembering with a chill of fear how Ambrosius and I had been pursued with hounds once before. They were the fearsome hounds of my homeland, great long limbed, shaggy beasts that fought alongside their owners and feasted upon the flesh of their enemies.

Reluctantly, I left the body of my friend, kissing his head and gently laying him back in the snow before trudging on, ever downwards until the slope gradually became more gentle and I came to a river crossing my path.

I turned left, following the river downstream towards the sea, aware that the sound of dogs was growing ever closer by the moment.

The high pitched screech of a bird caught my attention and I saw Lugotrix perched on a nearby boulder, his little head twitching to one side as he watched me struggle through the snow. No sooner had I set eyes upon him than he flew off, following the course of the river with a series of little whistles, soon vanishing out of sight and I felt a small ray of hope, knowing that at least Nivian and Morgana were safe for the time being.

I was painfully aware that time was against me and that I had to make it to the shore as quickly as possible, but my injured knee hindered my progress and I turned to see bobbing torches in the distance not too far away and I knew that I would never make it.

I decided that I would make a last stand where I was and take down as many Cruithne and Masraighe as I could before I was overwhelmed. I drew my weapons and shouted a challenge to the men in the distance, but the insistent chirping of Lugotrix behind me caused me to turn around and look downriver where I glimpsed a small, tapered rectangular sail coming towards me.

"Myrddin," I muttered, sensing hope return once more. Soon I was shouting the druid's name and waving my arms in an attempt to get his attention.

Just then something large struck me in the back and knocked me face first into the snow and I could feel strong, sharp teeth sinking into my shoulder. I fought with all the strength that I could muster to throw the shaggy, stinking beast off of my back as it snarled ferociously, its teeth unable to penetrate my mail shirt. I managed to struggle to my feet with the hound still hanging on my back, sliding my seax from its scabbard when another one jumped up and seized my right wrist, forcing me back down to the ground. I punched at the dog with my left hand, unable to release its vice like grip on my arm, its powerful jaws crushing my wrist painfully and causing me to drop my weapon, its teeth sinking into my flesh. With the last of my strength, I reached down and pulled Conmor's knife from my boot, stabbing the short blade into the dog's neck and I heard a whimper and felt immediate relief as the hound released its grip on my wrist. I threw the other one over my shoulder and it twisted around immediately, crouching, ready to strike again, its black eyes glittering with feral hatred in the moonlight.

I retrieved my seax just as the hound leapt towards me, swinging the weapon around and slashing it at the shaggy monster in mid-flight, feeling the blade bite deep into the dog's belly. Its momentum bowled me backwards as it struck me again, knocking me to the ground, its slavering jaws still working and snapping at my throat. I sawed the blade downwards, feeling the warmth of its blood spilling over me until finally its movements ceased and I threw its stinking carcass to one side and lay in the blood stained snow breathing heavily.

The other hound had limped off into the night whining piteously, but I could hear others approaching, along with the voices of their handlers.

I sheathed my bloody seax and looking downriver I saw Myrddin standing at the stern of the little curragh, guiding it towards me with the steering oar and I shouted to him and he raised a hand in response. Nivian and Morgana sat near the prow, their cloaks wrapped tightly around them to stave off the biting cold. Lugotrix, who was perched on Myrddin's shoulder, let out a high pitched screech as I plunged into the freezing river and waded towards the little boat.

The druid helped me aboard, placing his hands under my armpits and pulling me over the boat's side.

I lay in the curraghs bilge, cold, wet and exhausted, my body frozen and hurting all over as Myrddin slewed the boat around and headed downriver towards the sea. The curragh glided across the water, leaving our attackers behind, their multitude of orange torches bobbing on the shore. Soon we were in the open sea riding the waves, the twin peaks of Beinn Mhor vast, black and imposing against the moonlit sky.

I unfastened my helmet with unresponsive fingers and cast it into the boat's bilge, tentatively touching the throbbing wound on my face and I turned to see Nivian looking at me with concern.

"You are hurt," she said, moving over to me. "Let me take a look."

"What do you care?" I replied peevishly.

"You are the father of my child," she replied simply. She placed her hands gently on my face and turned my head so that she could see the wound. "It needs cleaning or else it will poison your blood and the fever will take you. As does that wound on your chest."

I grabbed her delicate wrists and removed her hands from my face. "Save your concern, Nivian. My best friend lies dead at the hands of your lover."

She looked at me with disdain. "I gave you fair warning but you did not listen, so why should I help you? You have killed my mentor and stolen me from my lord. I owe you nothing."

She carefully made her way back to her bench and sat next to Morgana who was swathed in a black cloak way too big for her and placed both arms around the shivering child in an attempt to keep her warm. Her eyes flashed with hostility as she glared at me.

"Take the steering oar, I'll see to you in a moment," Myrddin said, making his way over to the prow of the curragh and rummaging through his satchel.

I made my way to the boat's stern and took hold of the steering oar, my limbs feeling stiff and unresponsive. Myrddin reached down and removed a necklace, tossing it over to me.

"Hold it before you and follow the fish's tail," he said.

I looked down at the talisman in my hand. It was made of a strange black, pitted metal, crudely fashioned into the likeness of a fish. I held it out in front of me, letting it hang before my eyes and as I watched, the fish rotated, as though some strange force were moving it. I rotated my body experimentally, but the fishes head always remained pointing in the same direction.

"The fish will always look towards the North Star," Myrddin said.

"Where does it come from?" I asked with fascination.

"Distant lands, far to the south, beyond the Great Desert, where the sun always burns." He replied. Lugotrix let out a shrill whistle in response and bobbed his little head.

With the aid of the metal fish I guided the curragh over the waves. A biting wind blew over the sea and stung my face, but the sky was clearing and the moon shone brilliantly, reflecting off of the white crested waves.

"Where are we headed?" I shouted to the druid.

"South," Myrddin replied.

We sailed south, keeping the coast in view to our port side. Myrddin persuaded Nivian to tend to me while he took the oar and reluctantly she cleaned and bound my wounds, smearing them with a strange smelling salve of green paste from Myrddin's satchel after sewing them shut. I gritted my teeth and tried not to show any outwards signs of pain as she operated in sullen silence. Morgana looked on in quiet fascination, her eyes wide and bright. I smiled at her but she frowned at me and buried her face in her mother's cloak. At one point, Nivian was forced to lean her head against my chest as she bit through the thread and the scent of her hair, that same smell of pine resin and wild flowers brought memories flooding back, but the sharp tugging pain as she finally bit through the thread jerked me back to reality.

"The gods were with you," Nivian muttered grudgingly. "You are lucky to be alive."

"I'm sorry to disappoint you," I replied caustically. "But you can take comfort from the fact that my shield brother is dead."

Nivian looked at me with her deep green eyes. "I take no pleasure from seeing brave men die, despite what you may think. You loved him didn't you?"

I nodded in reply, unable to speak for the lump in my throat, my eyes clouding with tears. I diverted my gaze, looking up at the bright moon in the frozen northern sky.

Nivian looked down awkwardly at her hands. "I'm sorry," she muttered.

Myrddin looked up at the stars thoughtfully. "Carnun was with us. We have banished a great evil from this land. You did well, Fergus mac Fiontan."

"Fiachu still lives," I replied flatly. "Oengus and Brida have betrayed us. Geraint lies dead. I have failed in what I had set out to do."

"There will be other opportunities," Myrddin said. "Do not be so eager to throw your life away. The desire for vengeance will eventually destroy you if you are not careful."

I looked up at Nivian who was avoiding my gaze. "When Fiachu mac Niall is dead I will find peace."

Myrddin looked at me with his pale blue eyes burning intensely in his gaunt, bearded face. "Peace is not for you I fear, Tuan. I have foreseen much blood and turmoil along your path."

I shrugged impartially. "Such is the destiny of the warrior. That is not unusual in these tumultuous times."

"You will forge the bloody destiny of a king, yet your name will never be sung in the halls of your descendants," the druid said dreamily, his eyes becoming glazed as though he were remembering a distant dream.

"The Sword of Kings shall be yours, but you will give it to one unworthy of wielding it," Nivian interjected quietly. "I too have had prophetic dreams regarding your destiny. Remember when I first told you of the Sword of Kings?" My mind went back to that early summer's evening many years ago when I lay with Nivian in the cave, the day before our lives had changed completely. "How could I ever forget that?" I replied, looking into her deep set green eyes, my voice thick with emotion.

The briefest of smiles flickered across Nivian's face as she too remembered our time together, but her expression quickly soured and she avoided my gaze, looking out across the sea instead. "So what do you plan to do with me?" She asked, changing the subject. "Take my daughter from me and sell me into slavery? Keep me as a trophy of war? Kill me?"

I reached over and took hold of Nivian's fine hands. They were cold to the touch and I leaned closer to her. "Nivian, listen to me. I do not mean you any harm and I would never stand by and watch you come to harm. You will be free to choose your own path once this is all over. But Morgana stays with me. I will make sure she is well cared for and that she will want for nothing."

Nivian snatched her hands away and clutched our daughter close to her bosom, glaring at me with vitriol. The left side of her face was swollen and bruised where Geraint had hit her, but this did not mar her smouldering beauty. "You mean to murder my lord, take me from my home and my people and take my daughter from me? And you expect me not to hate you?"

"I am not taking Morgana away from you. I merely said she stays with me. What you decide to do is up to you."

Nivian's red mouth curled into a sneer. "I'd rather die than stay with you."

"Then you will never see your daughter again," I replied coldly, though with an ache in my heart.

We sailed on and Myrddin made a blood sacrifice to Manannan Mac Lir, the god of the sea, opening up the small cut on his palm and letting several drops fall into the sea while Nivian looked on contemptuously with Morgana fast asleep in her arms.

I remembered Dorbalos making the ultimate sacrifice to the same god, slipping into Manannan's cold embrace so that my sister and I could live and I thought about Jalmarr, captain of the Brimwulf with his libation of a horn of ale to his sea god and how poor Brother Carwyn and his monks had offered their prayers to the Almighty for safe passage and I found myself wondering which god truly did rule the sea or whether our lives were merely ruled by fate, or Wyrd as the Saxons called it. I drifted into an uncomfortable sleep and I dreamed of the Three Sisters that Jalmarr had once told me about, sitting at the foot of a huge tree whose branches disappeared into the clouds while they weaved and span and cut the destinies of every person who had ever lived and ever will live. The threads stretched out before them, countless millions, fine as spider's silk and shimmering silver in the starlight, stretching out as far as I could see. And as I watched the three hooded figures sitting there weaving, they each threw back their hoods in turn and I saw the first was Rhawn, my adopted mother from Penglyn who looked at me with a wistful smile. The next one was Nivian, her eyes intense but her expression unreadable as she stared at me wordlessly and then the final sister turned and pulled back her hood.

It was Sinusa, looking at me with her sunken, milk white eyes, her toothless maw hanging open as she let out a wheezing, mocking laugh. And as I looked on, unable to move, Nivian too joined in the laughter as Sinusa gradually became younger, her face altering before my eyes, going from a hideous crone to a striking young woman with raven black hair and then to a child, getting younger and younger by the moment until with horror I saw my own daughter, Morgana standing before me, chuckling with derision and with a malice in her eyes that I had never before seen in a child.

I awoke with a start, shivering with cold, my hair and beard frosted, unnerved by the dream that had wrenched me from my uneasy sleep. Nivian was curled up fast asleep with Morgana at the prow of the curragh under a pile of ragged blankets and sheepskins. A sealskin tarpaulin was stretched across the front half of the prow to make a crude shelter, large enough for a couple of people to have a cramped night's sleep. It was here that Myrddin had also stored our meagre provisions; a sack of hard black bread, dried fish and oats that would probably only last a couple of days.

I noticed that a mist was rising from the sea and mentioned it to Myrddin, who was still sat at the stern with one hand on the steering oar.

"Manannan mac Lir has answered our prayers," he said quietly. "He sends a mist to confound our enemies who are no doubt in pursuit of us."

"But how will we find our way in this mist?" I enquired.

The druid smirked and held up the fish amulet.

"It can see through the mist?" I said incredulously, watching it turn on its leather cord.

Myrddin nodded. "Take the oar please, Fergus. I must rest."

I sat at the bench in the boats stern, aching all over and took the oar while Myrddin wrapped a woollen blanket around himself and settled down on one of the rowing benches. "Keep the boat on a southward heading," he added.

I looked around at the heaving, foam flecked sea stretching out in every direction and wondered whether any of us would ever see a warm hearth again.

"But where can we go?" I asked. "We cannot return to Caer Cadwy or Caer Dor as they are both now under Gorlois' control and Penglyn no longer exists. We have nowhere to go."

"You forget what I am," Myrddin replied, wagging a long finger at me. "I am all that remains of a once highly respected order. Although many now profess to follow the Christ god, they still have an uneasy fear of the Old Ways. Few lords would turn a druid away from the doors of his hall, even now."

"So where do you propose that we go?"

Myrddin sat at one of the rowing benches and placed his long hands on his knees. "I hear rumour that High King Vortigern is in need of the services of a druid," he said with a smirk. "Therefore we should seek audience with him and with the will of the gods, maybe we can find out where your Lord Ambrosius and his half-brother Uther are being held before it is too late."

After two days of sailing we were cold, wet and hungry. We spied the coast of Ynys Manaw off of our starboard bow, the island home of the sea god, Manannan Mac Lir and Myrddin offered another prayer of thanks as we passed, pouring a small libation of ale into the deep green sea. I noticed that the druid stared wistfully towards the distant coast and asked whether he had any connection with the island, to which he only offered a nod.

"It was the home to my tutor and mentor, Dorbalos," I said quietly. "I only found that out shortly before he died."

The druid stared fixedly at the mist enshrouded island in the distance. "If my older brother thought your life was worth saving, then so must I."

"Your brother?" I echoed with a look of confusion.

The druid looked up at the scattering of stars overhead, at the misty band known by my people as Lugh's Chain and sighed with a deep sadness. "We spent our early childhood with our mother on Ynys Manaw, Manannan's island. I remember little about my childhood, save that it was safe and secure and we were loved, everything that a child needs," he looked over at Morgana, his pale blue eyes weary and distant. "I was barely six and my brother eleven summers old when the druids came and took us to Eire. Our mother had the gift of second sight and was often consulted by the villagers. Word of my mother's abilities spread until it reached the ears of the druids. They came for my brother initially, but they saw that I was the one who had inherited our mother's gift for prophetic dreams and that I could glimpse into the Otherworld and so we were both taken to learn the Hidden Ways. When we were older, we travelled far and wide but my brother eventually settled and stayed in Eire and became adviser to a local chieftain. However, I craved my freedom and became a wanderer, a travelling pellar and I continued with my wandering, always hungering for knowledge and delving into the secrets of nature."

I could barely believe what I was hearing. "Your brother was Dorbalos?"

Myrddin nodded slowly.

"But I knew Dorbalos all my life and he never once mentioned that he had a brother, until the very end, that is."

"He wouldn't have. He was ashamed of me. Both he and my mentors saw that I had great potential, that I had what it took to become the Arch Druid, but they thought that I was just throwing it all away by deciding to become a wanderer. They more or less turned their backs on me. I lost all contact with my brother until fate washed you up on the shores of northern Dumnonia."

I took a deep breath as I tried to assimilate the information. "So Dorbalos took us to Britannia to seek your aid do you think?"

Myrddin shrugged. "It's possible. I would like to think so anyway. The gods brought you to me, to continue my brother's work and to somehow do something that would have made him proud of me and to avenge his death."

I placed a hand on the druid's bony shoulder. "He would have been proud of you, Myrddin."

Eventually we headed towards the coast of the mainland and Myrddin guided the curragh into a small, secluded cove with a shingle beach and we hauled the boat ashore, hiding it behind a sandy bluff. Morgana was crying weakly from discomfort and lack of food, despite her mother's attempts to comfort her. I had tried to bond with the child, but every attempt that I made was met with stubborn silence and a cold stare, just like her mother and so I decided it was better to ignore them both. Also there was something in the child's gaze that unnerved me and despite the fact that she was of my blood and was a mere child, I found it hard to look into those piercing eyes as they regarded me with a knowing beyond her years, a sly malevolence that disturbed me deeply and reminded me of my unsettling dream. Myrddin too had proved uncommunicative, except with his little sparrow hawk, with whom he would hold entire muttered conversations, talking only when necessary with the rest of us and lapsing into long periods of contemplative silence, his eyes glazed as though he were looking into worlds invisible to the rest of us.

The landscape ahead was rugged and undulating, with mountains in the distance and no obvious signs of habitation anywhere.

"Where are we?" I asked Myrddin.

The druid raised his head and seemed to sniff the air. "Somewhere in the kingdom of Gwynedd I would say, though where exactly, I am not sure." He whispered to Lugotrix who was perched on his wrist and the little bird took to the air in a flurry of grey feathers.

We had not walked far, following the course of a swift running stream, when Lugotrix returned, circling above us and chirping noisily before settling on the druid's shoulder. The little bird chirped in his ear and Myrddin listened intently before turning to us. "Riders are approaching," he said.

My hand drifted towards the hilt of Octha's Ruin, but Myrddin placed a hand on my shoulder.

"There will be no need for that," he said reassuringly. "Let me do the talking."

Soon four men on horseback appeared over a grassy bluff, carrying small square shields and pennants bearing the symbol of a red bear on a green background. Each man wore a jerkin of studded leather and highly polished helmets of bronze, with plumes of white horsehair and cloaks of deep green, also bearing the bear crest. Like the Votadini and the Cruithne, they too were painted with swirling patterns that covered their arms and faces.

The lead horseman raised his hand as they approached and the other men stopped before us, their spears held at the ready.

"Who travels King Cunedda's lands without permission?" The lead rider barked.

Myrddin stepped forwards, leaning on his staff and greeting the man with a bow. "I am Myrddin Wyllt, priest of the Old Ways. And I am an old friend of your king."

The rider kicked his heels into the flanks of his black horse and rode around us slowly, looking at each of us with an expression of curious contempt. "Your name is known in these parts, druid. But who are these sorry companions that accompany you?"

"My apprentice and her daughter and my bondsman," he said, indicating us with a wave of his hand. "Forgive our threadbare appearance, but we have just come from the kingdom of Guotodin after serving your king's brother, King Cadlew of the Votadini. We were assaulted by Cruithne during our travels and barely escaped with our lives."

The soldier's eyes narrowed suspiciously and lingered on Nivian. "What proof do you have that you were in the service of King Cunedda's brother?"

I stepped forwards and unclasped my seax from my belt, handing it to him hilt first. "A gift to me from the king of the Votadini for our services to him. He gave this to me personally."

The soldier accepted the seax in its ornate leather scabbard and nodded in appreciation, drawing it halfway from the red scabbard so that the winter's sunlight reflected off of the finely honed blade. He looked me up and down as he handed it back with a frown, his eyes drawn towards Octha's Ruin hanging from my belt. "Where are you from?" He asked suddenly. "You carry the weapons of the Votadini and the Saxons but bear the markings of the Cruithne and speak with the accent of a Gael."

"I am a Gael, you are right. I crossed the sea long ago and found service with King Cadlew and now I serve Myrddin."

The man nodded again.

"Your King's hospitality would be much appreciated," I responded.

The man gave me a withering look. "Our King has little love for Gaels." He turned in his saddle to one of the other riders. "Bricius, take this woman on your mount, Jorred, take the child. You two will have to walk."

Nivian handed Morgana up to the rider before mounting the back of the other horse and then we set off, walking towards the rolling green hills in the distance and I wondered what sort of reception we would receive from King Cunedda. Although he was Cadlew's brother, he was also in thrall to High King Vortigern as the High King held his family hostage to ensure his loyalty. I wondered too how far behind us Fiachu mac Niall was and had no doubts that he would scour the four corners of the Earth for his woman and the audacious enemy who had stolen her from him.

****

Epilogue

By the time the old man had finished his tale, the sky was lightening in the east and the first birds had started to sing. The fire had died down to a glow and Godric's two thegns were snoring fitfully, swathed in their thick fur lined cloaks. Only he and the old man remained awake in the secluded copse of hazel and alder and Godric drew his cloak tighter around his broad shoulders in an attempt to keep out the chill of early dawn.

"Did the son of King Niall ever find you?" he asked after the old man had lapsed into a morose silence.

The bard looked up, blinking slowly and nodded. "He did."

Godric waited for him to continue, but instead the old man leaned heavily on his staff and climbed to his feet.

"Come, lord. We must be travelling onwards. Wake your men."

Godric watched the man with frustration as he rolled up his woollen blanket and attached it to his horse's saddle. He yawned wearily as he too rose to his feet and kicked his men into wakefulness.

The old man rummaged in one of his saddle bags and produced a smoke blackened bronze pot and a linen sack from which he scooped a few handfuls of oats, topping it up with water from a goatskin.

He patted his horse's neck and then limped back to the fire, poking it and blowing it back to life once again before setting the pot on a couple of thick logs over the flames.

"We must eat before we go on," he muttered.

Godric sat once again by the fire and huffed impatiently. "So are you going to tell me what happened next?"

The old man looked up with a wry expression and a twinkle in his eye. "In time, my lord. But now it is time to regain our strength for the journey ahead."

Lord Godric clenched his fists. The old man's elusive nature was grating on him and he was not a patient man at the best of times.

"I am not comfortable with travelling into Wealas territory and neither are my men," he blurted suddenly. "You said that you had something that could guarantee our safety?"

The bard nodded thoughtfully before fumbling at the elaborate dragon brooch that secured his tattered cloak. He tossed it to the Jutish warlord who caught it deftly. "It is yours, lord. Make sure you wear it so that all may see it. Tell anyone who asks that it was a gift from Fergus the Bard and that you wander these lands with his blessing and the blessing of the Horned One, master of the forests and of Brighid the Exalted One."

Godric turned the brooch in his hand, watching the early morning sunlight catch within the deep ruby eyes of the dragon. "And that will be enough to secure our safe passage home?"

The old man smirked as he removed the bronze triple spiral from around his neck and handed it to the warlord. "With this as well, most definitely."

Godric accepted the gift reluctantly. "But these are your most prized possessions. I cannot accept them, they mean too much to you."

Fergus mac Fiontan gave a sad laugh and shook his white haired head. "All that is of value to me is now gone. They are mere trinkets, nothing more. I cannot take them into the Otherworld, so what use are they to me now? I am passing them onto you, along with my memories, so that you may relate the truth of those times to any who would wish to know."

Godric stared down at the triple spiral in his hand, burnished with age to a brilliant sheen. It was warm to the touch, having spent several lifetimes against the old man's skin and as he held it, Godric could have sworn that it was growing hotter.

The old bard looked somehow relieved and he smiled serenely, as though a great weight had been removed from his shoulders. "Do not put on the necklace yet though, my lord. You must wait until my tale is finished. That is vitally important."

Godric shrugged and carefully placed the trinket into a doe skin pouch at his belt. "As you wish," he muttered.

After their simple breakfast of salted oats, they set off once again, travelling through lush but sparsely populated countryside until by midday they reached a wide river with high moors beyond.

"The River Isca," the old man said quietly as he pulled on the reins of his steed. He turned to look at Godric who stared impassively across the expanse of water.

"Is there a crossing?" he asked.

The old man turned in his saddle and pointed to the north.

"There is a bridge farther upriver, but I fear it may be guarded."

"Then how do we cross?" Godric demanded, unable to hide the annoyance in his voice.

The old man nodded towards the closest bank of the river where a ramshackle jetty protruded into the dark water. Tied to the jetty was a simple punt and a little farther down river was a tiny hut with a conical, moss covered roof.

A young man with dark hair emerged and his eyes widened in alarm when he saw the three Jutish warriors on horseback.

Fergus mac Fiontan raised a hand and called out to the young Briton whilst dismounting from his steed. He approached the young man, speaking to him in his own tongue and after a brief conversation the younger man appeared to relax. Fergus turned and smiled at Godric. "Young Glaw here has agreed to transport us across the river."

The Jutish lord nodded once, unsure whether he really wished to cross the river. The bard seemed to sense the lord's reticence and took a few paces towards him. "My lord, no danger will befall you in the lands beyond. You have my word. The gods are with you."

"Your gods old man, not mine," Godric replied.

After they had crossed the River Isca, they rode on across bleak and desolate moors until by the time the sun was touching the distant horizon they were looking down upon a vast forest that stretched as far as the eye could see in all directions, its deep green permeated by the meandering paths of streams and rivers that wound their way to the sea which appeared as an indistinct band of pale blue far to the north.

"Is this the forest of which you spoke?" Godric asked. He fumbled at his horse's reins and Fergus noticed a muscle flexing continuously in the man's jaw.

The bard nodded. "It is. Our journey is nearly over."

He turned without another word and kicked his heels into his horse's flanks, spurring down towards the foreboding darkness of the distant forest.

Godric paused for a moment, aware of his two thegns by his side, knowing that if he followed this strange old wanderer into those woods his life would never be the same again.

"My lord, it is not too late to go back," Deorulf, one of the thanes muttered. Godric considered the man's words for a moment. Deorulf was a plain speaker, a practical man who spoke his mind, which was why Godric liked him. They could leave now, return to the safety of their lands and forget that Fergus mac Fiontan had ever existed. He would eventually die and his extraordinary tale would die with him. Godric wondered what had possessed him to agree to the old man's request. After all, who was he but an enemy of his people, one of the hated Wealas who had killed more of Godric's kinsmen than he cared to count, or so he claimed. And what if his tale was nothing more than a bardic fabrication, a tall story of bluff and bravado pilfered from the deeds of more honourable men?

The warlord sat upon his steed in contemplation, staring out at the golden hued western sky, when a shrill whistle and a small, flitting object caught his attention. A tiny sparrowhawk swooped past his left ear, causing his horse to canter sideways and in that moment, Godric knew that the gods had spoken.

Silently he spurred his horse forwards and rode towards the Forest of the Horned One.

Part Three of Guardians of the Sword

Dragon's Exile

is available now.

Cast of Characters

Name	
Aldrien	King of Armorica, Great uncle to Ambrosius and Uther
Alwyn ap Glynn	Pendragon chieftain loyal to Drustan and later to Branwen
Ambrosius Constantinus	Romano British lord, son of Julianus and half-brother of Uther. Close friend of Fergus
Arwel	Lord of Lindinis, town south of Caer Cadwy
Avallach	Otherwordly lord of Ynys Wytryn
Awstin	Priest, adviser to King Erbin
Bradan Cionaodh	Clan chief loyal to Fergus' father and later to Fergus
Branwen Pendragon	Daughter of the warlord Drustan Pendragon and mother of Uther
Brendan mac Lauchlan	Deisi warlord loyal to Fiontan
Brida	Pict girl, captured by Fergus and companion to Oengus
Brithru	Commander of Eamonn O'Suilleabhain's army
Bron	The Fisher King, son of Rhawn and monk of Ynys Wytryn
Brynmor	Pendragon warrior and companion of Fergus
Cadlew	King of the Votadini of Guotodin, lord of Din Eidyn
Carwyn	Monk who accompanies Fergus and Ambrosius to the North
Catigern	Son of High King Vortigern

Ceneu	King of Rheged
Cletus	Sarmatian commander of Julianus' cavalry
Conmor mac Fiontan	Half-brother of Fergus
Constans Constantinus	Brother of Ambrosius, heir to Durotrigia and Caer Cadwy
Cornelius Varius	Commander of Caer Cadwy's infantry
Corryn ap Sel	Fergus' rival from Penglyn and son of Sel.
Cunedda	Votadini King of Gwynedd
Cynyr	Commander of Drustan Pendragon's forces
Demetrios	Pelagian Priest, friend of Fergus
Diarmuid	Companion of Conmor and later Fergus
Dorbalos	Druid of the Deisi, Fergus' mentor and teacher
Drustan Pendragon	Warlord of the Pendragon and the hill tribes of Dumnonia
Eamonn O'Suilleabhain	Clan chief of the Eoganachta, an Irish tribe
Eber	Friend of Corryn
Elena	Head of Julianus' household slaves in Villa Aurelianus
Enfys	Veteran Pendragon warrior
Erbin	Crippled young King of Dumnonia
Faustus	Youngest son of Vortigern, captured by the Deisi
Fergus mac Fiontan	Son of Fiontan mac Duggan of the Strongarm, Clan chief of the Deisi

Fiachu mac Niall	Dispossessed son of High King Niall, clan chief of the Masraighe
Fiontan mac Duggan	Chief of the Deisi Tuath, father of Fergus and Ygerna
Flavius Claudius Constantinus	The Usurper, who led the Roman legions from Britannia to try to claim the crown of Emperor Honorius, grandfather of Ambrosius and Uther
Geraint	Closest friend and companion of Fergus
Germanus of Auxerre	Romano-Gallic Bishop and ex general who came to Britannia to combat the Pelagian Heresy
Glaesten	Lord of Ynys Wytryn
Gorlois ap Gerdan	Duke of Cerniw
Gwyrangon	Dispossessed king of Cantia
Hefina	Kitchen slave in Villa Aurelianus. Girlfriend of Fergus
Hengest	Leader of the Saxon forces, brother of Horsa
Honorius	Emperor at the time of Flavius Constantinus' rebellion
Horsa	Hengest's brother, leader of the Saxons
Jalmarr	Anglii seaman, captain of the Brimwulf
Judoc	Gorlois' personal bodyguard
Julianus Constantinus	Battle Duke of Durotrigia, Lord of Caer Cadwy and descendant of the Usurper, Flavius Claudius Constantinus. Father of Ambrosius and Uther
Loegaire mac Niall	High King of Eire, brother of Fiachu
Lot ap Cadlew	Votadini prince, son of Cadlew
Lugotrix	Myrddin's sparrow hawk
Lugubelenus	Chief of the Coedwig Gwerin, the Forest Folk

Malbach	Dark druid, High priest of the Masraighe
Meinwen	Dumnonian princess, sister of King Erbin
Merrion	Drustan Pendragon's treacherous adviser
Morgana	Daughter of Fergus and Nivian
Myrddin Wyllt	Last of Britannia's Druids
Neirin	Abbot of Ynys Wytryn
Niall Noigiallach	High King of Eire, father of Fiachu
Nivian	Apprentice to Old Mother Argoel and lover of Fergus
Octha	Jute warlord, son of Hengest
Oengus mac Ruadainn	Irish bard, son of Ruadainn
Old Mother Argoel	Elderly mystic and wise woman from the forest of Coedwig dyn Bannog
Pascent	Son of High King Vortigern
Porcius	Priest, attached to Villa Aurelianus
Quintinia	Mother of King Erbin of Dumnonia
Rhawn	Fisherwoman from Penglyn, Fergus' ward
Rowena	Young Saxon wife of High King Vortigern, daughter of Hengest
Sarn	Pendragon warrior
Sel	Father of Corryn, head of Penglyn's militia
Severa	Daughter of Magnus Maximus the Usurper, first wife of High King Vortigern, said to have been poisoned by him

Sinusa	Masraighe sorceress and worshipper of Crom Cruach
Tiernach	Deisi warrior, helps Fergus escape Eire
Tigernmas	Ancient king of Eire, introduced the worship of Crom Cruach
Tuan	Fergus' spirit name
Ulfhere	Saxon captain of the Deopnaedre
Uther Pendragon	Son of Branwen, half-brother to Ambrosius and heir to the throne of Dumnonia
Vortigern	Corrupt High King of Britannia
Vortimer	Son of Vortigern, commander of his armies
Wulfraed	Saxon warrior, bodyguard of Queen Rowena
Wynfor	Clan chief who rebels against Branwen Pendragon
Ygerna mac Fiontan	Sister of Fergus

	Locations
Albion	Ancient name for Britain
Armorica	Brittany, France
Atrebatia	Wiltshire & Hampshire, Southern England
Avalon	Somerset Levels
Britannia	Latin name for Britain
Caer Baddon	City of Bath, North East Somerset
Caer Broga	Brent knoll, Somerset
Caer Cadwy	Cadbury Hill, South Somerset
Caer Dor	Castle Dore, Fowey, Cornwall
Caer Isca	Exeter, Devon
Caledonia	Latin name for Scotland
Cama	River Cam, Somerset
Cantia	Kent, South East England
Cerniw	Cornwall, South West England
Coedwig dyn Bannog	(Fictional) Vast forest between Hartland, Devon and Bodmin, Cornwall
Comeragh	County Waterford, Ireland
Connachta	Connaught, Western Ireland
Din Eidyn	Edinburgh, Scotland

Din Mhor	Beinn Mhor, Loch Lomond, Scotland
Din Tagel	Tintagel, Cornwall
Dinas Ffaraon	Beddgelert, Snowdonia, North Wales
Dumnonia	Devon and Somerset, Southern England
Durotrigia	Dorset & Wiltshire, Southern England
Dyfed	Pembrokeshire, South Wales
Eboracum	York, Northern England
Eire	Ireland
Forest of Celidon	Selkirkshire & Dumfries, Scotland
Gaul	France
Glevum	Gloucester, England
Guotodin	Lothian & Borders, Eastern Scotland
Gwynedd	North Wales
Lindinis	Ilchester, Somerset
Londinium	London
Mag Sleacht	County Cavan, Ireland
Penglyn	(Fictional) near Clovelly, Devon
Powys	Powys, Mid Wales
Prydein	Celtic name for Britain
Regia	Sussex, Southern England
Rheged	Cumbria and Lancashire, Northern England

Sliabh Bladhma	Slieve Bloom Mountains, Central Ireland
Tamesis	River Thames, Southern England
Verulamium	St.Albans, Hertfordshire
Villa Aurelianus	Bratton Seymour, Somerset
Viroconium	Wroxeter, Shropshire
Ynys Echni	Flat holm Island, Bristol Channel
Ynys Mannaw	Isle of Man
Ynys Mon	Anglesey, West Wales
Ynys Wytryn	Glastonbury Tor, Somerset

Glossary of Terms

808Aine	Celtic summer fertility goddess. Protector of plants and all growing things.
Annwn	Celtic name for the Otherworld
Aongus Og	Celtic God of love and beauty
Arawn	Celtic god of the underworld. Also the god of terror and vengeance.
Arianrhod	Celtic goddess of the Silver Wheel, a deity of the Moon, stars and retribution
Banshee	In Irish mythology, a wailing spirit said to portend death
Belenos	Celtic sun god
Beltane	Celtic festival of the Sun God, held on the 1st May
Bran the Blessed	In Celtic mythology, a giant who was the first king of Britannia and owned the Cauldron of Rebirth

Brighid	one of the Tuatha de Danann, daughter of the Dagda and goddess of spring
Cailleach	The Winter Hag, Celtic goddess of winter
Calan Awst	The British 'Feast of August', the beginning of the harvest season, also known as Lughnasadh
Calan Mai	Britons name for Beltane
Caledfwlch	Celtic name for the legendary sword Excalibur, the Sword of Kings
Caledonii	Pictish tribe
Cantref	A division of land in ancient Britain
Carnonacae	Pictish tribe
Carnun	Also known as Cernunnos, the Horned God and Lord of the Wildwood, Celtic deity depicted as a man with antlers
Ceffyl Dwr	See Fuath
Coedwig Gwerin	The Forest Folk, or First Men. The remnants of the first people to live in Britannia, who crossed over from mainland Europe after the last ice age
Cornovii	Celtic tribe from Cornwall
Creones	Pictish tribe
Crom Cruach	Ancient Irish deity also known as the Crooked One or the Bloody Worm. Crom's worship was marked by the sacrifice of a tribe's firstborn.
Cruithne	The Picts, barbaric painted people who lived north of Hadrian's Wall
Cuchulainn	Mythical Irish hero, known as the Hound of Ulster
Curragh	an early Irish boat consisting of a wooden frame covered with cured animal hides, sometimes with a sail
Cythraul	In Celtic mythology the realm of chaos
Dagda	Celtic father god, high king of the Tuatha de Danann
Danu	Irish Mother Goddess of the Tuatha de Danann

Decantae	Pictish tribe
Deisi	Fergus' tribe from the southern coast of Ireland
Donn	Celtic god of death, known as the Dark One
Druid	A Celtic priest with an affinity to all things natural
Elder Mother	A vengeful tree spirit, believed to dwell within the elder tree
Eoganachta	Rival neighbouring tribe of the Deisi, from the Comeragh mountains
Eormensyll	in Anglo Saxon mythology, the World Tree that gives structure to the universe
Epidii	Pictish tribe
Finn MacCool	Irish warrior hero
Fomoiri	A race of demonic creatures said to live underwater
Freya	Anglo Saxon fertility goddess
Fuath	in Gaelic myth, a supernatural lake dwelling monster
Gael	Ancient name for the Irish
Grian	Irish sun goddess
Heofenrice	The Anglo Saxon version of heaven or Asgard
Imbolc	Celtic spring festival, held in February, associated with the goddess Brighid
Kelpie	See Fuath
Liath Luacra	Warrior woman from Irish legend who lived in a forest and taught Finn macCool how to fight
Lleu	Ancient British deity hero, the equivalent of the Irish Lugh
Losgadh Famhair	The Burning Giant or Wicker Man
Lugh	'The Long Handed', Irish hero deity, skilled in the art of fighting

Lughnasadh	Celtic festival marking the beginning of the harvest. The feast of Lugh
Macha	Celtic Goddess known as the 'Death Maiden', one of the three aspects of the Morrigan
Manannan mac Lir	Celtic sea god
Masraighe	Fiachu mac Niall's adopted tribe. Worshippers of Crom Cruach
Milesians	Known as the Sons of Mil, one of the early people who came from Spain to settle Ireland, defeated the Tuatha de Danann and drove them into hiding
Morrigan	The Phantom Queen, Irish goddess of war and death, a triple aspect goddess
Nemeton	A sacred Druidic grove
Ogham	An early Irish form of writing consisting of a series of vertical, horizontal and diagonal lines
Otherworld	A mystical world which exists parallel to the real world. The realm of gods and spirits
Rath	In Ireland, a circular fortified settlement or ringfort consisting of banks, ditches and palisades
Samhain	Celtic festival marking the years end. Thought to be a time when the barriers between the world of the dead and the world of the living were at their thinnest
Seax	A single bladed knife, usually between 6 and 12 inches, carried by many warriors in the dark ages, but primarily by the Saxons
Shee (Sidh)	The mythical Fair Folk, Otherwordly beings related to the Tuatha de Danann who fled underground with the coming of the Milesians
Sisters of Wyrd	In Anglo Saxon mythology, the three sisters who sit at the foot of Eormensyll and weave people's fate
Smertai	Pictish tribe
Taranis	Celtic god of storms
Teulu	A British Celtic warband
Thunor	Anglo Saxon thunder god
Tir Na Nog	The Land of the Young, a mythical place said to exist off of the west coast of Ireland
Tuath	Old Irish term for a tribe or clan

Tuatha de Danann	Mythical people of the goddess, Danu, said to have an affinity for magic who dwell in a parallel world. Literally, the Tribe of Danu.
Ui Liathain	Celtic clan from Munster in Ireland
Vacomagi	Pictish tribe
Vate	A lower grade of Druid who performed sacrifices
Venicones	Pictish tribe
Wealhall	Woden's hall in Heofenrice, where those who have died in combat go to feast with the gods, later known by the Vikings as Valhalla
Wild Hunt	In Northern European mythology, a spectral hunt across the sky, involving phantom huntsmen, hounds and horses, usually led by the Horned God.
Woden	The 'Allfather' or 'One-Eyed Wanderer', Anglo Saxon god of wisdom, death and hidden knowledge
Wyrd	Anglo Saxon belief that corresponds to fate or destiny

Author's Note

5th Century Britain was a violent and turbulent place to live. Following the withdrawal of the Legions from the island and indeed for a century before, barbarians flooded in from all sides; Irish raiders attacked the west coast, Picts flooded down from the north and the dreaded Saxons, Angles, Jutes and Frisians came from across the sea for their share of what they saw as easy pickings, from what is now Germany, Denmark and Holland.

Rome, weakened by internal strife and by the incursions of the Huns from the east, had its own problems and was unable to offer any help. Britain was on its own.

It was during this time that a shadowy figure emerged, a Romano-Briton of noble birth by the name of Ambrosius Aurelianus. What little we know of this man comes from the writings of Gildas, a 6th century monk in his sermon, 'De Excidio et Conquestu Britanniae' (On the Ruin and the Conquest of Britain). He describes Ambrosius as "a gentleman who, perhaps alone of the Romans, had survived the shock of this notable storm. Certainly his parents, who had worn the purple, were slain by it. His descendants in our day have become greatly inferior to their grandfather's excellence."

It is obvious from this statement that Ambrosius was of noble birth and perhaps even the descendant of Roman emperors and that his parents (whoever they were) were slain in the upheaval of the 5th century.

According to the semi-legendary 'Historia Brittonum', Ambrosius was the enemy of Vortigern and half-brother to Uther Pendragon, father of King Arthur. The two are sent into exile to the safety of their uncle Aldrien in Brittany (then Armorica) to avoid the ruthless and murderous designs of Vortigern.

According to Geoffrey of Monmouth, Ambrosius was the son of Constantine III, the usurper who revolted against the Emperor Honorius in 409 AD. However, this would have placed him several decades too early in history, therefore I have made him the son of Julianus, another son of Constantine III.

The exploits of Fiachu mac Niall are entirely fictitious. He was the youngest son of Niall Noigiallach, but the historical Fiachu existed several decades later, according to the King List in the Book of Leinster. It is said that he refused baptism from St. Patrick and that he fought alongside his brother, King Loegaire. Whether he ever came to Britain, I do not know, though his father, King Niall was notorious for raiding up and down the west coast of Britain and is said to have taken the young St. Patrick as a slave, who escaped but then returned to evangelise Ireland. Legend has it that St. Patrick battled with Crom Cruach on the plains of Mag Sleacht and that the crooked stone representing the ancient god sank into the ground when Patrick struck it with his crozier.

I have taken many liberties with the traditional Arthurian legend to tie the entirely fictitious Fergus mac Fiontan into the tale; his sister Ygerna will become the mother of King Arthur and his daughter, Morgana will become the villainous sorceress of legend. But that is another story...

Jason Pope

Made in the USA
Charleston, SC
21 April 2015